T0303743

Praise for

Brian Duren's Ivory Black

In *Ivory Black*, Brian Duren takes us back to the last century—from hippie days to the Iraq war—and does it so powerfully and energetically that we can see it all in vivid color. This is a novel of enduring beauty and sorrow told by a master of the trade.

—**Mary Logue**, author of *The Streel* and *The Big Sugar*

In Big Bluff, Colorado in the '60s, young Richard sits in his father's art studio. He watches as a painting emerges from his father's concentration and strokes of paint: a mysterious, melancholy and magical process. From his father he learns to draw, knowledge he uses to make revealing caricatures, a skill that accompanies him through student years and adventures in France. Life follows its course until Richard becomes a high-up consultant behind the scenes of the Iraqi War. A coming-of-age story becomes Greek tragedy. Only the power of painting offers possible redemption. Brian Duren astutely explores what it can mean to be an artist working in the world. As Richard's father says, "You paint with your eyes closed so you can see the reality you have to paint."

—**Joyce Lyon**, Artist / Professor of Art Emerita, University of Minnesota

Rarely do I read a novel so compelling its multiple storylines are difficult to put down. We witness the main character making one mistake after another, but always leading with his heart. *Ivory Black* is a love story (in all its myriad forms), a war novel, a meditation on art, and the saga of a man who finally learns what is most important in life. It is a beautiful, hard, wonderful lesson to read.

—**Cary Griffith**, author of the novel, *Killing Monarchs*, and winner of the Minnesota Book Award for Nonfiction

Brian Duren breathes life into the classic artistic model of the solitary genius, showing two different ways a painter can be in the world. A father and his son follow separate trajectories and end up in the same place ... but with a twist. The novel's energetic plotline is accompanied by delicious descriptions of sights, smells and sounds which are a joy to the senses. *Ivory Black* celebrates the high romance of a certain kind of art life by putting an imaginary paintbrush into the hands of the reader and leading the way through an experience so real, it seems like more than a dream.

—**Nancy Robinson,** an award-winning surrealistic painter, has exhibited extensively in galleries, museums and other art venues

IVORY BLACK

A Novel

GUERNICA WORLD EDITIONS 62

IVORY BLACK

A Novel

BRIAN DUREN

GUERNICA
World
EDITIONS

TORONTO—CHICAGO—BUFFALO—LANCASTER (U.K.)
2023

Copyright © 2023, Brian Duren and Guernica Editions Inc.
All rights reserved. The use of any part of this publication,
reproduced, transmitted in any form or by any means, electronic,
mechanical, photocopying, recording or otherwise stored
in a retrieval system, without the prior consent of the publisher
is an infringement of the copyright law.

Names, characters, businesses, places, events, locales,
and incidents are either the products
of the author's imagination or used in a fictitious manner.
Any resemblance to actual persons, living or dead,
or actual events is purely coincidental.

Guernica Editions Founder: Antonio D'Alfonso

Michael Mirolla, general editor
Scott Walker, editor
Cover design: Allen Jomoc Jr.
Interior design: Jill Ronsley, suneditwrite.com

Guernica Editions Inc.
287 Templemead Drive, Hamilton (ON), Canada L8W 2W4
2250 Military Road, Tonawanda, N.Y. 14150-6000 U.S.A.
www.guernicaeditions.com

Distributors:
Independent Publishers Group (IPG)
600 North Pulaski Road, Chicago IL 60624
University of Toronto Press Distribution (UTP)
5201 Dufferin Street, Toronto (ON), Canada M3H 5T8
Gazelle Book Services, White Cross Mills
High Town, Lancaster LA1 4XS U.K.

First edition.
Printed in Canada.

Legal Deposit—First Quarter
Library of Congress Catalog Card Number: 2022944965
Library and Archives Canada Cataloguing in Publication
Title: Ivory black : a novel / Brian Duren.
Names: Duren, Brian, author.
Series: Guernica world editions ; 62.
Description: Series statement: Guernica world editions ; 62
Identifiers: Canadiana (print) 2022041159X | Canadiana (ebook)
20220411603 | ISBN 9781771838061
(softcover) | ISBN 9781771838078 (EPUB)
Subjects: LCGFT: Novels.
Classification: LCC PS3604.U7333 I96 2023 | DDC 813/.6—dc23

For Jane, Cathy, Neil, Michael and Daniel

CHAPTER 1

2005

I'LL ALWAYS REMEMBER THAT day. I was going home, as I'd dreamed so often I would. The streets of Bethesda and the trees and houses that border them unrolled before me like an old film I'd seen many times. Valerie turned into our driveway, and there stood our house, two-and-a-half stories tall, yellow, with white trim, green shutters, and dormer windows looking out from the attic. She followed the curve of the driveway around the garden, full of azaleas, the broken stems of last summer's Oriental lilies, and roses that had yet to bloom, and stopped in front. I threw my door open and set my cane on the concrete and pushed and pulled myself to my feet and gazed at the magnolia tree on one side of the house, the redbud on the other, and the green steps in front that lead to the porch and the wicker chairs, where Valerie and I would sit in the evening, talking, sipping cognac, listening to the cicadas, and breathing the air thick with the perfume of magnolias and lilies.

I hobbled along, trying to catch up to her as she mounted the steps and pushed open the door. When I reached the foyer, I stopped to look at the oak staircase ahead of us, the chandelier above my head, the painting of daffodils in the dining room on one side, and Dad's painting in the living room, on the other. I took a few steps toward his painting of the boy running through a world of shadows, felt Valerie's eyes on me, and stopped. She was standing at the foot of the stairs, her eyes cold, lips sealed. I opened my mouth, but said nothing.

She turned. I followed her, pulling myself along the balustrade. By the time I reached the landing, she'd already disappeared. I struggled to the second floor and found her in our room, next to our bed, facing me, waiting. She'd pulled back the covers and placed my pajamas on the pillow. I went over to the bed and sat down. She stood close enough for me to touch her, put my arm around her waist and draw her toward me, but I didn't. She took the medications out of a bag and set them on the night table, tossed some newspapers, a notebook, and a pen on the bed, and left, without even looking at me. I gazed at the empty doorway, and then looked down at the bed in which we'd slept for so many years and around at the chests of drawers and her vanity and the family portraits on the walls and the self-portrait I'd painted in college. Valerie reappeared, carrying a pitcher and a glass, walked past me, set them on the table, and as she left, I wondered why she wouldn't speak to me, why she'd refused for weeks to respond the few times I'd been alone with her in the hospital and had begged her to talk. I dug my fingers into the mattress and closed my eyes and took a few deep breaths, and when I calmed down, I put on my pajamas, lay down, stared at the ceiling, and remembered how I'd wanted to come home, wanted so much to never be alone, never again be without Valerie, Julia, and Jamie.

For months in the hospital, unable to see, speak, or move, I obsessed over crazy things. Memories and dreams and hallucinations seemed to weave together, and I had no idea what was real. A serpent would coil around me and sink its fangs into my face and rip it to shreds. And in my head I'd scream it wasn't fair, a man without a face. Other times the serpent would pull me down into the depths of a dark sea, illuminated by muffled explosions—bursts of red, yellow, blue, and green. The colors would shimmer, like music, like chimes. I'd hear a woman's voice repeating my name. Her voice was pure light. My name rippled toward me through the water and faded. Gone. And then there was just the snake, swimming deeper and deeper.

Sometimes I was flying in a helicopter, like the one in Iraq. A blazing ball of fire consumed the sky. The roar of the motors and the thumping of the rotor blades pounded against my head, and sweat streamed down my face and back. The sun kept getting closer. The lieutenant turned around, and his eyes bulged as he pointed at the helmet and body armor at my feet and screamed, "Sir, put on your gear. You don't want to become another sign of progress." His face exploded in laughter, hysterical laughter that rose above the roaring motors and the thumping blades. I looked down at the streets of Fallujah and saw the bodies of Iraqi men and boys. I put on the helmet and armor, and felt even more alone. I couldn't see anyone, couldn't hear anyone, couldn't get the armor and the helmet off, and I screamed for someone to help, but no one heard. The sun was going to hit us, and the heat and the noise were throbbing in my head, pounding my brain, and any second the helicopter would blow up.

I clenched my hand. And felt a hand resting in mine.

"You're awake." It was Julia's voice. "You're awake!" she shouted. "He's awake!" I was with Julia, in the hospital. I wasn't going to end up a charred corpse. She cradled my hand in hers, so soft and warm. I used to hold her hand, when she was a little girl walking next to me. Her small, delicate hand. A man's voice said they'd take the feeding tube out in a couple days, begin lowering the settings of the ventilator and decreasing the oxygen, and start taking me off the ventilator for fifteen minutes, then thirty, then forty-five … and then … and then I'd go home. They wanted me to be able to go home. I wanted to go home. My hand was still cradled in Julia's. She wasn't a little girl anymore. She'd gone off to college. I was going, too, drifting off in the black river, leaving my hand in the cradle.

I often heard Julia's voice whisper, "Dad, don't worry. Jamie writes. He calls. He's safe." Jamie would also whisper things in my ear, things about coming home for Christmas and playing soccer with me over spring break. My dad, even though he'd been dead for years, would murmur, "You're a great father. You love your children. Love is the most important thing." And Valerie's voice would say, "Dick, we have nothing to worry about. Everything's going to be fine. Each time Jamie calls, he sounds so happy. He's safe. He sends you his love." All the time I was strapped to the bed, my eyes covered with bandages, a breathing tube down my throat, morphine flowing into me—all that time I felt Valerie close to me, and I could speak to her night or day, awake or asleep, like a dream that never ended.

My mind held on to her and the kids when people would come for me in the morning, slide me like a side of beef from my bed to the gurney, and wheel me to the tank room. They would submerge me in the tank, scrape off my dead flesh, and irrigate my wounds. They called it debridement; I called it torture. They wheeled me back to my room, slid my carcass onto the bed, and secured my arms, tightening the straps so I couldn't claw my face, rip off what was left of it, or what had been added to it. Footsteps would leave the room, and I'd be alone again, inside myself, hearing only the hissing of the ventilator, the bleeping of the monitor.

As the weeks passed, I struggled to separate memories and reality from dreams and hallucinations. I'd boarded the helicopter in Oz and flew to Fallujah the day after the battle had ended and the mop-up had begun. We landed, and the stench hit me before I even saw the rotting corpses. What I saw, I never wanted to see again. But I did, every day, behind my bandaged eyes. We'd just taken off in the helicopter when fire blasted my eyes and lungs, and for months I saw the flames in the dark, and the dead returned. Some of them died because of me, because of the decision I'd made to go to Fallujah. And every time I wondered why I'd made that decision, my mind went blank, I saw the boy, his dark eyes fixed on me, accusing me, and I stopped breathing.

The day after a doctor removed the bandages over my eyes and the stitches from my eyelids, an orderly brought in a wheelchair, and the nurse, whose voice I'd come to recognize, raised the bed and pulled back the covers.

"Your first time on the parallel bars. A few days on the bars, and you'll graduate to crutches and walk every day, and soon you'll just be using a cane. And then you'll—"

"I want to see my face."

She looked at me, wondering perhaps if I'd lost my mind, and then left, the young man following her. She returned and handed me a mirror.

I took a breath, closed my eyes, and thought, *Oh, God.* I opened them, saw a face that wasn't mine, and stared at it, touched it. My skin was abnormally smooth. My eyes above my inflated cheeks seemed to have narrowed to slits, and my lips appeared to have spread into a weird smile and to protrude from the sunken skin around them. Even as tears welled up, my expression didn't change.

I closed my eyes and felt the mirror slowly move out of my hand. The nurse gave me a few minutes, and then took me to the parallel bars. Avoiding her eyes, I did whatever she told me. Back in my room, I waited for Valerie. For the first time in nearly four months, I was going to see her face, and see her face when she saw mine. I dozed. Sometime later I woke to the sound of high heels striking the floor in the hall. Valerie entered, stopped near the foot of the bed, and stared, her eyes revealing nothing.

"They took the bandages off," she said. "I guess that means you'll be coming home."

Valerie stood at the foot of our bed, a tray of food in her hands, the same impassive look she'd had that day in the hospital. "I brought you some dinner." She walked around to her side of the bed and set the tray next to me.

"You don't need to bring me food. I can come down to the kitchen."

She looked at me. Her green eyes had dulled, puffy dark rings sagged beneath them, and her brown hair combed back into a loose coil made her face appear thinner, her cheekbones more prominent.

"Okay," she said, and left.

I took my pills and ate some of the dinner she'd prepared.

The front door downstairs closed. I pushed myself upright, letting my legs slide off the mattress. My bare feet hit the floor, and the pain that stabbed my leg made me gasp. There was perhaps more metal than bone in that limb. I grabbed my cane, hobbled over to the window, and watched Valerie walk to the end of the driveway, down the sidewalk to the end of the block, across the street, and disappear. I stared at the corner, wondering why she'd left and where she was going. And if she was thinking about Jamie.

I went down the hall to his room, almost expecting to see him lying on his bed, reading a book. The sun was setting, but I could still see the posters of rock bands and soccer players that cover the walls, along with photographs of the teams Jamie played on. I'd driven him and his soccer buddies to games all over Bethesda and neighboring townships, Nirvana and Radiohead blasting from the CD player, and stood on the sidelines or sat in the stands, rooting for my boy and his team.

I sat on his bed and gazed at his bookshelves, on which he'd arranged his trophies, most of them featuring a gold figure dribbling a soccer ball. Above them hang gold and silver medals from red, white, and blue ribbons looped around tacks in the wall. The shelves are packed with books. He loved to read. When I'd come home from work, I'd find him slouched over an armchair or lying on the sofa, immersed in one of the Harry Potter novels. He might've turned eighteen, but he was still a boy, reading about a child wizard living in a fantasy world. It didn't seem that long ago I was reading *This Is the House That Jack Built* and Dr. Seuss to him.

When he was a toddler, I'd say, "Let's go, Satchmo," and he'd give me his hand and we'd go for a walk. We'd walk everywhere— through the neighborhood to a nearby playground, through shopping malls … Once, in an airport, when Valerie and I were taking the kids to visit Mom and Georgia in Denver, I let go of his hand, and he wandered off. I followed him, never letting him get more than three feet ahead of me. He looked up at the people walking toward him, at customers sitting in restaurants and standing in lines at food counters, and at the ads on the walls. He never looked behind, and if I hadn't taken his hand after a couple hundred feet, he would've continued walking away.

Shadows filled the room. I felt tired and went back to my bed to lie down. The house was so quiet I could almost hear it breathe.

When I awoke, it was dark. I lay still, listening. Distant, creaking sounds. *That must be Valerie, moving around in the guest room.* Then footsteps in the hall, and the light at the top of the stairs flashed beneath my door. *Is she worrying about Jamie?* I wanted to comfort her, tell her how much I love her, how happy we could be, if she'd just talk to me. I sat up and turned on the lamp. The curtains were closed. She must've drawn them shut while I was sleeping. I poked my feet into my slippers, grabbed my cane, opened the door, and stopped, listening to the silence, looking at the light from the living room that reached the landing half-way up the stairs. The steps creaked as I descended, and the light disappeared when I reached the foyer. I walked through the dark to the living room and stopped. Moonlight from the windows silhouetted her head. She was staring at me. I tried to see her face, but couldn't.

"Why don't we talk?" She remained silent. "I love you. I love Jamie and—"

"I want to be alone."

I took a step toward her. "I—"

"Please."

"But I—"

"Please."

"Why?"

She didn't answer. On the verge of tears, shaking my head, I went back upstairs and collapsed on our bed and sat there, wondering, *Will we ever be close again?* I raised my head, and my eyes wandered around the room to the framed photographs of the kids, of Valerie and me, and of all of us together. My eyes passed over my self-portrait, continued wandering, and then went back to the portrait, a few feet from the door just beyond the lamp's arc of light. I hobbled over and looked at my twenty-two-year-old face gazing straight ahead, neither smiling nor frowning, as if I were looking into a mirror, intrigued by myself, like I was the object of my quest. Deep-set brown eyes, a long nose, a narrow face, and dark brown hair that hangs in tangled waves down to my shoulders—that was the face I had when I met Valerie, two years after I'd done the painting. The face with which she fell in love. The eyes peering through time, through the semi-darkness, mesmerized me. I hadn't stopped to look at the painting in years. I extended my hand and touched the surface.

By the time I was fifteen, Dad had taught me everything I needed to know about sizing a canvas, laying the ground, composition and color, fat and lean, line and volume, adding glazes to give a sense of depth and varnishes to protect the surface. But he'd done more than just teach me the techniques of painting, he'd inspired me with his passion. I felt it every time he talked about the painters he admired—Rembrandt, Vermeer, de Chirico, Magritte, and Hopper—the painters of stillness and silence. The painter paints what cannot be said, cannot be described. He paints the inside from the outside. Look at how the figures in Rembrandt's paintings seem to rise from the deep, luminous, ivory black of the background, as if the painter were bringing all the silence of their lives right to the surface. And you can see it—it's right there. Right before your eyes. You must see his work, Richard. And I'd nod, my mouth agape, and he'd show me reproductions of Rembrandt's paintings, warning me they'd just give me an idea of what he was talking about. I had to see the originals.

Gazing at my self-portrait, I felt Dad's presence, his energy, the intense silence of his studio, and smelled the paint, the turpentine, and the linseed oil, and saw the brilliant white of the isolated figure he'd painted. I heard the brush dragging across the surface of the canvas, applying yellow ochre and flake white over the layers of ivory black and burnt umber. Streets and buildings started to appear. He pulled back, changed brushes, and concentrated on lines, details. Angles veering off in unexpected ways. An unreal space. A dream space. An open window. Empty. A closed door. Another empty window. An empty street. Dad working with the fury of a madman, stopping, pulling back, hovering above the canvas, and plunging again into his work. And then he returned to the figure in white.

I didn't dare make a sound, do anything that would break his concentration. If I did, he might've gone into a rage and screamed, "Get the hell out of here!" the way he had once before. If I was going to work in his studio, I had to stay busy and quiet. For a year he had me copy drawings from his folios—da Vinci, Rembrandt, Dürer, and other artists. I did what he told me to do—set the book upside down, position the easel so I could look at the subject and draw at the same time. Draw what the eye sees. I learned to trust my eye and my hand, learned how to copy lines without taking my eyes off them. But that day, after setting the folio upside down, I wanted to look at the feeling the lines created, and not just the lines themselves. I set the folio right-side up and gazed at Leonardo's drawing of a young woman, at the sparse lines and the gradation of the shading, feeling the beauty and the curiosity about life that seemed to come from inside her, and I wanted to do something more than just copy. I looked again at Dad's canvas. The white figure, seen from behind, in three-quarter view, from a slightly elevated position, as if from the point of view of someone looking out a second-story window, outside the frame—that figure had become a woman, in a luminous white dress that made her look like someone from a Greek myth, walking down the empty street, past the windows and the closed doors, along the edge of a dark shadow cast by a building. I wanted to draw Dad's energy and his manic concentration, the way Leonardo had drawn the young woman's beauty and sensuality.

I picked out a charcoal pencil from the cigar box, turned my easel, and started drawing Dad in three-quarter view. I wanted to capture the shifting fulcrum of his hips, the pivot of his upper body, the stretch of his shoulder, his grasp of the brush, the fixation of his eyes on the canvas—the energy that flowed through his body and into his work. I completed one drawing. It seemed awkward. I started another while Dad was adding a new detail to the scene—a woman, in a black dress, barely visible in the shadows of a room, staring out a second-story window at the woman in white, spying on her as she fled the city toward the open space and the butte in the background.

I finished the second drawing. It still didn't work, so I started a third. Dad's hand moved up and down, as if it were caressing the canvas through the brush, applying more strokes of viridian green and cobalt blue to the sky in the background. He mixed some viridian and cadmium yellow together, changed brushes and began to add more detail to the butte, his body bending into the canvas, his hand moving so fast it seemed to be jabbing at the rock, as if it would open the canvas, provide another dimension. I leaned toward my easel and into my work. I'd never felt this kind of rush before. After a while, Dad stopped and stared at the canvas. The extreme foreshortening had transformed the open space, which had seemed to offer a way out, into a closure, a trap. Eurydice, the woman in white, wasn't escaping anything. His arm, the brush still in his hand, slowly fell to his side.

He seemed subdued, defeated. He cleaned the brushes and walked from the garage to the house, lighting a cigarette on the way, and I followed. In the kitchen, he reached for the top cupboard, pulled down the bottle of Jim Beam, poured himself a glass, took a drink and a drag off his cigarette, another drink and another drag, and said, exhaling a stream of smoke in his sigh, "Let's see what you . got, Richard." He poured himself another shot, went into the living room, set the bottle and the glass on the table next to his armchair, sat down, took one more drag, and stubbed out the cigarette. I sat on the armrest, handed him the sketchbook, and waited.

Dad looked at the first drawing, made a humming sound, and nodded. He liked it. He extended his hand, I opened the cigar box, and he chose a pencil. He added lines to the hand holding the brush and more shading to the face and back. He looked at the second drawing and made similar changes. And then the third—the one in which I'd tried to draw what he had felt. He stared at it as he dropped the pencil back in the box.

"Very interesting, Richard. This time you drew the energy in my work."

"That's what I saw. I couldn't get it in the first two."

He smiled. "You've started drawing what the inner eye sees." He nodded. "It's a beginning." He handed me the sketchpad, took a drink, leaned his head back, and closed his eyes. He looked exhausted. He grimaced, took a deep breath, another drink, and let out a slow groan. "Well, Richard, you've got talent." He sighed, raised his glass, his gaze hovering above the clear gold of the whiskey, chuckled, and said, "You're going to be a great artist." He finished the glass and poured another.

I used to think being a great artist meant drinking a lot, drinking so much it could kill you. Sometimes I'd wake in the middle of the night to the sound of Dad in the bathroom, heaving his guts into the toilet. When I was younger, seven or eight, I'd pull my legs up to my chest and wrap my pillow around my head to muffle the sound of the retching and the wheezing. But later, about the time I did the drawings, I'd lie still and listen. The vomiting was just part of life. I didn't even flinch anymore when I'd go to the bathroom in the morning and see traces of blood in a yellow film of vomit that didn't get flushed.

Dad wouldn't eat breakfast after the nights of drinking. He'd just stare at his coffee mug on the table. Sometimes his eyes would make contact with Mom's, and they'd look at one another, before he lowered his eyes or grit his teeth. Georgia and I overheard conversations about drinking, money, and the kids, and Mom asking how we were going to make it, and Dad saying we'd find a way. His art dealer in Denver, a guy with a gallery who represented several artists, never got a lot of money for Dad's work and kept half of every sale. When the dealer organized a show for Dad and two other artists, sold all their paintings and skipped town with the money, Dad went berserk. Letting go of his paintings, like *Eurydice*, and then not even getting the fucking money! When he talked to the cops, he threatened to buy a gun and go after the dealer. But he didn't have the money, so he went on a binge.

A couple days later, he came out of the bedroom. Mom was standing in front of the sink, peeling potatoes. He walked up next to her and got a coffee mug out of the cupboard.

"What do we do now?" Mom asked.

"What the hell do you want me to do?"

"I want you to quit drinking and start thinking about your family," she said, while cutting a potato into chunks and dropping them into a kettle of water.

"You want me to quit painting? Is that what you want?" He glared at her. "Want me to get a job in the post office? Kill myself with customer service?"

"I want you to quit drinking."

"Oh, quit drinking, like it's easy. Like quitting ketchup. Yeah. No problem. Just quit."

She squared off and faced him. "Quit, George, or I'll divorce you."

"And what will our kids do for a father?"

Her eyes riveted his. "Quit, or I'll leave, and take the kids to my father's house."

"You can't!"

"The next time you drink, we're gone."

They glared at one another, until Dad slammed the mug on the counter and headed for the door, throwing a chair out of his way.

He started attending AA meetings, dropping out a few times and going on benders, and during his worst bouts he'd attack his work. The sound of a door slamming shut or a voice shouting in the garage would wake me, and I'd look out from my bedroom at the light coming from the garage windows. His voice would scream, "Goddamn," and I'd hear things smash against the wall or floor, or see a broken frame with a loose canvas fly past a window in a blur. He'd slam the door shut, leaving the light on, and storm back to the house, passing beneath my window. In the morning, he'd disappear into the garage. Later he'd come back and say, between puffs on a cigarette and while avoiding my eyes, "Maybe we should get to work." In the studio, I'd notice his empty easel. He'd stand close by mine as

I painted, ready to help, smoking as he watched over me, his hands trembling. Eventually, when the shaking stopped, he'd begin a new canvas, and I'd begin to breathe and immerse myself in my work.

He had me paint still lifes, and later, portraits. Mom hung three of them in the living room, and I saw them every day: Dad, in jeans and a long-sleeved shirt splattered with paint, sitting in an old armchair, his arms extended on the red velvet of the armrests, his hands hanging limp, his hips pushed forward, creating a gentle slope down his slim body to the hollow of his belly, his intense eyes fixed on me; Mom, in a white dress, with splashes of bright colors, her warm eyes gazing past me, because she couldn't look at me without grinning, her brown hair parted on the side and falling to a ring of frothy curls above her neck; and Georgia, in semi-profile, with that self-conscious look she got when she knew a mirror was nearby and wanted to steal a glimpse of her long, glossy blond hair, which she would pet, as if it were alive, while smiling to the Beatles singing "All you need is love" on her transistor radio.

I became aware of myself standing in front of my self-portrait. I took a deep breath and, feeling tired, lay down on the bed, stared at the ceiling, and remembered my life with Dad. Of course, it wasn't just painting. Summer and weekend days, I'd often work with him in the studio, but at night we'd watch old movies on TV—Bogie, Cagney, Edward G. Robinson, the tough guys. I saw some of the films so many times, I knew a lot of the lines by heart and would perform them for Dad. The movies were like a language for us. Our own. Like the time when we were all sitting at the table, I was eating with my mouth open, and Mom said, "Where did you ever get such awful manners?" And I did the scene from *The Big Sleep*, where Bacall, in her husky voice, says to Bogie, "I don't like your manners." I answered Mom in Bogie's gravelly voice, "I don't mind if you don't like my manners. I don't like them myself. They are pretty bad. I grieve over them on long winter evenings." Dad reared back and howled with laughter.

I loved movies, and projecting them might've been the best job I ever had. I hung around the theater, helping old man Lother whenever I could. He let me into the projection booth, and I watched him screen the movies, started helping out, and took over the job. I was fifteen when I flipped the projector switch the first time, my eyes following the shaft of light through the dark, from the lens to the screen, as if the lens were my eye, and the light and the image were coming from inside me. I saw Bonnie and Clyde, living fast, robbing banks, and killing people in Texas and Louisiana, and it felt somehow like a part of me. And when the end came, the different cameras shooting Clyde and Bonnie, from different angles and different speeds, I'd twist and pivot, like I was getting shot, and groan as the bullets hit me.

That film was always in my head. At home, I'd do my own shoot-out. I'd seen a picture of Dad, wearing a double-breasted suit and a fedora, looking cocky and handsome, like Cagney, the kind of gangster the ladies would die for. I snuck his suit jacket and fedora out of his closet and put them on in my room. The big-man shoulders of the jacket drooped from my boy shoulders, the sleeves reached my fingertips, the front was as loose as a sail unfurling, and the hat sunk so low over my forehead I could barely see. I hung a cigarette from the corner of my mouth and struck poses in front of the mirror, tilting the fedora at an angle, the brim over my right eye, raising my head, trying a sneer. *So cool*, I thought. *Yeah, women would die for me.* I turned, stood in profile in front of the mirror, looking at myself out of the corner of my eye, imagining other people watching me. Took a couple of steps and then, *Shit!* The bullets struck, and I jolted forward, back, forward again, contorting and dancing to death as the bullets pounded me. I crumpled onto the bed and lay there, dying.

By the time I was sixteen, I had a steady job projecting films. I'd walk home at night on lonely sidewalks lit by streetlamps. One night, like so many others, a ghostly light flickered through the window as I approached the house. I turned up the walkway, opened the screen door, and let it slam behind me.

"Richard!" Dad called.

I entered the living room.

"It sounded like someone fired a gun." He was just a figure in the dark, looking up at me. A burst of laughter came from the television.

My eyes adjusted to the eerie light and the shadows. His cigarette glowed, and the smoke flowed into the cloud above his head. He smoked constantly now that he'd quit drinking.

"You've got to see this, Richard. Hilarious!"

I looked at the screen. A round-faced, frustrated Costello asked in his squeaky voice, "Well then, who's playin' first?" And Abbott, the lean straight man, answered, "Yes." I'd seen the routine before, but I couldn't take my eyes off those jokers. Finally, an exasperated Costello screamed, "I don't give a damn!" And Abbott answered, "Oh, that's our shortstop."

"Brilliant!" Dad laughed. A laugh that turned into a bigger laugh, a huge laugh, and something caught in his chest, and he dropped the cigarette into the ashtray and clutched his handkerchief to his mouth, and the laugh turned into a cough, a deep rolling cough that bent him in half, ripped his lungs raw, and dredged up phlegm that he spit into the handkerchief. He gasped and wheezed, until his breathing became less labored, and said, in a raspy voice, "Don't worry, Richard." After a few more breaths, he added, with a snicker, "Life is overrated."

The screen door slammed shut, firing a gunshot right through me, right through the stillness of the day. I stopped in the entrance to the living room and looked at the armchair—a green overstuffed thing with big round armrests. It seemed to be waiting for Dad, a worn curve in the back where his head would rest. The television, silent. A blank face.

I remembered sitting near him in the dark, watching *film noirs*. He'd talk about the lighting, the beautiful shadows, the camera angles. The visually brilliant films I had to see—*The Cabinet of Dr.*

Caligari, M, The Passion of Joan of Arc, and everything by Man Ray, Eisenstein, Renoir, and Welles. And his caustic comments that punctuated any sentimental film scene—"Freedom, liberty, what crap! The only thing people have a right to is their own death." And the long silences, the thoughts that carried him off, the stained, sodden handkerchief always clutched in his hand. And in the hospital, his laughter, the love in his eyes, when I performed the "Who's on first" routine, days before he died. And then, as I gazed down at him, his lips still open from his last breath, he rose from the dead. He sat up. I screamed, "He's alive!" "No, it's just the muscles contracting, one last time," the nurse explained, placing her hand on my arm. He lay down. What a joke. What did he used to say? If God existed, he'd be a joker, a comedian. And death would be the straight guy.

I gazed at the green chair. He'd wanted to spend all the time he could the last few months in that chair, so he could be close to Mom, Georgia, and me. I wasn't even seventeen, but I could pick him up so easily, a sack of bones, bird-light, and carry him to his bed. I tasted blood. I'd bit my lip to stop crying.

One of his paintings hung above the couch. A butte, like the one outside of town, rose up in the left and center background, casting a deep shadow across the middle and foreground. Sunlight fell from the right background, knifing the shadow. Railroad tracks cut across the picture, separating the mountain from the town in the foreground. Windows and doors opened onto emptiness. A man, dwarfed by the mountain and the buildings, dressed in a black suit, shoes, and hat, walked into the light on his way out of town, out of the silence and the shadows.

"Where's the man going?" I once asked Dad.

"Anywhere out of this world."

The painting looked like a dream. The dream of a city full of violence—felt, but not seen. "You paint with your eyes closed," he'd say, "so you can see the reality you have to paint."

I walked down the hall to my parents' bedroom. Mom was sitting on the bed, staring at the floor, holding a rosary in her lap. She didn't move her lips, didn't finger the beads. Her flower-print dress hung on her wilted body. She looked at me, her red eyes wept dry. I sat down next to her, put my arm around her, feeling the sharp bones of her shoulder, and laid my hand on hers, on the beads woven around her hand like vines. She placed her other hand on mine, wrapping the vines around me.

The gray casket lay suspended over the open grave. I smelled the incense, saw the stare of the little altar boy, a fatherless kid from across the street, and closed my eyes. The priest, standing at the head of the coffin, intoned a prayer. Mom tightened her grip on my arm, her fingers squeezing through my coat, and Georgia clung to my other arm. I opened my eyes. The sun shone, a breeze blew across my face, a bird sang.

On the other side of the casket stood Archer, Mom's father, the rich guy from Denver. He showed up, first time ever, the day before, for the wake. Still, straight, and tall, he gazed past me in the direction of the butte. He wore a dark blue suit that fit him perfectly, unlike the suits people on Dad's side of the family usually wore—suits they got married and buried in. Archer raised his head, with its white mane, and pulled himself straighter and taller, as if he meant to measure up to the mountain. When he noticed me staring at him, he fixed his cool blue eyes on me, which seemed all the cooler and bluer because of his tanned skin, and smiled. I didn't flinch. He raised his head again and seemed to soar above us mortals in his own lofty realm.

Grandpa Rayburn, standing near the foot of the casket, a long way from Archer, wore one of those wedding-funeral suits, the black cloth worn to a sheen. Bald, thin, and stooped from years of working in a mine, he wasn't much more than a hanger for the clothes he wore. Grandma, who always looked malnourished, leaned on him and dabbed her eyes with a handkerchief.

Grandpa had said to Mom, "It's not right a man should have to see his own son buried."

"Eternal rest grant unto him, O Lord," the priest prayed.

I glared at him, and my mouth filled with all the words I wanted to scream. He'd told Mom and Georgia and me, after the last convulsion had racked Dad's body, that God had taken him and given him eternal life. Dad was gone, and nothing would bring him back.

A gust of wind, the priest's surplice fluttered, and something snapped. I cried, and rocked back and forth in the wind.

At the house, neighbors and friends had prepared a lunch. I wandered from room to room. Furniture, curtains, Georgia, the fatherless kid from down the block, small clusters of people—everything and everyone seemed unreal, ready to disappear. The door to Mom and Dad's room stood ajar. I touched it; it opened. Old man Archer had one hand around Mom's shoulder. In the other, he held an envelope. She was staring at it. Archer noticed me, his lips smiled, and his cool blues eyes warned me to stay out.

Chapter 2

Pain was throbbing through my head. I opened my eyes to the light entering the room from the window. I took my pills, rolled away, and curled into the fetal position, holding on to the knowledge the pain would end. When the semi-darkness began to feel like a peaceful harbor, I stretched out on my back and felt myself unmoor and drift off in the black river, wishing Dad had lived to know Julia and Jamie. I saw her, still a little girl, with blond hair like Georgia's, sitting on his lap, and Dad holding her hand and guiding a pencil as they drew, as he'd held mine when I was a little boy, my forehead resting against his cheek, feeling his whiskers, smelling the cigarettes and whiskey. And then his presence faded.

I lay still, listening for a sound that would tell me Valerie was in the house. I got up, put on my robe, looked for her in the other bedrooms, and went downstairs. As I walked through the dining room toward the kitchen, I saw her on the far side of the table, staring out the picture window at the backyard and the statue of Aphrodite standing on a rock, in an empty fountain full of dead leaves. Valerie had put a bowl, a carton of milk, and a box of cereal on the table.

"How long have you been up?" I asked.

"A while." She continued looking out the window.

"Thanks for breakfast."

She turned toward me, and her thin smile faded almost as soon as it appeared. "It's late. You must've slept well."

"The morphine helps."

Her eyes remained fixed on my face, and then she seemed to realize she was staring and looked away.

"Is Julia coming home?" My voice trembled.

"She's taking midterms, and then she starts rehearsals for *Streetcar*."

"*Streetcar?*"

"*A Streetcar Named Desire*. The play. She told you about it." She shook her head. "Fordham's putting on a production. She auditioned and got the role of Blanche."

"Oh." I bit my lip. "What about Jamie. You think he might call?"

She sighed. "I'm going for a walk."

"Valerie." I grabbed her wrist as she was about to pass me, without even giving me a glance.

She glared. "I told you last night, I need to be alone." She twisted her wrist out of my hand and left.

I watched her walk through the dining room, heard the front door slam, and collapsed onto a chair. I stared at the gardens, the broken yellow stems of lilies and hibiscus, the lifeless clematis that had woven its way through the lattice of the arched trellis, and Aphrodite, one hand reaching to conceal her breast, the other lying across her vulva. Valerie announced she was going for a walk the second I mentioned Jamie. If I didn't find a way of protecting him, she'd leave me. I checked my watch. It was after eight. I took my phone out of my pocket and called Ron Wolffe. A receptionist answered and said the Deputy Secretary of Defense was out of the office. I asked her to have him call me as soon as possible. It was urgent.

I gazed out the window at the statue and the brown leaves and felt like I was living in a dead space. I remembered the afternoon Georgia and I stood in front of the picture window, in the new house in Denver, the one Archer had bought for Mom and us, after he'd sold our house in Big Bluff, had our car towed away for junk, and bought us a black '70 Buick. As we stared at the new car in the driveway, at the ceramic pots on either side of the concrete walk, and at the wilting flowers that we hadn't watered since we'd moved in a few days before, I wondered, *What are we doing here?* Nothing made sense. We were so young, just sixteen and fourteen. And lost.

"I wish we still lived in our old house," Georgia said. "I always remember us there."

Tears wet my cheeks, and Georgia was crying, too. I put my arms around her and felt her body tremble, heard her breath catch. When the trembling stopped, I pulled back and took a deep breath. "We need to leave," I said. "I'll get Mom."

My steps echoed in the empty rooms. The house felt even emptier at night, when Mom's crying would wake me and I'd lie still, listening to her sobs and whimpers echoing in the dark. I knew Georgia was lying awake, too, listening, afraid of what lay ahead. We couldn't let go of Dad, couldn't let go of the old house, couldn't unpack all the boxes, all the shipping crates with Dad's paintings, couldn't hang anything on the walls. We didn't really live there. We might walk out the door someday and never return. Move back to our old house and find him waiting for us.

Mom stood facing the night table by her bed, staring at his picture, the one she'd always kept on the dresser in the old house. Now she kept it closer. I stood next to her and looked at him, a young man with a cocky grin, leaning against the side of a car, his head tilted back, his arms crossed in front of him, a cigarette in his hand. I'd always wondered what he was thinking, so I asked Mom. She blushed, laughed, and started crying again. After she recovered, I walked her toward the front door. She leaned on me, and I felt she might collapse if I let go. She paused in the living room and looked around. "Why couldn't he have given us a house like this when your father was alive?"

The question startled me. I didn't know what to make of Archer. A few days before, she'd tried talking to Georgia and me about him. "He's a good man, a good father, a good grandfather. He's making sure we have everything we need. Your dad and I, we didn't have a lot of money. Without your grandfather, we'd be living in poverty." She wiped the tears that welled up in her eyes with the handkerchief she always seemed to have at hand now. I asked her why he'd never come to visit us, and she licked her lips, as if she were getting ready to say a lot, and then, staring off, her mouth agape, her brow furrowed, said, "Your dad and my father didn't get along."

Georgia and I walked Mom to the car. She got in on the passenger side, Georgia sat in the back, and I drove. I pulled away from the three-bedroom rambler, a five-foot tree standing on either side of the driveway, and drove down the street lined with ramblers and trees just like ours. Thirty minutes later, we stood in front of the stone mansion Archer's father had built, with the fortune he'd made in mining. The walls rose like cliffs. It felt more like a monument than a house and looked exactly like Dad had described it, when he'd talk about the miners, or the mudsills, as he called them, on whose bodies the house's foundation had been laid.

A short, white-haired Latino opened the door and greeted Mom. "Hello, Ann."

"Hello, Jesús." Mom smiled. "It's wonderful to see you again, after such a long time."

"You look even more like your mother."

"Thank you."

"Your father's waiting for you."

We entered a large hall, and I stopped to look at a staircase, wide enough for four people to walk next to one another. The banisters that framed the stairs merged at the bottom with a pair of winged lions, sculpted out of the same dark wood as the thick handrails, each lion holding up one of its front paws, as if to greet the people who were about to mount the steps, or warn them to stay away. Jesús showed us into the living room, where shafts of pale sunlight penetrated the tall windows, dimly lighting portraits in gilt frames of men with mustaches, beards, and puffed chests, gazing off at something beyond the viewer. A life-size portrait of one of the men took up much of a wall. He rested a hand on a large globe as he smiled upon the world. In the background stood bookshelves lined with thick volumes. Mom stopped next to me.

"Who's he?" I asked.

"My grandfather."

Dad had told me none of the men in Mom's family were interested in books or art, so I found the books in the painting bizarre. Dad had also talked about the mansion full of portraits by "sycophant painters"—portrait painters, who made the rich look good, lofty, superior to commoners, to the mudsills—the painters who worked for money.

Archer, with his white mane and proud bearing, wearing a sport jacket, shirt, and slacks, entered the room, a tight smile on his lips, his intense eyes shifting back and forth. As he gave Mom a hug, she raised her hands and rested them against his shoulders, perhaps not wanting to get too close, and said, "Hello, Father," and when he let go, she wiped the corners of her eyes with her handkerchief. He beamed as he gazed at her and turned toward me and shook my hand with a firm grip, telling me how good it was to see me, and did the same with Georgia.

During lunch, he sat at the head of the table. Mom and Georgia sat at one side of him, and I at the other. He asked us if we liked our new house, and Mom said yes and thanked him, and looked at Georgia and me, and we responded, "Yes. Thank you, Grandpa." He talked about Mom's bedroom, the one she'd had growing up, in which everything was just as it had been when she'd last seen it, and about the neighbors who'd moved or passed away in the last—"How many years has it been?" he asked.

"Seventeen," Mom said.

He nodded as he repeated, "seventeen years," drawing out the syllables as his voice faded. Mom asked about two of her friends, but Archer couldn't remember who they were, let alone what had happened to them. Most of the time I focused on dinner, which included things I'd never eaten before—pheasant-and-wild-rice soup, roast bison, and a dessert that looked burned, *crème brûlée*. Jesús moved around the table, serving us, smiling at me when I looked up at him, and disappearing into the kitchen. Mom was drinking her coffee when Archer lit a cigar, leaned back, took another sip of his brandy, fixed his eyes on me and smiled and nodded, and then turned to Mom.

"Why don't you take Georgia upstairs and show her your room, show her around the house. Dick and I'll go to my office, where we can talk, man to man."

I looked at Mom and saw her furrowed brow.

"I just want to get to know the boy," Archer said in his gruff voice. He smiled, as if wanting to reassure her everything was okay.

Mom looked at me and, after a pause, nodded.

Archer guided me down a hall with huge paintings of Western scenes: Indians on horseback riding alongside a stampeding buffalo herd, one of them holding a bent bow, about to shoot an arrow into the flank of a buffalo; a cowboy on a horse that had reared back at the sight of a rampant grizzly, boulders and trees in the background; and other paintings, all of them framed with ornately carved dark wood and adorned at the bottom with a gold plaque and a title. We entered a large room, where strategically positioned lamps created rich halos of light. Built-in bookshelves, an elk's head, a stuffed wolf, a flying eagle, and more portraits lined the walls. Archer led me across a Navajo rug of red, green, black, and white toward a desk that stood in front of windows, which looked out upon pine and ash and a mountain rising above the tree line in the distance. He gestured toward one of two armchairs and sat down at his desk facing me. I sank into the chair and positioned my arms on the armrests to buoy me up. Archer leaned back, looked at me across the desk, puffed on his cigar, and blew smoke at me.

"Well, Dick. Finally, just you and me."

I wanted to leave, so it would just be him. I felt like a little boy.

"You don't mind if I call you Dick, do you? Your mother calls you Richard, but I bet your friends call you Dick." He smiled, crinkling the tanned skin around his eyes.

I shrugged, too intimidated to say anything.

"Well, we haven't had much opportunity to get to know one another. Now that you're here in Denver, we're going to have time. Lots of time."

I stared past him at the mountain. I could feel him looking at me. He leaned forward.

"Tell me, Dick, what interests you? What do you like to do?"

"I … I like to watch films. I worked at a movie theater, projecting movies. Until we moved here."

"Okay. What else?"

"I do imitations of actors, like Cagney, Bogie, Bela Lugosi."

"Well, that might be fun to do with your friends."

"I draw, too. I do caricatures."

"Ah, the caricatures." He chuckled. "Your mother told me all about them. They've gotten you into trouble. A caricature of the principal?" He grinned and shook his head. "Dick."

"I could be an artist, like my dad."

"You could. Do you want to?"

"I'm good at it. And it's something I like to do."

"Hmm. Can you make a living at it?"

"I …" I thought of the arguments between Mom and Dad that had so often come back to money.

"You know, someday you might want to get married and have children. You're probably not thinking about that now, but the day will come. Maybe sooner than you think. You never know when you'll meet that special person." Archer's eyes remained fixed on me. He smiled. "When I was about your age, I wanted to be a professional football player. I loved playing the game. I was a split end. That's what they called wide receivers in those days. Catching the ball, making a play, it was all about concentration. You had to be fast and know your routes, but, above all, you had to focus on the ball, be in exactly the right place at the right time. And when I'd make a great catch, there was nothing like it. It felt …" He shook his head.

"Well, I've rarely felt anything like it since. But, back then, you couldn't make a living playing football. Couldn't support yourself, let alone a family. I played for a while in college, and then my father had a conversation with me, kind of like the one I'm having with you. He talked about the importance of one day taking over his mining company and providing for our family, for future generations, and jobs for immigrants and the poor, so they can get by, and I understood what I had to do. I had to grow up. I dropped football and, instead of concentrating on a ball in the air, focused on what I had to learn to lead this company."

He nodded, staring past me, looking very satisfied with himself. And then he focused on me again, chewing on his lower lip and reflecting, before saying, "You know, Dick, before you were born, I offered your father a job, a path to success. I wanted him to be able to provide a good life for your mother, and for the children I knew she wanted to have." Archer shook his head. "All he wanted was to be an artist. I couldn't help him. But I can help you, your mother, and Georgia. Your lives are going to change for the better. They already have. And you'll never again have to go without."

I was going without Dad. He'd died just a couple months before.

Archer leaned toward me. "Dick, I want you to feel you have a future. That you can get married and have a family. I want you to have all the opportunities and privileges my grandson should have. A college education. A career. A profession worthy of a man." He paused. "What do you think of that?" I remained silent, and his smile faded. "Well, what do you think?"

"I, ah—I guess I just thought I'd finish high school, get a job, and work."

"Your life's going to be very different now. You can dream. You can be ambitious. In fact, I want you to be ambitious. I want you to accomplish great things." He waited for me to say something, and when I didn't, he got up and turned toward the window. A thin stream of smoke rose above his head. He turned around and, standing in an aura of sunlight and smoke, said, "Our family, after so many years, has finally come together."

My breath caught.

"Your mother is my only child, and you and Georgia, my only grandchildren. We're a family, and family means a lot to me."

I looked down at the floor, remembering Mom asking why he couldn't have given us that house when Dad was still alive.

"We depend on my company to provide our family with the wealth we need to lead our lives. Someday, Dick, I'm going to pass on. My business needs to stay in the family." He paused. "Dick, look at me." I looked at him. He smiled. "I want the two of us to work together, to prepare you to become the man who will take my place, who will hold the family together. You need to understand everything that's important—business, finance, law. You have to be ready to lead." He paused. "What do you think of that, Dick?"

I couldn't think. I mumbled, "Yeah."

"Yeah?" he repeated, a baffled look on his face. "That's all? 'Yeah?'"

"What you're talking about—I've never ... I don't know."

"I'm sure this is all so new. You've grown up until now with ..." His jaw clenched, and his blue eyes froze. He turned his back toward me, faced the window, and, in a tone seething with disgust, mumbled to himself, "... that Goddamn drunk."

I flinched, and clenched my fists. He probably thought I couldn't hear him.

He turned toward me and forced a smile. "It's time to move on, Dick. Time for us to work together. After you graduate high school, I'll send you to Colorado State for a couple years, because you have some catching up to do." He sat down at the desk and leaned forward. "After Colorado State, I'll put you through the best university you can get into. You'll do whatever interests you most—pre-law, business, finance. And then you'll get a law degree, or an MBA. And I'll pay for everything. Dick, you'll never have to worry about money again. And you can have all the fun you want." His smile morphed into a smirk, like we were buddies. "A guy can have a lot of fun in college. And you like to have fun, don't you?" He nodded, the smirk lingering on his lips. "And then, when you're done with law school or business school, you'll come back, I'll put you on the payroll as my assistant, and you'll learn how to run the business. And someday, it'll be yours. The business, this house, everything."

"I'll be rich, and so will Mom and Georgia?"

"And any children you and Georgia might have."

I thought of what it would be like to be rich and live in a mansion. Mom would never have to worry about money. I remembered the arguments between Mom and Dad, and the tense silence that would follow. But we'd been so happy. Mom and Georgia and I would give anything to be back in that house with Dad. I felt Archer's eyes fixed on me.

"Well?" he asked. When I didn't say anything, he added, "Most young men would give anything for what I'm offering you."

"Why couldn't you have given us a new house when Dad was alive?"

"What?"

"You could've helped us all those years, but you didn't."

"I tried to help your father. He didn't want my help."

"What about my mother? What about Georgia and me?"

His eyes narrowed, and his face flushed red. "I warned your mother."

"You warned her?"

He stared at me, as if wondering whether he should say what he was thinking, and then sneered. "I warned her, if she married him, she'd never get a dime from me. Not a dime."

"What was so wrong about my father?"

Archer leaned over his desk, like he might lunge at me. "He was a drunk. A lazy drunk, who never held down a job. And when he died … when he died, the world lost nothing."

I jumped up and shouted, "We lost everything. You're nothing. Nothing but a rich, selfish, disgusting old man."

"Get out!"

I backed into the armchair I'd been sitting on, fell into it, leaped up, and walked backwards screaming, "I hate you, I hate your guts." I turned and rushed out of the room, while Archer yelled, "Nothing. He was nothing."

By the time Mom and Georgia caught up with me, I was sobbing in the car, pounding my head against the steering wheel. Mom begged me to tell her what had happened. I told her what Grandpa had called Dad, and she fell silent. I kept on crying, repeating I was sorry, sorry for what I'd told Grandpa, sorry for throwing away everything he'd offered, but the way he'd talked about Dad …

She had me move over to the passenger seat and drove us home. That night, as I lay in bed, I heard her moving around the house. When Georgia and I got up Monday morning, she sat us down at the kitchen table and told us she was going back to teaching elementary school, and she'd take any job she could get—full-time, part-time, or substitute teaching. Georgia got a part-time job as a waitress, I found a job as a projectionist, and we sold the house and moved to a less expensive part of Denver.

I thought I'd never see Archer again.

CHAPTER 3

A s THE MONTHS PASSED, I came to accept that Mom and Georgia and I could never move back to our old house and find Dad waiting for us, and I started to feel like the man in the painting that had always hung in the living room, the man walking out of the city on his way to anywhere. I could go with him, because I no longer had a sun around which to orbit. I'd fallen in love with *Easy Rider*, which I'd projected a dozen times in Big Bluff, and sometimes, walking home at night in Denver, I'd hear the character Wyatt say to me, "You do your own thing in your own time," and I'd see him heading out on the highway, looking for adventure. I wanted to do my own thing in my own time and go wherever I felt like going.

During Christmas vacation, I met a girl from Minneapolis who told me what a great city it was for artists and leftists. She described it as a kind of Venice, with so many lakes, some of them connected by creeks and canals, and people swimming, sailing, and canoeing. She planted that description in my head, and it grew into a dream. I graduated high school, moved to Minneapolis, got a job as a projectionist, and, with help from Mom—and money for which she'd begged from Archer, who seemed to hover over our family—I attended the University. I never saw the young woman again, but there were others. One, in particular.

I was sitting in a classroom, bored, while the Ichabod lectured. A blonde stood in the doorway, off to the side, scanning the room, looking for an empty desk, and saw the one next to me. She sat down, glanced at me with her brown eyes, and I thought, *Faye Dunaway*. She gave me that Dunaway big-eyed look, as if to say, *Oh! Who are you? Why are you staring at me?* I smiled, and she smiled back. At the end of class, I asked what her name was. The next time Helen came to class, she stopped just inside the door, looked around until she saw me, and sat down next to me. The time after that, I walked in and found her already seated. She took her textbook off the desk next to her and invited me with her eyes to sit at the place she'd saved. We sat next to one another for the rest of the quarter. Winter quarter, my senior year.

Sometimes, on the open page of my notebook, she'd write questions, like, *Where are you from?* Big Bluff, Colorado. *How old are you?* Twenty-one. In addition to answering her questions, I did caricatures. I made her squirm the day I did a caricature of the prof—his big head, with his long nose and black-rimmed glasses, perched on a tall, angular, wispy body, and his eyes peering through shot-glass lenses magnified into huge marbles. She whispered, "Be careful," while trying to stifle her giggles. My caricatures had a reputation— some of them had ended up in the student newspaper, and one of them got posted all over campus.

A couple of weeks into the quarter, she wrote in my notebook, *Do you have a girlfriend?* I wrote, Yes. I added, I'm a serial monogamist. She drew exclamation points after monogamist. At the end of the quarter, I wrote in her notebook that I no longer had a girlfriend. We went out for coffee, and I invited her to the spring-break party my housemates and I were throwing.

I started the parties early in the evening by making martinis in the kitchen for my current girlfriend, my housemates, and their girlfriends, and then, when the crowd arrived, we'd switch to jug wine and a keg of beer. By the time I took Helen upstairs to my room, she'd had a martini and a few glasses of wine, we'd danced in the living room to the Stones, Led Zeppelin, and Pink Floyd, and she was giggling and giddy. I guided her with my arm around her back, my hand resting on her hip, and she leaned into me, laughing, trusting me to support her.

She stepped inside my room, stopped, and stared at my big brass bed that nearly filled the alcove in front of her. I closed the door, muting the pounding rhythms from the party below, and placed my hand again on her back. She arched her eyebrows and said, "Hmm," and gave me a look, as if to say, *You planned everything so well.* She'd heard a remark from one of my housemates when we'd headed for the stairs. I gave her a big smile, and she smiled right back, like she had a surprise for me.

She walked to the center of the room and looked up at the red veil with gold tassels that ballooned around the ceiling light and cast a red luminous haze. She approached the shelves, constructed of wooden boxes and boards, which held speakers, albums, a turn-table, and a red lava lamp. She gazed at each of my caricatures that covered the wall and stopped in front of the Led Zeppelin poster above the lamp. The caricatures surrounded the poster—a photo of Robert Plant singing on stage, and Jimmy Page next to him, point-ing his guitar toward the ceiling as he played—making it appear the centerpiece of a shrine.

"I saw them last year at the Met," I said, pulling down the shades on the windows behind the head of the bed and on either side. "Cool. Very cool."

She walked toward my desk, looking at the caricature hanging on the wall. "Oh! Here it is. The original."

The "original" was a drawing of a human figure with a round head, a curl on the top that evoked a pig's tail, a pig's snout, and what appeared to be a pig's anus under the snout with hams for cheeks. The words, MIRACLE OF NATURE, unfolded like a banner above the drawing, and at the bottom, the explanation, "An asshole from one end to the other." My friends, who had also taken the course from the pompous professor, loved it. They recognized his round fleshy face, the fat nose that turned up at the end, and the silly looking wave of brown hair on the front of his baldpate. Someone Xeroxed copies and stapled them to kiosks and taped them to walls around campus. They disappeared quickly. The cari-cature developed a reputation.

"You're such a devil," she said as she turned around, an admiring twinkle in her eye. She stopped, stunned, when she saw my self-portrait on the wall, just to the left of the door. She approached the painting. "I've never seen a face that big."

"I find myself infinitely fascinating."

She laughed. "I can see your whiskers. You didn't even shave for your own portrait."

"Yeah, well, I wanted it to be as realistic as possible."

"How did you get that picture blown up so big?"

"It's not a photograph. It's a painting."

"A painting! It looks so real. How did you do that?"

"A trade secret. All I'll tell you is that I started with a photograph."

Actually, I'd started with Chuck Close and did the painting in one of the art courses I'd taken for my minor. The course was easy for me. I'd learned how to paint with oil while working with Dad. With the self-portrait, I was experimenting with acrylic, just having fun. The instructor tried to talk me into majoring in studio art, but I'd chosen to become a historian and live in the ivory tower, as far from madness as possible.

"You're quite an artist," Helen said.

I feigned modesty and said, "Not really. The caricatures are just fun. And, as for the self-portrait, well, some morning I might wake up with an identity crisis. Oh, no! I'm a cockroach! And then I'd see my self-portrait and think, No, I'm just hung over, or, This has been one bad trip, man, but I know I'm that guy in the painting."

She wandered over to the opposite wall and stopped in front of a poster of Che Guevara, with his black beret and silver star and long black hair silhouetted by a red background, his deep-set eyes staring at something in the distance, like the liberation of mankind. I'd read a book by a historian named Albion on liberation movements in South America and decided that's what I'd focus on in graduate school. I'd listened to Dad talk about growing up poor in a mining town, scraping up what money he could to go to the University in Boulder, having to drop out after a couple years, and working odd jobs, painting, moving to Taos, and becoming friends with other artists. I hadn't forgotten where I came from, nor which side I was on.

Helen glanced at me, smiled, and gently shook her head as I tapped some dope into cigarette paper. She took a few steps toward another poster, one for the new movie, *Taxi Driver*, with Robert de Niro, shirtless, shot in profile from the waist up, pointing a gun, and the line, "You talkin' to me?" printed in white letters, at an angle, across the black and gray image.

"Ah!" Helen said. "That's where that line comes from."

I looked up from the joint I was rolling, got a crazed gleam in my eyes, and snarled, "'You talkin' to me? Huh? You talkin' to me?'"

She gasped, I grinned, and she burst out laughing. "You scared me! When we were downstairs, and you talked to me like that, I thought you were pissed. If you hadn't grinned …"

"Oh, yeah?" I'd recently projected *Taxi Driver* at the Varsity Theater. I figured she hadn't seen it. My friends and I had already used that line so often I thought it was useless, until I saw the effect it had on her.

I hummed, focusing on the joint I was rolling, while softly singing lines from Keith Carradine's song, "I'm Easy," suggesting she take my hand and pull me down. I licked the cigarette paper, lit the joint, and took a drag.

She moved closer to me, stopped next to the bed, tossed her purse on it, and said, "You like to do that to me, don't you."

I exhaled in a slow groan. "Like to do what?"

"Like to mess with me."

"You're so much fun." I handed her the joint.

She scolded, "tsk tsk," as she glided her fingers across mine and took the joint. "You're such an actor."

"Only in real life. You know, that crap about all the world's a stage, and we're just players."

She took a drag, her eyes descending from my face to my neck, and exhaled, blowing the smoke onto my chest. She took another toke, handed the joint back, dragging her fingers across my hand. She exhaled, got a look in her eye as if she could feel herself floating, and giggled.

"This is some good shit," I said.

"Yeah." She touched my cheek, her eyes following her fingertips gliding across my skin. "You belong on stage, Dick. Or in the movies." Her voice sounded dreamy.

"Yeah?" I took a drag, inhaled the dope a second time to get it deep into my lungs, closed my eyes, held it in for a long time, and exhaled. "You know, this acting stuff, it's something I started doing when I was a kid, just to have fun."

I handed her the joint, but she shook her head. I took another hit, looked at the joint, and chuckled. "God, this went fast." I walked over to the night table, picked up a roach clip, finished the joint, tossed the clip and the roach into the ashtray, and turned toward her.

She looked down at the bed and the American flag and then at me.

I laid my hands on her shoulders, moved them down her back, and drew her close. When my lips were about to touch hers, she turned away, pulled back, and looked up at me again.

"What's the matter?" I asked.

"When we headed for the stairs, one of your roommates said, 'Going up to the nooky nook?' He seemed to think that was real funny."

"You know, you really do have beautiful eyes. And such an unusual combination—brown eyes and blond hair. Like Faye Dunaway. Have you seen *Chinatown*?"

She drew her head back and removed my hands from her hips. "I've also heard your room referred to as the choir loft—because of all the singing."

I shrugged. "Yeah, well. I guess a few girls have kind of … practiced their scales. Hit a few high notes while they were here. Some very high notes."

"In the nooky nook."

I nodded.

"Was one of those girls Charlotte?"

"Charlotte?"

"Yeah, Charlotte. The way she was looking at you. How high did she sing? Soprano high?"

I grinned. Charlotte had immediately preceded my last girl-friend, who'd lasted about five months. As soon as any of them started talking about marriage, I ended it.

"You're used to getting what you want, aren't you?" She paused. "And you'd like me to get in the nooky nook with you." She grazed my chest with her fingertips. "You'd like to make me sing my hal-lelujahs, like I could feel the presence of the messiah." Her fingers wandered up my neck and traced the line of my jaw.

"Now you're messing with me."

"Oh, I'm definitely messing with you." She peered into my eyes. "So, why don't we just sit on the bed and talk?"

"Talk?"

"Talk. You know, utter words to one another."

I snorted a laugh.

"You can tell me about that little town you grew up in. What's it called?"

"Big Bluff."

"Colorado. Right?"

"Yeah."

"Then, if you're a good boy, maybe you'll get what you want. And maybe not. Depends on what I want."

I considered taking her back downstairs, but that would look like defeat. Besides, I liked her. So, bowing and gesturing toward the bed, I said, "After you."

She slipped off her shoes, snagged her purse, slid across the bed, propped a pillow up against the brass rails, and leaned back, setting her purse next to her. Once I'd settled onto my side of her purse, she took out a pack of Marlboro Lights.

"Cigarettes will kill you," I said.

"I'm trying to quit."

"They killed my dad."

"I'm sorry."

"It was a long time ago."

She put the cigarettes back in her purse.

"I didn't mean to—"

"It's all right."

She reached across the purse and laid her hand on mine. "So, tell me about Big Bluff."

"Big Bluff? Really?"

"Really."

So, I told her. The only big thing about the city was the bluff, and one of the few things to do was go to the movies. I talked about projecting *Bonnie and Clyde* and doing my dance of death at home, in my dad's suit coat and fedora, and as I talked, I got up, went over to the closet, got Dad's fedora off the top shelf and put it on. I snapped my fingers and said, "I need a cigarette." She took hers out of her purse and tossed me one. I bogarted it. Took a couple steps. The bullets struck my body. I jolted forward, backward, forward again, and collapsed onto the bed, my head landing on her thighs. She laughed and ran her fingers through my hair. I moved my hand over to the side of her thigh, beneath the hem of her skirt, and felt a flash of goose bumps. She clasped my hand and said, "I thought we were going to talk."

"Talk? Come on."

"So, you used to do performances like that in your bedroom?" She twisted one of the locks of my hair around her finger and gave it a little tug. "That's pretty funny."

"Yeah, I was a real clown." I told her how Dad and I used to watch old movies on TV, when I was in high school, and I'd do imitations of actors. I sat up and told her about the time my mother asked me about my grades, in front of my dad, and I did the scene in which the nightclub owner, the bad guy, Eddie, says to Bogie, "'Is that your business?'" I responded with Bogie's gravelly voice. "'I could make it my business.'"

"'I could make your business mine.'"

"'Oh,'" I shook my head. "'You wouldn't like it. The pay's too small.' Dad cracked up."

I could see him, laughing and shaking his head. And then, I felt tears in my eyes. I turned away and wiped them.

"What's the matter, Dick?"

I took a deep breath.

"Is everything okay?"

"Sure." I tried to look as if I'd been surprised by her question.

"You know, Dick, you could be almost anything—an actor, an artist—"

"Nah! We had one artist in the family—my dad. One in any family is enough."

"What was he like?"

"Why are we talking about me all the time?" I slid down on the bed, laced my hands behind my head, and looked up at her. "What about you? You never talk about yourself."

She smiled, but the smile faded quickly. And then it returned, exaggerated. "I'm just an ordinary girl, from an ordinary family in the burbs. My dad's a salesman, my mom's a housewife. I have two older brothers, who both went to the U. And that's where my mom and dad met. So, that's where I go."

"You didn't have anything to say about it?"

"Not really. I'm sure they think it's the logical step, so I can be just like my mother."

"Why do I sense you don't plan on being like your mother?"

"Maybe because you're smart. And perceptive." She paused. "When I was growing up, I always felt like two different people— the proper young lady, to whom my parents talked about marriage, kids, and church, and the other person inside me." Her voice took on a bitter edge. "They didn't even know that person existed. I didn't want to end up like my mother, with a husband and a family in the burbs, keeping a house and cooking meals, pretty dresses and church every Sunday. I want a lot more than that. A lot more." She slid down and lay next to me. "You're so lucky. An artist for a father. That's so far out! Someone over thirty you can talk to. Your life must've been totally different."

"Yeah, it was different."

She rolled on her side and laid her head on my shoulder. "What was it like?"

"Not all that great. My dad was a good painter, but he couldn't earn enough to support a family, even with my mom working."

"But, still, an artist understands the kinds of things that go on inside people. At least you had someone you could talk to about—"

"My dad didn't talk much. What I remember most about his paintings was the silence. He usually painted scenes of empty city streets. Everything seemed still. If someone did appear, the person was alone, dwarfed by the buildings and the shadows they cast. His paintings were like dreams. You know, the kind of dream in which everything is silent and still, and you can feel death. And you wake up scared out of your mind. That's what his paintings were like."

"But you must've had conversations."

"My dad and I had the movies. Above all, the last year, after he'd gone through AA. We had the movies. And my comic routines. I'd do my Bogie scenes for him. They'd crack him up." I stared at the ceiling. "He died. At forty-three." I closed my eyes. "It felt like suicide." I rolled away from her, got out of bed, took a couple of steps, and stopped. I felt tears welling up, wiped them away, and took a deep breath, and another.

"Dick?" She came up from behind, placed her hands on my arms, and rested her face against my back. "Are you okay?"

I heard a tremor in her voice. She was concerned about me. She cared.

I spun around, glared at her, and snarled, "'You talkin' to me? Huh?'"

She gasped and tensed up, brittle as glass.

I grinned.

"Dick!" She punched me on the chest and sobbed and laughed. "Oh, Dick!" She collapsed against me, repeating my name, laughing all the while.

I bent over her, her eyes fluttered shut, and I lifted her off her feet.

The last day of final exams for spring quarter, a Friday, I was in a West-Bank mood—as in, the west bank of the Mississippi, right across the river from the University's main campus, a playground of bars and after-hour joints for anyone wanting to have some serious fun. Helen and I had been talking about celebrating the end of finals, and what better way than going to The Mixers, The Triangle, or The Cabooze? Listen to some music, dance, drink, maybe do some dope. No time for acid. The big party was Saturday night.

I checked my watch. Almost eight-thirty. Where was Helen? I pulled on my buckskin jacket, rushed downstairs, threw the screen door open and leaped down the front steps. I got on my bike—a '52 Harley I'd had chopped to look just like Wyatt's in *Easy Rider*, minus the American flag. I turned the key and after a third kick the motor ripped. I twisted the throttle a couple times, making the air rumble around me. And then I heard Helen, shouting my name. I looked back and saw her running toward me, her purse swinging by her side.

She caught up to me, grasped my arm, and tried to catch her breath. "You weren't leaving me behind, were you?"

I slipped my hand under her blouse and skimmed it across the top of her hip and down the small of her back until my fingertips reached the crevice between her cheeks. "I was just going to look for you."

She slid on, I put the chopper in gear, and we roared off. We crossed the Tenth Avenue Bridge in the glow of the sun resting like an orange ball on the horizon, its light shimmering gold and red on the Mississippi. We parked on a street off Seven Corners and went into The Mixers. Students occupied all the booths and every inch of the bar, so I had to squeeze in sideways to the waitress's station to get the bartender's attention. People were talking and laughing, the jukebox was blasting, some kid was goosing the pinball machine and making it ping with testosterone, and pool balls were breaking and bouncing off one another with cascading clicks and careening toward the banks and thumping into pockets. We hadn't even finished our first beer when some drunk started a brawl in the middle of the crowd, and all hell broke loose. I bored a passage through the reeling bodies and got us the hell out. We finished our beers, left the bottles next to the wall of a shop, and walked down to The Triangle, where John Koerner stood on stage, hovering above the crowd, his fingers running, jumping, standing still, like spiders on speed, singing one of his folksy blues songs, everyone grooving and swaying to the music.

I squeezed through the crowd toward the bar, with Helen right behind me, got a couple beers, and then we moved away a few feet, where we had enough room to raise our bottles and drink. I wrapped my arm around her and pulled her close. We bobbed and bounced with the crowd, as if we all formed one huge organism, the rhythm of Koerner's "Everybody's Going for the Money" pulsating through us. The music, the crowd, the beer, the energy—I was flying high. I took a long drink and pulled Helen a little closer. She stood on her toes to catch a kiss and gave me a sexy smile, like she couldn't wait to make love.

I was watching Koerner perform, when I felt Helen's body stiffen. I looked down and saw her staring at the bar. I followed her eyes to some unshaven, grungy guy in a green army field jacket and jeans, with a rat's nest of dirty blond hair. He was sitting on a stool, looking down at his beer, oblivious to the music.

"Who's that?" I asked.

She kept staring at the guy.

"Who the fuck is that guy?"

"Let's go." She looked up at me with panic. "Please." She tried to set her bottle on a nearby table, but it tipped, beer spilled, and one of the guys sitting there shouted, "Hey! Watch it!" She rushed off. "Bitch!" another guy screamed.

"Shut the fuck up," I snarled, slamming my bottle on the table.

"Fuck you, asshole," he shouted as I walked out the door.

I caught up to her.

Tears wet her cheek. "I want to go home."

"Who is that guy?"

She kept on walking.

"Why are you so upset?"

She continued, head down, arms wrapped around her body.

We walked up Cedar, past The Mixers, to the street where I'd parked my chopper. When we got home, she went straight to my room and to bed. I lay down next to her and turned off the light, and she pulled close to me.

"Who was that guy?"

"Just hold me."

I held her. Held her until she fell asleep. And then I rolled away, tried sleeping, shifting from one position to another, got up and read, went back to bed, tossed around, got up, and went back to bed again.

I took a sip of coffee, set my mug down, and looked across the table at Helen's plate. She hadn't eaten any of her pancake, hadn't even poured syrup on it. She looked past me, as if I wasn't there. I stared at my coffee. When I looked up, she was staring down at her cup, her lips separated, as if she wanted to say something, but couldn't. I laid my hand on hers.

"It might help if you talked."

She shook her head. "I have to go."

She stood up, headed for the front door, and tried opening it, but it wouldn't budge. I reached over her shoulder, flipped the dead bolt, and laid my hand on her arm, gently turning her toward me. I tried to peer into her eyes, but she looked down.

"Are you coming to the party tonight?"

"The party?"

"Yeah. Remember? We've been talking about it for two weeks."

She looked away, as if she were trying to understand something. Finally she said, "I don't know," and left.

Watching her walk away, I wondered again who the man was and what he meant to her.

I returned to the kitchen, stopped at the table, and stared at the uneaten pancakes.

"You're up early."

I spun around.

Mike was standing next to the coffeemaker. "Ah! You left me some coffee." He took a mug from the cupboard, poured some coffee, held the mug to his lips, just in front of his black Van-Dyke beard, blew into the steam and took a sip. "Where's Helen?"

"She had something to do."

Mike approached the counter, not walking so much as gliding. Everything he did was smooth. Smooth, smart, and poised, he never lost his cool. "What did you do last night?"

I tried to look relaxed, resting one hand on the counter and the other on my hip, while thoughts about the night swarmed in my head like bees. "Not much. Went to The Mixers and The Triangle, came back here and went to bed. Kind of a shitty night. Everyone's talking about how The Mixers is going to close and reopen as a fern bar. Can you believe it? A fucking fern bar! And The Triangle." I shook my head. "I heard the other day it's been sold to some fucking real-estate agency. Everything's dying. The whole West Bank's gonna die. Pretty soon it's gonna be just like downtown. Or the suburbs. Gotta live fast, before they destroy everything."

"Man, what's eating you?"

"Nothing," I snapped. "Just didn't have the greatest night, that's all."

Mike studied my face. "Yeah. Well, don't forget, we've got the party tonight." He grinned. "And you're making martinis, Bogie."

I went up to my room and stared at the papers and books lying around my desk, wondering if Helen would call. I checked my watch. A little after ten. She hadn't been gone an hour yet. Was she calling that surly looking asshole, with the rat's nest on his head and a face covered with old-man stubble? Was she on her way to him now? I couldn't sit still, so I left the house and walked the streets, staring at the sidewalks, the same questions playing over and over. When I finally looked up, I was standing in front of the little brown house with white trim where Helen rented a room. I rang the doorbell. Rang it again. Looked in the front windows, but saw no one.

When I returned home, I found another housemate, Ron, sitting in the living room, a newspaper spread out on his lap. He said Helen had called and wanted me to call her back. I called. No answer. I checked my watch. Nearly two. Called again. Checked my watch and called yet again. Gave up, walked the neighborhood, came back, lay down on my bed, took some deep breaths, and told myself to focus on the party, on being with my friends and having fun.

A few hours later, I looked over my audience of Mike, Terry, Ron, and their girlfriends on the other side of the counter. Charlotte was standing close to me, her eyes sparkling, her Farrah-Fawcett-blond waves cascading to her shoulders, and her tanned, taut breasts holding up the top of her white strapless dress. I lined up the martini glasses. She moved a little closer. "Can I help with anything?" she asked. She rested her hand on mine and gently ran her fingertips across my skin, reminding me of what had once been. I ignored her touch. Ken, another housemate, peered over one of her shoulders and rested his hand on the other.

I told her I had everything under control and was about to turn my attention back to the gin and vermouth, when Helen's face appeared behind Charlotte and Ken. She flashed me a smile that zapped my tension and left me grinning like a kid. I could do anything now.

"'Of all the gin joints, in all the towns, in all the world, she walks into mine,'" I snarled.

"That's the way you greet me?" Helen grinned, squeezing into the space between Charlotte and me, placing one hand on my back and the other on my chest. "Ooo! A white tuxedo jacket and blue jeans! How cool!"

"I fled all the way to Casablanca, and look who shows up in my gin joint."

Helen raised her face toward mine, her eyes shining. As I bent over and kissed her, I felt for a second as if I'd slipped deep inside her, while the voices of our friends, from a long way off, called me a ham, and Mike shouted, "He just loves to say gin joint."

Helen pulled back. "I know. We went to see *Casablanca* at the Campus this week, and all the way through the film he was performing the lines." She smiled at me. "You drove me nuts."

"First time I've seen you in a black dress. You look elegant."

"You told me to dress for martinis, so I went shopping."

"That's where you were? I was wondering if you were coming."

She looked puzzled. "Didn't Ron tell you I was coming?"

I shook my head and kissed her again, letting my hand slide down to the small of her back and feeling her breast press up against my ribs. I loved how easily, how naturally our bodies came together into such a close fit. I pulled away, saw the gleam in her eye, and wished the whole evening would fly to the end, when we'd go to bed.

I announced to cheers and laughter that Father Dick was ready to perform the transubstantiation of gin and vermouth into the most sacred of all drinks, the martini. And when I finished with my jokes, snarling like Bogie and pontificating like a priest, and everyone had a martini, we raised our glasses to toast the end of the quarter and, for some, the end of college.

Terry proposed we drink to the great adventure he and I were setting out on. Someone asked, "What adventure?" And he said, "Dick and me are hitting the road on our bikes. It's easy rider all over again."

"Let's hope not," I said. "I don't feel like getting blown away by some redneck."

"Is Helen going to be your easy rider?" asked Charlotte.

Helen looked over her shoulder at Charlotte. "I'm always his easy rider, even when I'm not riding with him."

"I bet he ends up with an easy rider in all fifty," Charlotte said with a taunting grin.

"Helen's the easy rider of my dreams," I said, and kissed her, tasting the cold martini on her lips.

After the party, when Helen and I were lying in bed in the dark, she said she didn't want any secrets between us, wanted to tell me about the guy in the bar. They'd fallen for one another and started living together, and then everything fell apart because of drugs. This was the first time she'd seen him since they'd split. While she was talking, I was trying to understand what I'd gone through, from the moment we'd seen him in the bar to her appearance at the party. When I'd thought she might've left me, I'd panicked and felt like I was going insane. I needed to see myself in her eyes, and when I did, I felt happy, and strong, and confident. I needed to see myself in a woman's eyes.

After we made love, I lay next to her on my back, and she laid her head on my chest and whispered, "I love you." She hadn't said that to me before. "I love you so much."

"I love you, too." Aside from my mother, I'd never told a woman that.

She pulled herself tight against me, squeezed me, like she'd never let me go, and held on to me even as she fell asleep.

I wondered, *Is that what love is, seeing yourself in the eyes of another? And what if the other leaves?*

CHAPTER 4

L YING IN BED, STARING at the ceiling, I heard Helen's voice say, "I love you so much," and regretted what had happened years ago. Those feelings faded in the sunlight that filled the room. I'd already eaten the cereal Valerie had set out for me in the kitchen, gone back to bed, and dozed a while. I hadn't seen her at breakfast, hadn't heard a sound that might've suggested she was in the house, but now footsteps mounted the stairs. I sat up and grabbed the *New York Times*. She entered the room, stopped at the foot of the bed, and asked if I'd like to read today's paper. I told her I was reading it. She said, "That's yesterday's." She set the tray with my lunch and today's papers on my lap, walked around to the other side of the bed, gathered up the rest of yesterday's papers, and left. No smile. No questions about how I was feeling. I stared at the empty doorway, wondering if she'd ever forgive me.

I leafed through the *Times* and stopped at an article by Maria Cutler. Like many of her syndicated pieces, this one lambasted the decision to invade Iraq and ridiculed the people who'd made it, with the usual references to Puppy, her nickname for the president. It had caught on, and now some people routinely referred to him as Puppy, because he was the vice-president's puppy dog and took orders from him.

Maria had visited me in the hospital. I'd felt her touch, smelled her perfume, and talked to her. After a while, I realized she hadn't been there. I'd hallucinated her presence. I hallucinated a lot of things during those weeks, after I'd come out of the coma. The warmth and affection I'd heard in Valerie's voice when she'd whisper to me—I must've hallucinated that, because it was only when she whispered that her voice sounded affectionate. And Jamie, he couldn't have whispered anything to me. The little boy in Fallujah, he didn't whisper anything either, but his dark eyes stared at me—that was a memory.

And so was Maria. The first time I saw her was in a beer garden in Austin, Texas, in 1976, the year I graduated college and did my easy-rider trip. I was sitting alone, drinking a beer, and looking around at the college-age kids at the other tables, in the shade beneath the boughs of live oaks and the vines that weaved through the trellises overhead. I leaned back and stretched my legs and was about to take another swig, when I noticed a woman, in a halter top, with long black hair falling to her shoulders, sitting alone. From time to time, she'd glance off to the side, in the direction of the door to the bar, and then her eyes would wander, and a couple times our eyes met and fixed on one another, and then we looked away. However, when she wasn't looking my way, I'd gaze at her as she stared off, or as she checked her watch and looked at the door for the person she was expecting. She shook her head and appeared to sigh and then, resting her elbow on the table and her chin in the palm of her hand, stared at something off to my side and beyond me, and I wanted to capture her distant gaze.

I opened my sketchbook to the first blank page and took a pencil out of my pocket and started drawing her face, using a lot of heavy shading to suggest the darkness and the depth of her eyes, the thickness of her brows, and the volume of the heavy waves of black hair that fell from the part in the middle of her head to her shoulders. As I studied her eyes, fascinated by what I saw, she became aware of my stare and tilted her head to the side and gave me a look that seemed to ask, *What the hell are you doing?*

I decided to apologize for my invasive stare and explain why I'd been watching her. I got up, with my book in one hand and my beer in the other, and started walking toward her, toward the eyes fixed on me, feeling one second that I was walking a tightrope leading

me right to her, and another that I was risking ridicule and em-
barrassment and should go back. I reached her table and said, "Hi.
I can explain." She didn't say anything. I asked, "May I sit down?"

"Do I know you?"

"Not yet."

"Not yet? Really?" She chuckled. "You're making quite an
assumption."

"I guess I am. Sorry to've bothered you."

I was about to leave when she said, "Sit down," and gave me a
coy smile.

"All right." I sat down and gazed at her warm, dark-chocolate
eyes. "I apologize for staring. I was fascinated by your face and
wanted to draw it."

"That's an interesting line."

I opened the sketchbook to the page with the drawing and set
it in front of her.

She studied it, looked up, and said, "I'm flattered. You're a good
artist." She took another look and slid the book back across the table.

I tore out the drawing and handed it to her. "It's yours. Think of
it as my penance for gawking at you."

We both chuckled. I leaned back in my chair and watched her
as she looked again at the drawing and then set it down and glanced
at the book.

"It's full of drawings?"

"Yeah. I don't take pictures when I travel. I draw. Drawings give
me more of my feeling for what I see."

"Really. And what did you see when you were looking at me?"

"A beautiful woman with a dreamy look in her eyes. A woman
who's not hiding anything," I said, grinning, "because she doesn't
know someone's watching her."

"You wanna know what I see when I look at you?"

"Uh-oh." I laughed. "Sure."

"You remind me of those pictures of Jesus. You know, hippie
white Jesus with the long brown hair. Only you're wearing a buckskin jacket and jeans, instead of a robe."

"This is my easy-rider jacket," I said, grabbing a lapel in each hand.

"Easy rider." She shook her head. "Well, Mr. Easy Rider, do you have a name?"

"I do. Dick. Dick Rayburn. And yours?"

"Maria Cutler." She paused, as if waiting for me to say something other than happy to meet you. "Well, Mr. Rayburn, you're a Yankee. I won't hold it against you. I've known a few. Some of them have been very sweet. Some. But, I'm wondering, What brings you to Austin?"

"Before I answer that question, I'm wondering why you looked at me the way you did, when you told me your name."

"Because a Texan would recognize it and have a response. My daddy's Warren Cutler. Everyone knows who he is. But, you're a Yankee."

I was struck by her use of "daddy," which made her sound like a little girl, and by the father's implied status. "Must be a powerful man. Where does he get his power?"

"Daddy's got two homes. One in Houston. That's where he does his oil business. And one near Austin. That's where he does his oil politics."

"Business and politics are doing well?"

"You're in Texas."

"So, they go hand in hand, like lovers."

She arched her eyebrows. "That's good."

Her mouth opened, like she was about to continue speaking, when something grabbed her attention, her breath caught, and she exclaimed, "Jimmy!"

I looked, following her eyes to the door, and saw coming toward us, swaying, drunk, a lanky kid in his early twenties, with brown hair hanging over one of his eyes, in jeans and a T-shirt and an unbuttoned shirt with the sleeves rolled half-way up his forearms. He dropped a newspaper onto the table, collapsed into a chair next to Maria, hit the paper with his fist and moaned, "He's dead. Raúl's dead."

Maria cried, "What!" As Jimmy leaned back, his eyes brimming with tears, she scanned the front page of the paper and said, "Damn it." She put her arm around Jimmy's back and pulled him toward her while murmuring, "I'm sorry, Jimmy."

I leaned forward, resting my arms on the table, and she looked up at me.

"It says here that the night before last, his friend, Raúl, got killed. He was running away from a cop, who was pursuing him with his gun drawn. The cop tripped, the gun went off when he hit the ground, and he shot Raúl in the back. From a hundred feet."

"That's quite an accident."

"Yeah. Some things never change."

Jimmy set his arms on the table and collapsed on them, turning his head to the side, facing Maria, and closed his eyes. She put her hand on his back and gently rubbed.

"I should get him home. Can you help me walk him to his truck?"

She put on her sunglasses, the kind that conceal the eyes while reflecting the outside world, and we hauled Jimmy to his feet. I wrapped his left arm around my neck and my right arm around his waist, and as she extended her arm to place it on his back, her hand grazed mine, and I felt the touch of her skin. We walked Jimmy past the gawking customers in the bar and got him into his pickup. She revved the motor, and I leaned against her door and looked up at my reflection in her glasses and said, "I'd like to see you again."

"Well, you're traveling, and in a couple weeks, I'm going back to school on the East Coast."

"So, we should get together soon. Before we both leave."

"We should?"

"So we can get to know one another. How about dinner tonight?"

She shook her head. "Can't."

"Breakfast tomorrow?"

She shook her head again.

"Lunch?"

"Why?"

"I can entertain you with the story of my trip."

"Your easy-rider trip?" She smirked.

"Yup. Where would you like to have lunch?"

"You're doing the invite."

"You're going to have to choose, because I don't know this town."

"That's right. You're a stranger." She reflected. "The Old Pecan Street Café. Ask anyone in town, they can tell you how to get there. About one." She looked at Jimmy and back at me. "I need to get him home."

"I can follow you, if you want, help you get him into his place."

"Thank you, Mr. Easy Rider, but I can manage."

I returned to my motel room, threw myself on the bed, and re-lived the experience of looking into her dark luminous eyes. After a while, I sat up, noticed the phone, and remembered my promise to call Helen every night, a promise I'd kept until the last three days. She'd always answer on the first or second ring and want to know everything I'd done, and I'd hear the excitement in her voice when she'd tell me she couldn't wait for me to come home. But she wasn't the only reason I had to get back to Minneapolis. Within a week, meetings would begin for new TAs in the University of Minnesota's History Department, where I had decided to attend graduate school and where I'd be teaching recitation sections for lower-division courses. And I'd promised Helen I'd return two days before the meetings. Time was getting tight. I'd spent a couple extra days in San Francisco, and a detour through Taos had taken an-other three days, a detour that had led to the mountains, where I'd hoped to find the cabin that Dad, Mom, Georgia, and I had stayed in when I was fifteen and we explored Ghost Ranch.

Instead of that cabin, I ended up in another, where a bunch of hippies lived, and they took me swimming in a pool in a mountain stream. While we were drying off in the sun, I gazed at a girl's long hair splayed like wet ribbons on her bare shoulders, her skin covered with goose bumps, her nipples erect. Our eyes met. She smiled and turned away. That night she came to me in the dark, slipped under the covers, and gave me her warm, soft body. Free love, we called it then. It felt so natural, I thought it couldn't be wrong. When the sun started to come up, she slipped out and glided back to her room, like a ghost in the gray light of dawn. It wasn't until I was on the road that I felt what I'd done was wrong, that I'd been unfaithful to Helen, and I tried to assuage my guilt and quiet the voices whispering accusations in my head by rationalizing that I had to follow my curiosity wherever it might lead, that's what an easy-rider trip was, and that's what I was doing when I made love to that woman. She had intrigued me, just as Maria did.

I tried to escape my conscience by hopping on my chopper and riding down to Sixth Street, where I visited a few bars and got a little drunk. When I returned, I called Helen. She was so happy, she started crying. A kind of laughing cry, as her tension shattered. She hadn't been able to sleep, she'd been so worried. I told her I'd gotten sick and had tried to make up for lost time by riding until late, and by the time I'd checked into a motel, it was too late to call. She said she'd been imagining the most horrible things and pleaded with me to never do that again, to call her no matter what the time. I promised her I would. I also promised I'd leave the next day.

In the morning, as I stood in my room, looking at the door and wondering if it was time to go home, I remembered that line from *Easy Rider* and decided I wanted to do my own thing in my own time. I rode downtown, entered the Old Pecan Street Café, and saw Maria sitting at a table on the other side of the room. I sat down, peered into her eyes, and said, "You're beautiful."

She shook her head. "I'm happy to see you, too."

"I thought maybe Jimmy would be with you."

"Jimmy and I are friends. That's all."

"He seems to be going through a hard time."

She sighed. "He's been going through a hard time for many years. What's frustrating is there's nothing I can do about it. I can't make him stop drinking." She looked down at the table. "All I can do is show him my love." She looked up at me. "Let's talk about something else. You were going to tell me about your trip, right?"

I didn't just tell her about my trip, I performed it, expressing the excitement of it with my voice and gestures and adapting my narration to what I saw in her eyes, performing as I'd been doing since I was a kid. I told her about projecting *Easy Rider* in Big Bluff and about Terry and me setting out from Minneapolis on our choppers and riding across the plains, pursuing the setting sun through the Badlands and the Black Hills and the mountains of Montana, and heading south from Seattle along the coast, feeling we were born to be wild as we rode along cliffs jutting out over the Pacific. "We dropped acid in Frisco in the morning and couldn't stop laughing at the absurdity of life. And when I told some guy we met I loved martinis, he said, 'Man, you want a great martini and see a little of the absurd, you gotta check out this funky Persian bar called the Aub Zam Zam, on Haight. You gotta do it, man.'"

"The Aub Zam Zam?"

"Means The Fountain of Youth. That night, Terry and I stand in front of the place. It has a green and pink exterior, a Moorish arch, and a couple of minarets on a lintel above it. We go inside." I dropped my voice to a dramatic whisper. "Quiet as a crypt. A few dim lights glowing in the dark. A dozen people sitting at the bar, not saying a word, like they're in some sacred place. And then Bruno emerges from the shadows, looking like Boris Karloff in *The Mummy*." I assumed Karloff's deep voice. "'I shall awaken memories of love and crime and death.'"

She laughed. "Who's Bruno?"

I intoned again in Karloff's voice, "The high priest of Thoth, the martini god, mummified alive for having once made a vodka martini."

"The bartender?"

"Yeah. And the martini god condones only gin martinis. Man, I was scared."

"Why?"

"Because if he didn't like your looks, or if you ordered the wrong thing, like a vodka martini, he'd tell you to leave. Like you had to measure up to get served."

"That's the craziest thing I've ever heard."

"The guy's weird. Doesn't talk. Just stares. And he hates hippies. He runs the best martini joint in Frisco, it's located on Haight, and he despises hippies. Go figure!"

"We've got some folks like that here."

"Well, Terry and I must've passed the test, because Bruno serves us. Best martini I've ever had. We relax, get used to the dark, and look around. Bottles behind the bar, all different colors, glowing like they're lit from inside, and above them, this mural, with an Arabian prince pulling in the reins of a horse to stop for a veiled woman. Probably a scene from the *Arabian Nights*. I'm tripping out, and Terry's flying high. He can't stop talking about how funky the place is. Finally I say, 'Hey, Bruno, how about another round?' And Terry says, 'How about some mescal? I wanna make the worm turn.' Bruno gives us his Boris Karloff look, I feel like we're in *The Mummy* again, and he says, in his deep voice, 'I think you'd be happier at the Gold Cane.' And Terry says, 'We're happy here, man. I just want something other than a martini.' And Bruno says, 'The bar's closed.' And glares at us like we're unspeakably vile.

"We get outside, and shit! Terry's chopper's gone. The next day I take him to the airport, and then I split. I'm totally free. Freer than I've ever been. I cut across California and Arizona and into New Mexico. And I see some of the most incredible land formations, and unbelievable colors—red, magenta, blue, gold. I take a detour up to Taos, look around a little, and pick up a hitchhiker. He invites me to stay with him and his friends in a cabin they'd found, up in the mountains. So I spend the night, and the next day the hitchhiker and I and a couple women go swimming in a pool with a cold creek flowing through it, the water as pure and clear as air. I leave the following morning and come to a town, where a guy's sitting on a blanket spread out on the ground next to a gas station. He's got long hair and skin that looks like wrinkled brown leather, like he's been sitting in the sun for years, and he's wearing a necklace with rattles hanging from it. Rattles from rattlesnake tails. I sit down in front of him and the bead and leather jewelry he's selling, and he tells me about his peyote visions and the spirits of ancestors that speak to him in the wind and tell him what the eagle sees and appear to him as coyotes and flames burning in the night. Every time he moves, the rattles click against one another, like old bones, like death stirred into life. And then ... then ...."

She was staring at me, probably wondering where all this was going.

"Sometimes I wish people would just tell me to shut up. You gotta do it, or I'll talk forever."

"Don't worry. It's a pleasure to listen to someone who can put words together."

"I'm glad you're still here. I'm not just glad, I'm ecstatic. We should have musical accompaniment. A soundtrack. Someone playing, 'The world will always welcome lovers as time goes by.' And then Bogie says, 'Play it again, damn it.'"

"What are you talking about?"

"The movies. When you feel like this, there's music. You don't just say things. You've got music to make the words really mean what they need to mean."

She laughed and shook her head.

The waiter stopped at our table. I ordered the same entrée she did, but instead of a glass of wine, I decided to have a margarita, and told the waiter to hold the mix. He furrowed his brow and said, "Would you like that margarita, hold the mix, on the rocks or straight up?"

I grinned. "Make that a double margarita, hold the mix, straight up."

Maria bit her lip as she stifled a laugh.

The waiter said, "Huh, okay," and shook his head.

"Oh, just serve it in an ordinary glass."

The waiter repeated, "In an ordinary glass—yes, sir," grinned, and left.

"I don't know why I did that. He probably thinks I'm nuts."

"Dick, calm down. Relax. You've made it to first base. Okay?"

"I've made it to first. I've made it to first. That answers the question, Who's on first? Who's not on first, I'm on first."

She shook her head, a baffled look on her face. "What are you talking about?"

I performed the skit for her, and she laughed. She looked so happy, I said, "Well, did I make it to second?"

"I think you're trying to steal third."

I called Helen that night to tell her I'd blown the engine on my bike and was stuck in Austin until it was repaired, with nothing to do but wander around, and described what I'd seen of the city, mostly the University's campus and the downtown area. I told her I loved her, missed her, was so sorry I couldn't leave right away, and couldn't wait to see her and hold her again. After we said goodbye, and she hung up, I continued holding the phone, paralyzed by guilt. I finally set the receiver down and tried to sleep.

I woke up late the next morning and rode my bike over to a Mexican restaurant on the east side called Cisco's to have lunch with Maria. The sign over the front door featured a picture of Cisco, a Mexican Groucho Marx, with black-rim glasses and a cigar sticking out of his grin. I found Maria sitting at a table where she could see me enter. Above the table, on the wall, hung a green toilet seat that functioned as a picture frame, and inside the frame, an old black-and-white photo of a young guy in a military uniform, like what the cavalry might have worn in the 1920s or '30s, standing next to a horse. The caption under the picture read, "Rudy Cisneros and His Horse. Rudy on right, horse on left." Maria explained Rudy was Cisco's real name.

I sat down across from her, looked around, and said, "Yeah, it's funky all right."

The wall by our table was covered with pictures of people with big names who'd hung out at Cisco's, like LBJ, who'd meet his cronies there to talk politics, at least until he became president. While we ate our *migas* and red sauce and biscuits, she told me about her mama, who came from the *barrio* and used to wait on tables here, and her daddy, who was talking with LBJ over breakfast one morning, when Mama waited on him, and he found her beautiful, and courted and married her.

I had nothing as romantic as her story. I told her I didn't know how Mom and Dad had met. Probably at the university in Boulder, where Mom was a student. Dad moved back and forth from the art colony in Taos to Boulder, in love with his work and my mother. After a couple years, she used the money her father had given her for college to marry Dad, and from then on her father refused to talk to her. Dad succeeded in becoming an artist, even though his parents had no education and no money. I wanted to end the story there, when I felt emotions welling up that might overwhelm me, but something in Maria's eyes made me trust her, and I kept on talking about Dad, describing his paintings, how they often made me feel as if I were in a dream.

"There was a part of him that I didn't understand, and probably never will. But he loved us, and he was a good father. I think he felt guilty about not being able to give my mom and my sister and me a better life. That seemed to weigh on him. I used to wonder if he would've been better off without the responsibility of a family. He could've just walked out on us. A lesser man would've done that. But not Dad. Maybe that's why I was so angry when he died. Angry at him for abandoning us, as if he'd chosen to die. Sometimes I felt he had. I so wanted him to live, to talk with me, help me understand who he was, who I was, who I am." I shook my head. "This might seem strange, but I felt most confident in myself when I was in his studio, where he taught me to draw and paint, and where the two of us would work close to one another, and I'd get into this zone, this mental state, where I was what I was painting or drawing." I paused. "When he died, six years ago, it was like the core of who I am was blown away."

She placed her hand on mine, her warm touch and compassionate gaze held me together, and I felt relieved after having told her more than I'd ever told anyone else.

I walked her to her car, and she followed me to my motel, where I left my motorcycle and rode with her. We ended up strolling, hand in hand, on Lady Bird Trail, along the Colorado River, and I told her about my experiences working in the studio with Dad, and she told me about her desire to get away from Texas and explore the world, and her concerns about Jimmy, whose condition seemed worse each time she returned home. She fell silent, and I saw a wistful look in her face. I asked her how they'd become friends, and she said she'd known him since the two of them were toddlers. His parents lived in the house closest to hers, and when she and Jimmy were kids, they rode to school together. He was like a brother. When I asked what had happened, she looked away, and when she didn't answer, I rephrased my question and said, "Why do you think he's like that?"

"His brother, Jeb." She paused and took a breath. "He was killed in Vietnam."

Like everyone, I knew of people who'd gotten killed in Vietnam.

"Jimmy's never again going to be the sweet little kid I grew up with, and the rest of his family is never going to be the same. Because that boy died in a war. A war that shouldn't have happened, that our fucking leaders shouldn't have lied us into." She shook her head. "When you talk to his parents, they get this distant look in their eyes, like they see you, but they can't stop seeing their dead son somewhere off behind you." She sighed. "Poor Jimmy. Always the second son. Never good enough. His daddy lost his first son, and instead of turning to the second and giving him his love, what does he do? He just kind of dies." She shook her head again. "God damn him." I put my arm around her, and we continued our walk.

I didn't call Helen until late. I acted angry about my bike not having been repaired yet. How could it take so long to get new pistons? I couldn't bring myself to tell her the truth. Maybe I didn't want to admit it to myself.

The next afternoon, Maria picked me up at my motel and took me to Barton Springs Pool, a spring-fed pool about the length of three football fields. It had a grassy bank on one side, where adults sun-bathed and women went topless. As we lay next to one another on our backs, my fingers resting against her thigh felt the heat of the sun in her skin, and I let go of everything. Nothing could make me move. Nothing but Maria.

Her body shifted, she lay on her side, and her fingertips glided across my chest.

"You're smiling," she said.

"I smile when I'm happy. It's a weird habit I've developed."

"What are you happy about?"

"All the topless women I'm going to see when I sit up."

"Men are such fetishists." She pulled away.

I opened my eyes and sat up. She had removed her bikini top. Her hands rested, palms down, on the ground just behind her bottom, thrusting her chest forward.

"A penny for your thoughts," she said.

"You have beautiful eyes."

"You do, too. They're green, like emeralds."

"Yours make me think of chocolate. Warm, melted chocolate. Last night I dreamt I was swimming in chocolate. But it wasn't thick, just warm and dark. And you were swimming, too. I could feel your body."

"What did we do?"

"I had this feeling our bodies were exploring one another. I could touch yours, but couldn't see it, because we both disappeared in the chocolate."

"We could've drowned."

"Hmm. Death by drowning in chocolate, with a beautiful woman."

We remained silent. A cloud passed across the sun, casting a shadow over us and the few people sitting or lying on the bank that sloped down to the pool and the heads of a couple swimmers bobbing in the water. I could feel the end of summer. There was always something in the air, when people tired of going to beaches and pools and prepared for the beginning of the school year. The vacation was coming to an end, reality was setting in, and I was going to have to leave her. *She's just my easy-rider girl,* I told myself, but didn't believe it.

"I have to leave the day after tomorrow," I said, changing in an instant my plan to leave the next day. "That'll give me just two days to get to Minneapolis."

"The day after tomorrow? You just got here."

"I have to attend a meeting at the University for new TAs. And you have to return to that college back East. What's it called?"

"Smith."

"Smith? Now there's an unforgettable name. What's it like?"

"It's a great school. Very small."

"Maybe I should've gone there."

"It's just for women."

"So, you can't meet any men?"

"We get men in our classes from other colleges. And we can attend classes at their colleges, too. It's very easy to meet men. What's hard is meeting a cute Christ, who arrives one day like a holy man coming out of the desert. On a motorcycle."

I leaned over and ran my finger under her chin. "You have a drop of sarcasm there."

She grinned.

"So, the guys from the other colleges, what are they like?"

"They're nice."

"What does that mean, 'nice'?"

"They're polite."

I remembered something I'd learned from a woman I'd dated for a while, a theater major, who was a mime. "They ever do something like this with you?"

"Like what?"

I slid around so I was facing her. "You see my needle and thread?" I held up my hand, my thumb and index finger pressed together as if they gripped a needle.

"Of course I do."

"So, I'm going to sew us together. Let me know if it hurts. I'll start with my foot." I pretended to penetrate the skin on the top of my foot with the needle and then, when I pulled the needle taut, my foot popped forward, as if pulled by the thread. I leaned toward her and poked her foot with the needle; she feigned pain and cried, "Ow!" I pulled the needle, and her foot popped forward, too. I continued sewing our bodies together, pinching skin so the needle had something to penetrate. When I got to the hands, she held one of hers to mine, and I sewed them together. I pulled my hand a few inches in my direction, and her hand followed. I lifted my foot off the ground, and her foot came with it. I asked her to dance. Holding her hand with mine, I used my other hand to push up and get my footing. She rose with me. Once we were standing, I held my hands out and up, level with my head; she mirrored my movements, her body just a few inches from mine. I started to move, as if doing a slow waltz, and she followed, mimicking every move. I sped up the waltz; she followed me. I slowed down; she did too. I stopped and looked around, the way mimes do, with an immutable gaze.

She moved her hand; my hand followed. She moved the other; my other hand followed. She started to do a pirouette; I panicked. Then, oops, my left arm didn't follow her. She froze. I looked at my arm, then at her, then back at the arm. She looked terrified. I moved my arm; hers didn't follow. The thread had broken. I got the needle and thread out of the invisible pocket of my invisible shirt and started sewing my hand and elbow to hers again. I grimaced in pain as I ran the needle through my elbow, accidentally hit a nerve, and grimaced again as I wiggled my fingers. She commiserated, with a sad look in her eyes. Then I pulled the thread, panting, as if in agony, and passed the needle through the skin over her elbow, while she grimaced. When I finished, we started to waltz again, moving in unison around and around until we got dizzy, staggered to a stop, and I pulled her close.

"Those guys out East who come panting after you, did they ever sew you to them?"

"You're still thinking of them?"

"Did they ever dance with you like this?"

"No."

"They ever go swimming in chocolate with you?"

"No."

"They'd better not have. Because we were both nude."

"Oh, being nude should stop me from swimming with them? What about you and those hippies you went swimming with? The women, I bet they were nude." She studied my eyes, looking for a reaction. "I bet you made love with at least one of them."

I blushed.

"That's pretty ... far out, man." She put the "far out, man" through a drawl and followed it with a smirk. "That's what happened, right?"

"Not exactly. I was just ... Well, there's this scene in the film, *Easy Rider*, when Wyatt and Billy come to a commune, and they end up going swimming with a couple of women. I imagined meeting some women at a commune, going swimming with them in the raw, and making love with one of them."

"So, did you?"

"In my imagination."

She laughed so hard she dropped my hands and nearly doubled over. "How many of the other stories happened only in your imagination?"

"They all happened. Sometimes not quite the way I said, but not much difference."

"Well, like the guy you met, with the necklace of rattlesnake tails and the peyote visions. Was any of that true?"

"I did meet a guy with jewelry spread out on a blanket and a rattlesnake necklace, and the way he talked he could've eaten some peyote."

"So, you made up the rest."

"I might've gotten carried away. I was reading B. Traven and, well, you know."

She laughed.

"You liked the stories."

Her eyes shimmered. "I can listen to you talk all day long, even if the stories only happened in your head." She put her arms around me and raised her lips to mine.

When Maria dropped me off at the motel, she said she wanted to do something special to commemorate my last night in Austin and invited me to have dinner with her and Jimmy at his place. The next evening, I coasted down his street in sunlight filtered by the tall, arching limbs of sycamores and elms and a canopy of live oak, past two-story houses, some with colonial columns, and ramblers sprawling across expansive yards with colorful gardens. The street paralleled the Colorado, and the backyards of the houses led to the river. I hadn't expected Jimmy to be living in a neighborhood like this. I pulled my chopper to the curb in front of a split-level house and walked up and rang the bell.

Maria opened and stood in the doorway, dressed in a sleeveless blouse and jeans, her hair pulled back in a ponytail. She caught her breath and blew a loose strand of hair away from her mouth. Perspiration gleamed on her forehead.

"It's hot," I said.

"Sorry. I shouldn't make you stand there. Come in." Exasperation resonated in her voice. She stepped aside so I could enter.

"Jimmy's got quite a house," I said, as I walked into the living room, furnished with a couch, armchairs, and a coffee table. Nothing fancy, but new. Someone was taking care of him.

She shut the door and stood next to me.

"Jimmy must be into gardening. Not many guys I know have roses in the front yard. And those bushes with the red flowers."

"Crape myrtle. Jimmy's daddy pays a gardener to take care of the yard."

I looked around at the bare walls. "I guess Jimmy's not into interior decorating."

"He lives in his head."

"That can be dangerous. Where is he?"

"Out. I think he'll be back late. If he comes back." She sighed, looked around the living room and then at me, as if her mind were returning to the present. "Well, sorry it's so hot. I opened all the windows to air the place. You wouldn't believe what I found when I was cleaning. Dirty clothes scattered everywhere. Half-empty beer bottles, dirty dishes, with pizza, and roaches—both kinds. And a bare mattress, full of cigarette holes. And the stains! Oh, my God. Lucky I thought ahead and brought clean sheets." Our eyes met, and she blushed. The dance we had started at Barton Springs Pool was continuing.

I followed her through the living room, past a half-flight of stairs leading to a hall, and descended three stairs to the dining room, bright with sunlight. A plate-glass wall and door looked out on a sloping lawn, a weeping willow, and the sun shimmering on the river's surface. In the kitchen, we grabbed a glass of cold white wine. She told me we were having red snapper for dinner, a fish I'd never heard of before. I joked, "Is it aggressive? Does it snap back? Get revenge?" We grilled it outside and ate at a picnic table. She wondered if Willie Nelson would cover "London Homesick Blues" that night at the Armadillo and recited a few verses from her own version of the song, "NoHo Homesick Blues"—NoHo being short for Northampton, where Smith was located. A hundred feet away, the branches of the willow trailed on the surface of the water, like a woman's fingers on a man's back, and a canoe floated by in the lazy current, voices and laughter carrying in the stillness of the evening.

A few hours later, after drinking and watching Willie perform at the Armadillo and driving back to the house, I tried gazing up at the stars and walking at the same time, swaying as I followed her toward the front door, while singing Willie's iconic song about getting back on the road. She spun around, threw her arms around my neck, and told me I wasn't going on any fucking road. She plastered herself against me, and we nearly toppled over. We made love on the bed in the guest room, lay in a daze, and made love again. We wrapped ourselves around one another, exploring each other with our hands, our lips, our tongues. I was drugged by the feel and the taste and the smell of her. During moments of stillness, sounds would come through the open windows as if from another world—chimes in the backyard, the cry of a bird, a voice on the river.

The next afternoon, after the last orgasm, I lay exhausted, sprawled on the bed like a corpse, her head resting on my out-stretched arm.

"I have to pee," she moaned, "but I don't know if I can stand up."

I heard the words, but they came from a long way off. She rolled away and staggered out of the room. Later, the toilet flushed, and a long time after that, I felt her lie down next to me.

Hunger finally roused us. We got up and dressed and, when we left, she joked about walking as bowlegged as a cowboy. We drove to a restaurant she liked, got something to eat, returned to the house, and found Jimmy lying asleep on the living room floor, along the front of the couch, his head turned toward us, his mouth open. He'd probably lain down on the couch and rolled off. She knelt next to him, felt his forehead, and ran her hand across his hair, pushing long strands off his cheek and away from his eye. There was something maternal in the way she bent over him. I remembered Dad, passed out on the floor once, and Mom bending over him like that.

"What should we do?" I asked.

Maria stood up. "Just let him sleep it off." She gazed at him. "Oh, Jimmy ..."

Someone needed to care for him, but I had to leave for Minneapolis. When I asked her if it was time for her to go home, she said, "You think I'm going to let you go before I have to?"

"But your parents. They're expecting you."

"I'm twenty-one. A big girl. I might want to mount my steed, go for a ride."

I laughed. "It might be a painful ride if you're as raw as you say."

She pulled up close and whispered, "Let's go to your motel," and as we kissed, I calculated how much time I'd need to get from Austin to Minneapolis, about twelve hundred miles. At sixty miles an hour, I could do it in a day, and if I left early the next morning, I might make the TA meeting. Might even have time for a couple hours of sleep. We finished kissing, and I said, "Let's go," but she wanted to call home first and went to the kitchen to use the phone.

Jimmy drew a deep breath, exhaled a loud sigh, and regained his death-like stillness. His long hair had slid down over his eye again. I walked over, knelt next to his head, and as I brushed his hair back, I heard Maria say, "Laura Lee's just not feelin' too well, Mama. And she wants company. Can't blame her. Poor thing." A minute later, Maria returned with a grin.

"You think she believed you?"

"I don't know. But Mama trusts me to take care of myself more than Daddy does."

We were about to leave, when she stopped at the door. "This doesn't feel right. We should leave a note with the number of your motel, so he can call if he needs me."

Within a half-hour we were sitting on my bed, leaning against the headboard, and Maria was talking about her fear that someone she loved might drink himself to death, or kill himself, and there was nothing she could do but show him she loved him. She couldn't imagine what it would be like to have a child who was addicted to alcohol, and sometimes she wondered if that's why his parents didn't seem to pay attention to him, not just because they'd lost one son in Vietnam, but also because the other could end up dead from drinking, and, who knows, maybe they woke every morning wondering if he was still alive. She knew if Jimmy were her child, that's what she'd be doing. When she was at Smith, she'd call him sometimes, just to be sure.

A few hours later, the phone rang, I answered, and a man asked for Miss Cutler. I passed the phone to Maria.

"Jimmy?" She looked frightened. "What happened?" She shook her head. "Oh, no. I'm on my way." She passed the receiver to me. "Oh, God!"

"What's going on?"

"It's the guy who runs the pool hall downtown." She started getting dressed. "Jimmy got into trouble. We need to go."

I followed Maria past the bar and through the poolroom, where dark clouds of cigarette and cigar smoke filled the air, lights with green shades hung over each table, and guys, drinks in hand, chalking a cue, or bending over to take a shot, paused to watch the two of us pass by. We rushed into the office in the back, where an old bald guy was reading a paper spread out on a desk. On his other side, Jimmy lay passed out on a leather couch cobwebbed with cracks. Maria cried, "Jimmy," repeating his name as she knelt next to him and placed her hand on his forehead.

"He's gittin' worse, Miss." The old man stood up. "Someday he's gonna do something like what he did tonight, only in the wrong place, or with the wrong people. And he'll end up …" He shook his head.

"What did he do?" I asked.

"He came in drunk, in a foul mood, lost a game and tried to bash a guy's head in with a cue. Like I said, he's gettin' worse. If you could talk to his daddy or his mama."

Maria thanked him for looking after Jimmy and asked to use the phone. He set it near the edge of the desk. She dialed a number, waited, and said hello to someone named Peggy.

"Whoa! Now hold on, Miss Cutler. I don't want her down here. No way."

Maria put her hand over the receiver. "She's not coming down here."

After Maria finished talking to Peggy, we dragged Jimmy past the players and slid him into the back seat of Maria's car.

"So, who's Peggy, and why doesn't that guy want her coming down here?"

"She's Jimmy's sister, and an assistant district attorney, who doesn't know when to stop prosecuting."

I drove Jimmy's pickup and followed Maria to his house. There was a black Lincoln in the driveway. Maria parked in the street, I pulled up behind her, and we walked Jimmy up to the door. Before she could touch the handle, the door swung open. A woman with brown helmet hair and tight lips stepped aside so we could enter. She studied Jimmy's face as he staggered past her like a zombie. We got him to the couch and let him collapse.

"Who are you?" Peggy asked me.

Maria introduced us, and Peggy took my measure, as if I were a piece of merchandise, while Maria explained she was at my place when the man called.

Peggy asked, "Where do you live?"

"I'm staying at a motel, down on Congress."

"Well, that's none of my business. What *is* my business is Jimmy. You two can go."

"You know, Peggy, every summer I come home, I spend time with Jimmy. This summer, he's been worse than ever."

"You don't need to tell me."

"He should be in a program for alcohol addiction, and someone should be looking after him all the time. Otherwise ..." Maria shook her head.

"It's all because of our goddamn father. I so wish I could prosecute that man, but there's not a law against parents who have no love for their children." Peggy looked at me. "People don't have any idea how much a father influences his son, how he can make him and break him, how he can make him feel ..." Her gaze drifted toward Jimmy. "How he can make him feel so empty. So worthless." She drew a little closer. "This is my baby brother. The little boy with such a beautiful smile, such a lovely laugh. Look at him now. Half the time he's too drunk or stoned to do anything but listen to music, and then everything's groovy, far out. There's nothing left of that boy but the husk."

"He's still alive," I said.

"Barely." She looked me over. "Have you met Maria's daddy, yet?"

"No. I'm leaving tomorrow for Minneapolis."

"Well, if you meet him someday, I'd love to be there. It would be interesting." She looked me over again. "Very interesting."

Maria got us out of there, and we drove to a place where we could park and look out over the river. I tried to get her to tell me what Peggy meant about meeting her father, but she didn't want to talk about that, it was nothing to worry about. I let it go. We hugged and kissed and talked about calling and writing when she'd be away at Smith and I'd be back at the University. Concerns about Peggy, Jimmy, and the two fathers faded with the last rays of the sun behind the hills, and night settled on the black river.

CHAPTER 5

I DRESSED FOR THE FIRST time since leaving the hospital and was about to go downstairs for dinner, when I noticed the *Times* with the article by Maria on the bed and took it with me. I entered the dining room and found Valerie had set a place at either end of the table. Before everything had gone to hell, she'd put my setting at the head, hers to my side, and wine glasses next to our plates. Now, a water glass stood next to mine and a wine glass next to hers. I placed the *Times* on the table, sat down, hooked my cane onto the armrest of my chair, and stared at Valerie's place, at the china, crystal, and silver glowing in the fading evening light.

I took a deep breath and gripped the armrests. It felt good to be sitting in my chair. I looked around at the paintings on the walls—on my right, the yellow daffodils, like those we'd seen along the highways as we traveled through France with the kids; behind me, between the two windows that look out onto the porch, the field of bluebonnets; and, on the left, a painting of a girl, sitting in a high-chair, at a round table with a white cloth, a vase with yellow and pink flowers, an orange, a white coffee pot, and a book that Valerie recognized as the collected poems of Wallace Stevens. She'd studied his poetry at Smith, where she hoped our little girl would go.

Valerie entered the room bearing a platter and a bowl, set them down, and went back and forth, carrying food, a pitcher of water, and a bottle of wine, never looking at me. Finally, she sat down and poured herself a glass of wine.

"I'd like some, too."

Her eyes fixed on me. "Take morphine with alcohol, and you might not wake up in the morning. That's what the doctor said."

"One glass won't do me any harm."

Valerie noticed the newspaper near my plate. "She's got a lot of nerve." She glared at me. "It's easy for her to criticize and ridicule. 'We know they have weapons of mass destruction, because they got them from us.' She probably thinks that's really funny. And that business of calling the president Puppy, because he can look into the eyes of the American people and tell one lie after another with big puppy eyes. She makes a joke of everything. She doesn't have any skin in the game. If she did, she wouldn't be writing that trash." Valerie took a drink, gazed off to the side, pursed her lips and shook her head.

"Are we going to go through this every time Maria publishes an article?"

"I don't know. I didn't plan *this*."

"You know, I'm just as worried—"

"Stop it! You can worry all you want, that won't get Jamie out."

She stood, walked to the foyer, pivoted and sneered. "Maybe you can call that heartless bitch and ask her to stop writing that crap. I'm sure you could get through to her. Remind her of how close we used to be. Tell her she might not have any skin in the game, but *we* do." She stomped upstairs.

My fist tightened with each step, and when the door to the guest room slammed shut, I pounded the table. *Why the hell hasn't Wolffe called? He's the only chance I've got of getting Jamie out.* I got up, worked my way with my cane to the other end of the table, and took a drink from the bottle. The wine tasted sweet and strong. I took another drink, and another, felt dizzy, and collapsed in her chair. Even if I knew Maria's number, I couldn't call her. I wouldn't be able to think straight. After all these years, I still need distance. But there was a time when I couldn't tolerate any distance, and I'd follow her anywhere.

During my first year of graduate school and Maria's last year at Smith, I got to see her three times, each for a week, when she came to stay with me in Minneapolis. She laughed at my housemates' jokes about the nooky nook, rolled her eyes and shook her head, said she wasn't surprised, and looked at me in a way that made it clear she loved me and knew I loved her. When we weren't together, we wrote and called. During my second year, she lived in Paris with her college roommate, a trip that was a graduation present from their parents, and sent me letters and photographs. I came to love her more with each letter I received and wrote. It was as if the separation caused her to grow inside me, and I wanted her more every day. I re-read the letters, gazed at the photos, and made love to memories of her and to my fantasies that blossomed from the pictures.

I decided to do a Ph.D. in history at the University of Texas, so I could be close to her when she came home, and so I could work with Albion, the history professor who'd published articles and books on liberation movements in South America. I'd planned on teaching that summer in Minnesota before moving to Austin, but by March I knew I couldn't wait until August to see her. So instead of teaching and having enough money for the move and my first month's rent and still have some left over, I sold my chopper, bought a ticket on a charter flight, knowing the second I'd written the check I'd done something crazy, and flew to Paris.

I was standing one morning in a little park, wedged between two streets a hundred feet apart. One street ran along the quay that bordered the Seine, and on the other stood the bookstore in which I hoped to live for the next eight weeks. I looked up at the sun filtering through the trees, felt its heat and the burden of my easy-rider jacket, and turned my gaze toward the bookstore entrance and the big green letters above it that spelled *The Common Good*. I imagined myself pushing the shutters open on the second floor, just above the sign, and turned and saw, as if I'd just opened them, the cathedral of Notre Dame rising from the island, like a sculpted mountain, with its bell towers, gargoyles, flying buttresses, and a crowd of tourists funneling toward the entrance.

I looked back at the bookstore, tapping my hand with the sketchpad I was holding. Maria had told me her roommate's fiancé had dumped her in March for another woman, and the roommate didn't want a man living with them, so I'd have to stay at a youth hostel. And Maria and the roommate had planned a trip to Spain and would be gone when I arrived. I'd be on my own, in a foreign city, with little money. I moved into a hostel, in an area of Paris called Pigalle. It didn't take me long to find the Latin Quarter, where young people hung out, and one of them, a poet named David, told me about a bookstore, owned by a guy named Frank Morris, where writers could stay for free. I was going to try to convince Morris to let an artist stay there. I had to succeed, because when I got to the metro that morning, I discovered someone at the hostel had stolen the money in my wallet. I still had traveler's checks, but not enough to cover living expenses in Paris for eight weeks.

A snore snagged my attention, and I looked down to see a *clochard*, a homeless man, lying on a park bench. He had tousled gray hair, stubble on his cheeks, and heavy lips flapping in the snores. A soiled T-shirt had ridden up, revealing his flabby gut, and an old suit jacket, the stitching coming undone at the shoulder, covered his side and back. The exposed skin of his neck and swollen hands and ankles was of a weird pink that darkened to a bluish purple around some boils and looked taut as if it was ready to split open, and the odor of stale piss rose from his soiled pants.

I stepped inside the bookstore and saw two men talking near the windows that looked out on the street. One of them, with brown hair and a mustache, bore a vague resemblance to Hemingway, while the other, tall and wispy, reminded me of the English prof I used to call Ichabod. I walked past an antique desk and down one of the aisles between two rows of bookshelves, scanning the titles, until I came to the back, where a steep wooden stairway led to the second floor. On the front of one of the steps at eye-level, someone had painted, "Live for Humanity," and I nodded, thinking that was consistent with what David had said about Morris.

I walked down another aisle toward the front and stopped halfway, where I could see the two men talking. I opened my pad and started sketching. My hand moved quickly, and the sparse lines took shape. After a while, the men said goodbye, and as soon as the tall one left, I approached the other. When he asked if he could help me, I said, "Hello, Mr. Morris. My name's Dick Rayburn." Unsure what to say next, I extended my hand, hoping he'd take it. He did, and then asked what he could do for me.

"I've heard you allow writers to stay here, if they need a place."

"Who told you that?"

"A poet I met a couple days ago at that jazz club, over on *rue de la Huchette*."

Frank's eyes lit up. "Oh, that must've been David. He's so talented. And how about you, Dick. What do you write?"

"Ah, I don't write, unless you consider a Master's thesis in history writing. But I do drawings, and I'm a good caricaturist." He didn't look impressed. "I didn't bring any of my work from home, but …" I extended my hand, offering the pad.

Frank glanced down at it and up at me, leaving it suspended between us.

"I hadn't planned on … Well, I stopped off at that big bookstore, the one over on the *Boulevard Saint-Michel*."

"*Gibert Jeune*."

"Yeah, and I did some sketches from the pictures of authors on book covers, just so you could see." I opened the pad to the first sketch and handed it to him, and this time he took it.

He smiled, murmured, "Rimbaud," nodding in recognition, and turned to the next page, arched his eyebrows, and said, "Nice. Very nice." He continued turning the pages. "Baudelaire. Ah! Hemingway. Hmm." He smiled. "You definitely got the intense eyes, that square jaw of his, and the strong character." Frank turned the page. "Papa Hemingway. The stout face perched on the pullover. Everyone's grandpa. Hard to see the man who committed suicide, isn't it?"

I'd forgotten about the suicide, but I nodded in agreement. I was desperate and would've nodded at anything he said.

"And Fitzgerald."

"David told me you grew up on the same street as Fitzgerald."

He continued studying the drawing. "And what else did he tell you?"

"You chose to go to Princeton, because that's where Fitzgerald went. You loved everything about the American expatriate writers in France, and that's why you wanted to open this bookstore."

"David told you a lot." Frank flipped the page and lingered over the sketch, a smile forming on his lips. "Richard and me." He looked up. "You did this just now?"

"Yeah. While I was waiting."

He looked at the sketch. "Ha! Hilarious. Richard is kind of willowy, isn't he? I didn't realize I was that much shorter. Of course, this is a caricature." He smiled as he gazed at the drawing, then closed the book and handed it back to me. "You're very talented."

"Thanks. David told me writers frequently give readings here, but, when I looked around, I just saw a few photographs of writers. Like Ginsberg and Burroughs over there." I nodded in the direction of the aisle I'd just walked down at two signed photographs, one at the end of each bookshelf. "I was thinking I could do some drawings, or caricatures, of writers as they do their readings. Just sit in the back, where I won't distract anyone, and draw. Then you could hang them up, or give them to the writers. Or whatever."

"And why would you want to do that?"

"In exchange for staying here. I'm not a writer, but I would be contributing something for writers. For everything you're doing here."

Frank considered my offer for a few seconds. "You said your name is …"

"Dick. Dick Rayburn."

"Where are you from?"

"Originally, Colorado. But I just completed a Master's in history at the University of Minnesota."

"You mentioned a thesis. What's it on?"

"Nicaragua, the Sandinistas, and the people's struggle for liberation."

Frank's face lit up. I knew from the name of the bookstore he was a leftist, and the title of my thesis opened the door to his political heart. In no time he was telling me about talking with Sartre in a café and seeing him sell *L'Humanité* on street corners, and I was telling him about my admiration for Che Guevara and the influence on me of my father, who'd grown up poor in a mining town and had gone to school with the children of immigrants and migrant workers.

Finally Frank said I was welcome to stay. David had left the day before, so all three beds were available. I had to get up before the bookstore opened, so people could come in and browse. I assured Frank I would. David had told me everything.

"So he probably told you about the rules, too."

"Yeah, he did."

Frank reviewed them as he led me up the staircase to the second floor and the kitchenette, stopping to point out the sink and the little stove I could use to boil water for tea and coffee. He guided me through a warren of dark passages and nooks, lined with bookcases, and containing an occasional narrow bed that served as a couch during the day. In one of the nooks, a lamp stood in front of an old, tarnished wall mirror, a red velvet spread covered the bed, and a few cushions lay propped up to form a backrest. The atmosphere reminded me of my nooky nook in Minneapolis. I dropped my sketchbook on the bed.

Frank led me out of the warren, and, as we passed through the kitchenette again, I noticed black letters on the wall overlooking the landing: "Be not inhospitable to strangers, lest they be angels in disguise." I wondered how many angels he had helped, and how many had just used him. I saw him standing in the sunlight that flooded the large room in the front and joined him. He pulled open one of the windows that looked out on Notre Dame, and the previously muted clamor of voices from the street below and of cars driving along the quay flooded the room. I gazed at the park, the river, and the cathedral, and felt the life of the city vibrate inside me.

Three weeks later, I was at the antique desk, keeping an eye on the audience seated in front of the lectern at the other side of the room. I checked my watch: five after eight. The reading, which had generated the best turnout since I'd been living in the bookstore, was supposed to have started at eight. I went upstairs where Frank was sitting at the table in the front room, across from a man in his early thirties wearing a baseball cap. Tim Blake was going to read from his new novel. Frank looked at me.

"They're getting restless," I said.

"Tim, this is Dick Rayburn, the artist I mentioned. You've gotta look at his sketches."

Blake stood up and told me he was happy to meet me. His lips spread into a smile, sending ripples into his cheeks, while his brilliant eyes mesmerized me with their warm intensity. The grip of the short, thin writer sent a charge through me, and I felt the tremendous energy that seemed to rise through his body and burst out in an explosion of wild curls from beneath his cap.

"Dick," Frank said, "why don't you show Tim your sketchpad?"

"They're getting impatient."

"It'll just take a minute."

I rushed downstairs, grabbed my pad off the desk, announced to the crowd that the reading would start in five minutes, rushed upstairs, and gave the pad to Blake.

He turned the pages, nodding in recognition, smiling at the caricatures, until he got to a page where he stopped, stared, and burst into laughter. "This is you and Richard!"

"Yeah," Frank said. "Richard Wilkins."

"What a great caricature! The long face. And the arms—he might start flapping them and fly off." Blake shook his head. "Has Richard seen this?"

"No," Frank said.

"If he ever does, I'd like to be there." Blake looked up from the sketch, a mischievous grin on his face. "We'd find out if he has a sense of humor." He looked back down at the drawing. "Brilliant!"

Frank smiled at me, the way Dad would, when I'd go back in the house after working in the studio, and he'd look at my pad, with copies of Leonardo's drawings from the *Notebooks*, or Goya's *Caprichos* or *The Disasters of War*, and I'd see how proud he was of me. If he'd lived, he might've said to a friend, "Hey, you gotta see my son's drawings. He's truly gifted." I could hear Dad saying that. It felt so good, as if it had really happened.

"Are you going to test my sense of humor?" Blake asked.

"Am I going to what?"

"I'm wondering what you're going to do with me. Or to me."

"He'll show you after the reading," Frank said, beaming with pride.

"Yeah, I'll show you."

"Good," Blake said. He handed me the pad. "Do you know David Levine?"

"I know his work." Dad had subscribed to the *New York Review of Books,* so he could stay current on the publication of folios and books about art.

"I'll mention you to him, next time I'm in New York."

I was so giddy fantasizing the caricaturist Levine looking at my work, I almost fell as I descended the steps.

I looked over the heads of the audience at Blake as Frank introduced him, and I started sketching, while listening to Blake's opening remarks about his novel that suggested a surreal adventure, as if the American soldiers in the novel had fallen down a rabbit hole and ended up in Vietnam. I finished a sketch, a realistic rendering of the author, and turned to a new page.

The thing that had struck me about Blake, from the first moment I'd seen him, was the energy that seemed to rise through his short, wiry body and burst into a broad smile. I started drawing the energy that expanded as it rose from his feet to his upper body, swelled his chest, engorged his head, radiated through his eyes, and cascaded as curls of brown hair from beneath his cap. The cap seemed to define something about him, so I exaggerated its size, above all the visor, which needed to be big, assertive, coming at you. The head, the cap, and the visor filled the top half of the page and dwarfed the body that filled the bottom half. A little more shading, and I finished the caricature. It was good. It could go on the wall.

Blake read a passage in which young soldiers slogged their way through the jungle, and his voice enclosed me like a cocoon. I could hear brush trampled and pushed aside, feel the heat, the sweat, and the breath of the man behind me as I followed the man ahead. He finished reading, everyone applauded, and the Q and A started. In response to a question about the influence of his experience on his writing, Blake talked about endless marches along country roads and through the jungle; about friends alive one second, gone the next; about guys going off the deep end and killing everything in sight, or propping up an enemy corpse and talking to it as if it were alive; and about the surreal sense of humor people developed after becoming intimate with death, how they befriended it with terms of endearment, confided in it, whispered to it, as if to a secret lover. As Blake talked, he seemed to stare beyond the audience. Fixed upon something miles and years away, his eyes revealed sadness beyond anything I could remember. The ebullient character I had drawn—gone. The force I had thought pushed this little guy into the world and made him write and publish and establish himself as a literary hero—gone. Loss powered this man. Irreparable loss. Writing was his way of living with the dead.

I turned to a new page and set to work drawing the eyes, trying to capture the gaze turned inward and the sadness, the loss, the mourning they reflected. The smile had faded, the cheeks collapsed, and the visor now seemed to close around the forehead. As I worked, I felt myself drawn in deeper and deeper, until the eyes existed in my mind as much as on the paper. Dad used to say about the artists he loved, they paint the inside from the outside. I drew the inside of Blake. I gazed at the drawing until the Q and A came to an end.

After the second round of applause, the audience stood up, and a few people flocked toward Blake, copies of his novel in hand for him to sign. Frank, who had been standing off to the side, came over and squatted next to my chair.

"Must be quite a book," I said.

"It's extraordinary. The scene in which the soldiers go through a tunnel, fall down a hole, and come out in this jungle, where their dead friends and dead Vietnamese join them, tell them jokes about being dead—it's amazing. After a while, the dead seem more alive than the living." He paused and seemed to reflect about what he'd said. "Well, let's see what you did."

I opened the pad to the caricature and handed it to him. "He never took his cap off."

"I've never seen him without it. He probably sleeps with it on. Kind of like your easy-rider jacket."

"I take it off, if it gets hot enough."

"It must have to get pretty damned hot." He handed the pad back to me. "Let's frame this one and find a place to hang it." He stood up and turned around. "I'd say on the wall, behind the desk. But not too close to the Lowell." He nodded in the direction of a signed photograph of Robert Lowell. "I wouldn't be surprised if Blake wins the National Book Award."

I should've felt excited about having done a caricature of a famous writer that people would look at every time they entered The Common Good, but I couldn't stop thinking about the third drawing of Blake.

I followed Frank to the opposite side of the store, where Blake, his coterie of friends gathered behind him, signed one more copy of his book for a reader. Frank and Blake talked for a few minutes, and then Blake turned to me and asked if he'd need a sense of humor. I showed him the caricature. He chuckled. "That visor looks like it could be dangerous." He returned my pad and said he'd be sure to mention me to Levine, next time he saw him.

Frank and I watched Blake and his friends leave the store and walk past the window, Blake flashing us one last smile.

"What a great reading," Frank said. "Shall we go upstairs and have some tea?"

"I think I'd rather have wine. I've got some *vin de table*, vintage 1978."

"The people's wine. I'll stick to my tea."

I followed Frank up the steep steps to the narrow space of the kitchenette. He put water on to boil and started washing the cups and glasses that had accumulated in the sink. I offered to help, but he waved me off.

I went to my nook, sat down on my bed, and looked at the drawing of Blake, at the intense eyes that seemed to sink into the face, as if pulled inward, and at the mouth, partly open, gasping at what the eyes saw. I'd captured the feeling of an internalized distance, where the war lived on in Blake, in all its surreal horror. Dad would've been proud. Maybe I should keep on doing this. Be an artist, like him. But I thought of the unhappiness. The drinking. The depression. The imminence of death in everything he'd done. And even if he had become famous and made a lot of money, would that have made a difference? It didn't help Rothko or Pollock much. And how happy was Blake? Would he ever stop writing about the war? About loss? It was inside him. And every time he wrote, he returned to it and lived it again. I knew what I wanted—happiness, which meant Maria, and a career as a history professor. Or maybe as a caricaturist, like Levine.

The teakettle whistled. I took a last look at Blake's eyes and closed my pad. I stopped in the kitchenette, poured my wine, and joined Frank at the table in the front room. Sitting down together after closing had become routine. I felt at home with the old couch, the roll top desk, and the photographs of writers. As Frank puckered his lips and sipped his tea, I gazed at his thin face, at the almost feminine wrists and hands extending from the sleeves of his tweed jacket, and at the long, delicate fingers that held the cup, and found laughable the resemblance I'd seen to Hemingway, the tough guy, the big-game hunter, the man's man.

"I really like that caricature," Frank said. "What you did with the baseball cap and the visor was perfect."

"Why do you think he always wears a baseball cap?"

"Well, it's not just the cap. It's the whole outfit—the jeans, the shirt, and the cap. I see it as an embrace of one part of American culture and rejection of another part—the part that's focused on money and power."

"He has money, though, doesn't he? I mean, he's making money from selling books, teaching, giving talks."

"That's not what's driving him."

"Did you ever think about becoming a writer?"

"Yeah. But never for long. I'm perfectly happy with what I do."

"You think Blake's happy?"

"I don't know. He carries a lot inside."

"Maybe he could have chosen not to focus on what he carries inside."

"I don't think it's that simple, Dick. I didn't become a writer because I don't have anything that compels me to write. Blake does."

"But, if he didn't focus on the war, and he didn't focus on his memories, he probably wouldn't feel compelled. It's a choice he's made. I think one can choose to be happy. You, for example. You listen to authors read, and then you close the bookstore and go home. You have your wife and daughter. And," I said, feeling cocky, "you serve the common good."

"You make it sound so simple. What about artists? Can they just decide, Oh, I want to be happy, so I won't paint, because I might have to deal with something I'd rather not think about?"

"Why not?"

"Don't you want to be an artist?"

"I love doing caricatures. You analyze what you're drawing, but you're always staying on the surface. They're fun. They make people laugh. And you can use them to make a point."

"Is there anything that compels you to do something?"

"Just the desire to be happy."

"Anything beyond that? Anything more important?"

"No. I love teaching history, because it's a subversive act. Students come into class thinking one way, and I get them to think a different way, just by providing facts. Historical facts they can't dismiss. When I'm done with my Ph.D., I'll teach courses on liberation movements in South America. I can't wait to do that. But I have no interest in being a revolutionary. They don't always end up happy. Look at Che."

"But you could be an advocate for revolution."

"In an academic way, yeah. That would be fun. I could do that, get married, have kids, and go home every night to my family, and be happy, and serve the common good. Like you. I don't wanna die for anything."

He nodded. "It'll be very interesting to watch you develop."

Frank and I left the bookstore and set off down the *rue de la Bûcherie*. He said I didn't need to walk him to the metro, but I told him I had a lot of pent-up energy. We crossed the *rue du Petit Pont* and walked along the quay, past the closed shops and the restaurants with their intimate spaces lit by the glow of table lamps and candles.

"You know, Dick," Frank said, pulling close to me, "you're welcome to stay in the bookstore as long as you want, in exchange for your caricatures. I know a lot of people in publishing who could help you. You could build a career here."

"That's really generous of you, Frank."

"You do good work. And it would serve the common good."

"You won't let go of that, will you."

"We can talk about it tomorrow."

We reached *Place Saint-Michel*. I said goodnight and watched him disappear down the stairs beneath the art deco sign, *METROPOLITAIN*. Then I weaved my way through the throngs of people strolling down the boulevard to the pedestrian crossing.

On the other side of the *Place*, as I searched for Maria, a woman threw her arms around me and pressed her lips to mine. When I pulled back, I recognized Maria. Her long black hair was gone. Not entirely. Just cut to about a half-inch in length.

She struck a defiant pose and said, *"Je me suis libérée du regard de l'Autre."*

"What?"

"I have liberated myself from the gaze of the Other."

I couldn't take my eyes off her short hair as she led me to a table on the terrasse of the café, where she had been waiting for me. She had sent me a postcard, in care of American Express, telling me she would meet me there the evening of her return. We sat down, leaned into one another and kissed, the way people do all over Paris. A waiter arrived, and I ordered a beer.

"What do you think?" She turned her head to the side and raised her chin, so I could see her haircut in profile. It had horizontal cuts that contrasted with the downward flow of the hair. I had never seen anything like it before. Maria explained that a famous stylist on the *Champs Elysées* had cut her hair with a razor—*une coupe au rasoir,* she said, with another flourish of her French. The *coupe* had been inspired by Hélène Cixous, "such a great feminist." Maria and her roommate had read her essay, "The Laugh of the Medusa," and, when they learned she was teaching at a campus of the University of Paris, attended a few of her classes.

"The first time we arrived late, and Cixous had already begun talking. I wish you could've seen her. This beautiful woman, with dark hair, cut short, and aqua-blue eye make-up on her eyelids that tapered off like wings, and heavy black liner on her eyebrows. She was standing in front of the class, wearing just this smock dress, but she looked like a queen."

I thought of cracking a joke about Liz Taylor's Cleopatra, but decided not to as I watched Maria's eyes glow with adoration while describing the packed classroom and having to stand in the doorway, looking around people's heads, and the students listening in rapt silence beneath a thick cloud of cigarette smoke.

"Cixous was talking about the women in the paintings of the pre-Raphaelite artists, and the fullness of their long hair—the energy, the abundance, the excess that the hair symbolizes. And then she talked about the severed head of the Medusa, and the snakes, and Freud's idea that the Medusa represents man's fear of castration, and she said it's not the castrated female that men fear—it's not what women lack, it's what they possess in abundance, and women can't allow themselves to be defined by the phallogocentrism of males, or by the gaze of the Other, and I thought I'd always had long hair because I believed it looked beautiful, but that's a male concept of beauty, so I decided to get all my hair cut off, because I knew I'd lack nothing."

"So, it's like flipping the bird."

We laughed and kissed again. She left her arm draped across my shoulder and ran the fingertips of her other hand up and down

the sleeve of my jacket and said, "Hmm. Your easy-rider jacket. Still
wearing it." She fingered some of the fringes on the sleeve and the
areas where they were missing and shook her head. "This thing's
falling apart." She let go of the sleeve as if it were filthy and gazed
at the streams of people flowing in front of our table, laughing and
talking, a few isolated words rising above the hubbub like fish leaping out of a fast-flowing brook. "Wow. Paris. And you're staying in
that bookstore, right in the center of the city."

"Pretty cool, isn't it?"

"Yeah. And all because you met that poet."

"Well, I had something to do with it. I had to convince Frank
to allow a caricaturist to stay there. He'd never allowed anyone but
writers before."

"Of course, my little Dicky." She laid the palm of her hand
on my crotch and leaned forward to conceal what she was doing.
"You're so clever," she crooned, "so cocky." She'd read *The Female
Eunuch* and had no intention of being one. She puckered up her
lips and feigned a loud, sloppy kiss. I leaned into her and soaked
up a real one.

We finished our drinks, and I led her across the *Place* and down
the *rue de la Huchette* and the *rue de la Bûcherie* to the bookstore,
pulled her inside, closed the door, and proclaimed, as if I were a
child showing off a hidden-treasure cave, *"Voilà!* My bookstore."

She took a few steps, stopped, and scanned the room in the
light from the street. I walked over to the desk and turned on the
lamp. She looked at me, smiled, and wandered around, gazing at
the signed photographs and chuckling at my caricatures that had
already been framed and hung. I led her toward the back of the
store and the stairs. She stopped at the sight of the words, "Live
for Humanity," and said, "That's so cool." When we reached the
second floor, I told her to turn around and gestured toward the
sentence, "Be not inhospitable to strangers, lest they be angels in
disguise." She asked me if it was a quote. I didn't know, but it said
a lot about Frank.

Maria beamed. "He found an angel."

"If angels live here, it's because this place is paradise."

I showed her the front room and pulled open a window, like a magician pulling back a curtain. Her mouth agape, she moved toward the sill, drawn to the scene she beheld. Nearly midnight, and people still wandered the streets, talking and laughing, and headlights darted along the quay. The Seine, like a black mirror, reflected the moonlight; streetlights lit up the white stone bridge; and floodlights on the ground illuminated the walls of Notre Dame as they rose from the island. The moon glowed above the clouds that drifted slowly across the deep black sky, just beyond the bell towers. Men had built those towers seven or eight hundred years ago. Hundreds of years ago, others had stood here, in this same place, maybe a couple like us, and gazed up at the towers and at the clouds gliding across the sky like ghost ships. And hundreds of years from now, another couple might stand here mesmerized by this sight. The longer I gazed at the cathedral walls and towers, the lighter they appeared, as if they might at any second rise from the earth and glide away with the clouds. I felt as light, as otherworldly, as one of those ghost ships. I could rise and sail away. Another breeze, and I'd be gone. A chill came over me. I placed my arm around Maria's back and held her, as if I would anchor her and prevent her from drifting off. She leaned her head against me and murmured, "It's so beautiful." We continued gazing, until someone laughed in the street below. The air caressed my skin, and I pulled Maria closer to me. She was all I wanted.

I guided her into my little nook and turned on the lamp on the bookshelf. The light glared on the dull surface of the tarnished mirror. Our eyes met above the center of the glare, she smiled at me, and looked down at the red velvet cover and the cushions.

"Not as atmospheric as your nooky nook, but I'll take you wherever I can have you."

After we made love, I lay on my back, and she along my side, her head on my chest.

"Lucky we love each other," she said. "Otherwise we couldn't sleep in this bed together."

I felt her breath, the moisture of her mouth on my skin as she talked.

She asked what Frank was like, and I told her how smart, kind, generous, and trusting he was. Probably the most trusting person I'd ever met. How could he know I wouldn't go through the place, help myself to whatever I wanted, and walk off? Maria murmured she didn't know. I could feel her beginning to drift off. I kept on talking, until she ran her fingers through the hair on my chest, tightened her hand into a loose fist, and then relaxed and murmured, "Good night, my little Dicky darling. I love you." She fell asleep. After a while, she pulled away and lay on her side, her back to me.

I lay awake, staring into the dark, thinking about Frank and the offer he'd made, when we were walking together. I could see myself living in the bookstore, doing caricatures, working for the magazines and newspapers and publishers where Frank had connections, and making money. David Levine had to be making a good living, and if an artist like him could afford to live in New York, I'd be able to live in Paris. I'd get my own apartment. Instead of going back to school in journalism at Texas, Maria would move to Paris. Her parents had enough money; she could do whatever she wanted. We'd get married, and invite Mom and Georgia. And Maria's parents. And Frank, his wife, and daughter. And Frank's writer friends and magazine editors. We might have to start out with a modest apartment. Maybe a studio, like the ones I'd seen advertised. But we'd succeed. We'd live in one of the old buildings in the Latin Quarter or on the *Ile Saint-Louis*. An apartment hundreds of years old. And every night we'd sleep together in our own bed. And as I fell asleep next to Maria, feeling we were in our bed, in our apartment, I heard voices, hushed voices, fragments of conversations, of intimate moments, from years or centuries gone by.

CHAPTER 6

I FELT VALERIE'S PRESENCE AND looked up to see her standing in the doorway, staring at me. I smiled, hoping to entice her in, but she didn't move.

"I saw you drank a lot of wine," she said. "But you didn't eat."

"I wasn't hungry."

She nodded. "Do you need anything before I go to bed?"

"No. But it's nice of you to ask."

She almost smiled. "How are you feeling?"

"Well," I said, chuckling, "with all the medications"—I nodded at my night table—"it would be a miracle if I *could* feel any pain."

"I mean, psychologically."

I shook my head and sighed. "It would help if we could talk."

"The psychiatrist told me he'd suggested you try journaling, to help with your recovery."

"That's the only thing I remember him saying."

"He said you wouldn't remember much from your meetings. That's why he wanted to talk to me. So, have you tried journaling?"

"Yeah." I paused. "I found that what I'm writing takes possession of me, and then my memories carry me off, and I stop writing. I just continue remembering."

"Hmm."

"Do you remember when we first met?"

The tiny glimmer of warmth disappeared from her face. "I'm tired. I don't want to stay up all night talking. Try to get some sleep."

She left.

I heard the door to the guest room close. Close on my love, my happiness.

I felt loved that night in Paris, as I fell asleep next to Maria, thinking we were embarking on a magical adventure together. Sometimes the past haunts us, sometimes it's a place to which we can escape. That night had both. But the next morning …

Someone shook my shoulder. I tried to shrug off the grasp, but the hand wouldn't let go.

"Dick! Get up!"

I awoke and saw Frank's eyes riveting mine.

"Come on! Get up!"

"You'd better get up," Maria whispered. She'd pulled the cover up to her neck, as if it might protect her.

"We can talk in my office," Frank said.

He left. I got dressed and found him staring out the same window from which Maria and I had gazed at Notre Dame the night before. He turned toward me.

"You're my guest, and you violated one of the few rules I have. You can't invite people to spend the night. This isn't your bookstore. I learned the hard way what happens when guests have friends over. Things disappear. I told you that."

I bit my lip and nodded. I had no defense.

"I want you and your friend out of here. I trust she's dressed by now. And I want the key. Bring it here before you leave." Frank walked over to the table, picked up a stack of mail, and leafed through the envelopes. He looked at me. "What are you waiting for?"

I started to turn around and stopped. "Look, I know I shouldn't have done that. I'm sorry."

"Get out!"

I returned to the nook and found Maria dressed and sitting on the bed. I said, "Let's go," threw on my jacket, slung my knapsack over my shoulder, walked into the front room, where Frank was still looking at his mail, slammed the key on the table, and left the bookstore with Maria running after me.

"Slow down!" she shouted.

I stopped in the park and waited for her to catch up.

"You don't have to run away from me!"

"I'm pissed. I should've talked to him. Then maybe everything would've been okay." I started walking again. "Now what the fuck do I do?"

She grabbed onto my sleeve to try to keep up with me. "Let's go to a café and see if we can come up with a plan."

"I need to walk." I pushed my way through the crowded streets, with Maria hanging on, cursing myself for disappointing Frank and turning him against me. I had nowhere to live. I could survive in the hostel for five weeks, but I'd be broke when I went back to the States. The *METROPOLITAIN* sign appeared, and I realized we'd arrived at the station.

"There's a nice café just across the street from my apartment," Maria said. "We can have breakfast and talk."

I couldn't think of anything else to do, so we took the metro. Twenty minutes later we climbed the steps of the station and walked up the narrow *rue Saint-Ambroise*, past cars parked bumper to bumper and the stone walls of apartment buildings. We stopped in front of a café on the corner of a T-intersection. "This is it," Maria said, pointing across the street at a new building, with glass walls on much of the first floor, and plate-glass windows and doors that led to balconies for every apartment on the five floors above. She told me she'd meet me in a few minutes in the café, crossed the street, and disappeared through the entrance to the building.

I entered the café, sat down at a table near a pinball machine, and ordered an espresso. I checked my watch. A couple of workers came in and ordered a *petit Muscadet*. The barman poured the wine, and coins clinked on the metal surface. I took the sketchbook out of my knapsack and started sketching the workers as they leaned against the bar. I hadn't drawn more than a few lines, when I thought of Frank and the opportunity I'd lost and snapped the book shut. The workers glanced at me and then returned to their conversation. I wondered what Maria was telling her roommate. Some teenagers entered the café and swarmed around the pinball machine. One of them started playing, thrusting his hips at the machine as if he was screwing it, and every bounce of the ball pinged, and every ping pricked my nerves.

Maria appeared in the doorway and nodded at me. I joined her outside the café, and she summarized the conversation with her roommate. I glanced at the apartment building and saw a woman watching us from the doorway to a small balcony. Maria and I crossed the street and took the elevator to the second floor. She unlocked the door, and I followed her into the foyer and saw the roommate standing in the kitchen, leaning against a counter, a coffee cup poised in her hand. Tall and slender, with long brown hair, and eyes that looked right into mine, she held her chin raised, as if she had readied herself to deal with the reality of living with a stranger in her apartment.

She looked me over. "He doesn't resemble Christ, certainly not with that buckskin jacket. Excuse me, that 'easy-rider jacket.'" She smirked. "So, Dick, you've apparently run out of bookstores where you can stay."

"I've only found one with the philosophy, 'Be not inhospitable to strangers, lest they be angels in disguise.'"

"The owner found you're not one of those, so now you're looking for a place to live." The dry-ice tone of her voice made her feelings clear. "Maria has told you about our agreement. You're welcome to stay for a while, until you can find your own place."

Valerie left, and as soon as she closed the door, I said to Maria, "I thought she was okay with me staying here for the next five weeks."

"Don't worry. I've been talking to her all year about you. She'll come around."

The next morning, I was standing in the open door of the small kitchen balcony as I watched people below carrying their shopping baskets, bustling along the sidewalks, maneuvering to avoid one another, creating a constant hum of greeting and conversation. Spasmodic ringing burst from the café across the street, where someone was playing the pinball machine. Peals of laughter, high-pitched cries, and a few kids broke ranks from their mothers and ran past the bakery, on the opposite corner from the café, and headed down the street for the playground in the square. From the depths of one of the apartments, a couple floors above the café, crackling like the soundtrack of an old film, rose the ghostly voice of a woman singing.

"And," Maria said, standing behind me, next to the stove, "what I find amusing about shopping with you is the shopkeepers saying, '*Monsieur-dame, que désirez-vous?*'"

I looked at Maria, who was holding a teakettle above the porcelain cone on the coffee pot, waiting for the hot water to filter through the grounds.

"*Monsieur-dame.* Mister-Missus. It's like we're one person. Or like we get married every time we enter a shop, the way they couple us together. *Monsieur-dame,*" she sang, as she resumed pouring. "But they never say, *Dame-monsieur.*"

"Sounds like damn *monsieur.*"

"They always put the *monsieur* first. Cixous said something very interesting in class one day. She held up a copy of the magazine *Le Nouvel Observateur* and read the biggest headline on the cover, 'Israel and the PLO,' and said, 'Why is it always Israel and the PLO? And never the PLO and Israel? Generally, when we list two things, the first is considered to be more important than the second. Fathers and sons. Mothers and daughters. Husbands and wives. Israel and the PLO. *Monsieur-dame.* Just reverse the order, and you'll see the hierarchy. So, the next time we walk into a shop, if there's a woman and a man, I'm going to say, *Bonjour dame-monsieur.*"

"Maybe you should just say, *bonjour,* and to hell with the hierarchy."

Maria set the kettle down and approached me, grinning. "Cixous also said, 'It's men who love to play with dolls.' We were talking about a story called 'The Sandman.' The main character, a man, falls in love with a female automaton. A doll. And all it can say is, 'Ah, ah.'"

"Cixous, Cixous, Cixous."

Maria put her arms around my neck. "Do you love to play with dolls? I bet that's what you were doing in your nooky nook. Hmm? Playing with dolls. Undressing them, propping them up, laying them down." She pulled her arms tight. "I love to play with dolls, too." She kissed me, running her hand across my butt. "Maybe we should do breakfast later."

"Oh, no. I'm starving. I've got to eat something."

"Okay. Have a *tartine au beurre.* And then I'll be your *tarte.*"

"Isn't Valerie going to be back soon?"

"We'll take a chance."

Maria lay next to me in a daze, her head on my outstretched arm. We'd closed the window before making love, so the children playing in the courtyard wouldn't hear us. The heat had accumulated, and sweat trickled down my face and chest. I got up and pulled open a window. The kids in the courtyard were hopping and skipping, screaming and punctuating their play with bursts of laughter. I took a deep breath of the cool air that was evaporating the sweat off my body. A happy moan came from the bed. Maria, nude, the bed-clothes kicked to the bottom, had rolled over on her belly and lay on the space I'd just left, her face turned to one side, her raised fore-arms framing her head, a smile dimpling the corner of her mouth. I wondered if Cixous had said women should express themselves more freely when having an orgasm, because Maria had screamed and laughed as never before. I was thinking of getting my pad out of my backpack and drawing her, when I heard the apartment door close. Valerie shouted, "Anyone home?"

I sat on the bed and placed my hand on Maria's shoulder. "We'd better get dressed."

She rolled over on her back, reached toward my face, and traced my lips with her fingertips. "I could stay like this all day. Above all, if you'd come back to bed."

I placed my hand on her breast, and she placed her hand on mine.

Footsteps came down the hall and paused a few feet from our door.

Maria called, "We'll be out in a minute."

The footsteps retreated toward the living room.

"I bet she wishes she had someone like you," Maria said.

She put on her underpants and a silk kimono, I pulled on my jeans and a shirt, and we went out on the balcony, the large one off the living room. Valerie was sitting next to a small table, holding a croissant in her hand. She wore jeans and a shirt, with the top three buttons undone, revealing the tanned skin of her chest and a glimpse of the pale skin of her breasts.

"Thanks for leaving me a croissant," she said, picking up her mug of coffee.

Maria and I sat down next to one another, across the table from her.

"Well, Dick, your first morning here and you seem to have adapted very well to your new environment. Oh, my God! You're not wearing that jacket."

"Yeah, I usually take it off when I go to bed. And I never wear it in the shower."

"You do take showers. Good!" Valerie grinned at me over the top of her mug.

"Only when I really need to. Just let me know if I start to stink up the place."

Shaking her head, she set her mug on the table, took a cigarette out of her pack of Dunhills, lit up, leaned back in her chair, and exhaled.

"Cigarettes will kill you," I said.

She looked me in the eye and sang, "*Je fume pour oublier que tu bois.*"

Maria snorted and guffawed. "She got you, sweetie!"

"She did? What'd she get me with?"

"I smoke to forget you drink." Maria frowned. "Doesn't sound good in English."

"I think it needs to stay in French," Valerie said.

"It's from a song by Alain Bashung, the newest French cutie," Maria said. "You've got to be careful with Valerie. She'll always come back at you."

Valerie took another drag and gazed across the street. "Oh, there he is. Our *jules*."

A man in his fifties, salt-and-pepper hair and moustache, in a white undershirt, leaned on the railing of a window ledge in an apartment across the street, looking down at the people on the sidewalk two floors below. He took a drag of his cigarette.

"How do you know his name is Jules?" I asked.

"Oh, dear," Valerie said. "Do we have to teach this boy everything?"

"It's not his fault. He just doesn't know any better."

"Why do I have the feeling that everything going on here is at my expense?"

"Your expense?" Valerie asked. "You're living here for free!"

"Sweetie, *jules* is slang for man, or ol' man. Like when a woman says …" She reached for Valerie's pack of cigarettes and asked, "May I?"

"Of course."

Maria dangled a cigarette from the corner of her mouth, let her jaw go slack, and growled at me, "*Eh! Mon jules!*"

I cracked up.

She blew me a kiss and rolled her eyes. "*Mon jules!*"

"A *jules* can also be a pimp," Valerie added, looking at the man in the window, "but we'd never accuse our *jules* of being one of those."

"No," Maria said, "although we suspect he's quite a lady's man. Oh, listen."

Her face lit up, and she started singing along with the recording coming from the man's apartment and bouncing her head to the tune. Valerie snickered and joined in. I listened intently, unable to understand the lyrics. Every few seconds, Maria and Valerie would stop, bounce their heads in time, and shout, *gori-i-i-i-yuh*. When the song ended, I asked them what it was about. They launched a cacophony of raucous comments and laughter, trying to shout over one another. I caught something about a male, virgin gorilla, and old ladies who came to the zoo to see his private parts. And there it was, the phallus, at the center of everything, and those women were nothing but eunuchs. And the guy who'd written the song ended it with a line about the gorilla choosing a judge over one of the women and sodomizing him, and at the moment of being sodomized the judge hears the voice of a man being decapitated shouting, "Mama," and that was so typically male, intercourse and castration and the precious phallus, and the writer was a closet phallogocentrist, but there was no such thing as closet phallogocentrists, because they were everywhere but in a closet.

Maria and Valerie laughed and giggled and, when they finally came to the end of their attempts at being sophisticated and witty, Maria leaned back, closed her eyes, smiled and crooned, "Oh, the sun feels so good." Valerie gazed at the opposite side of the street, her elbow resting on the back of her chair, her raised hand twisting, untwisting, and re-twisting a lock of hair around her fingers.

She became aware of me looking at her and asked what Maria and I were planning on doing, and when I said we were going to the Louvre, she quipped, "Ah, the pilgrimage to the temple of art." I mentioned my father was an artist, and she wanted to know more about him, so I told her about Dad's work and the artists whom he admired and whose paintings I wanted to see, because he'd talked about them with such passion. I could see in her eyes that she wanted me to keep on talking, so I told her about how he'd taught me everything a painter needs to know, right down to the origin of paints, like black made from bone or ivory, and other paints made from earth pigments, such as umber, and still others from minerals, such as lead. And how dangerous they could be. How Whistler had fallen ill because of the lead white he'd used in the "Symphonies in White." And my dad also used the lead-based paint in his paintings.

I fell silent, wondering if he knew how dangerous the paint is, if he was oblivious to that danger, because there was something suicidal in him, and that's why, when he drank, he didn't just drink to relax, or be with other people, he drank to obliterate himself. And what about his family? How could he have loved us, and yet wanted to be dead? I became aware of Valerie's eyes watching me and felt as if she could sense what I was thinking and turned away so she couldn't see.

"And tomorrow?" she asked.

"Tomorrow?" I looked at her. "Tomorrow, we're going to the Cinémathèque. They're doing a Truffaut retrospective."

"Oh, *Jules et Jim*. Another *jules*!" she exclaimed.

"I think we've had enough *jules* for a while," Maria mumbled, her eyes still closed.

Valerie dipped her cigarette into her coffee mug, where it sizzled to extinction.

The three of us would usually have breakfast together on the balcony and talk and crack jokes and laugh. Then we'd set out to explore Paris. We'd go to the bookstores—French and American—and Valerie and Maria would buy books by authors they felt they just had to know. Determined not to be left behind, I found a translation of "The Laugh of the Medusa" and something by Derrida. We'd wander around Montparnasse, in the neighborhoods where Cixous and Samuel Beckett lived, or hang out at some of the famous cafés, brasseries, and restaurants, like *Le Select*, *La Coupole*, or *La Closerie des Lilas*, hoping to catch a glimpse of our idols. One day we found ourselves on the *rue d'Ulm*, staring through the grill fence at the *Ecole Normale Supérieure*, the university where Derrida taught, as if he might be there during summer vacation. We went to the museums during the day and at night we'd go to movie theaters and the cinémathèque. Once, after having seen Godard's *Band of Outsiders*, we tried to run all the way through the Louvre and break the record the three characters in the film set out to break, nine minutes and forty-three seconds, but the guards stopped us before we even got past the *Mona Lisa*. We rented bikes, took a train out of Paris, and went bicycling through the countryside, just like the characters in *Jules et Jim*. A magical day, flying down the country roads, past fields and through woods, feeling the air flowing through our hair. Like we were in flight, totally free.

And then, one day, I entered the apartment, closed the door, and shouted, "I'm home!" No one answered. I glanced in the kitchen. No one. I entered the dining room, shouting, "Hello!" Still no answer. I walked through the living room and was about to enter the hall that led to the bedrooms when I heard voices from the street, noticed the balcony door was open, and saw Valerie sitting with her back to me. I stepped onto the balcony. She looked up, sadness in her bloodshot eyes, and down, and took a drag off her cigarette. Her limbs appeared contracted into a defensive position. She bit her lip and sniffed. Tears trickled down her cheek.

"What is it?"

"I saw my fiancé, my former fiancé, and his wife."

Valerie dropped her arm, the ash on the cigarette falling to the floor, and placed her other hand on her forehead, partially covering her eyes. She sniffed back tears and swallowed her pain. "In the bookstore, near the *Place de la Concorde*."

"I'm sorry," I said. "I really am."

She forced a smile. "You're a sweetheart, Dick." She dropped the cigarette to the floor, stepped on it, and stood up. "I'm going to lie down."

I put my hand on her shoulder as she started to walk by. She leaned into me, I held her, and felt her body tremble in my arms. She took hold of herself, walked down the hall to her room, and closed the door.

The next morning, I was sitting at the kitchen table, drinking coffee, eating a *tartine au beurre*, and wondering if Maria had been up part of the night with Valerie, because she was still in a deep sleep. I heard a door shut at the other end of the apartment and footsteps approach the kitchen. Valerie appeared, her face gray with grief. She got a cup out of the cupboard, poured some coffee, opened the door to the balcony, and leaned against the doorframe, looking out. After a couple minutes, she poured her coffee in the sink, said she was going for a walk, and left.

In the silence of the apartment, I sensed the ghost of her pain.

Over the next few days, I'd find her slumped in a chair, staring off into space, or gazing out a window, as if she could see in some far-off place the happiness she'd lost. I'd put my arm around her shoulder, or squat down in front of her and look into her eyes and say, "We're going to have a great Bastille Day."

She'd force a smile and repeat what I'd said.

The day arrived with an explosion that shattered my sleep and hurled me out of bed so fast I staggered and nearly fell. Maria cried, "What was that?" I scanned the room, trying to find, among the shadows and obscure forms in the gray morning light, a clue to what had happened. Had a war broken out? Valerie came to the door and announced a *mirage*, a French fighter jet, had buzzed the neighborhood. We dressed and joined her in the kitchen and sat down at the table, where she had set plates, cups, a baguette, butter, and jam. She laughed when Maria described our response to the jet. It was the first time she'd laughed since the day she'd seen her former fiancé. I admired her, the tall, lithe girl, with square shoulders, pointed chin, and determination to go on. She sat down, leaving the balcony door open to the sounds of the neighborhood—the teenagers goosing the pinball machine, the voices and laugher of people milling about, stocking up on food and wine for the holiday, and kids screaming as they ran to the square.

While we ate, we planned our evening celebration. Should we have dinner *Chez Amar*, over by the *Place de la République*, where you could get the best couscous in Paris for ten francs? Or maybe that funny little restaurant in the *Quartier Latin?* The one where the waiters responded to questions such as, How's the *cassoulet?* With answers like, *c'est dégueulasse*, it's disgusting, or *c'est merdique*, it's shitty, and a recording of the French national anthem played in the dining room every time someone flushed the toilet? Or the *Brasserie de l'Ile Saint-Louis*, with its garnished sauerkraut and Rhine wines and the long tables where everyone ate and drank together and ended up talking to one another? Valerie and Maria had heard the best *bal du quatorze* took place on the île, the island.

And then Edith Piaf's voice erupted from the apartment of the *jules*, singing, "*Non, je ne regrette rien.*" It seemed to contain all the energy of the street, of the *quatorze*, and of a new beginning. Maria, and then Valerie, started singing along with Piaf. I tried, too, but could manage little more than repeating, "*Je ne regrette rien.*" The women taught me what they thought was the most important line in the song, "*Je me fous du passé*"—I don't give a damn about the past. And we sang it over and over.

That night, we ate and drank at the brasserie, danced together in the street, danced in a long line that weaved through the crowd at the tip of the island, danced until two in the morning, and then, having missed the last metro, staggered home drunk, Maria and Valerie leaning into me while we sang, "*je me fous du passé!*"

As the days passed, we talked less about phallogocentrism, Freud, and Cixous. She was an inspiration for Maria and Valerie, but they hadn't read anything by her other than *Le Rire de la Méduse* and *La jeune* née, which they'd struggled through in French. We'd read a little of Derrida in translation and learned enough to proclaim that deconstructing the binary oppositions of the reigning ideologies was like dynamiting the basements of tall buildings and watching them collapse. Oh, we were brilliant. It was like the '60s had finally found their way. We had created our pantheon of cultural heroes—Cixous, Derrida, Lacan, and Deleuze, with his cape and inch-long fingernails. Like kids, we would dress up in their rhetoric and prance around, as if we were getting ready for Halloween. And like kids, we got tired of the costumes, threw them off, and left them where they fell.

Our world closed in around us, and we spent more time at home, talking and reading newspapers and books by authors other than our fading idols. One afternoon, Maria left Valerie and me alone in the living room while she ran an errand. Sitting on the couch, my legs stretched out on the coffee table, I was reading Blake's novel, while Valerie sat on an armchair near the window, *The Bell Jar* resting on her lap. I turned a page and happened to look up and see her face in profile, as she stared out the window. Fascinated by her reflective gaze and wondering what was going through her mind, I went to the bedroom and got my drawing pad and returned to find her still gazing out the window at whatever inside her had captivated her thoughts. I sat down, opened the pad by chance to the drawing I'd done of Blake, paused to look at it for a second, then turned to the next page and looked up to see Valerie watching me.

"Well," she said, "I guess that's what happens when you live with an artist."

"I'm not really an artist, just like to do drawings. Do you mind?" I started drawing.

"No."

"What were you thinking about?"

"The life I was living. If everything had gone as planned, I'd be married now. And my husband would probably be here, in this apartment, if we weren't traveling around Europe."

I continued drawing her head and her eyes, her face and her neck, and the bangs and the long hair that fell to her shoulders.

"That life was full of dreams, and those dreams carried me off into the future. A future in which I believed. And then one day, I got a letter, and that life ended. And for the next few months, I felt like I'd died. You know"—she looked at me, as I darkened the hair—"every book I've read lately deals somehow with suicide. But I didn't think of killing myself, because I was already dead. I felt nothing. And then, sometimes memories would come back, and I'd breathe, and feel alive, and then I'd realize again he was gone. Forever. That day in the bookstore, when I saw him with his wife, my life with him died for good." She fell silent. I continued with the gradation and shading of the cheeks and darkening and deepening the eyes. "Now, I'm living another life, and I have new dreams."

"What are they?" I retraced the lines to sharpen her chin and jaw.

"I've always loved books. And one of my dreams is to be an editor and work with writers. Like Sylvia Plath."

"Hard to work with someone who's dead."

"Oh, I'm sure there are still letters to edit, new collections of her poems to publish. An editor can work with someone who's dead."

"Any other dreams?"

She gazed at me. "Someday I'd like to have a family."

"You need a husband for that."

"That helps."

The front door opened, and Maria entered the foyer, saw us, and came into the living room, plopped down next to me on the couch, and looked at the drawing. Valerie came over and sat next to her, and Maria took the pad so Valerie could see the drawing. As I listened to them talk, I wondered why I'd once again been intrigued by the look on the face of someone drawn inward by loss. I remembered that first day on the balcony, when I was talking about Dad and his influence on me, and I sensed Valerie could perceive my feelings about him. I looked over at her and Maria marveling at the drawing, at how it seemed to have captured something inside Valerie.

I smiled at her and said, "If you like it, it's yours."

She looked up, surprised, and thanked me.

Our friendship continued to deepen, and the three of us became so inseparable that leaving Valerie at night to go to bed with Maria felt awkward, like we were abandoning her. Making love with Maria, I'd feel Valerie's presence, as if she were in the room, and after Maria had fallen asleep, I'd lie awake in the silence, wondering if Valerie had listened to us and what she was thinking, feeling, doing. I no longer wished she'd find someone to replace the love she'd lost, because I'd replaced him. It's possible to love two people at once. And make love to two people—even if one is in the other room.

A week later, the three of us were sitting at the kitchen table, talking about what we wanted to do, when the phone rang—a ring that always felt like a dentist's drill bearing down on a molar. Valerie rushed to the living room.

"Dad! Hi! How are you?" I couldn't hear any more of the conversation, until she said, "In three days!" And then I heard my name mentioned. A few minutes later, she returned to the kitchen, a shocked look on her face. "He's going to be here in three days."

"I thought he was coming in two weeks," Maria said.

"He's on his way to someplace in the Mediterranean, so he thought he'd make a detour and visit us. And get this: he wants to take the three of us out to dinner. At *Le Grand Véfour*!"

"*Le Grand Véfour*!" Maria repeated.

"The three of us?" I asked.

"Yes," Valerie answered Maria. "It's his favorite restaurant in Paris. He always says, 'If it was good enough for the emperor, it's good enough for me.'" She shook her head and grinned. "That's my dad!" She looked at me. "He wants to meet you."

"Wait a minute," I said. "What emperor?"

"Napoleon," Valerie answered.

"Sweetie," Maria said, "this restaurant's two hundred years old."

"Why does he want to meet me?"

"I told him we see you all the time, because you and Maria are engaged."

"Not yet." Maria blushed.

"You will be."

Maria blew me a kiss.

"If he likes you, I'm sure he'll invite you to join us on the yacht," Valerie said.

"You have to meet him sometime," Maria said. "You can't just show up at the yacht and say, 'I'm too cute to be left behind.'" She looked me over and wrinkled her nose. "And you're going to need some new clothes. Jeans and an old Led Zeppelin T-shirt just won't do."

"And the buckskin jacket, with those tassels." Valerie eyed me, shaking her head. "No, not at *Le Grand Véfour*."

"This jacket's been with me from Minneapolis, to Seattle, to Austin, to Paris. I can't—"

"It looks it." Maria touched my hand and peered into my eyes. "It's falling apart." She touched the front of my jacket. "It's missing half its tassels."

"And your hair," Valerie said.

"I bet your daddy isn't wild about guys with Jesus hair." Maria looked me in the eye. "That's so '60s, and this is 1978."

"I can recite a list of rock stars with long hair today."

"Are you thinking what I'm thinking?" Valerie grinned at Maria.

"I think so."

"*Une coupe au rasoir,*" Valerie said.

"Then people can see how really cute you are," Maria said, gently pressing my long hair against my head.

"Wait a minute!" I looked at the two faces grinning at each other. "Stop treating me like some kind of doll. I have something to say about this, too."

"Of course you do," Maria crooned, while holding my arm. "But, you do want to have dinner with us at the *Grand Véfour*, right? And you do want to make a good impression on Valerie's father. Right?"

"Because you do want to go sailing on the Mediterranean with us, don't you?" Valerie smiled seductively at me. "We really want you to come."

"We do," Maria said, "grazing my cheek with her hand."

Her touch softened my resistance. I thought about the yacht, the wind in the sails as the ship flew across the waves, the heat of the sun as Maria and I made love on a beach, and the ship's gentle rocking as we collapsed below deck in post-coital bliss, and the stupidity of selling my chopper and coming all this way, and then not being able to continue because of my hair and my clothes. I told myself I'd just be doing this for the performance—like an actor, getting a haircut and wearing a costume. Maria traced my lips with her finger, tickling them into a smile.

"Okay," I said. "I'll go along with this."

Maria and Valerie took me to a salon in the sixth arrondissement, where a man, with an impeccably groomed black beard that evoked a Renaissance portrait of a prince, proceeded to give me a *coupe au rasoir*. The rapidity with which the razor blade flew about my head and slashed through my hair made me sit stone still. Once I felt confident I wasn't going to get scalped, I relaxed and watched the Jesus locks in the mirror fall to the barber's sheet, revealing my bare neck and the contour of my head. A new me emerged, replacing the easy rider. When I wondered if I'd sold out, I reminded myself this was just temporary, I could always go back. The coiffeur finished and handed me a mirror. I thought I looked chic.

The ladies paid and took me to a men's clothing shop on the *Champs Elysées* and had me fitted with white linen pants, sport jackets, a suit, and shirts of various colors, and picked out a pair of white canvas shoes that would be perfect for the yacht. I posed, turned, and posed again, looking at myself in my new clothes, from every angle in the three mirrors. Another twinge of conscience made me wonder if I was selling out, and I paused in mid-turn. But in my mind's eye, I saw John Lennon in his white suit, his eyes gazing at me through round wire-rimmed glasses, holding up two fingers—*Peace, brother*. I smiled at myself and struck a confident pose while the sales clerk raved, "*C'est très élégant*" and "*Ça vous va parfaitement.*" I took a last, lingering look at myself in the mirror before I followed Maria, Valerie, and the clerk to the counter. He was folding the new clothes and placing them in boxes tied with ribbons, when he looked up at Maria and, with his hands hovering above my jeans, T-shirt, and easy-rider jacket, asked if she'd like him to wrap them. She shook her head and told him he could throw them in the trash.

"Whoa!" I cried, glaring at Maria. "He can't throw those away!" I looked at the clerk and said, "Wrap them up," and, when he gave me a blank stare, gestured what I wanted him to do.

The clerk gingerly touched the old clothes as he folded them and arranged them in a box. He added up the purchases, and Maria and Valerie laid down a few thousand-franc bills while telling me not to concern myself about the money, this had been so much fun.

When we got back to the apartment, they led me into the living room and asked me to change out of the white linen pants and blue

short-sleeved shirt I was wearing and into my other outfits. I was
about to head for the bedroom, when Maria said, "You don't need to
go to the bedroom to change. It'll take forever. Do it here."

"You can put on a show for us," Valerie said.

"Yeah. We paid for it," Maria said.

They grinned like imps. I decided the fastest way to finish that
farce was to cooperate. I set the bags down on a chair, pulled my
clothes off and tossed them on the couch. Maria pointed out my
"cute legs" and my "cute ass," and the two of them ooo-laa-laad and
laughed as I stood in my underpants.

"I'm glad you're finding this amusing," I snarled, while button-
ing a linen shirt. I slipped on a pair of pants and a matching jacket.

"Don't you feel like a different person?" Maria asked.

"I feel like a gigolo."

"Ohhh," Valerie purred, as she stood behind me, pulling the
shoulders of my jacket taut, while Maria, gazing up at me, stroked
my hair with her fingertips.

"You're right," Valerie said. "He does have a cute ass!" She
touched my butt. "What an asset!"

"Stop it! God damn it!" I spun away. "Stop treating me like some
Ken-doll." I sat down on the couch and glared at Maria. "Who likes
to play with dolls? Huh?"

She sat down next to me, put her arm around my back, and gazed
at the side of my face. "I'm sorry, Dick. It's just that Valerie and I want
you to come with us on the yacht, and we think her father will be
more likely to invite you to join us if he's impressed with you."

"And your appearance is part of what will impress him," Valerie
said.

"I know." And then it hit me, the performance I had to pull
off. "Oh, man, I'm going to feel so uptight meeting your father in
that restaurant. And with more silverware than I'll know what to
do with."

"Don't worry about the silverware," Maria said. "Just relax and
be yourself."

"Dick," Valerie said, "you have style on your side. Look at you:
you've got class."

I looked down at my white linens, got up and walked back and forth and down the hall to the bathroom, where I looked in the mirror. I turned around, glanced over my shoulder, turned back toward the mirror, and returned to the living room, did a little pirouette and said, "Yeah, man, I got style. Got class." I nodded my head. "I'm cool."

"And Dad's going to love you. I know he will."

"So, I meet you at the *Grand Véfour* at …?"

"Eight," Valerie said. "We'll arrive a little earlier, so Dad doesn't think we're living together."

"Okay. That'll give you time to talk me up. Not too much. I don't want to fall off a cliff."

The evening of the dinner, I passed under the arch that connected the *rue de Rivoli* to the gardens of the *Palais Royal* and strolled down the arcade, beneath the hanging lamps, past the lush flowers and the fountain and the splashing water and the statue of a naked boy seated on a rock, rehearsing what I'd say to Valerie's father. I had an extra spring in my gait. I didn't need anyone to wind me up; I couldn't wait to step on stage.

I entered the restaurant and froze, in awe, as I looked at the dining room and saw wall panels and square columns covered with gold borders and filigree; neoclassical paintings, under glass, of women standing on gold pedestals, bearing loaves of bread in their hands and baskets piled with fruits and vegetables on their heads, and wearing dresses that amounted to little more than soft veils draped to reveal their breasts; ceilings covered with gold stucco garlands surrounding more paintings; gold chandeliers with globes of light glowing above the diners; tables covered with white cloths and china and silver; and mirrors, on opposing walls, multiplying to infinity the glow of light and the vibrant gold, reds, and pastels.

Just as the *maître d'* approached and asked, *"Monsieur?"* I saw Maria and Valerie, in black evening dresses, seated at a table with a partially bald man in a dark suit. Following the *maître d'* to the table, I experienced a moment of vertigo as I saw my reflection repeated ad infinitum in the mirrors. Maria and Valerie looked up and greeted me, and Valerie introduced me to her father as a friend and Maria's fiancé. I sat down across from him.

He told me he was delighted to have the opportunity to meet someone his daughter and Maria had spoken so highly of and to just call him Alex, instead of Mr. Nash. He seemed friendly, charming, his face always ready to break into a smile, his eyes sparkling. He asked me what I'd like for an aperitif, and I said a Johnny Walker, having watched Frank drink it with his guests. A waiter appeared, and Alex pointed toward his glass and nodded in my direction and said, with a strong American accent, "*La même chose pour lui.*"

I relaxed, guessing his French wasn't better than mine, and launched a conversation. "Valerie told me about the work your firm does with countries in the Middle East, helping governments convert oil revenue into programs that improve people's lives. I'm so impressed."

"Thank you. I'm very moved that you appreciate the work we're doing."

I was about to ask how his firm worked with those governments, when he said, "Valerie tells me you've just finished your Master's at the University of Minnesota. Congratulations!"

"Thank you!" A glass of scotch appeared in front of me, and I took a drink.

"What did you do your degree in?"

"History."

"Really?" Alex furrowed his brow. "Why did you choose history?"

"Because history's the study of power over time: who had it, how they got it, what they did with it, what they did to hold onto it, who wanted to take it from them, the battles for it, and the consequences of retaining or losing it. I think that's fascinating."

"A very interesting definition. Is that your definition?"

"Oh, yes. It's mine."

Alex nodded. "A trip to France is a great way to celebrate."

"Actually, I'm combining work with pleasure. I'm doing a study of the United States of Europe."

In my peripheral vision, I noticed Maria's eyes widen with surprise and Valerie's eyebrows arch. I was enjoying myself, feeling quite cocky about my chances at succeeding. As for Alex, he looked stunned.

"But there's no such thing."

"There will be. That's obvious."

"Perhaps. One day."

"Oh, I think there definitely will be a United States of Europe."

"Why?"

"Europe evolved from warring principalities to warring nations. And then it got a look into the abyss in World War II and saw where the rivalry between nations leads. I think Europe has come to understand the importance of a union. Of some kind of federation. People are writing about this. They see the economic power Europe will wield if it can evolve into a United States of Europe. It's going to become a reality. In the twenty-first century, the important thing will be this: Which nations have come together to form economic blocs that can generate the most revenue and provide their people with the highest quality of life? A union of European states will keep people happy and earn their support."

"And how does the United States fit into your vision?"

"Well, I don't know about us. To me, it's obvious with Europe. But the U.S." I shook my head. "I'm afraid we didn't learn our lesson in Vietnam."

"Which was?"

"Well, there were a lot of lessons."

"I know one," said Maria. "This country must never allow itself to be lied into another war."

Valerie smirked and shook her head as she looked down at the table.

Alex arched his eyebrows.

"Another lesson," I said, "is that we didn't have enough confidence in what we were creating in the United States. After all,

Vietnam just wanted to be free of other rulers—first the Chinese, then the Japanese, then the French, and finally, us. If we had invested in ourselves, in our people, and not in that war, we could have been a model for the Vietnamese to emulate, instead of an enemy to kill."

"Hmm. Rather idealistic," Alex said. "Vietnam is communist. You can't just ignore the communist agenda. World domination. The end of democracy. Of our way of life."

"From what I've read, the French seem far more concerned with the CIA. They look at what we did in Chile and—"

"We have a lot of ties to South America," Alex snapped.

"Yes, we do."

"We can't allow a communist state in our backyard." He smiled.

"I understand. Ties can be very lucrative."

"Yes, they can," Alex said, nodding. "Tell me, why did you choose the University of Minnesota for graduate school? Someone as articulate and knowledgeable as you could have gone anywhere."

"Like HYP," Valerie said.

"Yes," I said, not knowing then that HYP meant Harvard-Yale-Princeton. But I didn't let that bother me. I was on a roll. "My grandfather has been a major contributor to the University's endowment, so it was just expected that I would go there. He's very committed. And so am I. I think our family has behaved admirably with its generosity."

"I see." Alex looked me over, nodding and smiling.

He picked up his menu, looked at the three of us, and suggested we order. I recognized *pâté de foie gras* among the *entrées* and *poitrine de poulet* among the *plats principaux*, so, when my turn came to order, I announced them to the waiter. Wine arrived, and the conversation flowed smoothly. Alex asked about the next step in my career and appeared impressed with my choice of the University of Texas for my Ph.D. and talked about Austin—such an interesting city—and how lucky I was to have found a woman like Maria. He found a way to flatter all of us. Finally, he invited me to join them in a week on the Mediterranean, for a cruise on a yacht that a young

Saudi prince was providing. I said I hoped to have my work on the future federation of European states finished by then and would be happy to do so.

I glanced around the room and basked in the mirrored reflections of light and gold and color and beauty and elegance and, in the midst of it all, me, dressed in white linen. I belonged there. I lifted my snifter and swirled my cognac, held the glass to my nose, inhaled the intoxicating perfume, and drank the cognac in a gulp. It flashed through me, and I felt my face glow.

I reclined on a *chaise longue*, gazing up at the cliffs that rose from the sea, at the stunted trees with their gnarled, twisted roots and trunks that grew from the crevices and crowned the summit, and at the blue of the sky—so pure, so deep.

The captain—a Saudi, like all the crew, who spoke English with a British accent—had dropped Alex off at Monte Carlo, where he planned to "mix a little pleasure with some business," and then sailed west along the Côte d'Azur, with its beaches and cliffs always in view. He'd anchored the yacht in a cove, between Monte Carlo and Nice, so Maria, Valerie, and I could go for a swim.

I'd thought I was on vacation when I was in Paris. But here, on the yacht, my life entered a different rhythm—that of the sea. My first three days on board, I found myself falling into a deep sleep early in the evening, drugged by the sea and the salt air, and sleeping until late morning. I smelled the sea every time I breathed, tasted it on my lips, felt its gentle rocking of the ship at anchor, and heard its waves rolling and breaking on the shore all day and all night, its hypnotic rhythm putting me in a trance.

I wiped sweat from my forehead and reached for the glass of water on the table, took a drink, and gazed at a gull wheeling above the towering mast. I set my glass down and glanced at Maria, stretched out on her *chaise longue*, and at Valerie, lying next to her, their eyes concealed by dark glasses, their lips smiling. I closed my eyes and sank into the warmth of a sun-induced stupor. I was in paradise, with two beautiful, wealthy women. One of them in love with me. Maybe both. I felt at home in their world of privilege.

I'd never lived in poverty, but money had always been tight, until now. Which did I prefer, wealth, or the lack of it? Wealth. Life becomes a menu. You order whatever you want. Or someone can order for you. Like, Daddy. Yeah, Daddy. Daddy snaps his fingers. The waiter appears, bows, and says, Your wish is my command, and hands Daddy a menu. Daddy's little girl leans over and whispers something in his ear. He smiles, nods, and says to the waiter, I'm looking at your graduation presents. My little girl's graduating from Smith. She'll have a year in France. And she'd like that to include trips to Spain, Italy, Germany, Holland, and England. And, let's see, maybe end the year with a cruise on the Mediterranean, on one of your yachts. And the waiter says, Yes, my lord. I got a real kick out of this fantasy, until I remembered Mom sitting on the bed, in the silence of that house, looking up at me and saying, "Why couldn't he have given us a house like this when your father was alive?"

I opened my eyes and saw the mast rising into the deep, calm, infinite blue. I took a breath. I'd learned how to get by on a TA's salary and take care of myself. I didn't hold anything against Archer anymore. Yeah, he could've helped us when Dad was alive. But Mom and Dad had both made decisions, and they'd paid a price. I couldn't let Dad's life determine mine. The life I had, I'd earned. I closed my eyes, and all the tension that had taken hold of me dissipated in the gentle rocking of the boat.

I'd almost fallen asleep, when I felt fingertips gliding back and forth across my belly. I opened my eyes and saw Maria's dark eyes smiling at me over the frame of her glasses.

"I'm so hot," she said. "I need to go below, or I'll burst into flames."

"If we go below, I might just stoke the fire in you."

"Oh, I'd love a good stoking." Maria stood up and said to Valerie, "We need a break."

Valerie grinned. "Have fun!"

"We shall," Maria said, as she took my hand.

Afterward, I lay in bed with Maria, listening to the lazy lapping of the water against the hull. I rolled over on my side, facing her. She had a blissful smile.

I said, "You have that freshly fucked look."

"What?" She laughed and opened her eyes. "What did you say?"

"You have that freshly fucked look."

"And what does that look like?"

"Go look at yourself in the mirror."

"Where did you get that?"

"A woman. She stood in front of a mirror and said that." I chuckled, while trying not to think of Helen standing nude, saying those words and looking over her shoulder at me.

"And who was the woman?"

"I don't remember."

Maria didn't believe me and continued to try to get the name. I diverted her attention with kisses and caresses, and we made love again. Afterward, I lay next to her, watching her eyelids flutter and close, listening to her breathing coming in longer, deeper waves.

I had to piss. I put on my bathing suit, started down the galley toward the head, and was about to pass Valerie's cabin, when I saw her standing nude in the doorway, her hand pulling a towel off her back. She must have just turned away from the mirror on the wall and would've been out of view, if she hadn't stopped. We gazed at one another. My eyes descended to her neck, her breasts, her pubic hair, and down her long legs and back up to her face.

"I thought my door was shut. The rocking of the boat must've opened it."

I had my heart in my throat. She didn't move. Finally, I said, "Sorry."

She smiled.

I nodded, and continued to the head.

After we'd returned to Paris, I was drinking an espresso one morning on the terrace of *La Palette*, a popular café on the *rue de Seine*, a narrow street on the Left Bank, near the *Ecole des Beaux Arts*, a prestigious art school. The café had been a hangout for artists like Cézanne, Picasso, and Braque. I stretched out on my chair, like a lizard absorbing the warmth of the sun, and was watching people go by, when I recognized a fellow graduate student from the University of Minnesota. I called to him. He saw me and looked confused. And then he recognized me, shouted my name, and came over. We shook hands and patted one another on the back. His eyes shifted from mine to my white linen jacket and slacks, and then, once we'd sat down, he looked me in the eye again, shook his head, and said, "Wow, you've undergone a metamorphosis."

"I decided it was time to let go of my hippie past."

"Must've been an expensive change."

"Nothing's cheap in Paris, but, ah, I managed. It's been an incredible summer."

I leaned back and told him about exploring Paris with Maria and Valerie, having dinner at the *Grand Véfour,* and sailing on the Mediterranean, while never mentioning who'd paid for everything. A break in my monologue allowed him to start talking. He was happy, too. His wife had gotten a good job about a year before, they were on a two-week vacation, their first big trip together, and he'd been admitted to law school.

"Man," he said, "the idea of taking two more years of courses and writing a dissertation, and five years from now, if I'm lucky, having a Ph.D.—for which there's no market. None. And then trying to get jobs teaching as an adjunct, for peanuts, and being dependent on my wife. That really depressed me. I don't like being dependent. It's humiliating. Money's going to be tight for a while, but then I'll be making fifty thousand a year." He grinned. "That'll be cool." After he'd dwelled on his thoughts about his happy life, and I'd dwelled in my mind on my humiliation, he asked, "And how about you? Going to stick it out? Do your Che thing, teach revolution?"

His smile felt condescending. And then Paris disappeared. I felt sick in the empty silence. I'd heard what he was telling me, I knew everything he knew, but I couldn't think about it, because I couldn't see a way out. I could only see one way forward. I became conscious of his presence, saw him looking at me, waiting for a response, and said, "Yeah, I'll do my Che thing. I don't give up."

I walked into The Common Good and stopped. No sign of Frank. I looked around at what had been my home. Footsteps descended the stairs in the back, and Frank emerged from the shadows. He said hi and asked if he could help me.

I put my hands on my hips and waited to see how long it would take him to recognize me.

He stopped a few feet away, a baffled look on his face. "Dick?"

"Yeah. It's me." I waited for him to say something, but he just stared.

Finally he asked, "Where's the easy-rider jacket?"

"At home."

He nodded, looking me up and down.

"I'm leaving tomorrow. Going back to the States. Just wanted to stop by and say hi."

I was trying to decide how to talk to him about his offer of letting me live in the bookstore in exchange for drawings. I'd often relived the fantasy of marrying Maria and living in Paris and working as an artist, and I'd remember the way Frank would smile at me, the way a proud father might smile at his son. But I also remembered the look in his eyes when he shouted at me to get out. Now each second of silence seemed to push him further away.

"I want to thank you for letting me stay here," I said. "For being so kind." The words weren't helping. He seemed further away than ever. "You know, I'm really sorry. I shouldn't have …" I felt tears welling up and clenched my teeth. "I hope … I hope everything goes well for you." I took a couple steps toward him and extended my hand.

He reached across the divide and took my hand in a loose grip. "It looks like you've made some decisions. I hope they work out for you."

"Yeah." I hesitated. "Well, I've got to get going. It was good seeing you again."

"Likewise. Oh, I almost forgot. Tim Blake wrote. He said he'd mentioned you to David Levine. Levine would like to meet you."

"Thanks. If I ever get to New York, I'll look him up."

Frank nodded.

I walked out, entered the little park in front of the store, heard a raspy, drunken voice snarl "*Amerloque*," and saw a *clochard* leaning back on a bench, his eyes following me with contempt. I went from the Left Bank to the Right, while thinking about the likelihood of ending up an adjunct, working for peanuts, being dependent on my wife, living a life of humiliation, feeling trapped. Frank had offered me an opportunity to build a life in Paris as an artist, be independent, and feel proud of myself. I could have done that with Maria.

I walked as fast as I could, and faster still, swerving around people, crashing into an oncoming shoulder, ignoring complaints, charging through the crowds, stopping at the blast of a horn just before a car nearly hit me at a pedestrian crossing, reliving that night Maria stayed with me in the bookstore and the next morning, and wondering, *Why didn't I talk to Frank about her? Why didn't I confide in him? Frank, Frank, dear, kind, generous Frank. Why did I throw everything away?* I had no answers. No defense. Nothing. I looked up from the sidewalk and saw the yellow walls and the red awning of Goldenberg's Deli and stopped. I was on the *rue des Rosiers*, in the Jewish quarter. How in the hell did I get here? I heard voices, people talking, weaving around me, sitting in the cafés that opened onto the street, driving their cars at a walking pace with their radios blasting, stopping for mothers and children crossing back and forth.

I was walking up the *rue Saint-Ambroise*, when Maria called my name. I saw her smiling down at me from the balcony. Her smile tamped down my anger and depression. Maria, Valerie, and I decided to go *Chez Amar* to celebrate my last night in Paris. "Couscous and a bottle of Sidi Brahim," Maria said, knowing I loved the strong Algerian wine. "The perfect going-away dinner."

At the beginning of our dinner, while I nodded and smiled and acted as if I were engaged in the conversation, I continued to feel depressed about the dream I knew would never come true. But as I ate my couscous and drank my wine and raised my glass to toasts, the fantasy and the depression faded, and I felt joyful in that intimate space, gazing at the women, their faces beaming above the soft glow of the candle on our table. Toward the end of the evening, I felt Maria's hand on my thigh. I placed my hand in hers and looked into her eyes and saw in their luminous warmth my happiness ... and the purpose of my life.

The next day, I flew back to Minneapolis. When I unpacked, I couldn't find my easy-rider jacket. I looked and looked. Gone.

CHAPTER 7

THE SERGEANT SCREAMED AT the old man on his knees, "Ali Baba, where are the mujahedeen, motherfucker? Where are they? We're going to kill the boy if you don't talk. You better be scared. We'll kill your fucking little Sinbad." My body tensed. A burst of gunfire, and the old man beat his head and wailed like an animal flayed alive. The boy stared at me, dark eyes wide with terror. The eyes stopped my breath. Accused me. I'm guilty. Guilty of everything I see in them.

My eyes snapped open. I looked around, still feeling the boy's stare, until the forms in the dark reassured me I was home, in my room. I'd been asleep; now I was awake. The dream I'd had so many times in the hospital seized me on just my second night home, and I could still feel it lurking in the darkness, ready to return if I closed my eyes. I got up, grabbed my cane, and opened the door. Light seeped beneath the door of the guest room, where Valerie was staying. I hesitated, took a couple steps toward the light, and stopped. I'd never talked to her about Fallujah. I took a couple more steps and stopped again. I remembered how she'd glared at me, when she said Maria might not have any skin in the game, but we do. How could I talk to her about the war? She wouldn't listen. She'd just attack.

I turned away from her door and went downstairs to the living room. The moon provided enough light through the windows for me to make my way to the liquor cabinet and pour myself a glass of scotch. I took a drink, sat down in the armchair at the end of the coffee table, faced the windows at the front of the house, and took another drink. The memory returned of Maria, smiling at me from the balcony in Paris, an act that had made me feel I was a good person, worthy of love, at a moment when I felt I wasn't. A smile that opened the door to happiness.

After Paris, I returned to Minneapolis, packed my things in a moving truck, and followed Maria to Austin. She'd found a furnished apartment for me, the second floor of a house, eight blocks from the campus of the University of Texas. The day I arrived, she was waiting for me, excited to show me my new place. She ran up the exterior staircase ahead of me, threw open the door, and we followed the sunshine in. She guided me through the rooms, her eyes darting back at me as she talked up the best features, like the armchair with the matching ottoman where I could sit for hours and read, the cherrywood table in the dining room, and the window that framed a beautiful tangle of oak branches in a way that I thought resembled a Japanese painting. We entered the bedroom and forgot about the tour and made love.

We got up an hour later, rushed to unload the truck, assembled the shelves, set up the stereo system, and hung my self-portrait and the drawing of Blake on the living room wall. While I shelved books, she flipped through the records and found *Roulette russe*, the album by Alain Bashung we used to listen to in Paris, put the LP on the turntable, and set the needle on *"Je fume pour oublier que tu bois."* Bashung began singing, and she turned to me and shouted, "For Valerie!" We sang the lyrics about life being like an overdose—"You take everything at once, you die and fast"—and started to dance and danced until we collapsed to the floor and made love again. After we'd lain there for a while, taking deep breaths and humming our ecstasy, she roused herself and said she'd better get dressed.

"Dressed? I thought you were staying here tonight."

"Oh, I'd love to. But Daddy wants me to drive him to the airport in the morning."

"I'm losing you to Daddy?" I laughed. "That sounds weird."

I walked her to the street, she got into her Buick Regal con-vertible, and I watched her drive away, two taillights glowing in the dark, getting smaller and smaller.

The week before classes began, I settled into my office and met my three office mates, also Ph.D. candidates. They cracked up when they saw the Che poster above my desk and exclaimed, "Another Che!" They said some of the right-wing members of the Texas legislature referred to my adviser, Professor Albion, as "Che the Great Liberator," and one of them had made the comment, re-peated in the *Austin American-Statesman*, "We thought he'd been killed in Bolivia ten years ago, but he showed up at the University alive and well." There'd been an effort by some politicians to get Albion fired, because of his criticism of American foreign policy, but most of the faculty and the administration had supported his right to free speech.

When I finally entered his office to meet him, I didn't encoun-ter a young guy with a beard and a beret, but an old man with white hair, who apologized for the mess while nodding at piles of books, scholarly reviews, and papers piled high on a conference table. "I'm afraid I still haven't developed those organizational skills we tell our students are so important." His eyes twinkled. We sat down at the table and talked. He seemed gentle and kind and interested in everything about me, and I could see why students loved him so much. But I was the only one doing a dissertation under his direction. As one of my office mates said, "There aren't many uni-versities looking for specialists in South-American revolutionary movements."

The following Saturday, Maria and I were to have dinner with her parents, and I'd meet them for the first time. Knowing they were wealthy, I decided to wear the white linen suit I'd worn to the *Grand Véfour*. Maria picked me up, and we followed a road west out of Austin and into the hill country, over dry terrain sheltered by the boughs of live oak. As we climbed hills and wound our way around huge boulders, Maria pointed out and named the different cacti—yuccas, prickly pears, and agaves—and slowed down so I could get a good look at a juniper tree, its twisted trunk and sparse branches and green spikes and berries outlined by the sky.

"I love that tree," she said. "It looks like it should have—I don't know—some kind of mythical meaning."

"You mean, like a metamorphosis?"

"Yeah. Like a god decided to punish a human by turning him into a tree. And the person twisted in agony at the moment his limbs transformed into wood. Look at those boughs. Don't they look like arms?" She pulled the car over to the side of the road and leaned toward me. "See that shelf, just beyond the juniper? If you stand out on the edge, you'll be looking down a thousand feet to the valley."

I gazed at the twisted tree and beyond at the panorama of hills, bluffs, and strange rock formations—a view I'd never expected to see in Texas.

She exclaimed, "Look!" and pointed up at two bald eagles, gliding above the shelf, their wings tipping slightly one way and then the other as they circled the same area, but in opposite directions, so that their flight paths crossed. After completing a few circles, one eagle flew away, the other tipped its wings and followed, and they disappeared in the distance. I'd heard bald eagles mated for life and felt what I'd seen was a good omen.

I sensed Maria's eyes on me and looked at her. She sighed, as if she felt guilty of something. "One thing I haven't told you. My parents think we met in Paris this summer. They don't know we've been in love for over two years."

"Why didn't you tell them?"

She beamed. "You're my secret lover."

"Okay." I smiled back. "I'll keep the secret."

We kissed and set off again, reached a plateau, passed through a clearing, and turned onto a driveway lined with live oak that led to a yard and, about a hundred feet ahead of us, a two-story stone house, of the same creamy color as the rock formations I'd seen on our way up. The house seemed to emerge from the earth and sprawl, like something at once primeval and elegant.

"There it is—home!"

"Unbelievable!"

"Not if you know Daddy."

We drove through a sea of green with scattered islands of roses and stands of redbuds, of crape myrtle ablaze with reddish-pink flowers, and of other blossoming trees and shrubs. The house and garden made the few estates I'd seen in this country look like bungalows.

"My granddaddy has a big house in Houston. He put an oil derrick in his yard, so before you see the magnolias and the crape myrtles and the beautiful house, you see that rig from his first oil well. That's a tradition in Texas. The University put the rig from its first well, the Santa Rita, on a corner of the campus, where everyone can see it. But Daddy wanted to create a different world. No oil rigs."

"Looks like paradise."

"Daddy was probably thinking along those lines. When I was at Smith and learned about Louis the fourteenth, the Sun King, I said to myself, That's Daddy, the Sun King of Texas."

"'Sun King of Texas,'" I repeated, imagining a guy in poofy robes and six-inch heels, with a foot-high white pompadour wig. My gaze drifted across the gardens, and I said, "This is as impressive as Versailles."

"Daddy gets what Daddy wants. That gazebo you're looking at, near the magnolia trees, that's where Daddy and Mama like to take their mint juleps. In the spring, when the magnolias are in bloom, you can practically get high on the perfume, just sitting in there."

She pulled the car to a stop. I got out and followed her up the walk, as she pointed at the different shrubs and flowers with names like skyflower, mistflower, and rain of gold. I gazed at the colors in the garden, at the walls of the house and the light rose hue that the sun brought out in the cream-colored stone, and at the casement windows that reminded me of windows I'd seen in old French houses. The low eaves seemed to weigh the house down, pushing it toward the ground, while the stone created a feeling of something ethereal rising from the earth. I thought of old man Archer's house. That was monolithic. This was otherworldly.

I followed her toward the massive door that opened magically—the magic provided by a man in a white shirt and black slacks, whom she addressed as Pedro. He stepped aside and smiled as he greeted us. We entered the foyer and walked past a grand piano on one side and potted plants on the other, and down two steps into a sunken living room. I stopped to take in the massive stone fireplace that rose to the ceiling and divided the room, and the soft glow of lights, placed along the base of the walls and in the ceiling, that lit up murals of flowers and warmed the interior, making it feel like a sacred space. I turned in a semi-circle, gazing at the flowers and colors that reminded me of the gardens outside, and thought of Monet's water lilies in Paris. When Maria shouted that we were there, the high pitch of her voice seemed almost sacrilegious.

My gaze drifted from the murals to the grand piano in front of one of the large windows next to the foyer. I asked Maria who played the piano. She did. I asked her to play something. After some hesitation and what sounded like excessive modesty, she sat down and started playing Lennon's "Imagine," and we sang the lyrics. About halfway through, when we faltered, she stopped and said, "Do you know this?" She started singing in a sultry voice a song about inviting a boy to dine on her fine finnan haddie, and adoring him asking for more, but her heart belonged to Daddy. She broke off the song and said, "Isn't that weird? I can't imagine giving my heart to a sugar daddy."

A voice behind me said, "Where did that come from?"

I turned and saw a woman who resembled Maria, only older and a little plump, bestowing a beatific smile on her daughter as she shook her head. She wore a dress with embroidered flowers and a lot of gold—rings, bracelets, and earrings.

"Hi, Mama. A woman performed it at Esther's Follies. In a fur coat, and almost nothing underneath." Maria batted her eyelashes, like a vamp. "It's a Cole Porter song."

She introduced me to her mother, who told me to call her Cristina. She led me into the living room and gestured toward a couch that faced a coffee table and a loveseat. She sat on the loveseat facing me, and Maria on an armchair at the end of the table, between her mother and me. Cristina said she'd heard I was teaching at the University, and I explained I was working as a TA in a two-semester course on Latin American History. I was grateful to have something to talk about and probably would have described the course in detail, if I hadn't noticed Maria's eyes fixed on something. I followed her gaze and saw a man in a sport coat looking at me.

Cristina said, "Dear, this is Dick."

From the way Maria had talked about her powerful father, I'd imagined him tall and built like a Greek god, but as I shook his hand, I found Warren Cutler to be physically unimpressive.

"Dick was just telling us—"

"I heard." Warren's thin lips spread in a tight smile. "Who's the faculty member you're assisting?"

"Professor Albion."

"In History?"

"Yes."

"I don't know him. I know the president, of course, and some of the deans. And a few of the faculty have done consulting for us. But no one in History."

Warren suggested we sit down. Cristina moved over so he could take her place on the love seat across from me and next to Maria. His eyes met hers and lit up and then froze when they focused on her short hair. He looked at me.

"So, you're grading papers for this, ah …"

"Professor Albion. I also teach a recitation section, once a week."

"Hmm. Recitation section. And what do the students recite?"

I looked into Warren's eyes, trying to determine if he really didn't know, and saw a poker face. "They don't recite anything. I

don't know why they're called recitation sections. I lead discussions
of the material in the textbook and of the points that Albion covers
in his lectures."

"Ah!" Warren smiled, as if he now understood—or had satisfied
his sense of humor. He glanced at Cristina and back at me. "What
do I know? I'm just a businessman." The smile never left his lips.
"You enjoy that?"

"Teaching?"

Warren nodded.

"Yes. I love teaching. It's very rewarding."

Warren repeated, "very rewarding," and nodded again. "Now,
when you finish your Ph.D. ... That's what you're working on,
right? A Ph.D.?"

"Yes."

"And you're being trained to teach this kind of course?"

"Yes. And I came here because Albion is one of the top scholars
of South-American history. We're going to use one of his books
next semester, when we focus on the period from the end of the
Spanish conquest to today."

"So, why did you choose this field?"

And so it went, even after we moved from the living room to
the dining room, on the other side of the fireplace, where I found
myself sitting across the table from him, with Maria next to me. The
questions became increasingly difficult to answer without revealing
more than I wanted to about myself. History was kind of risky,
wasn't it? Did I think I could make a decent living at it? What did
your father do? Was he able to make a living as an artist? And on
and on.

As I looked into the eyes that never stopped smiling at me, I
had the feeling I was looking into the eyes of a snake hypnotizing
its prey. Warren was trying to get as much information out of me
as he could, and sooner or later I'd say something that would reveal
too much. I realized why Maria had postponed this encounter. The
Sun King's approval of the man she loved meant everything to her,
but she knew where I came from—the grandson of a miner, the

son of a painter, who'd never made much money, and smoked and drank himself to death, and of a mother who had to finish raising her children and putting them through college on a teacher's salary and money she begged from her father. No, I couldn't let the snake hypnotize me like some prairie dog. About halfway through dinner, while Warren was savoring a forkful of roast dove, I said, "Maria tells me you're originally from Maine."

No, he said. His father was born and raised in Connecticut. The family had a summer home in Maine. His daddy, his uncles, and their families went back to Maine every year, but they had all wanted to create their own lives in places like New York, DC, and Houston. His daddy had served in the First World War, and after he'd come home, he learned about the Texas oil boom, moved to this state, discovered oil, built the East Texas Petroleum Company, and then expanded it to Texas Petroleum. I'd interject an occasional exclamation, making him think I was impressed, and he'd continue talking, totally wrapped up in himself.

I'd found a way of controlling the flow of information: asking questions, awaiting each response with a fascinated look, and hoping Warren's narcissism would make him want to talk about himself all night. Soon I had him reminiscing about his childhood memories of the summer home in Maine, where the family had a yacht and a golf course; of his Uncle Elias, a U.S. senator from Connecticut who'd stood up to the Emperor's efforts to get Social Security and Glass-Steagall through Congress and turn this country into a socialist state; of the success of his grandfather, his great uncles, and his uncles on Wall Street, and of the power they had accumulated. Warren punctuated his spiel with a glassy-eyed, far-off gaze as he nodded his head at the thought—that seemed to have almost taken human shape, somewhere beyond me—of the wealth and power his family had accumulated.

My greatest achievement was getting Warren and Cristina to talk about how they'd met. For the first time since her husband had stepped on stage, Cristina talked.

"It was after Warren finished his junior year at Yale."

"The men in my family all went to Yale," Warren interjected.

"He was home for the summer. I was working as a waitress, at Cisco's. Do you know it?"

"I've heard of it," I said.

"Cisco's real name is Rudy. He and my papa were friends. So, one day, I was waiting on tables and noticed this very handsome *gringo*. He was sitting with LBJ, who—"

"I was not sitting at a table with LBJ. I was with someone else."

"*Sí, sí, sí.* You were sitting with LBJ. I remember."

He shook his head. "I wouldn't sit with that—"

"*Sí*," she beamed, gazing at Warren.

He took over with his version of the story. "I was with some-one, I don't remember who, and saw this beautiful Mexican woman waiting on tables. I caught her eye and held up my cup."

"And when I served him, he gave me such a look." She shook her head. "He came back the next morning and drank so much coffee, I thought he'd get sick. He asked me out. I told him I had a boyfriend, Felipe. Just a boy, so young." A wistful look appeared in her eyes and then faded. "But Warren wouldn't give up. He kept coming back." She grinned at him, as if he were still a mischievous kid, and then looked at me. "Felipe got called up and shipped off to the war. He wrote at first, but then the letters stopped coming. Not long before the end, his sister called and told me he'd been killed at Iwo Jima." She sighed and shook her head, sadness washing across her face. "He died so young."

"The poor guy," Warren said. "All of us were worried about get-ting called up at the end of the war and being the last man to die."

Cristina nodded. "When I got the news, Warren was at Yale. He came home to comfort me. And that summer, when he re-turned for good, we started seeing one another every day. We got married in September." She beamed, as if to say, And we lived happily ever after.

Pedro removed the plates.

"I'm a very fortunate man." Warren fixed me with his serpen-tine stare. "Of course, one makes one's own fortune, good or bad. And good fortune can cost a fortune." He paused. "We're so happy to have Maria back home with us, after four years at Smith and a year in France. We missed her. She's like an only child to us. So, when she told me she wanted to get a degree in journalism, I said I'd be happy to pay for it." He looked at her, and she basked in his gaze. "Our good fortune." His eyes turned toward me. "But on the condition that she live at home for a year, to make us happy. I even bought her a new car, to sweeten the deal." He smirked and repeated his line about good fortune costing a fortune, and I knew he knew I didn't have one. I would later learn he'd put Maria on a small allowance, to have more control over her.

When we rose from the table and moved toward the foyer, I noticed Warren was wearing cowboy boots and realized that even the powerful in Texas wore boots and that my white linen suit probably made me look prissy. Maria and I reached the front door and were about to leave, when Warren acted surprised she had to drive me home, and then appeared to remember I didn't have a car. I assured him I'd buy one soon. He explained that he and Cristina didn't like the idea of Maria driving through the hill country at night, it could be dangerous.

Maria and I slid into her convertible and, as we sped off, my body decompressed and sank into the seat. She shouted over the rush of air, "Oh, my God! I've never heard Daddy talk so much!"

"Yeah, amazing. You think I passed the test?"

"A-plus. They really like you."

I had the impression Cristina liked me, but Warren? As I went back and forth across the conversation between us, trying to determine what he thought of me, I stumbled on a comment that had surprised me. I looked at Maria. "Your father said you were like an only child. That implies you're not."

After a brief silence, she said, "I have an older sister, Anita. She doesn't have anything to do with my parents, and they don't have anything to do with her."

"Why?"

"I don't know. She didn't confide much in me when she lived at home, and I haven't talked with her in years." She paused, and added, "I don't like to talk about this."

A few minutes later, she pulled into my driveway. I leaned toward her, and we kissed. When I opened my door to get out, she didn't move.

"You coming?"

"I know Mama. She'll call Jimmy's, just to be sure I arrived safe, and if I'm not there, she'll go crazy."

"Why would she call you there?"

"Daddy made arrangements with Jimmy's mother for me to stay there, on days when I might leave campus late."

So, Daddy knew all along she wouldn't need to drive through the hill country at night. "Well, maybe we can both stay at Jimmy's."

After a long silence, she answered, "I guess we can."

"You don't sound very happy."

"It's just … When I come home, I start behaving like a good little girl." She laughed. "Maybe I'll break the news someday to my mother that we've lived together."

"Should I get out?"

She put her hand on my neck and pulled me close to her.

The next morning, I looked around at the walls covered with posters that Maria had purchased in museums in Europe and that reproduced some of her favorite paintings, such as Vermeer's *Woman in Blue Reading a Letter* and Van Gogh's *Starry Night*. I glanced over at Maria, lying on her back and gazing at me, her lips spreading in a smile as she pulled me toward her, but I was too interested in seeing Jimmy to make love again. We got up and dressed and went downstairs to the dining room, where we found him sitting at the table, facing us, his back turned toward the glass wall and door that looked out onto the lawn and the river. Tapping the tabletop with a constant roll of his fingertips next to a plate covered with smears of egg yolk and jam, and bouncing one leg crossed over the other, he seemed to be staring at something behind me. I turned around, saw nothing, looked back, and found him grinning at me.

"Long time, no see," he said.

"Yeah. Two years."

"Ya look real good. Y'all want some breakfast? I got eggs and toast. Cereal, too. Let me get you some coffee." He stood up, tall and lanky, in a T-shirt and a pair of jeans, and shuffled in his bare feet to the kitchen.

Maria sat down at the end of the table, where she could be close to both of us, and I sat across from Jimmy's place. He returned with two mugs, sat down, noticed his own was empty, filled it, sat down again, poured in milk and sugar, slurped a mouthful, pushed his chair back, crossed one leg over the other, bouncing the top leg again, while his eyes darted around the room, before focusing on us and repeating, "Y'all want some breakfast?" Maria said she'd just like to talk for now.

Jimmy pulled a cigarette out of the pack on the table, snapped a lighter open with a flick of his wrist, lit up, took a drag, and another, and rested his hand on the table, tapping his fingertips again, and flashed a smile, as if something funny had gone through his head.

"Maria told me you've been clean," I said. "How long's it been?"

"I haven't done drugs or had a drink in a year." He took a drag.

I looked at his index and middle fingers, stained a sickly yellowish brown, and thought of Dad and his chain-smoking after he'd quit drinking. "And cigarettes?"

"Aw, man," he said, shaking his head, desolation on his face. "Two packs a day. At least."

"But you're clean, and you've got a job," Maria said.

"First time I ever held onto one." He grinned and nodded repeatedly.

I asked about his job, and he described what it was like working with the ground crew at the University, and then fell silent, and his smile turned into a distant stare.

Maria leaned forward, placed her hand on his, looked into his eyes, and brought him back again. "And you're making money."

"Yup! I pay for my own groceries. And books. I've been reading books."

"What books have you been reading?" I asked.

He rubbed the stubble on his chin, leaned back, sighed, folded his arms and shook his head. "Can't remember. Something about Vietnam. Did you go to Vietnam?"

"No."

Jimmy nodded. "You're lucky." His gaze drifted past me.

Maria got up, placed her hand on his shoulder and looked down at him, like a mother at her little boy, and brushed a lock of hair away from his eyes. She glanced at me and smiled and said she'd make us breakfast.

And then the phone rang. It was Cristina.

A week after the dinner with Maria's parents, we hosted the first of many parties at the Sun King's paradise. Actually, it was Maria who did the hosting. I was just there, like an extra. The parties, generally on Saturday nights, blur in my memory, but parts of the first one remain distinct. I was reading a book, when I heard footsteps rushing up the stairs. Maria threw open the door and struck a pose, bending one leg slightly, dipping her head, and looking up at me while fluttering her lashes. And she had lashes to flutter. The mascara was thick. All of the makeup was thick. Bright red lips, heavy black eyebrows, and blue eye shadow. And a black dress that covered her from her breasts to her hips. Fluttering her lashes, she asked, "You like?"

"Put on a pair of black stockings and a bowler hat, and you could do *Cabaret*."

"Liza Minnelli?"

"You're a lot sexier." I stood up. "Now, look at me. See anything different?"

She looked me over, commenting that she liked the combination of my jeans with the white linen jacket and shirt, and then, when her eyes reached my feet, she exclaimed, "Boots!"

"In Texas, if you're a man, a real man, you wear boots."

She crouched at my feet and ran her fingers across one of the hand-tooled black boots and said, in a reverential tone, "They're beautiful, Dick."

"You can lick them if you want."

"You're incorrigible."

A short time later, Maria and I flew through the entrance to her house and into the living room, where Cristina greeted us.

"That was quick," she said to Maria.

"Hi, Mama! Yeah, I didn't lick his boots." Maria snickered.

"What?"

"I was admiring his new boots, and he told me I could lick them if I wanted."

"Oh, dear." Cristina grinned and shook her head, and then asked me how everything was going. I talked about the recitation section I was teaching and the courses I was taking. She remembered Maria was sitting in on one of those courses and asked what it was.

"Latin American Revolutions," I said.

"Ah!" Cristina exclaimed. She looked as if she wanted to say something, and then changed her mind. "Well, let's see if everything's ready for the party."

She led us through the house to a patio with round tables and chairs, and we continued toward a long table, where Pedro was arranging wine glasses. While Cristina talked to him, Maria locked her arm in mine and guided me around the table toward a swimming pool with palm trees at one end.

"At night, the pool's lit from inside, and it glows like an emerald. It's beautiful."

"It's huge!"

"Fifty meters. Daddy thought one of his daughters might be an Olympic swimmer. No one can say he doesn't have high expectations."

"And the palm trees."

"He decided if palms could grow in Austin, they could grow here, too."

We'd strolled past the palms and were wandering toward a cluster of pomegranates, when a voice called, "Maria!" Two women approached us. Fay, a blonde, and Bonnie Mae, a brunette, would attend every party and always wear shorts, or a skirt, and a halter-top.

They gave Maria a restrained hug, not wishing to press their hair-dos sprayed to perfection against her skin. While Maria introduced us, informing me the three of them had been friends since grade school, the two women gazed up at me with big eyes. Like Maria, they also had bright red lips, thick black eyebrows, and fluttering lashes that made me think of Barbie dolls, and the similarity made me wonder if Maria reverted to a former self when she partied with her old friends.

"So, Dick," Bonnie Mae said, "Maria said you met her in Paris, and the two of you went to the Riviera together and sailed on a yacht." She spoke in a melodious drawl, pausing after each clause and looking as if she might faint at each exhilarating thought.

"On the Mediterranean!" Fay exclaimed, in a high-pitched twang. She looked at Maria, arched her eyebrows, and grinned. "I want to hear *all* the details."

Maria left us to greet a few more women dressed like Bonnie May and Fay, accompanied by young men with hair flowing over their ears. Bonnie Mae opened a purse and pulled out a pack of cigarettes, and the women lit up and smoked as they eyed the newcomers.

"She hasn't been divorced more than a month, and here she is already, with a new man," Bonnie Mae drawled as she watched one of the women.

"He doesn't look like much to me," Fay said.

"If that's who I think it is, his daddy's gonna make 'im rich."

"She always finds a way." Fay glanced over her shoulder, gave me a look that said, Oh, you're still here, and said to Bonnie Mae, "Let's get a glass of wine."

They headed for the bar, and I walked over to Maria, who was talking to a woman with red hair. Maria introduced me to Maureen, who rolled her eyes and told Maria I was *so* good looking, she'd better not take her eyes off me, and then they both took their eyes off me while Maureen talked about her experience working on the Governor's staff, a job her daddy arranged for her after she'd finished her degree at Mount Holyoke. Another staff member was an old friend who was shacking up with some guy. Maria hoped he would work out better than the preceding one.

When the two women started gossiping about another friend, I headed for the bar, where the candles in the globes lit up the glasses and the bottles. A crowd was standing in front of the table, and I got stuck next to a couple of heavy drawlers, swigging Lone Stars and talking about Texas beating OU, the kind of football conversation I'd been overhearing all week among my students. I edged past the guys, caught Pedro's attention, and ordered a martini.

A familiar voice said, "Hello there, Dick."

I turned around to see Warren. "Mr. Cutler, I didn't know you were here."

"I just got home. And call me Warren. 'Mr. Cutler' sounds so formal."

"Sure." When Pedro said, "Here you are, Señor Rayburn," and handed me my martini, I told him to just call me Dick.

"I didn't know you were a martini man," Warren said.

"Bogie inspired me. You know, in *Casablanca*."

"Ah, Bogie," he smirked. "Say, I, ah, I don't mean to harass you about this, but I was just wondering if you'd looked into buying a car yet."

"As soon as I have enough money, I'll buy one. That's my top priority."

"Great. Well, have a wonderful evening."

He smiled, like everything between us was perfect, and moved off, stopping to chat here and there. When he got to Maria, he put his arm around her shoulders and talked with her and her friends, while she gazed up at him, and then continued to the house.

I finished my martini, had Pedro fix me another, and wandered among the guests, ready to respond to anything that might snag my attention and make me feel I was having a good time, but all I heard was more talk of football and cheerleaders, my daddy this and his daddy that, dove hunting in the fields and rattlesnake hunting in the hills. It was getting dark. I rejoined Maria, tired of the gossip, circulated again, and stopped near the pool. A couple of young men in bathing suits rushed by and jumped in, and as they swam in the luminous emerald-green water, I remembered swimming with a woman in the mountains of New Mexico and her coming to me in the night. I raised my eyes and took a drink and noticed Maria watching me. She smiled as soon as our eyes met, and then turned her attention back to her group.

Noticing the party was winding down and people were leaving, I joined Maria and her closest friends, who were reminiscing about the parties they used to have, and Maureen recalled how Maria would play the piano and they'd sing along. Some of the women asked Maria to play for them, so we moved inside to the living room, she sat down at the piano, and everyone gathered around. She asked what she should play, and someone shouted, "Stand by your man." Maria tried a few bars of the song, said she couldn't remember it well enough, and then started playing "Let's do it," batting her lashes as she performed the playful naughtiness of Cole Porter's song. When she finished, the blonde with the twang, Fay, shouted, "Stand by your man," and some of the other women turned the words into a chant. Maria positioned her fingers above the keyboard, tried a few chords, seemed to find the song in her memory, started playing, and a few women sang along with drunken confidence about the need to give your man something warm on those nights he's feeling cold and lonely. Maria became more tentative in her playing and then stopped, while Fay and Bonnie May continued to the end. Maria stood up and said they'd have to do this more often, it was so much fun.

In her car on the way to Jimmy's house, she talked about the party, repeating some of the gossip her friends had told her, while I stared into the dark, steeped in a sullen state. She fell silent for a while, and then said she hoped I hadn't been bored. She went way back with a lot of her friends, like Maureen, whom she'd known since first grade. Maureen told her some of the girls from their high school had gone to UT together, joined the same sorority, and scheduled all their classes around their favorite soap operas. "Isn't that funny?" She fell silent again, and then said, "It's kind of like a soap opera, isn't it. The party, I mean. Who's getting married, divorced, having an affair, moving to Dallas or Houston, whatever."

"Yeah," I sighed, ready to agree with whatever she said, so she'd stop talking.

From that night on, I referred to the parties as Saturday night soaps in paradise. Or rather, that's how I referred to them in my internal rants. With Maria, I just smiled and thought about my next martini.

One night, a few parties later, Maria was driving us back to Austin, and I, having had one too many, was focusing my attention on the black pavement coming at us in the headlights, when she asked me if I'd had a good time. I remained silent, thinking about how I felt like a mudsill among her guests, who all seemed to have daddies who'd put them through college and positioned them to get whatever they wanted, and they felt they were entitled to everything. I might've understood even then that resentment mediated my perceptions, but I couldn't talk about my prejudices with Maria. So, when she asked again if I'd had a good time, I said, "Yeah."

"Hmm. You disappeared for a while. Where did you go?"

"Just wandered around the yard, on the other side of the pool."

"All by yourself, in the dark?"

"I had an interesting conversation with myself, about that film we saw the other night."

She fell silent, and I continued to focus on the road as it curved around the hill.

"Did you talk with anyone tonight?" she asked.

"Yeah, your daddy." I looked at her. "He wondered if the University paid its TAs enough for them to buy a car, and when he got done with that subject, he moved on to another one of his favorites—Did I think I could get a job after I finished my dissertation? When I told him the market was a little tight, but I could succeed, he said, 'Good boy!'"

"You see, he has confidence in you."

"Really? You don't think he might've been playing with me?"

"Why do you always interpret everything in the most negative way?"

"I've already told him the market sucks. That's why he loves to talk about it."

We reached the bottom of the hill, she put the pedal to the metal, and we flew down the blacktop, trees near the side of the road flashing by in the headlights. When we reached Jimmy's house, we went straight to bed, she on her side and I on mine.

I awoke in the morning and found her gone. I threw on some clothes, rushed to the top of the stairs, and heard voices coming from the dining room. When I entered, Maria and Jimmy fell silent and stared at me. She said, "Look who finally woke up. Want some breakfast?" She nodded toward my place at the table, where a plate and a coffee mug had been set. Jimmy, sitting in front of a partially eaten stack of pancakes and a bottle of maple syrup, had a big grin on his face. He cut a wedge of pancakes three layers thick and stuffed it, dripping with syrup, into his mouth and munched, managing somehow to smile and chew at the same time.

I sat down. Maria took my plate, disappeared into the kitchen, returned with a stack of pancakes and set it in front of me, and moved behind Jimmy, resting her hands on his shoulders. "I want my boys to have a hearty breakfast," she said, in a weirdly euphoric voice. "I want them to be happy." She tousled Jimmy's hair and pulled his head back between her breasts. "That's what every mama wants for her boys. Right?" Jimmy hee-hawed with his mouth full until he choked.

CHAPTER 8

I BECAME AWARE OF MYSELF sitting in the living room, in the moonlight, staring at my empty glass, wondering, *Why do we remember what brings us pain? Why can't we just forget?* I wanted to go to sleep, but if I went to bed, I knew I'd lie there, awake, reliving the past. I checked my watch. It was after one. I went to the liquor cabinet, poured another scotch, and sat down again. And thought about Maria.

I sometimes felt the woman with whom I'd fallen in love had disappeared and a stranger was inhabiting her body. At the Saturday night soaps, she seemed to regress to a teenager, or Daddy's little girl, an angry girl. But there were also times when I felt the woman with whom I'd fallen in love reclaimed her body, like when we'd go out for coffee after Albion's course, alone, or with her friends in Journalism, or mine in History, and talk about politics and feminism and our other interests, or when we'd have a quick dinner and see a film and discuss it afterwards.

I was anticipating that kind of evening one Friday, when I returned to my office after class, tossed my textbook on the desk, flopped down in my chair, and propped my boots up. I picked up the *Austin American-Statesman* I'd left there, spread it open across my legs and leafed through it, scanning titles and bylines, until I came to an article on the opinion page that stopped me: "Listen Up, Austinites," by Maria Cutler. The title was so Maria.

She maintained a tone of defiant, prophetic revelation throughout the article as she described the lives of the unemployed who'd lost all hope, of those who worked minimum-wage jobs and didn't earn enough to live, of the school dropouts heading for nowhere but trouble, of the alienated and the abandoned, and of the people who should be seeing doctors, but couldn't. She challenged Austinites to get their act together and move their city to create a sense of opportunity and hope for the young and turn them away from despair and violence. Her voice sounded so sincere. How about free daycare centers, so parents could go to work without having to worry about their children? Or free health clinics, so people wouldn't be afraid to seek medical help? And why not develop in-school and after-school tutoring, and a broader range of extra-curricular after-school programs, so we can get kids moving in the right direction, instead of down the well-trodden paths to unemployment, poverty, welfare checks, crime, and—for way too many—prison? And what if? What if? I could hear the down-home drawl, the twang she used when she wanted to come off as a true Texan, one of the clan. The article ended with a vision of what the city could be—poverty eradicated and everyone leading meaningful lives and giving back to the community. "Now, wouldn't that be cool?" she concluded.

Cool? The article wouldn't lead to anything. The liberals would eat it up like raspberry sorbet, and the rednecks would lift a leg and piss on it. There might be a few friends who'd say, *Oh, did you tell 'em!* Or, *Way to go, girl!* But the others—above all, the Barbies—would smile real polite and drawl, *Saw your article in the paper, Maria. You write so good. I wish I could write like that.* Anyone who had power would dismiss it. But Maria had a good heart. That counted. Counted for a lot. And she did write well. I folded the paper and tossed it onto my desk.

"Ooo, look who I found, tucked away in his office." Maria slid through the partially opened door and onto my lap and wrapped her arms around my neck. "My little Dicky darling."

"I wonder how I'd explain this to some student who might walk in."

"We're smart. We'd think of something." She kissed me and nestled her head in the crook of my neck. "I missed you," she whispered, her warm breath caressing my skin.

"It's only been a few hours."

"It may as well have been years." She pulled back and looked at me. "You know what Jimmy said at breakfast this morning?"

"I should know. I was there."

"When you went to pee."

"Oh. What did he say?"

"He thinks you're the man for me, and we should get married."

"I think he's right. What did you say?"

"I said, when the time's right, I think you should ask Daddy."

"Ask your father?" I snickered, imagining the look on Warren's face. "Are you kidding? Isn't that something we decide?"

"Yeah, but there are benefits that come with a father's blessing. And, besides, it's the right thing to do."

"Maybe in the nineteenth century."

"I think it shows respect."

"And what if we were to get married, and then tell your parents?"

"That would hurt them."

"Okay," I sighed. "I'll ask his permission. After we get to know one another better." She rested her head on my shoulder. "You know what I was thinking?"

"Tell me."

"I thought maybe we could have dinner, and then go to the student union and see that film about revolution and counter-revolution in Chile."

"Let's do it!"

She slid off my lap, and I stood up and gathered my things.

"And then, since it would be much too late for you to drive on those dark roads back to your parents' house, we could spend the night at Jimmy's."

"We spent last night there."

"So?"

"I promised Daddy and Mama I'd live at home this year. That was the deal." She stiffened. "They've given me everything I've ever wanted. I'm their little girl. I'm all they've got. And I'm not going to disappoint them."

"They've got another little girl. Why can't she move home for a year?"

"I don't know. And it's irrelevant."

"You're going to turn twenty-four in a month."

She glared at me. "You know, you're right. By the time we get out of the movie, it'll be too late for me to drive home. So, I'll go home right after dinner."

I tried to push her too far, and if I continued pushing, she wouldn't even have dinner with me, so I apologized, saying she should keep the promise she'd made. After we made up, we went to the Old Pecan Street Café for the first time since the day after we'd met, two years before.

I was holding a shot of tequila and watching her sip her margarita, when I said, "So, the city should create public daycare centers for low-income families?"

"You read my article."

"I finished it just before you came."

"What did you think?"

"I agree with the content, and I love your sassy tone. Hey, listen up folks. There's a problem, something needs to be done, and I'm going to tell you what it is. Very cool."

"But ..."

"What?"

"I know you've got some criticism you're holding back."

"Certain people will ask how you're going to pay for the goodies."

"What people do you have in mind?"

"Who do you think?"

"Let's think about dinner. Shall we order a bottle of wine? I feel like letting loose."

After dinner, instead of seeing a film, Maria wanted to go to the Armadillo and hear Stevie Ray Vaughan perform with his band, Double Trouble. She'd known about him since high school, when he first started performing in Austin, and claimed he was the best blues guitarist ever, so we went. When he played "Voodoo Chile," a hurricane tore through the crowd, swept us into a mass of flesh, pulsating with music and glistening with sweat. Maria rolled her big eyes and sang, "I'm your voodoo chile," and I responded with, "crazy chile." I saw a couple of my students gawking at me as if to say, *Is that our TA?* I waved to them, and they collapsed in giggles. When a slow number came, Maria pressed herself up against me, laid her face on my chest, and she grooved into me, hot and sweaty, and murmured, "You can take up all my sweet time anytime you want." We were just sober enough to make it to Jimmy's house.

In the morning, the phone rang. Maria, lying next to me, flinched. She was sure it was Mama. The phone stopped ringing, then started again. She glanced at the alarm on the night table and said, "Five minutes after nine. I bet she's been sitting next to the phone, waiting for nine o'clock to come." She rushed to the kitchen in time to answer and returned a few minutes later. "I told her we were having brunch at Cisco's, and it would be so much fun if they'd join us."

"When did we decide to have brunch at Cisco's?"

"We didn't have time to talk about it, so I thought I'd tell her we would, and then if we decide not to, I'll call her back."

"Like, now I'm going to say no?"

"If you absolutely do not want to go …"

"I have a hangover."

She ran her fingertip across my lip, tickling me. "There's no cure for a hangover like brunch at Cisco's."

"Oh, yeah? Says who?"

"Me. I say it all the time." She leaned over and kissed me. "Oh, and don't forget, you didn't stay here last night. I picked you up at your place this morning."

"Oh, my God. I have to lie, with a hangover?"

"I've got one and I'm going to lie."

We headed for the east side of town, parked near Cisco's blue brick building, went in, and joined Maria's parents at their table. Warren glared past me, like I wasn't there, and I wondered what was bothering him. Maria, next to me, caught my eye and grinned, like everything was going great, and leaned forward to talk with Cristina. Maria's lips moved, then Cristina's, as if their lips had a life of their own. I felt like I was watching a poorly post-synchronized film.

Too hungover to talk, I stared at the wall behind Warren and at the framed, grinning faces under glass, with hand-written dedications to Cisco, and recognized LBJ, his deeply lined, flabby face smiling with a look that seemed to say, please forgive me for Vietnam, and still the chant came back, "Hey, hey, LBJ, how many kids did you kill today?" And John Connally, wounded during the Kennedy assassination, and John Tower, who looked like he was trying to talk and smile at the same time, and Chill Wills, with his cowboy hat and goofy grin, and the Texas outlaws—Willie Nelson, Kris Kristofferson, and Jerry Jeff Walker. All together, with their big smiles, they looked like a freak show. I could hear their voices—the pols, twanging and drawling, Willy's sky-blue singing, and Chill Wills' donkey-braying. What a concert!

Cristina was looking at me, saying something with her out-of-synch voice. I leaned forward and concentrated all my attention on her eyes and lips as I smiled and nodded, trying to follow what she was saying—something about offshore oil drilling in the gulf. It was Warren—no, Warren's daddy, who'd set up the first offshore rig in 1937. "Really?" I said. And about ten years later, he set up the first offshore well in the gulf beyond sight of land. "Wow!" I nodded, while my head throbbed, and I barely succeeded in suppressing a groan. All the while Warren sat there, tight lipped, probably furious he had no one to talk to but me.

The waiter came and took our orders, and then I stared at Warren, irritated by his passive hostility, and decided to go after him. "Warren," I said. He continued looking away. I raised my voice. "Warren, have you had a chance to read Maria's article?"

He scowled. "Yeah, I have." He recomposed his face and looked at Maria with a benevolent gaze. "You write so well, if you wanted to, you could convince people day is night and night is day." He smiled a pontifical blessing upon her. "You're very talented"—he paused for emphasis—"and you're going to make a great journalist."

"Oh, Daddy, that's so sweet of you. But what did you think of the points I made?"

Yeah, Warren, I wondered, *what did you really think?*

"Well, the article shows, maybe, a little bit of the influence of your education. I mean in the, ah, that East-Coast liberal way of seeing things. But the logic, the development of the argument, if you accept, you know, the premise, it's strong as steel." He beamed. "I've always said, you're so talented, the sky's the limit."

Someone said Warren's name. I looked over my shoulder and saw a thin man with gray hair and a mustache, in a black button-down shirt and jeans, with his hands on his hips, looking down at Warren. "Welcome to Austin." He looked at the pictures and back at Warren. "Come to see your ol' friend, Lyndon?" The man chuckled.

Warren glared with his reptile smile, like he'd strike any second and sink his teeth into the man's neck, and said, "Cactus, you're just as prickly as ever," accentuating the first syllable of *prickly.* "One thing I'm thankful for is I've never had to suck up to politicians to get interviews. But, hey, someone's gotta do it. Right?"

"You haven't lost your sense of humor," Cactus said. "That is what you call it, right, a sense of humor?" Cactus grinned and shook his head.

"What are you doing here? There are other Tex-Mex restaurants in Austin."

"Oh, I just love to come by and see my picture on the wall of fame here." He nodded toward a picture of himself. "I'm in good company. LBJ, Willie, and a lotta folks who done a lotta good for people. Sometimes I wonder why you ain't up there."

"Maybe I like to keep the good I do to myself."

"You probably keep half the state o' Texas to yourself. Oh, and speaking of good company, this your family?"

"Yeah. My wife, Cristina. My daughter, Maria. Her friend, Dick."

"Cactus Pryor. Happy to meet y'all." He beamed. "Well, my better half's waitin' on me." He nodded at a table across the room, where a woman with gray hair smiled at us. "I better go. Hope y'all have a wonderful life. And Warren, I'll be sure to say hi to Lady Bird for you, next time I see her."

Cactus walked away, and Warren spat, "Jackass."

"I don't mean to change the subject, Daddy, but Dick and I have decided to get married."

Warren's mouth dropped, like he'd just gotten kicked in the crotch. "What?"

"Dick and I have decided to get married."

Warren's eyes darted from Maria to me. "Is that true?"

"Ah, yeah. We've talked about it."

"You think you're marrying my daughter?" The muscles in Warren's cheeks twitched, as his eyes bore into me. And then his gaze softened, and he said to Maria, "Sweetheart, when did you decide this?"

"You frightened me, Daddy. I thought you were upset."

"Just surprised. It's not every day my princess tells me she wants to marry someone. Let alone …" He sighed and smiled.

Cristina beamed. "That's wonderful. Have you talked about a date?"

"Oh, Mama, we haven't gotten that far. We're just, you know, it's still so new."

"Yeah," I said, "it's all so new."

"I'm happy for you," Cristina said.

Warren nodded and looked at me. "Well, Dick, you'll have to get that Ph.D. done, so you can get a job, and do what a man has to do." He grinned.

I felt like telling him I knew what I had to do, but just nodded and grinned back.

As soon as Maria and I got in the car, I said, "What was that?"

She started the car. "What?"

"You wanted me to ask your father's permission."

"I did what you wanted me to do."

"Why didn't you warn me?"

"You're never happy with anything I do. Maybe we shouldn't get married."

"I'm not saying that."

She floored it, and we pulled away. We rode in silence, until she stopped in front of my apartment. We made up, but there was a bitter aftertaste.

I wondered sometimes if Maria couldn't see that her father despised me. Or that I wasn't the only person she loved for whom he felt contempt. He had a way of making people feel his disgust that could be so humiliating, it could be deadly. That became clear at the party he and Cristina hosted to celebrate Maria's twenty-fourth birthday.

She couldn't give me a ride, so one of her friends from a wealthy Texas family came by in his Corvette to drive me. We glided past the cars parked along the driveway, swung in front of Maria's house, and parked facing the lawn and the stage that had been erected for Stevie Ray Vaughan and Double Trouble. About a dozen round tables had been arranged between the stage at one end of the yard and a row of serving tables at the other. Behind those tables stood cooks and servers and a couple barbecue smokers. We headed for the house and found Warren and Cristina standing inside the entrance, talking with a couple. I had the feeling I'd seen the man with the woman before. He was a tall, thin, dignified looking guy, with waves of white hair.

Warren beamed as he greeted Maria's friend and told him how good it was to see him and asked how his daddy and mama were doing. Learning they were doing just fine, he said, "Good, good," and told him the young folks were in the back, by the pool, and to just make himself at home. While he was shaking the guy's hand, Cristina turned toward me, gave me a hug, and said she was happy to see me. And then Warren shook my hand.

"Dick, you found your way here again. Maria's gonna be pleased."

"Thanks, Mr. Cutler."

"None of that Mr. Cutler stuff. Remember? Just call me Warren. And let me introduce you to my dear friend, Senator Earl Hunt." I recognized the politician who'd recently won re-election. "Earl, this is the young man who wants to marry Maria."

"I'm so happy to meet the young man who wants to marry Maria," Earl said, glancing at Warren with a complicit smirk as he shook my hand.

Warren looked at the woman standing next to Cristina and said, "And I'd like to introduce you to this lovely woman, Mrs. Hunt."

"When's the happy day?" she asked.

"Oh, they don't know, yet," Warren said. "He's still saving up for the engagement ring."

I pressed my fingers against my jacket pocket and felt the ring box.

Earl cleared his throat, licked his thin lips, which always seemed to stick together in the televised interviews and debates, and said, "Where you from, Dick?"

"Minnesota. Most recently."

"Ah! A Yankee!" He feigned astonishment, as he looked around at his wife, Warren, and Cristina. "I hope he's not here to tell us how to run our state, I forgot to bring my notebook." Warren and Mrs. Hunt laughed. "Just kidding, boy. What brought you to Texas? Aside from wanting to marry Maria."

"I'm doing a Ph.D. in History, at the University."

"Hmm," Earl hummed, "who you working with?"

"Professor Albion."

Earl's smile disappeared. "Uh-huh. The Che."

"The what?" Warren asked.

"Well," Earl said, "I wish you the best o' luck." He looked away.

Pedro appeared with a tray of drinks, and Warren handed mint juleps to Cristina and the Hunts, and took one for himself.

I announced I'd go find Maria and bowed my head, as if I were some kind of servant.

"She's probably by the pool," Warren said. "And if she's not there, well, you know your way around."

I nodded, told Cristina it was good to see her. She gave me another hug. I turned to the senator and his wife, told them it was nice to meet them, bowed my head again, and wanted to kick myself in the ass.

I went through the house, out the back door, and into the under-thirty crowd standing in clusters and milling about, drinks in hand, while servers, in black slacks and white shirts, circulated among them. I surveyed the crowd and saw a group of Maria's closest friends, chatting and laughing, and heard Fay's twang resonate above the other voices, and then, after a burst of laughter, Bonnie Mae's languorous drawl surfaced. One of the women left, and through the gap her departure created I saw Maria, standing next to Maureen. I touched the box in my pocket and considered walking over to her, but thought of the diamonds some of her friends wore and decided to wait. I navigated my way around groups, placing my hand on a shoulder here and there, flashing a *hi, how are you, good to see you*, to people I'd met at previous parties, and when I reached the bar, I sighed and had Pedro make me a martini. I was staring at the evening shadows beyond the pool, when someone touched my arm, and I looked and saw Maria.

"Finally, I get to be alone with you," she said. We hugged.

And then I saw Jimmy, in a white Nehru shirt, standing at the edge of the patio and looking like a little boy whose mother had spiffed him up. Peggy, Jimmy's sister, in a staid blue dress remarkable for revealing nothing of her cleavage, was standing next to him. Maria and I went over and greeted them. She told Jimmy she was happy to see him wearing the present she'd given him, informing me his birthday was just six days before hers. He beamed and extended his wrists, so we could see the green stems and leaves and the blue flowers with the orange stamen embroidered on each cuff. And then he said he wanted to show Maria her present, an Eiffel Tower, just like the one in Paris, and when he'd get it set up, it would stand six feet tall and be covered with lights, so Maria could use it at her parties to light up the night. He wanted to set it up right away, but she suggested they wait until the next day, it was almost time to sit down for dinner. Jimmy glanced at me, gave me a mischievous grin, and asked what I'd gotten Maria.

"Yeah, what did you get me?"

I put my hand in my pocket, rummaged around, and pretended to panic, as if I'd lost her present, while Maria's eyes darted back and forth, from my bulging eyes to my pocket. She begged me to stop teasing her, so I pulled out the present and gave it to her. She opened the box and gazed at the ring, her eyes wide with joy, her voice trembling as she sighed. She slid the ring onto her finger and held her hand out so we could see the gold band, with tiny leaves in relief, and a gold rose that seemed to blossom in the center. As Maria, Peggy, and Jimmy marveled at the ring, I remembered how enamored I'd been of the idea of gold coming to life in the form of a flower, and I felt the kind of pride I'd felt when I was a boy, and Mom would open the presents I'd bought for her birthday, or Christmas, and she'd look so happy as she discovered a scarf with bright colored flowers, or a bar of lavender-scented soap, or a glass coffee-warmer with a gold stand. Maria threw her arms around me, whispered in my ear the ring was gorgeous, and she loved me, loved me so much. When I let her go, she extended her hand again so she could admire the ring, sniffling and wiping tears from her eyes. I whispered I could get her one with a diamond later, after I'd bought a car. She said it was the only ring she wanted and ran off to show her friends, with Jimmy following her.

I was alone with Peggy. I felt awkward, never having been alone with her before. All I could think of saying was that it had been a while since I'd seen her, and she said, Yeah, she'd been busy. Thinking I might try to have some fun, I said, "The prosecution business must be good," and she answered, "It's always good in this county." Realizing she had a sense of humor, I said, "Too busy pros-ecuting to go to parties, eh?"

"That, and someday I might end up dealing with some of the guests. Or their daddies."

"Interesting. Anyone in particular?"

"No comment."

"What about Warren?" I blurted, surprising myself.

She arched her eyebrows and shook her head. "No comment."

"A couple years ago, you said you'd love to be there the day Warren and I meet for the first time. I think I understand why."

She snickered and said, "I saw Maria's piece in the *Statesman*. She's smart, writes well, and she's got a handle on some of what goes on here. Some. If she can ever see through the façade of certain people, she could become one hell of a journalist."

I asked her what she meant by "the façade of certain people."

She shook her head.

Maria rejoined us and said everyone loved her ring. Peggy asked where Jimmy had gone. We looked around, but didn't see him. Servers announced that people should seat themselves, dinner would be served soon, so we walked up the incline toward the rows of tables, while looking for Jimmy. We reached our table, on the perimeter of an open area in front of the stage, and turned around and surveyed the guests, the sun propped like a glowing red ball on the tips of the trees. Peggy mumbled, "That's the trouble with trying to keep track of Jimmy—he's always wandering." She left Maria and me to look for him. We sat down, reassuring one another he'd show up. A waiter circled the table, pouring wine, left a full bottle, and moved on to the next. And then Jimmy appeared, laid his hand on the back of Peggy's chair, next to the chair where he was supposed to sit, looked around with a cocky grin, as if he knew something the rest of us didn't, and said, "Hi, y'all." Maria said, "Jimmy, this is your place here," and nodded toward the chair next to her. He shrugged and grinned at her, sat down in Peggy's place, filled her glass with wine, and took a drink.

"Why are you drinking?" Maria asked.

"I'm a big boy. I can take care of myself."

He looked at Maureen, who was sitting on his other side. Or rather, he looked at her red hair, and his face broke into a grin when she looked at him. She said she hadn't seen him in a long time and asked how he'd been. She continued asking questions, trying to fill the silence between them. Eventually he started talking about his job. He said he was saving money and might go back to college.

"Have you ever gone?" she asked.

"A long time ago. But I stopped."

"Why was that?"

"Do you like Double Trouble?"

"I love them."

He nodded and stared at her with a grin. As Maureen turned her eyes away from him, she noticed me watching, arched her eyebrows, and looked at Bonnie Mae, on her other side. Jimmy finished his wine, refilled his glass, and lit a cigarette. This was a new Jimmy. Whenever I'd seen him before, he was drunk, stoned, or passed out, or sober, awake, and fidgeting. I'd never seen him pay attention to a woman, aside from Maria and Peggy, but I knew he'd had relationships.

While a server moved around the table, setting salads in front of everyone, Jimmy kept his hand and his eyes on his glass, as if he were afraid someone might take it from him. He announced, "I told Stevie Ray I think he's the greatest. Even greater than Jimi Hendrix. Me and Maria saw him play when we were in high school. He didn't remember us, though. Said he didn't hang out with the kind o' kids who are here tonight." Jimmy looked at Maria, his eyes dilated. "We had a good time, Stevie Ray and me."

Peggy appeared, stopped behind her chair, and stared down at him. When he leaned his head back and looked up, she asked him where he'd been.

"Just going around saying hi to folks."

"You're drinking."

"I'm old enough to do what I want."

"Maybe we should go home."

"I'm having too much fun." Jimmy drank his glass dry and filled it again.

Peggy sat down between Jimmy and Maria. When the server returned to remove the salad plates, Jimmy asked him to bring another bottle of wine. The server fetched the bottle and then served the main course—slices of Russian boar with roast squash. While Jimmy drank and chain-smoked and stubbed his cigarettes out in his squash, Peggy, Maria, and I ate in silence, and Maureen, Fay, Bonnie Mae, and the others ate and talked and laughed. I could feel Maria's apprehension, and had no doubt Peggy was scared, too. The silence on Jimmy's side of the table seemed to weigh on Maureen and the others, and they stopped talking. By the time we finished eating, the sun was setting, and the candles and lanterns provided most of the light. The faces at the tables started to take on a saintly glow, or an eerie look.

Servers were clearing the tables, when someone tapped a microphone. Warren's voice blasted out of the speakers, "Can everyone hear me?" The guests responded with a resounding yes, followed by laughter, as if they were amused by the volume of their own response. Warren talked about how much he and Cristina had missed their daughter during the four years she'd spent at Smith and the year in Europe, and how grateful they were to have her home. They were so proud of the person she'd become: a woman of learning, who believed the world could be a better place and would work to realize that belief. "I'm sure you've all read her article in the *American-Statesman*. While each of us might see the problems she addresses in that article differently, the strength of her convictions is clear. Because we feel so blessed to have a daughter like Maria, Cristina and I wanted to show her our love and appreciation by giving her the best birthday party ever. That's why you're here tonight. Thank you for coming. Now, Maria, let's see if you have enough wind left—after your article—to blow out your candles."

I was stunned. Warren hadn't even mentioned Maria's engagement to me.

She walked to a multi-tiered cake standing on a table, in the center of the dining area. The candles on the top layer glowed in the encroaching darkness. She blew out most of the candles, and with a second and a third try got the last of them. The crowd applauded, and she returned to her place. I put my arm around her and kissed her. Servers brought the first slices of cake to our table, and then served the others. I leaned back and looked up at the sky, where the first stars appeared, and wondered if Warren would ever accept me as Maria's husband.

And then the lights went on in front of the stage, and Stevie Ray and the other musicians appeared, and Jimmy, a big grin lighting up his face, shouted, "Aw right!" His eyes appeared even more dilated, as if he'd been drugged by the excitement in the air. Stevie Ray, wearing a black hat with a flat brim, a lavender sports jacket, and black jeans tucked into cowboy boots, picked up his guitar, struck a chord, sending energy rippling through the crowd, and said, "Y'all ready to party?" A roar went up. He turned to the other musicians, they nodded, he turned back, wished Maria a happy birthday, and lit into his bluesy rock version of "Pride and Joy."

Maria leaned into me and said she'd like to dance, but was worried about Jimmy. I felt as long as Peggy was there, we could leave him. We began dancing in the open space, in front of the band, and looked over at our table from time to time to make sure he was still there. And then, halfway through the next song, I looked up and saw his lanky body bobbing up and down as he danced. He noticed me watching him and beamed, looking proud to be dancing with Maureen. She shrugged her shoulders, as if to say, What am I to do? When the music stopped, Maria and I found ourselves next to Jimmy and Maureen. Maria said she didn't know he could dance so well, and Jimmy responded by humming, uh-huh, uh-huh, uh-huh, as if keeping time with the music in his head. Maureen agreed he was a good dancer. He took her hands, bounced them up and down, and when the music started, he led her away, and she grinned back at us over her shoulder. Stevie Ray finished the first set with a fifteen-minute version of "Voodoo Chile." After the last chord, Maria and I, exhausted and sweaty, found ourselves next to Jimmy and Maureen again. Maureen said she had to use the bathroom, and Maria went with her.

I put my arm around Jimmy's shoulder and started walking him back to our table, when I noticed Warren, standing close to a blonde server. His head bent, his mouth close to her cheek, he seemed to be whispering something to her; she looked up and whispered back. He grinned, raised his head, and caught sight of us. He said something to the server; she looked at me and walked off. Warren headed for the gazebo. His path intersected with ours, and Jimmy, when he saw him, froze. Warren asked if we were having a good time, and then scrutinized Jimmy's face.

"You've been drinking."

Jimmy wilted.

Warren's face wrinkled with disgust. He sneered, shook his head and spat, "Pathetic," and walked away. Jimmy stared at the ground.

I said, "Come on, Jimmy. Let's go back to our table," and took his arm, but he wouldn't budge. He said he needed to go to the bathroom. I offered to walk with him to the house, but he pulled away and headed toward the side entrance, his head bowed.

As I returned to our table, I saw Peggy watching me. I sat down and told her everything, except the encounter with Warren. She checked her watch repeatedly, while staring at the house, where I told her Jimmy had gone. When I repeated what Warren had said to Jimmy and wondered why he would've treated him that way, she glared at me and said, "Don't you get it?"

"Get what?"

"Why do you think Maria's so close to Jimmy? Because they grew up near each other? I thought you were smart."

"What?"

"We have to find him. Now."

Her panic startled me. I told her to stay at the table, in case he returned, and I'd go look for him in the bathrooms. On my way to the house, I ran into Maria and Maureen and asked if they'd seen him. They hadn't. Maria wanted to know what was the problem, but before I could answer, Warren's voice called her. I turned around. He was walking toward us, looking at Maria, as if Maureen and I didn't exist. He told Maria that Senator and Mrs. Hunt wanted to say goodbye and pointed at them as they stood next to Cristina, in front of the stage. Maria said she'd be right back. As she walked off with Warren, I wondered what she'd say if she knew how he'd treated Jimmy. Maureen went back to our table, and I headed for the bathrooms. There were two on the main floor, a short line of people to each door. I asked them if they'd seen Jimmy. Most of them didn't know who he was, so I described him. No one had seen him. I waited a few minutes to make sure he wasn't in one of the bathrooms, and was about to return to the table, when the door to the den opened and Stevie Ray and his band members came out.

As he walked by, I asked him if he'd seen Jimmy.

"Jimmy?"

I described him, and he said, "Oh, that dude. Yeah, he stopped by." He shook his head. "Kind of weird."

Stevie Ray and the band continued toward the stage. I went down the hall to the den and stepped inside. Wisps of smoke floated above the couch, the coffee table, the bottle of Jack Daniels, the mostly empty glasses, and the traces of coke on the table. I left the room and went outside. It was almost dark, and the people standing beyond the candlelight on the tables were becoming nebulous forms. If I was going to find Jimmy, I'd have to walk up and down each aisle. I wanted to tell Peggy that Jimmy wasn't in the house, but I had to find him.

Double Trouble began their second set as I searched. I'd stop to ask guests I recognized if they'd seen Jimmy. Some had, but it had been a while. The band's music was getting louder, more frenetic, and Stevie Ray's solos lasted longer, and his playing had a sharper edge. The candles on the tables farthest from the stage had been blown out and the lanterns extinguished. I walked toward dark figures, some standing, some sitting, and inhaled the smell of dope and heard someone snorting coke. I approached a couple guys and asked if they'd seen Jimmy.

"Who the fuck are you?" one of them said.

A smaller form squeezed between them, and a woman with cadaver-white skin, dilated eyes, and black hair drawled, "He's Dick, the birthday girl's boy."

"Do you have any idea where Jimmy is?" I asked.

She laughed and disappeared.

I continued moving among the tables, until Maria appeared. We returned to our table, found Peggy, and the three of us weaved through the crowd to the gazebo, where we had an elevated view, but could only see where the candles were still lit. Stevie Ray performed the opening chords of the "Star-Spangled Banner," and I heard in my mind the words, "Oh, say can you see, by the dawn's early light." But then his guitar shrieked, and the chords became jagged and screeched with pain. Maria cried Jimmy wasn't there, and I shouted I wanted to take one more look and forged ahead, sometimes bumping into people in the dark, while Maria and Peggy followed. In the discordant, strung-out chords, I heard rockets exploding, bombs bursting in air, and planes whining as they crashed to earth. And then real rockets whistled and burst in the air, and flaming streams of blue and green showered toward the ground. As Stevie Ray's guitar continued to wail, fireworks gashed the night, turning it into day. Night, day, night, day, the fireworks felt as if a god were flipping a switch, and people looking upward would appear and disappear. Stopping each time the darkness returned to give my eyes a second to adapt, and then moving forward, I reached the slope leading to the back of the house and the swimming pool and heard Stevie Ray play the chords for the land of the free and the home of the brave, but his playing felt more like a wail of unbearable suffering. And then salvo after salvo of fireworks exploded, followed by darkness and silence, and the swimming pool appeared before me, like a liquid emerald shining in the night. And in the middle of that emerald, a man floating, facedown, his arms outstretched. I ran, stumbled down the slope, got up and kept on running and jumped into the pool and waded in water up to my chest toward the outstretched hands that touched my shoulders, as if to embrace me. On the white sleeves, on the cuffs, embroidered flowers.

Jimmy returned often over the following days and nights, his body floating toward me, his arms closing around my neck, his cold face pressing against mine.

He haunted Maria, too. She was never the same. If we went to the Armadillo or one of the bars to listen to music, she'd toss down shots of Jack Daniel's or tequila. If we went out for dinner, she'd drink martinis until she could only stagger out the door, and I'd hold her up, the way I'd held Jimmy that day in the beer garden. If we went to a movie or a play, we had to go to a bar afterward. Her eyes would glaze over, and sometimes she'd wonder, "Why? Why?" She seemed to be drinking herself to death, out of empathy with him. I'd try to help her by getting her to talk, and sometimes she would. She'd go on about what a good person he was, but he didn't know it, and she'd talk about his father ignoring him after he'd lost the son he loved in Vietnam. I'd ask about her parents and how they felt about Jimmy. Mama had always been kind to him. And your father? She'd shake her head and fall silent, or she'd go off on a tangent about him being unforgiving and controlling, no one messed with him.

A few weeks after Jimmy died, I stopped by Peggy's office and had coffee with her. She invited me to visit her at her home so we could talk about what was going on with Maria, and I spent a couple evenings with her, over a glass of wine. We talked about Jimmy's suicide, and Warren telling him he was pathetic, and I wondered why he had so much power over Jimmy, and what she meant when she told me I was an idiot for not understanding. What didn't I understand? She shook her head, didn't remember saying that, and didn't know why she would've. What about the other daughter, Anita, why did she leave home? And why don't the parents talk about her? "Anita had the audacity to become a hippie, flaunt her independence, and move to San Francisco. She no longer exists for Warren."

"Was there something more to Anita's flight from home?"

"Like what?"

"Like abuse."

Peggy scrutinized my face, shook her head, and said, "I don't know."

Another evening, I got her talking about wealthy, patriotic Texans who'd hid their boys in the Texas Air National Guard during the Vietnam War, and the bitter tone of her voice reminded me that one of her brothers had died in Vietnam. I said it was amazing what the rich could get away with and mentioned Felipe, the young Mexican whom Cristina had loved, who was called up not long before the end of World War II and got killed at Iwo Jima—so convenient for Warren, who was at Yale. Might he have had something to do with that? She seemed mystified, and asked, "How?" "Well, his Uncle Elias, the U.S. senator, might he have had Felipe sent off?" She had no idea. I got her to talk about oilmen and the law. If she ever went after them, it was usually for bribes or violations of campaign finance laws.

"What about Warren? Has he ever been prosecuted?"

She stared at me.

"Is he going to be?"

She smirked and shook her head.

I didn't get what I'd wanted from Peggy, but sometimes Maria would surprise me and lash out at Daddy, and I'd feel she was on my side. One night Warren said, "Fortunately the Ches of the world don't live long." And Maria responded, "Fortunately for the world, many of the Ches, like Professor Albion, do." But when we were alone, and I agreed with her criticism and vented my pent-up anger, an argument ensued, and we ended up screaming at one another.

I'd hoped to end one of Warren's constant digs when I bought a '68 VW Beetle. I set out for the Sun King's paradise early one evening, envisioning with glee the surprised look he'd have when I'd pull up in front of the house. I cruised up the lower slopes, but when I started following the steep, winding road up his mountain, I had to downshift to third gear, then to second, and once to first, the engine screeching from its labor. Cars and pickups pulled up behind and honked and passed me on the first straightaway, the drivers and passengers staring at me, sometimes laughing, or giving me the finger. When Warren saw the bug parked in front, he asked, "You expect my daughter to ride in *that*?" But he didn't repeat the question. He probably had the same nightmares I'd had, of Maria drunk and driving off a cliff.

Maria and I had planned on celebrating Christmas with her parents, but she suggested, given the tension between Daddy and me, it might be best if I went to my mother's house. The only money I'd saved, for anything other than Christmas presents, was for a tune-up of the Beetle. A ticket to Denver at the last minute before Christmas would consume most of my savings, but I couldn't stand being in Austin without her, so I went. The day after Christmas, I returned, and that evening drove to her house. She greeted me in the foyer with a kiss, and then extended her right hand to show me a ruby, mounted on a gold band and surrounded by diamonds. "Isn't it beautiful! And look at this." She held up a ruby pendant that perfectly matched the ring. She had the jewels to surpass those of all of her friends.

"It's gorgeous," I said.

"Yes it is," Warren said, appearing by her side. "We asked the jeweler what were the most beautiful rubies in the world. He said Burmese, so that's what we got."

"You're so sweet, Daddy."

As we drove off, I wondered if there were any poisons that were sweet. Wasn't antifreeze supposed to be sweet? Could it be mistaken for sweet vermouth? I fantasized serving Warren a Manhattan with antifreeze and watching him die.

I was on my best behavior that night. We had dinner at a restaurant, she didn't get drunk, and we didn't fight. We went to the student union, saw a film, and returned to my apartment. As we made love, she dug her nails into my skin and started crying when she reached orgasm. She pulled away from me, lay on her side, and I spooned her. She took my hand and, still sobbing, bit my finger until the pain obliterated my anxiety about losing her. We slept like the dead and, in the morning, I washed the blood off, bandaged my finger, and made breakfast for her. We ate, drank our coffee, talked, smiled, and kissed like we'd just fallen in love. A few days later, after Warren made another snide remark, I vented in the car, and she lost her temper and hissed, "You're always looking for something negative," and told me to take her home.

Days before spring break, Maria and I had another fight, and she decided to go to Padre Island with some of her girlfriends, instead of with me. Remembering how things had gone when I'd returned after Christmas, I didn't worry. When I picked her up at the airport, she asked me to take her immediately to my place. We started stripping one another before we even reached the bedroom. Later, exhausted, we lay in bed.

"I've been thinking about us," Maria said, looking at me. "We should get married."

"When?"

"The first Saturday after final exams. When we can really be together."

"Okay. I want whatever you want."

"I want you." Her brows furrowed. "We love one another. Why do we fight all the time?"

"I don't know."

"It has a lot to do with Daddy. It would be better if we lived somewhere else. We should move this summer."

"Where to?"

"New York." She rolled onto my chest and gazed into my eyes. "I was thinking about this all the time I was on the island. Valerie lives in New York. We could stay with her until we find jobs and an apartment, and we can finish our degrees, and then, when everything's going well, we can have children." Her eyes glistened. "You'd make a fantastic father." She laid her head in the crook of my neck. I stared at the ceiling and thought about the reality of earning a living in New York, and the cost of finishing our degrees, and her naiveté, because she'd never had a job, and neither of us knew what it meant to raise a child. But I didn't want to say anything that would cause her to pull away. I'd do whatever she wanted, even if I knew we were heading for disaster. She murmured, breathing the words onto my neck, that we should announce the wedding at the first outdoor party of the year. The first since Jimmy's suicide.

A few nights later, I was ecstatic as I left my place, knowing this wouldn't be just another Saturday-night soap. I sped out of Austin and headed up the mountain, shifting down to third, and then second, and then back to third. It was, as always, a humiliating experience—people driving past me, shouting at me to get a real car. I didn't care. Maria and I loved one another, we were going to get married, and nothing else mattered. I saw the juniper tree, the one Maria loved so much, and downshifted to second as I rounded the curve and accelerated as I started up the steep incline. I heard a loud, whirring sound, as if something were spinning rapidly, causing a huge amount of friction, and then the motor died. The car came to a halt and started rolling backward. I slammed on the brake, put the car in neutral, and tried starting the motor. The starter cranked, but the motor wouldn't turn. I smelled something burning. I let the Beetle roll toward the side of the road, got out, and smelled the stink of something like oil burning. I raised the hood. A wave of heat hit me, followed by a clicking sound, as if the engine were a ticking time bomb. The clicking was probably the sound of hot metal cooling. I must've burned a valve.

I started walking, with over a mile to go in near ninety-degree weather. When the top of the hill was finally in sight, and my shirt soaked, a car pulled over next to me. I kept on walking. The driver honked once, and again. I looked and saw Maureen at the wheel. She motioned for me to get in. The cold blast of the air conditioner gave me the chills and made me feel sick. She asked what had happened. I wiped sweat from my face as I explained. By the time we arrived, I'd stopped shivering. I followed Maureen inside. Cristina greeted us, said I looked pale, and wanted to know if I felt all right.

"I found him on the side of the road," Maureen said.

"Did the bug die?" Warren showed up with his smirk.

This piece of humiliation hit me like a fist in the gut. I shot back, "It might be a bug, but I didn't have to have my daddy buy it for me."

Maria had rushed in and stopped just as I snapped at Warren. The joy on her face vanished. She looked back and forth at us, then smiled, came to me and took my hand and said she was wondering why I was late. Her abrupt change of mood stunned me. She looked around at her parents and Maureen, said we had a big announcement to make, and pulled me toward the rear of the house. Warren and Cristina must have been stunned, too, because they didn't move. Looking back and seeing them standing still, Maria shouted at them to come. We walked out onto the patio and to the table in front of the pool, where Pedro was pouring champagne.

Maria hollered, "Listen up, everyone." Maria's friends gathered around. "Dick and I have an announcement to make." Everyone fell silent. "We're getting married in May." When the expressions of joy and surprise died down, she added, "And in June, we're moving to New York." Everyone stared at Maria in disbelief. I did, too, not knowing she'd planned on announcing the move.

Maureen held up a glass of champagne and proposed a toast. One toast led to another, and to hugs, handshakes, and tears. The sun started to set, the emerald green pool began to glow in the encroaching darkness, and Maria, anxiety resonating in her voice, implored everyone to go inside, where Pedro had set up a bar. The champagne flowed, and the party got louder. Maria drank and waved her glass around as she talked and laughed. When she sprinkled champagne on my neck and chest, I laughed and said, "Careful."

"Oh dear. Oh my." She bit her lip, looked contrite, and then burst into laughter. "Mustn't waste champagne!" She drank what was left in her glass and went to the bar for another.

I sensed someone's presence, looked aside, and saw Warren out of the corner of my eye. He'd moved behind me, close to my ear, where he could speak softly enough for just me to hear.

"My daughter's beautiful, isn't she?"

"She is," I murmured.

"And you have the *cojones* to think you're going to marry her?"

"I have the *cojones* to *know* I'm going to marry her."

"Why would I want my daughter to marry you?"

I snickered. "I didn't know you did."

"Why would I want her to marry a hustler? A gigolo? I know how you lived off the girls in Paris. I know your grandfather tried to make something of you, and then disowned you. And I know you're interested in Maria because of my money. I've learned a lot about you, Dick, and none of it's good."

I struck back, raising my voice to make sure every word hurt. "Oh, yeah? And what about you? Your uncle did you a favor and had a man by the name of Felipe called up near the end of the War. Remember Felipe? The guy your wife was in love with, and who was in your way?"

When I turned toward Warren, I expected to see him in shock, and I'd have a smirk on my face, like the one he loved to flash my way every time he humiliated me. But it wasn't his eyes that caught my attention, it was Cristina's. She'd joined him. She dropped her champagne glass, and I felt it shatter. She stared at me, her mouth agape, and then touched her cheek, like she was making sure she was awake and had really heard what she thought she'd heard.

"Mama," Maria said. "Mama, are you okay?"

Cristina's eyes fixed on Warren. "Is that true?"

"Of course not. He's just trying to make trouble."

Maria glared at me. "There's never going to be an end to this, is there."

Cristina turned and walked toward the stairway to the second floor.

"Mama," Maria pleaded, as she followed her.

"Leave me, Maria. Please."

Maria looked at Warren and me and headed for the bar.

I caught up to her and grabbed her arm. "I can explain."

She twisted her arm away, snatched a glass of champagne at the bar, and headed for the piano. She sat down and played a few chords. I leaned on the piano and tried to make eye contact. She took a drink and said to no one, and everyone, "This party's boring. Shall we liven it up? How about some Cole Porter?" She played a few chords of a piece I didn't recognize and shouted, "Does everyone like Cole Porter?" Her friends fell silent and gathered around the piano.

I said, "You remember that time at Esther's Follies—"

"The time when that woman performed those Cole Porter songs? What a wonderful night! Let's see, I could play, 'Let's Misbehave.'" She played the opening and stopped. "But we do that all the time. Or, 'I've got you under my skin.' That's a real problem, having someone under your skin. What if you don't want him there?" She moaned and shook her head. "Or, 'I get a *kick* out of you.' Getting a kick from someone who's under your skin must really hurt. Let's see. I know. 'Love for sale'—'old love, new love, every love but true love.' That might be for down the road. Oh, I've got it. Listen up, everyone. Y'all know this song? Wait, I need another drink." She said to me, "Be a gentleman, get me another glass of champagne."

"I don't think that's a good idea."

She spotted a nearly full glass that someone had left on the piano, grabbed it, and raised it for a toast. "To all my friends." The friends who had gathered around drank to her. "And to Cole Porter!" The friends drank again.

And then she started to play, leaning back, rolling her head slowly from side to side. She fluttered her eyelashes, laughed, and sang about a time when she used to date young men who hunger after pretty girls, but now she's in a love affair so sweet, and I thought, That affair is with me. But as she continued singing about dating men, I wondered, Why are you gazing at me with such a derisive smile? Why did you choose this song? Why are you singing it to me? And then she sang the refrain, and I remembered the title—"My heart belongs to Daddy." It pierced me, and my breath caught. She sang the refrain over and over, and replayed stanzas just so she could repeat it, and smirked with each repetition. The friends chimed in and sang "My heart belongs to Daddy," until the refrain became something of a chant, an article of belief, a cause.

I turned away and saw Warren's serpent smile.

CHAPTER 9

SITTING IN THE ARMCHAIR, gazing at the moonlit window, I heard Maria singing, "My heart belongs to Daddy," and saw Warren's smile, and felt my pain cry out and echo in the hollow space I'd become as I walked down the mountain in the dark. And I remembered fingers touching my shoulder, Maureen's voice gently repeating my name, her hand tightening its grasp, and me, becoming aware of myself standing on a rock shelf in the moonlight. I looked down into the darkness and realized with two steps, I'd be gone. She repeated my name again, pulled me toward her, and walked me past the twisted juniper tree to her car.

I remained in my apartment for days. Every time I wondered if I'd ever see Maria again, I'd think of Warren, whose ability to combine love, support, control, and manipulation made her totally subservient to him, his little girl. She was aware of his power and knew we had to move away from him, if we wanted to save our relationship. But we didn't move. Maybe it was impossible for her. And if we had, would it have saved us? Were there other problems I couldn't see? All I could see was Maria, gone.

A few days later, I received an envelope with her handwriting, opened it, and stared at the ring. The gold that had seemed to come to life in a blossoming rose was nothing but metal.

I was sinking into depression, and the only thing that lit up my world were the suicide scenes that flashed through my mind like film loops. I'd see myself driving a car up the road to Maria's house, stopping at the twisted juniper, and hanging myself, where she'd see my body when she drove by. On the plane to Denver, I fantasized opening the emergency door and being sucked out at an altitude of thirty thousand feet. And when my sister, Georgia, drove me from the Denver airport to Mom's house, the urge to open the door and leap into traffic almost overwhelmed me.

I walked into the house, and the first thing I saw was Dad's painting, the one that had hung in the living room of our old house, with the butte in the background and the man in black walking out of town on his way to anywhere out of this world. I sat down to dinner with Mom and Georgia, and we'd just started eating when Georgia asked, "What do you think you'll do now, Dick?" Before leaving Austin, I'd gone to see Albion to let him know I was dropping out of the Ph.D. program. I didn't want to spend the rest of my life working as an adjunct. He commiserated with me, said the job market was awful, and if I quit, it was a loss for the profession. So, what are you going to do, Dick? My friends asked the same question. And so did I. *What was I going to do?*

It was Valerie who saved me. The memory of her and of a time when I was happy and felt good about myself; of the three of us on Bastille Day, dancing on the *Ile Saint-Louis*, dining in Versailles-like splendor at the *Grand Véfour*, and sunbathing on the yacht in the Mediterranean; of her weeping in my arms on the balcony, after she'd seen her former fiancé in a bookstore with his wife; of drawing her as she gazed out the window, a copy of *The Bell Jar* on her lap.

I finished my glass of scotch, made my way upstairs, turned on the lamp on Valerie's side of the bed, and looked at the portrait on the wall. I remembered asking her as I drew what was going through her mind, both because I wanted to keep her still and wanted to know, and her answer wandered from the life she would've been living if her fiancé hadn't ended it, to the novels she was reading that dealt with suicide, to her dream of becoming an editor and working with authors she admired, to her desire of someday having a family. As I gazed at the drawing of her young face, of the reflective look in her eye, of her lips parted as if she were anticipating whatever lay ahead, I recalled her telling me a few years ago that the portrait made her look beautiful, and I told her it reflected the love I'd already begun to feel.

I left the room, saw no light beneath her door, and stopped, imagining what she'd do if she were to wake while I was next to her. I decided to take the risk. I pushed the door and saw the foot of the bed, the form of her legs and her torso beneath the covers, and her head lying on the pillow, facing upward. The moonlight through the lace curtains over the windows cast a pale glow on her face and neck. The rocking chair, in which she'd nursed Julia and Jamie, was nearby. I pushed it close to the bed, sat down, gazed at her face, her hair falling away from her cheek and splayed across the pillow, and wanted to get on my knees and kiss her. I listened to her breathing, watched her chest rise and fall. Childlike innocence and peace replaced the tension and anger I'd seen over the last two days. I started rocking, and the tension in my body melted like ice in a warm hand. She took a deep breath and rolled over on her side, facing me, as if responding to my presence.

I called her. After I'd been at Mom's house for a couple weeks, I called her to talk about what had happened. And to hear her voice. She was shocked and commiserated with me. When I told her I didn't want to go back to Austin or live in Denver, she said if I wanted to try to build a life in New York, I was welcome to stay with her, if I didn't mind sleeping on the couch. By the time I'd paid for the plane ticket and the cab that took me to her apartment on the upper West Side, I was low on money. Once again, I was going to have to live off her, and with the salary of an assistant editor at Doubleday, she wasn't making a lot. I looked for a job, but a Master's in History didn't impress anyone.

I felt awkward at times, and not just because she was supporting me. Maria was always on my mind. I would talk about her, reliving moments, bringing them back and letting them go, and Valerie would listen, and sympathize, as if we were one in mourning the death of my relationship with Maria. Valerie would touch my cheek, pull my head onto her shoulder, and press my body against hers, all to console me, and I'd inhale her fragrant perfume.

And then came the day she told me her parents had invited us for dinner at their apartment on Fifth Avenue, and I thought, *Oh, shit!* I knew Alex would've figured out I'd lied to him during our dinner at the *Grand Véfour*. I tried to conceal my dread. After we got out of the cab, she pointed up at a picture window on the third floor of the building in front of us and, looking at Central Park across the street, raved about the view from her parents' apartment. I looked at the stone wall that bordered the park, the walkway winding among the trees, and an old man sitting on a bench, leaning back as if he were opening himself to the ambient sounds and smells and the sun filtering through branches, and wished I could've been him. Valerie talked about her mom and dad having a home in Bethesda, too, because her dad liked to be where the action was, and for him the action was in New York and DC.

We entered the apartment, and her mother told me how happy she was to finally meet me, and Alex shook my hand and said it was about time I came to visit. During dinner, anxious to please, I performed, telling anecdotes about my former students, the breathless Barbie dolls with their lashes fluttering like dragonfly wings and the men drawling on about the Texas Longhorns beating Oklahoma, and felt more confident every time they laughed. After dinner, Valerie and her mom disappeared into the kitchen, while Alex and I moved to the living room. As we drank our cognac, he recalled the evening we'd met at the *Grand Véfour* and said he'd seen something in me that set me apart.

I asked what it was.

"You're very astute," he smirked and arched his eyebrows. "And you're a gifted liar."

"What?"

"That story about the wealthy grandfather donating money to the University of Minnesota, and that's why you went there—I believed it, at first. But there was a little voice in me that whispered, *He's not wealthy.*"

Alex leaned toward me, treating this as an intimate matter.

"It had to do with the clothes. You didn't wear them the way someone would who wore them all the time. And I remembered catching a glimpse of you looking at yourself in a mirror, admiring your appearance. So, when Valerie came back from France last August, I asked her, and after a while I got the truth."

"I'm sorry. I put on that show because—"

"Oh, I know. You don't need to explain. When you talked about your grandfather, your concept of history, and the work you were doing on the United States of Europe, I admired your intelligence and performance. You're very articulate, Dick, and very convincing. You pulled it off with panache, the way you delivered your lines with such sincerity, and all the while, so charming. Those skills can't be taught." He nodded, pleased with what he saw. "You can convincingly present an argument that is untrue but serves a worthy end. Which is to say, you'd make an excellent professional."

"A professional what?"

"We need to talk about that sometime, but this is not the time."

"Why not?"

"Let's get together for lunch. We'll talk then."

He gave me the name of a restaurant where he wanted to meet in a few days. I was baffled. On the way home in the cab, Valerie asked what her dad and I had talked about. I repeated his comments. She said, "Oh, really? That's bizarre." I could see her smiling at me in the dark.

A few days later, Alex and I met at a restaurant on his side of the park. While eating his salad, he told me that what he saw in me in Paris, in addition to my exceptional communication skills, was my knowledge of Latin American countries. He talked about his consulting firm and the work he'd done with some of the Gulf nations, enabling them to use their oil revenues to modernize. He wanted to expand his business into Latin America and work with poor countries that were rich in oil and minerals, but didn't have the money or the technical ability to extract and market them.

"We could provide the money and the know-how and enable those nations to generate wealth and use it to ensure a better life for their citizens." He smiled. "And end poverty." He paused to let his words sink in. "But, some of those governments are corrupt, and whoever is doing the negotiating might have to present arguments that might not be entirely true, but will obtain a result that's good for the people. I think you demonstrated that night at the *Grand Véfour* that you have that ability." He paused again. "Are you interested?"

Was I interested? He had ignited my fantasies of liberation. I blurted, "Yes!" He offered me a job as his assistant, I accepted, and, after we left the restaurant, I walked through the park, my spirit singing with the birds.

Alex's company helped me find an apartment in DC, and Valerie started visiting me on weekends, staying in the guest room. I talked about Maria less ... and felt Valerie's presence more. At night, I'd hear her in her room, getting into bed, and I'd wonder what she was thinking as she lay there, so close to me. During the day, my hand might brush across her skin, or our thighs touch as we sat next to each other on the couch looking at a book, and I'd feel awkward, maybe guilty, but less so each time. And then that Sunday morning, I made scrambled eggs and coffee, while she took a shower. After I'd heard her turn the water off, I went to her room to tell her breakfast was ready. The door was open, and she was sitting on the bed, naked, a pair of underpants in her hand. She looked at me as she had that day on the yacht. I entered her room ... and we got married a few months later.

I felt as if I'd been settling for months into the role of son-in-law, because, even before the wedding, her parents treated me like one. Her mother bought me new shirts, ties, and bottles of fine wine, and Alex offered me the position in his company. That time when Valerie and I were planning the wedding, and I talked about how kind and generous her parents had been, I saw in her grin, and then in the giggles she couldn't control when I asked what was going on, that she'd been concealing something from me—she'd known by the time we'd sailed on the yacht that she was in love with me. After I'd called and said I wanted to start a new life, she'd told her parents she wanted to marry me and asked them to support her.

I became Alex's protégé. And soon realized that to understand his business, I had to understand him, because his company reflected his character. I knew from the conversation we'd had at the *Grand Véfour* that he and I were at opposite political ends. His responses to my comments about the Vietnam War and what the U.S. had done to Chile had made that clear. What I hadn't realized was the extent to which he was invested in his politics. I'd tried to clarify those politics at the beginning of the conversation that night, when I said I'd been impressed by what Valerie had told me about the work his firm had done with governments in the Middle East, but after expressing his happiness at my appreciation of his work, he changed the subject before I could ask any questions. I soon learned that, while he had indeed used his influence to do good in the Middle East, that had not been his primary objective. No, he had another side to him. One Valerie didn't seem to know, or want to know. He was an arms dealer.

And an elitist. From conversations I had with Valerie and others, I learned he'd come from a wealthy family and had gone to the right schools—Exeter, Yale, and the Harvard School of Business. When he was still young and cultivating relationships with school and university friends, as well as members of his extended family, he recognized the Middle East would be ravaged by one war after another, and he could make a fortune working with the weapons industry. He drew closest to those friends and family members who eventually became powerful in that industry and in presidential administrations.

He developed a bond with a Saudi prince—the Playboy Prince, as he called him—and the two of them became close associates. With his contacts in DC and in the military-aviation industry, and the Prince, who operated as the representative of the King of Saudi Arabia, he set up the first deal between the Saudis and the U.S. for the sale of F15s. Just the beginning of a collaboration that would bring in millions for him and, over the years, a fleet of fighter jets to the Saudis, second in the Middle East only to Israel's. And the Playboy Prince was just one of his many close associates.

Aside from me, all the core members of his staff were also HYP graduates, who came from the right class and the right prep schools. I always felt out of place when I'd join them during coffee breaks or for lunch, because they'd talk about encountering a relative or an old college friend, who had a father or an uncle who was a chief of staff, or a CEO, or a lead member of this think tank or that lobbying firm. The only important person I knew was Alex. Someone who should've been a member of that fraternity was Elliott, the staff member Alex assigned to work part-time with me. Elliott had gone to Phillips and Harvard, where he'd earned a degree in economics.

My work consisted of identifying countries in Central and South America that were rich in oil and minerals and work with leaders in those countries and our contacts in American corporations to create proposals for developing the resources and submit them to the World Bank for funding. Alex provided the contacts, or the contacts to develop the contacts, and Elliott, with his mathematical brilliance, created economic projections that would convince anyone the GDP in those countries would double or triple if my proposals were implemented. Alex had trained Elliott, and I came to see that the projections were often exaggerated, but I worked with them nevertheless in developing my proposals, because I believed we were about to liberate the poor and transform the world one country at a time.

But it wasn't easy for Alex to recognize my accomplishments, and when he did, it was usually in the context of a reminder of everything his company—that is to say, he—had done to position me to succeed. While he was patronizing toward me, he seemed callous in his dealings with Elliott. I saw this when he had Elliott give a presentation to his staff on Iraq, its estimated oil reserves, potential oil production and revenue per year, and projects that could be undertaken with Iraqi funds and American corporations to modernize the country. The staff would then discuss the importance of developing a working relationship with Iraq, by whatever means possible, to create a new stream of revenue. Not just a stream, a river, because Iraq represented the grand prize of the Middle East.

Elliott was visibly nervous, and his voice trembled as he clicked from one slide to the next and explained the numbers. Alex repeatedly asked him to explain things in greater detail and shook his head as Elliott became increasingly nervous and stumbled over his words. I could see him sweat as his eyes darted back and forth from the screen to Alex's scowl. At one point, he interrupted Elliott mid-sentence to say, "That will do." I felt Elliott's humiliation as he left the room.

After Alex provided the staff with his own explanation of the data and dismissed us, I went to Elliott's office, found the door closed, knocked, and knocked again. A quavering voice told me to come in. I found him with his elbows on his desk, his head in his hands. I sat down. When he finally looked up at me, I asked how he was doing.

"I'm not good at talking in front of an audience."

"You're not good at doing that when Alex is present. You're fine when he's not." Elliott's mournful air remained unchanged. "I'll talk with Alex. Tell him you've been crucial to my projects in South America. Maybe I can convince him to let you work with me full-time."

"You think that's possible?"

"Alex wants to see new revenue streams flow in."

Within a year, I had Elliott to myself.

Not long after that, Valerie pulled a surprise on me. We were in bed, I'd just finished describing a project Elliott and I were working on, and she said, "How do you feel about having children?"

"What?"

"I'm wondering how you feel about having children." Her eyes were open wide, as if to say, *Well, come on, tell me.*

I was only twenty-nine and hadn't thought about children. I asked, "Why?"

"My period's late. Very late."

"Well, do you want a child?"

"I do."

"What about your career?"

"I'm not editing anything that inspires me. And I'd rather stay home with my baby. I can always go back to work later."

I would've been perfectly happy without a child, but if she wanted one enough to put her career on hold ... "Well," I said, laughing, "let's have that baby."

As her belly swelled, I could see an elbow or a knee poking against her skin and feel with my hand the body inside her, and I started falling in love with our baby, and my love for Valerie deepened as our baby grew. I was with Valerie when she gave birth to Julia and nursed her for the first time. Valerie grimaced in pain as Julia latched on, and relaxed and closed her eyes after Julia found her rhythm. At first it was the sight of our daughter suckling at Valerie's breast that moved me, but soon it was the smile on Valerie's face—a delicate smile I'd never seen before, one that seemed to come from deep within. She relaxed, her lips spread, and a low humming sound came from her throat. When she opened her eyes to gaze at Julia, her smile broadened, emanating from her eyes as well as her lips. This wasn't just an expression of happiness. It seemed rapturous, blessed, and sacred, and I thought of it as her beatific smile. I wondered if Mom had looked at me that way, imprinting my memory, so that when I saw Valerie's smile, I remembered hers. Perhaps. But what I know is that I fell in love with Valerie—really fell in love—while gazing at that smile. She felt my gaze and looked at me and asked what I was thinking. I shook my head and said, "I'm just happy." That happiness became my reason for living.

Our infants became toddlers and the toddlers became running, jumping, screaming little kids. No matter how upset I got with Alex at work, when I walked into the house, and Julia and Jamie came running up to me shouting "Papa" and threw their arms around my legs and wanted me to pick them up and hug them, the anger from everything I'd put up with from him evaporated.

Julia craved our attention and became even more of a performer than I was growing up. When we still lived in the townhouse, she'd get up from the bench in the alcove of the kitchen on which she sat for meals and act and sing and dance, and do a fancy bow when we applauded. And then she started going off to theater camps and participating in grade-school and high-school productions—those wacky, melodramatic comedies, like the one in which she recited lines full of hilarious hyperbole, and dramatically swooned, collapsing like a ballet swan, and was carried off-stage by the hero. Days, weeks, months later, Valerie and I would reminisce and laugh. But Jamie, he wasn't a performer. Not until he discovered soccer, and then he was performing all the time—on the field. I'd never been involved much in sports, but his passion for books, that's something he picked up from both of us.

And drawing and painting? I'll never forget that summer we took the kids to Denver to visit my mother, and Jamie, when he learned I'd done the portraits in the living room of his grandmother, of his aunt, and of the grandfather he'd never known, asked his grandmother how I could've done them, they looked so real, and she looked at him and Julia as if she had a marvelous tale to tell and went on about the thousand hours my father had spent teaching me to draw and paint, and how I continued painting all the way through college. "Have you seen that beautiful self-portrait hanging in your mom and dad's room?" she asked rhetorically, knowing they'd seen it. "Well," she beamed, "he did that in college. Maybe someday he'll start painting again."

She showed the kids my old drawings and paintings, and they seemed impressed, and interested, so, when we got home, we bought them sketch pads and paint kits, and I taught them to draw and paint, and by the time they'd each finished a portrait of the other, they'd lost interest. I blamed myself for not communicating the same passion to them that Dad had to me, but I also felt relieved, because my work consumed so much of my life. We gave the kids' portraits to my mother for Christmas and she hung them on her bedroom wall. They're not great works of art, but they were done by her grandkids, and that's what counts for her.

I'm amazed Julia will soon turn twenty, and Jamie nineteen. My years with my family seem to have flown by. Maybe because they've been the happiest of my life.

I must admit that whatever unhappiness Valerie and I have experienced has come from my relationship to Alex. I needed to gain independence from him, and I knew doing so would cause her pain, but I had to.

I couldn't have done it without Elliott. Poor Elliott. He had no siblings, his mother had died when he was young, and his father lived in a retirement home. If he had any uncles, aunts, or cousins, he kept them secret. I never met anyone so bereft of love. He became like a brother. The kids even called him Uncle Elliott. He'd join us for Thanksgiving and Christmas Eve, and attend the kids' birthday parties, put on a cone-shaped birthday cap and grin like a happy little boy. When the kids got older, Elliott would join me on the sidelines and root for Jamie's soccer team, and bring back gifts from his travels, like the gold carnival mask from Venice that he gave to Julia and that she hung on her mirror.

Valerie's parents also came to the house, but that changed the year the grandkids turned five and four and I decided to launch my own firm. With Elliott's help, I'd succeeded in generating new business in South America and later in Sub-Saharan Africa that would someday rival Alex's in terms of revenue, and yet he refused to discuss promoting me to vice-president.

"He's left me no alternative," I told Valerie one evening, when I talked to her about my desire to start my own company.

"But how can you do this to him? Where would we be without him?"

"Where will our family be if I continue to work for someone who refuses to recognize my accomplishments?"

She didn't have an answer, other than to turn cold toward me for the next few days. And then, on a Sunday night, she said, "If you have to do it, then do it. But try to find a way of doing it with kindness. Tell him how grateful you are." She shook her head, started crying, and mumbled, "I feel like I'm stabbing my own father in the back."

I walked into his office Monday morning and told him we needed to talk.

He looked at his watch, leaned into his high-back chair, and said, "You must've been thinking about something over the weekend."

"I've decided to resign."

"Really. And how, may I ask, do you plan on supporting your family?"

"Same way as now. Only as the president of my own company."

Alex sneered. "That costs money. You need a staff. And, above all, you need contacts."

"I've got all that. By the way, Elliott's coming with me."

"So, you, my son-in-law, you're taking what I've given you to provide for my daughter and my grandchildren ... you're taking my investment in you, and using it to start a company."

"Aside from Elliott, everything essential that I'm taking is in my head."

"With my contacts, my support, my guidance, and my staff."

"I've paid you back a hundred times over. All you had to do to avoid this was make me a partner. You couldn't do that. You're incapable of appreciating anyone's success but your own."

He glared at me through the thick lenses of his glasses, and I realized how much he'd aged. He seemed to have shrunk into his chair, his head tonsured like a monk's.

"I assume I'll still be allowed to visit my daughter and grandchildren."

"Of course, Alex. We're family."

Valerie's parents didn't visit us again for over a year, we didn't receive an invitation from them for the next Christmas-Day dinner, and for each invitation not offered or ignored, she'd make me feel her pain. Eventually her parents came back, and the biggest problem was finding a way for them and Elliott to share time with the kids. My new business continued to succeed, and within three years I was able to offer Valerie a new home in Bethesda—the beautiful house where we live today. Elliott, whose self-esteem seemed to improve with our success, found a caring, loving woman, who nurtured him and seemed to make him whole. Within a few years, they had two little girls, and he came less frequently to the house.

I got so caught up in my life with Valerie and the kids, it was as if nothing existed prior to her, and that mindset made the eruption of people from my past into the present all the more surprising, and sometimes shocking. Like that afternoon in 1992, shortly before we moved into our new home. I was standing in a cashier's line in a bookstore and noticed a man in front of me who looked familiar. He had a black Van Dyke, threaded with gray. I said, "Mike?"

He gave me a quizzical look.

"Mike, from Minneapolis?"

"How do you know my name?"

"I'm Dick. Dick Rayburn."

"Dick. Wow! You've changed."

My old housemate looked me over, trying to reconcile the neatly groomed thirty-nine-year-old with the easy rider he'd known. The only difference I could see in him were the glasses and some gray in his hair. We paid for our books, went to a nearby restaurant, sat down at the bar and ordered a couple beers.

"So," I asked, "what are you doing these days?"

"I'm an English professor at George Washington University. How about you?"

I explained the work I was doing with the World Bank and American corporations to develop the resources of developing countries and enable people to rise out of poverty.

"The old theme of liberation." He grinned. "But, how does that work?"

"You mean how do the poor benefit?"

"Yeah."

"Well, the projects we get funded usually include the development of health-care services and schools and infrastructure, which benefit everyone." I should've stopped there, but something made me go on. "With a lot of these countries, though, we're dealing with corrupt governments. The powerful take a cut, and when they get done, well, that's life." I took a deep breath and sighed, releasing a little of the anger I felt every time I thought about what I was and wasn't accomplishing, and reminded myself it was a complex world, the good was often difficult to separate from the bad, and sometimes I had to do what once I would've thought was wrong to accomplish what was right. I wondered how Mike felt about being a professor and asked him.

"I love teaching, but the politics of academe—don't get me started. The best part of my life is my family."

"Oh, yeah? Have you got kids?"

"Three."

"I've got two." I paused. "You know, one of the amazing things about kids is that we see them in four dimensions. I look at Julia and Jamie and see them through all the years of their lives—infants, toddlers, little imps. They're only nine and eight now, but I suspect when they get into their twenties, it'll be the same thing."

"Yeah, we've got pictures of the kids all over our house, just in case we need reminders of how they looked at any age."

We got emotional, ordered another round of beers, and reminisced about old housemates and girlfriends. And then I asked a question I wish I hadn't.

"What about Helen?"

He shook his head and sighed. "She committed suicide."

"What!"

He took a deep breath. "Yeah. My wife's family is from St. Paul, so we go back fairly often. Last time, I ran into our old housemate, Ron, who's still in touch with Helen's husband, Tom. Remember him? He lived with us for about a year. Teaches history at—"

"Did Ron say why she did it? Or how? Or …"

"No. He just said Tom and the kids have been struggling. I can't imagine dealing with something like that. I mean …"

As Mike continued talking, I remembered the day in September, at the end of my easy-rider trip. I pulled up in front of the house in Minneapolis, and Mike and Ron were sprawled out on the couch on the front porch, having a lazy afternoon of beer swilling and bullshitting. I joined them, and was having a beer, when Mike went in the house and returned with an envelope.

"She's been calling every day. She's going crazy worrying about you."

I set my bottle down, looked at the envelope, tapped it against my thigh a couple times, put it on my knapsack, picked up my bottle, took a swig, and said, "So, when's the next party?"

Later, I tossed my knapsack on my bed, opened the envelope, took out a birthday card, and saw Ingrid Bergman, in a close-up from *Casablanca,* gazing at me with love in her eyes, as if I were Bogie, and in a speech balloon she wished, "Happy birthday, darling." I opened the card and found the words, "I never knew what love is, until I found you. Forever yours, Helen."

Mike knocked and opened the door. "You going to talk to her?"

"How do you tell a woman who loves you that you no longer love her? Or you thought you did, but you don't?"

"Just tell her the truth."

"I feel like an executioner."

And that's how I felt when I went to her house. She opened, her eyes fixed on me, and by the time I'd entered and stood in the foyer, the expression on her face had morphed from joy to dread to agony. She could see my shame. I looked down so I wouldn't have to see her eyes.

"You told me you loved me," she said. "I believed you." She shook her head and cried, "I loved you, loved you so much." I glanced at the door, wishing I weren't there. She said, "Are you scared to look at me?" I looked up, and she pierced me with her eyes. "You're like a little boy. A scared little boy." She shouted, "You'd better run, little boy. Run! Run run run!"

I ran. Ashamed. For the first time in my life, I cried after breaking up with a woman, cried most of the way home. I swore I'd never hurt a woman again. Never.

I heard Mike's voice talking about Helen's children, a boy and a girl, who seemed to be close in age to Julia and Jamie, and thought,

What would that do to my kids, if I were to end my life? I wondered if Helen had thought about that, or if the pain that had led her to kill herself was so great, she couldn't think about anything else.

I became aware again of the bar and of Mike. We remembered some of the good times we'd had and went our separate ways with smiles on our lips, telling one another we should stay in touch. I never tried to contact him. Sometimes I'd think of Helen and wonder what had led her to do it.

Maria also came back into my life. And in Valerie's, too. Around the beginning of the new administration in 2001, her column started to appear in the *New York Times*, her articles lambasting the new president and his politics. When I'd get home from the office, I always knew if Valerie had seen one of Maria's articles in the paper, because she'd have a scowl on her face and something caustic to say. I'd try to avoid reading them, but sometimes I did, and I'd remember the smart, cocky, naïve woman Maria had been, and following her to Paris and Austin, and going along with all her impetuous decisions, like the unexpected announcement of our engagement and our wedding and our move to New York. I did whatever she wanted, tolerated every humiliation, couldn't make her happy, but still clung to her, trying.

That day I was driving Valerie and the kids from the Denver airport to Mom's house, I remembered being driven by Georgia on the same highway twenty-two years before and looking out the window at the cars alongside us and feeling the urge to open my door and just end it. And as I continued driving, the flow of the traffic, the angle of the late-afternoon sun, and the hypnotic effect of the hum of the wheels on the road felt as they had that day with Georgia, and I relived the pain of turning away from Maria and walking past Warren's smile.

"Dick. Dick, are you there?" Valerie was leaning forward, looking at me. When she saw my face, she looked frightened and asked, "Are you okay?"

"Sure. I'm fine. Why?" I looked back at the road.

She said something about the kids wanting to know if Grandma would come with us to Rocky Mountain National Park. I answered,

"Probably," gripping the steering wheel, my eyes fixed on the road, my mind trying to stay focused on getting us to Mom's house.

After we'd given Mom a hug and carried our things into the house, I found myself alone with her and asked for Grandpa Archer's phone number.

"Why?"

"I have something to say to him."

"What? You haven't seen him in over thirty years."

"He destroyed something important to me."

"What did he destroy?"

I stared at Dad's painting on the wall, the one with the man walking out of town.

"Aside from that awful day at his house, what did he ever do to hurt you?"

I shook my head.

"My father and I get along. He's helped you kids. He gave me money for Georgia when she needed a down payment for a house, and when she went through a divorce. And he gave me money to help you when you were an undergraduate."

"And what did you have to do to get it?"

"He wanted me to remain close to him. That's what every parent wants."

I handed her my phone. "Will you please dial his number for me."

Her eyes beseeched me. "Remember, he's an old man. He can't hurt you. But you could hurt him." She dialed his number and handed me the phone. "Be kind."

A woman answered, and I asked for Mr. Archer. When she asked who was calling, I said, "His grandson," and when she asked which one, I said, "He only has one."

After a long silence, a rasping voice said, "My grandson. You've finally decided to call."

"I want to talk to you."

"Go ahead."

"In person."

"All the better. When?"

"Now."

I'd visited a few mansions over the years, and the walls of Archer's house no longer seemed to loom above and intimidate me. I rang, the door opened, and a woman led me through the foyer, past the staircase with two lions, and into the living room, where she gestured toward an armchair and told me I could wait there. I remained standing and looked around at the tall windows, purple drapes, dark woodwork, and portraits of men with stern faces gazing into the distance. I looked up at the portrait of my great-grandfather, his hand resting on a globe, bookcases in the background, and thought the painting a pathetic attempt to impress the viewer.

I was wondering how long the caretaker had been gone, when she entered and told me Mr. Archer would meet me in the study. I followed her down the hall, with the paintings of Western scenes on the walls, and into the room lit by sunlight, and across the Navajo rug toward the two leather armchairs with a small table in between. She gestured toward one of the chairs. I sat down and faced the desk, which didn't look as big as it had before, and the windows, which didn't look as tall, and the mountain rising above the tree line in the distance. She walked out of the sunlight, into the shadow, and out the door. I stood up and looked at the walls beyond the reach of the light and at the things attached to them that seemed to lurk in the dark—the mounted animal heads, the flying eagle, and the portraits. I turned around, walked past the desk to the window, gazed at the mountain, looked down at the desk and the chair where Archer had sat, and found nothing impressive. I returned to my chair.

A low whirring sound caught my attention. Archer, in a wheelchair, came out of the shadow and entered the sunlight, the caretaker following him. The white mane that had struck me the first time I'd seen him had thinned to wisps that lay across the top of his otherwise bald head, and his facial skin looked pale and flaccid, with reddish blotches and mushrooms, and his eyes were a watery blue. He ignored me as he drove past, stopped, and pointed at the chair across the table from mine. The caretaker moved the chair so he could park where it had been and face me. I was surprised that he chose to sit there and not behind the desk, which had given him so much power the first time. I moved my chair to face him. Thin and frail, in a shirt, a charcoal cardigan, and slacks, he stared at my face, like he was trying to read the story I'd lived, and finally said he was happy to see me, wheezing as he spoke. He asked if I'd like a cognac, I said okay, and he nodded to the caretaker.

"So, after all these years, you want to talk. Why?" His raspy voice caused a tremor in the wattle hanging from his throat.

I felt embarrassed, going there to confront an old man. I had Valerie, Julia, and Jamie. I couldn't be happier. I thought of excusing myself and leaving.

The caretaker returned carrying two snifters, one with twice as much cognac as the other, set the glass with more near me, the other near Archer, and left. Archer picked up his glass, inhaled the aroma, as if this breath might be his last, and made a humming sound.

"I want to talk about what you did to me twenty-two years ago." My voice quivered.

About to take a drink, he paused, and studied my face.

"It's interesting," I said, "how some things that happened years ago, you never really forget. And what I can't forget is Warren Cutler, the father of the woman I was going to marry, telling me my grandfather had tried to make something of me, and then disowned me. And my grandfather had told him I was interested in his daughter solely because of his money."

Archer took a drink and set his glass down. "You want to talk about that?"

"You lied. You didn't try to make something of me, because I wouldn't let you. You didn't *disown* me, because you never *owned* me. And I certainly wasn't interested in Maria because of her father's money. I didn't give a shit about that."

I must've been looking at him like I wanted to hit him, because he raised his hands toward me, as if preparing to defend himself. And then a smile crept over his face. "Okay. Good. You got that off your chest." He laid his hands in his lap. "I'm happy to see you." He gazed at me in silence, then licked his gray lips. "I vaguely remember what you're talking about. If what I said did you any harm, I'm sorry."

"You're sorry? Do you know how much harm you did me?"

He shook his head. "I truly am sorry, Dick."

Is that all? I thought. I felt like berating him, but he'd already said he was sorry, and, as Mom had said, that was all so long ago, and he was just an old man, with sagging cheeks and a wattle and a raspy voice, bound to a wheelchair, living in his mansion with portraits of dead people. I wondered if he had any friends. The longer I sat there, the more I felt his vulnerability. It would be inhumane to try to get revenge. And revenge for what? I was *happy*.

"Thirty-one years ago, in this room," Archer said, "you sat right where you're sitting now, and I sat behind the desk." He shook his head. "After you ran out, I thought I'd lost my daughter. Ann didn't talk to me for almost a year. But we talk now. She's very proud of you. She says you have a lovely wife and two kids, a beautiful house in Maryland, and your own company. I'm happy for you." He paused, looked toward the pool of light on the floor, licked his dry lips again. "I'm hoping you and I can start over."

I was confused. I'd come to this house to vent my hatred of him, and he just wanted to have a good relationship.

"The reason I agreed to see you today is that you're my grandson. And you and your wife have brought my great-grandchildren into the world. I'd love to meet them."

"Why?"

"They're my family."

"Family didn't mean much to you when my father was alive. And after he died, you called him a goddamn drunk, and said the world had lost nothing. I'll never forget those words."

"I shouldn't have said those things. I was angry. I'd gone through years of frustration. It hurt, being excluded from my own family." He paused, sighed, and licked his lips, his eyes wandering off to either side, as if he were looking for help. They returned to me, resting in their swollen pouches. "But, you know, your father might've had a better life, if he'd taken what I'd offered. And you and Georgia and Ann might've as well. That's what I wanted, happiness for all of you. And for me to be part of that happiness." He fell silent.

I was having trouble reconciling this old, fragile, gentle being with the monster who'd screamed at me.

"You're surprised I'm talking about how important family is to me."

"I am."

"Imagine what it's like to lie awake at night in the silence of this house and hear voices, words I can't forget, things I wish I'd never said." He bowed his head.

I felt like reaching across the table and touching his hand.

"Enough of that. I'm curious about your business. Ann's told me a little, but I'd like to hear it from you. What do you do?"

I told him, and he listened with an air of fascination, nodding his head as he saw how the pieces fit together. I felt increasingly proud of myself, and by the time I finished, I could hear myself boasting. I picked up my glass of cognac, felt like toasting myself, and took a drink.

"What an amazing accomplishment," he proclaimed. "You've helped the poor and ah … you've apparently done well for yourself." He chuckled. "You know, I could say that about my mining company—which I sold a long time ago. I provided jobs for a lot of immigrants, people who'd come over from Italy and Greece. Desperate people, who might've died if it hadn't been for my company. So, like you, I helped the poor."

I looked away, thinking about what I'd heard from Dad and his father about mining companies exploiting immigrants, and how the miners were nothing but mudsills for those bastards who owned the companies.

"You're a successful businessman," he continued, while studying my face. "You've changed so much. I think you and I have a lot in common. Now you might understand where I was coming from, when I tried to talk to you. I wanted you to be successful, just as you are now. I might have been a little clumsy, I guess, in the way

I handled the situation. Your mother told me, when she started talking to me again, that I just didn't know how to talk to young people. I certainly didn't know how to talk to her when she was growing up. Maybe I have to wait until people reach a certain age. What do you think? Do we talk better with people as we get older?"

"Maybe."

"You know, if you ever need investors, I'd love to invest in a company that's doing so much good."

"I don't need investors," I snapped. He flinched. I felt like I'd slapped him. I took a breath and, when I calmed, said, "You know, maybe we can talk about that again sometime." I was thinking of leaving, but there was something I'd wondered about and decided to ask. "The first time I met you, you said you loved playing football when you were young and wanted to be a professional football player."

"I told you that?"

"You did. Was it true?"

"Huh! You thought I'd made it up?" He shook his head, his lips spread wide, and he seemed to light up. "I loved playing football."

"Why?"

"Oh, the obvious things, I guess. Being part of a team, that was huge. And the crowds, the cheering when I'd score a touchdown. I played split end. Did I tell you that?"

"You did."

"I loved making a catch in midair and being able to hit the ground running." He shook his head. "There was something exhilarating about that kind of concentration, nothing else existing but my hands and the ball, and being exactly where I needed to be to make the catch. That was perfection. And then I'd get clobbered. Football's a murderous sport. But I loved it, even after I had to let go of it and get to work." He licked his lips. "That's one of the things I like to remember, when I'm awake at night, in that silence that goes on forever, full of regrets for all the things I can't change." He stared at the floor, then looked up, his eyes afloat in their pouches. "Do you ever wake up in the middle of the night, wondering what might've been?"

I thought of the nights I'd lie awake, obsessing about projects that didn't culminate in the liberation of which I'd dreamed. "We all do." I nodded. "Well, I should probably get going."

"Next time you come, bring your wife and children. I'd love to meet them."

I stood up, placed my hand on his shoulder, and said I'd bring the family over sometime the next few days. He placed his hand on mine and said, "You're a very smart man, Dick. You know how to hold a family together. If you can do that, you'll never be alone." He smiled. "And thanks for having a drink with me. My doctor said I shouldn't. It's bad for my vocal cords and digestion." He laughed, and his laugh morphed into a cough that rattled his chest and left him gasping for air.

I squatted in front of him and asked if he was going to be okay. He caught his breath, nodded, and said, "It was good. Every drop."

I followed the caretaker out of the room and down the hall. I slowed down as we approached the winged lions and ran my hand across the mane of one of them and thought of the old man whose long mane was now just a few wisps lying across his bald head.

When I got back to Mom's house, she asked, with an apprehensive look, how it had gone. I told her he thought he and I had a lot in common.

"What?" she asked.

I summarized the conversation and said maybe I should take Valerie and the kids for a visit.

Mom nodded and said, "Amazing."

The next day, she got a call from the caretaker. Her father had died during the night. I hoped he wasn't awake and alone in the dark. I felt sad, and yet relieved, because I'd rid myself of a monster—not Archer, but my perception of him that day, thirty years before.

Archer wasn't the only person impressed by my success. A little over a year after I'd visited him, the Lowell Group, the most powerful private equity firm in the United States, named me a member of its advisory board and its point man in Iraq for the upcoming occupation. I knew Alex would envy me. Iraq was the grand prize he'd coveted. It had as much oil as Saudi Arabia and the best water resources in the Middle East. And it was strategically positioned, surrounded by Iran, Kuwait, Saudi Arabia, Jordan, Syria, and Turkey. During the 1980s, Alex had had some opportunities to work in Iraq, but Saddam had always gotten in the way. Alex would rant about that SOB, who the hell did he think he was? Doesn't he know you don't fuck with America? Does he want to end up like Mosaddegh, spending the rest of his life under house arrest? Or going down in a bloody coup, like Allende?

The day I learned we were going to invade Iraq, I was ecstatic. The moment had come. I called Elliott into my office and, while waiting, stood gazing out the window at the Hay-Adams Hotel, where foreign dignitaries and men of power stayed. Built in the early twentieth century to resemble an Italian-Renaissance mansion, the hotel looked out across Lafayette Square toward the back of the White House. I'd positioned myself well. Now I would capitalize on that position to pull off the biggest deal of my life. A shot at the grand prize. The Lowell Group had swatted Alex aside like a fly and chosen me to handle its interests in Iraq. I chuckled, and saw my smile reflected in the glass, until it waned, as I thought about what I'd have to do.

I heard Elliott enter the room and turned to see him sit down on the couch and pour a glass of whiskey from the bottle on the coffee table. He held the bottle over the other glass and looked up at me. I nodded, and he poured my whiskey. I sat down on the arm chair, on the other side of the table, and we raised our glasses to one another.

"Well, Elliott," I said, leaning back into the chair, "we're going to liberate Iraq."

"Hallelujah!"

"We're going to open that country up, get rid of Saddam, and replace him with people we can work with, and get things done." I paused. "And we're going to get rich." I laughed. "So fucking rich, we'll never have to work again."

Elliott snorted a laugh. "You're already worth millions."

"A few," I chuckled. "You know, several years ago, I started thinking I'd love to be able to retire when I turn fifty and do something else with the rest of my life. But first I'd have to make enough money to put the kids through college. Well, if I commit to the Iraq project for three years, I'll be able to retire at fifty-two."

"I have a hard time seeing you just sitting around the house. What'll you do?"

"I don't know. I've fantasized all kinds of things. Traveling, taking up painting again. How about you? What are you going to do?"

"I don't know. Maybe retire when you do. Move to Florida. My wife would love that. So would the girls. We could take them to Disney World as often as they want."

"That sounds great. Here's to a wonderful life in Florida." We tipped our glasses again and drank. I smiled, but my happiness ebbed. "One reason I want to retire early is because of all the years of telling myself, 'Stay focused on the positive, on the good you're doing for people, and not on the corrupt politicians and the rich and the corporations and the …'" I sighed and shook my head. "I'm so fucking sick of that. And here we are, involved in a project that includes invading a country and killing people. We've never been part of anything like this before."

"Let me remind you of what you tell me. You and I are not invading the country. That's going to happen, regardless of what we do."

I nodded. "Yeah." I took a deep breath and sighed. "You know, whenever I think of the millions of people we've helped over the last twenty years, I feel good. You should too. You developed the economic models that got everyone on board. Oil, construction, communications, the World Bank. They all lined up, because you performed magic with numbers."

"That's a bit of hyperbole."

"And we made a lot of money, while doing good. And we'll do good in Iraq, too." I paused. "I have to keep that in mind tomorrow at the meeting of the advisory board, when I talk about creating opportunities for American corporations." I paused again. "You know, Elliott, sometimes I'm amazed I got this position. I'm sure Alex wanted it."

"He might be a little old for it."

"Yeah, but as we know, he never got over the frustration of Saddam getting in his way. I mean, Iraq's the mother lode. The mother lode of black gold. It might be even bigger than Saudi Arabia … Saudi Arabia. What a perfect set-up. The U.S. helps the Saud family develop their oil industry; they guarantee us oil and sign an agreement to buy our weapons. They become despised by the Wahhabis for being too close to us, the infidels. They get nervous, want to buy more weapons from us, and want to sell us more oil. We sell them F15s; the Wahhabis get pissed; the family gets anxious. We put air bases over there, and the Wahhabis get really pissed; the family buys more weapons, creating even more tension, and …"

I snapped my fingers. "Bingo! We have a perfect system that can work for decades. Alex understood that situation and milked it for God knows how many millions. He's smart. He knows how all this comes together. If the Saudis are dependent on us, we're also dependent on them. How do you increase your power in a dyadic relationship? You introduce a third element—Iraq. With us fully controlling the Iraq oil industry, the Saudis will be even more willing to please us. Having the two largest oil reserves in the Middle East in our hands, we'll control the oil markets. Our government will be thinking in terms of increasing our power throughout the Middle East, and Alex would be thinking—among other things—of the fighter jets that black gold can buy." I chuckled. "But his son-in-law got in the way."

"You like getting in his way."

I smiled and nodded. "And his Playboy Prince is going to be at the meeting tomorrow. The Playboy Prince … What a nickname! He gets on a plane, and as soon as it takes off, out come the scotch and the women." I laughed, and then sneered. "If an ordinary Saudi got caught doing that, he'd end up in Chop Chop Square." I take a drink. "Can you imagine, if bin Laden and Al Qaeda were to take control of Saudi Arabia, they'd come for the heads of every member of the royal family, and they'd make the Reign of Terror look like a school picnic."

"I'm sure the Playboy Prince has been funneling money into foreign banks for years, just in case." Elliott paused. "About the meeting tomorrow, is there anything you need from me?"

"No. And from now on, forget about numbers. I need you to work with me more as an adviser and a confidant, and accompany me on my flights to Iraq. It's not going to be easy, ensuring the Lowell Group's corporations take advantage of all the opportunities."

After Elliott left, I returned to the window and gazed at the evening light splayed across the walls of the Hay-Adams, until I noticed the reflection on the glass of my troubled expression. Did I pounce on the opportunity to serve on the advisory board of the Lowell Group and represent its interests in Iraq just to outdo Alex? My efforts to always look at the positive and remind myself that I was doing good for others, were they simply a way of enabling myself to do what I would have condemned twenty years ago? Was I obsessed with money and power? I reminded myself again that we were liberating the people of Iraq from a cruel dictator and his sons and installing a political system that would provide equal rights to everyone, and so much more.

I sighed and wondered if I'd ever learn to accept that the world is not defined in simple terms of good and evil, and never the two shall meet. I shook my head. There was nothing wrong with getting wealthy from doing good. Wealth had enabled me to provide a home for my family. And every time I'd think of Valerie, every time I'd remember her beatific smile as she nursed one of the kids, or the kids screaming "Papa!" as they'd come running up to me and throw their arms around my legs, and I'd pick them up and watch them giggle and scream, every one of those memories made me feel a happiness that effaced all my concerns.

I became conscious of my image reflected on the glass and saw my smile, felt my happiness, and knew I was doing the right thing.

My reflection gave way to a view of the hotel, and I started thinking of the meetings I'd arrange over lunch or dinner in the hotel's restaurant, with Cabinet members, CEOs, and other powerful men, and I reminded myself that Valerie had wanted me to do this. She'd wanted it as much as I had.

The lunar glow on Valerie's face had faded in the gray light of dawn. I gazed at her closed eyes and parted lips, stopped rocking the chair, listened to her breathe, and thought, *We've built a life together. And nothing is more important to me.* I got on my knees, lowered my face toward hers, until my lips nearly touched her skin. *Someday, someday you'll return to me. We'll sleep in the same bed again. And our love will make us feel whole.*

CHAPTER 10

M Y ROOM WAS FLOODED with sunlight by the time I woke and went downstairs. I called Valerie's name. No answer. She'd left a box of cereal and a bowl on the table again, but no note explaining where she'd gone. I stared out the window at Aphrodite and the leaping dolphin touching the calf of her leg. Before everything had gone to hell, Valerie would've left a note. I pulled my phone out of my pocket and called Ron Wolffe again. The receptionist answered and said the Deputy Secretary wasn't in.

"I called yesterday morning and left a message for him to call me ASAP. It's urgent."

"He's out of town and won't be responding to messages until tomorrow or the day after."

"It's extremely urgent."

"I'll make sure he gets the message."

I was still sitting at the table when I heard the front door close. I turned and saw Valerie's face as she walked through the dining room. Her eyes met mine, and then she looked past me toward the window as she went by.

"You have physical therapy this afternoon at three," she said.

"Already? I just got home two days ago."

She went over to the sink, set her purse on the counter, and drank a glass of water.

"Where have you been?" I asked.

"Running errands."

"Why do you disappear all the time?"

She took another drink.

"Why won't you talk to me?"

She shook her head.

"Is it my face?"

"Yeah, it's your face. I can't stand looking at it. And the cane, the way you limp around, like some cripple. It makes me angry."

I looked at my leg and the cane and asked, "Why?"

"I don't know." She turned and glared at me. "I'm looking at you."

"Is something else bothering you?"

"Bothering me? I wake up worrying about him, worry about him all day long, and fall asleep worrying about him."

"I worry, too. I—"

"Don't. Don't you dare."

Her phone rang in her purse. She dug it out and, as she spoke, her voice waxed warm for the first time since she'd brought me home. "That's all right. I'm with him now. Do you want to talk to him?" She came over and handed me her phone. "It's Peter." She didn't move.

I said into the phone, "Peter."

"Sorry I haven't been by to see you yet."

"That's okay," I said, thinking of the look on people's faces when they saw mine.

"I want you to know I'm looking out for your interests here. I'm going to meet with the Board of Directors to discuss your severance package. I'll get back to you with an offer I think you'll like."

When the call ended, I gave the phone back to Valerie and seized her extended hand. "Why can't you talk to me the way you talk to him?"

She yanked her hand away and riveted me with her eyes. "Peter's never done anything but help us." She headed for the front of the house. I assumed she was on her way upstairs, until she shouted from the foyer she'd be back to pick me up for my appointment. The front door slammed, and I slammed the table. "Fuck!"

I shook my hand stinging with pain. "God damn it!" I envied him, the way she talked to him, but she was right. I shouldn't begrudge him the warmth I'd heard in her voice. He'd done nothing but help us, and his friendship had changed our lives.

I had the feeling it would from our first encounter, at the banquet hosted by the Lowell Group, at the Fairfax Hotel on Embassy Row. Less than a year before the invasion. People from the IMF, the World Bank, and American corporations, as well as current and former cabinet members, and entrepreneurs like me, we were all there to schmooze. I'd never worked with the Lowell Group and wondered who could have been responsible for the invitation I'd received. When Valerie and I approached the table to which we'd been assigned, Peter, whom I knew by reputation, rose to introduce himself, his smile crinkling the skin around his eyes. Wearing a blue suit, he had dark hair combed back in waves and a tan that made me think of yachts and tropical islands. We shook hands, and I got a whiff of his cologne. He introduced us to his wife, Marie-Thérèse, a blonde with big brown eyes, who looked at least twenty years younger than him.

We sat down and began talking. He knew who I was, because he'd served as President of the World Bank before heading up the Advisory Board of the Lowell Group and had read some of my proposals. I ignored the other two couples and focused on Peter, laughing at his jokes, telling amusing anecdotes about foreign leaders we'd both worked with, even doing a few impersonations of some of them. After he finished addressing the audience on the need for free and open markets in the developing world, an orchestra started performing arrangements of popular songs, and Peter, Marie-Thérèse, Valerie, and I took to the dance floor. Toward the end of the evening, he and I switched partners, and I knew we had established a bond.

He called the next day to say he wanted to discuss something with me. The call confirmed my guess it was no accident we'd been assigned the same table as Peter and Marie-Thérèse. When I entered his office, he approached me with a bit of a strut, his chest puffed out, his extended hand revealing a gold cuff link with a red jewel. Again, I got a whiff of his cologne. He smiled up at me through his gold-rimmed glasses, gestured toward two armchairs on either side of a small table, and we sat down. His secretary brought in a coffee set, put it on the table, and left. He poured me some coffee, and we talked for a few minutes about my work experience.

And then he said, "Dick, the reason I want to meet today is because of your experience. Now, what I'm going to tell you is confidential." He paused, and I nodded. "The Advisory Board supports the administration's decision to invade Iraq." He paused to see how I was responding; I tried not to reveal my emotions, which were intense. "The administration will sell the invasion to the American people by stating that Saddam is involved with Al Qaeda and is developing weapons of mass destruction—perhaps even nuclear weapons—and thus poses a threat to the United States. The invasion will be easy, because the people of Iraq want to be liberated from Saddam and his psychopath sons. Through a proconsul, we'll rule Iraq for at least three years, transform their government into a democracy, and create free and open markets that'll generate wealth, which can be used to benefit everyone, including the poor. Now, what we, the Lowell Group, need is someone who has learned how to work with Third World countries, corrupt governments, and corporations to develop projects that'll benefit the people of a country, while appeasing certain individuals and entities with a cut of the wealth." He chuckled. "As I think you've learned, doing all these things is a delicate balancing act. You have to support different interests simultaneously. That's not easy."

"No, it's not."

"I'm offering you a position to represent the interests of the Lowell Group and of all the corporations in which we're invested, and which will play a major role in developing a new Iraq. Your principal responsibility, if you accept, will be to ensure that our corporations benefit as much as possible from the rebuilding. But—and this is why I think you're the ideal person for the job—I also want someone who can see the big picture, see how everything comes together—or should come together—for the benefit of everyone. And keep this in mind. Iraq will stand as a model for other countries in

the Middle East, and we will encourage those countries to follow
that model." He paused. "Does that sound interesting to you?"

"Very much."

"Do you have any questions?"

"Yeah. Does the administration have proof to back up its claims
about WMDs?"

He humphed. "What do you think?"

"I'd be surprised."

He nodded. And then engaged me in a conversation about
some of the details of the work I'd be doing, while returning to what
was important—our glorious goal of liberating the people of Iraq
and of the Middle East, as if we were bringing salvation. He knew
from my proposals which words to use to entice me into accepting
the position. I was flattered. A man as prominent and powerful as
Peter seeming to admire me! Why wouldn't I want to work with
him? The seven-figure salary, stock options, and bonuses also flattered me. Nevertheless, I asked for time to think about his offer.
"Sure," he said, "take as long as you like, but we need to get started
right away." Before I left, he invited Valerie and me to his home in
Georgetown for dinner.

It was already dark when we arrived at the Federal townhouse
on N Street, a few doors down from the one in which JFK and
Jackie had lived when he was a senator, campaigning for the presi-
dency. Peter opened the door, and Marie-Thérèse welcomed us with
her French accent. They led us into the living room, which had walls
as white as those of an art museum and white rugs on the hard-
wood floors. Color came primarily from the abstract expressionist
paintings on the walls. Among them was a Rothko—one of the
few abstract expressionists who survived my contempt, which I'd
inherited from Dad. "No tension," Dad used to say. Which for Dad
meant the painting was devoid of content, and therefore a picture
of nothing. When I expressed my admiration for the Rothko, Peter
insisted on showing me the paintings in his office.

After he finished effusing over a Clyfford Still, he asked me if
I'd reached a decision about the position, and I said I had. The four

of us celebrated with champagne. As the evening progressed, and we finished the champagne and moved on to wine with dinner and cognac after, everyone got a little happier and a little more play-ful. The conversation turned to French politics, and Marie-Thérèse made a comment about the corruption of Chirac. He had not suc-ceeded in winning fifty percent in the first round of the presidential election, and now, in the run-off between him and Le Pen, the choice was between the crook and the fascist.

Peter said, "Sometimes she gets a little too French."

"What?" Marie-Thérèse asked. "Too French? You mean I care about people. The people who would be *baisés* by those *salauds*."

"Fucked over by those assholes? Now, now, Mother Teresa," Peter admonished her, with a playful grin.

"Now, now, Napoléon," she responded.

On the way home, Valerie and I replayed the scene and got a good laugh out of it. She said Marie-Thérèse had told her she came from a working-class family in one of the suburbs of Paris and had obtained a Master's at the University of Paris and a position as a French instructor at Georgetown University.

I said, "She's got a lot of pluck."

"I bet he plucked her like a flower."

"Maybe he plucked her flower."

She laughed. "I can imagine how easily handsome, wealthy, so-phisticated Peter, with that seductive smile, charmed her right out of her panties … She's so young. It's bizarre, it's like partying with my own daughter."

"Your daughter?"

"Oh, my God, what a thought!"

"You would've been a ten-year-old mother at her birth."

"You think he gets a younger one with each marriage?"

We saw the possibility of developing a friendship with Napoleon and Mother Teresa, as we referred to them when we were alone, and invited them to our place in Bethesda. After a few get-togethers,

Valerie and I would fly to New York to have dinner with them, go see a play or a musical, spend the night at their apartment on Fifth Avenue, and have breakfast with them in the morning before returning home. Peter would entertain us with stories about his early years sailing on Chesapeake Bay and yachting along the Atlantic coast to the Caribbean, sunbathing on the white beaches of Costa Rica and the islands, dancing in night clubs, and drinking sweet, colorful rum cocktails. Valerie, who'd led a similar life, would respond with stories about her travels with her parents, and later without them, to Europe and the Mediterranean. What I'd done as a kid—working with Dad in his studio and projecting films— seemed out of place, so, like Marie-Thérèse, I'd remain silent and smile. Eventually Valerie and I got together enough money to buy an apartment on Central Park West, so we could spend more time with our friends.

Peter and Marie-Thérèse also invited us to receptions and parties, at which Peter introduced me to members of the Lowell Group Advisory Board—high-ranking people from previous presidential administrations, CEOs, and one former U.S. president, whose cold eyes and smile froze me the first time I met him. I learned to face him, smile back, and ask questions that might appeal to his narcissism, such as how he'd managed to bring the Cold War to an end—as if he had. I created a buffer zone between him and me by referring to him in my mind as Pappy, the nickname Maria had given him in the scathing articles she'd written about him and his son, the current president, whom she claimed could've never become president without Pappy. I'd continue thinking of him as Pappy, but my reason for doing so would change.

Another Texan, James Coker, who'd served under Pappy as Secretary of State, looked me over as if he were sizing me up, determining if I was worthy of serving on the Advisory Board and representing its interests in Iraq. I casually took a drink of champagne and told Coker I admired his handling of the first Iraq War, as if I were his equal and in a position to compliment him. Alex had already introduced me to Frank Bartolli, a small, compact man with a reputation for being an inside brawler, who'd served as Secretary of Defense in Pappy's administration, before becoming CEO of one of the major defense contractors. We talked about the good old days, when he and Alex worked together on some projects in the Middle East. And then there was Jonathon Earle, the Advisory Board's resident neocon, known as both the Prince of Darkness and the Pope, who looked at me with a smirk. According to Peter, Earle, unlike most humans, had grown up in a think tank.

Sometime in October, I went to the Lowell Hotel in New York and knocked on the door of one of the luxury suites. Peter greeted me and led me into the conference room. About a dozen men were sitting around a long table, and another man, BlackBerry in hand, was standing, his back turned toward the group, in front of a window that looked out on East Sixty-Third Street. Peter led me to the head of the table, where we sat down. Looking over the Advisory Board members, I recognized the Playboy Prince at the opposite end, his dark thick hair and neatly trimmed beard threaded with gray. I'd seen him a few times in meetings with Alex, but had never had a conversation with him. I'd heard he had a fondness for Cuban cigars and single malt scotch, and had a magnificent estate in Arlington and a palace on the Côte d'Azur. He was talking to Pappy, seated next to him, while Coker, on Pappy's other side, was talking with Gordon Minor, the former British Prime Minister. Next to Minor sat Bartolli, who was leaning over an empty place at the table, trying to read a document that a suave-looking man with waves of gray hair, glasses, and a bow tie was studying. I realized this man, dressed in a pinstripe suit and vest, was none other than Arthur Boyd, the former head of the SEC and later of the NYSE.

Most of the other board members at the table had gone through the government-corporate turnstile, having held positions as Secretary of State, Defense, or Treasury, or CEO of corporations that would be involved in the occupation. I'd never seen so many powerful people assembled in such a small space, and all of them were going to focus on me. I felt a rush of stage fright. *Channel it*, I said to myself, *Channel it and ride it.*

"Gentlemen," Peter intoned in a bright key. The men paused their conversations to look at him. "We've had a very busy morning. A lot of items on our agenda, some of them difficult. So I think it's time to interject a report that will give us much to be happy about. I'm delighted to introduce someone who, for many of you, needs no introduction: Dick Rayburn." All eyes turned toward me. The man standing in front of the window pocketed his phone, turned around, and Jonathon Earle took his place at the table between Bartolli and Boyd. "Dick has done admirable work in such countries as Columbia, Bolivia, Ecuador, Guatemala, Angola, and Nigeria, enabling them to develop their resources, with help from corporations in which we've invested. He has established a reputation at the World Bank for the creative thinking behind his proposals and his thoroughness in preparing them. This is a man who understands the world we live in and"—he looked around the room—"knows all the points where we connect."

While Peter extolled my accomplishments, everyone at the table stared at me. I'd first heard of these men years before and had met some of them as I worked myself into position to succeed and move up. Now here I was, after years of progressing from one circle to the next, having arrived at the innermost circle, face to face with the nucleus of the Lowell Group—not the Board of Directors, but the Advisory Board, the men behind quite possibly the most powerful global asset management and investment firm in the world, who could make their priorities the priorities of this government and rearrange the world as they desired.

"As a major element of our support for the new government that we'll set up in Iraq," continued Peter, "Dick will work closely with the Director of Private Sector Development, who will report to the Proconsul, who in turn will report to the President. Obviously Iraq is very different from the other countries Dick has worked in. It's not as if the Iraqis never developed their resources. As we know, Iraq is one of the crown jewels of the Middle East." I looked up and noticed Peter's eyes fixed on the Prince's. "We've talked for months about what it would mean to open up the Iraqi economy and introduce a free market system, while replacing the tyrant with a democratically elected government with which we could work."

The Prince nodded.

"We know the administration will be handing us and our associates no-bid contracts for every service we can provide. The question then is how do we make sure there are no needs for services going unmet? No opportunities overlooked? Having someone on board who knows how we connect through our firms and those of our associates is crucial to taking full advantage of the opportunity Iraq will provide. That's Dick's role. Many of the reports that I've provided to you these last few weeks on the Iraq project have come from Dick. Today, he's simply going to give us a brief update on some points."

Several men nodded. Pappy and Coker continued staring at me as they waited to see how I'd perform.

I looked each man in the eye and said, "Gentlemen, it's an honor to serve this organization, which provides leadership to the world in private-sector development. First, let me say what a pleasure it's been to work with Peter. He's always brought to our discussions an open mind, a wealth of experience and knowledge, and a remarkable willingness to commit time and energy to difficult problems. Another man I should thank is someone who is not here: Paul Brunswald, whom some refer to as our proconsul." I glanced in the direction of Coker, who, according to Peter, had been the first to use the term. "Brunswald is going to make my work easier. One of the first things he'll do as proconsul is issue orders that will supplant the laws of Iraq. Indeed, one of the orders will state essentially that Iraqi law has been set aside." I noticed the consternated look on Boyd's face and paused. "That order will stipulate there will be criminal charges brought against anyone, regardless of nationality, who violates any of the other orders."

Boyd said, "This business of setting aside Iraqi law troubles me." His gaze shifted from me to the other men sitting around the table. "I'm concerned this will be a violation of international law. Mr. Minor, I've been told that the United Kingdom's Attorney

General advised your successor that replacing an occupied country's legal system is illegal under international law." He took out a document from his vest pocket. "It violates the ... here it is. 'The Hague Regulations of 1907, the Geneva Conventions ...'"

"The Geneva Conventions," Earle repeated, his cupid lips curling into a sneer.

"'... and the U.S. Army's field manual, The Law of Land Warfare.' The AG went on to say, 'the imposition of major structural economic reforms would not be authorized by international law.'"

Coker smiled benevolently. "Arthur, we are the only superpower, and as such, we have the right—some would say, the responsibility—to correct the things in the world that need correcting."

Earle said, "So we can offer the world the *Pax Americana*."

Coker added, "And if the international community is offended by what we do, what is it going to do?"

Boyd stared at the table, embarrassed and humiliated.

Coker continued, with dramatic indulgence. "We can always find a way to explain everything we do. And the world, in the end, will accept our explanation."

Boyd looked at Coker. "I'm sure you're right."

Coker nodded.

Boyd bowed his head, took his handkerchief out of his suit pocket, and wiped the lenses of his glasses. Pappy's cold eyes remained fixed on him for a few seconds, before he turned his attention to me, giving me a nod to continue.

"I was talking about how Brunswald's orders will make things easy for us. One of those orders will shut down the two hundred state-owned enterprises that provide for all the needs of the Iraqi people—water services, electric utilities, schools, hospitals, prisons—you name it." I paused, and fixed my gaze on the two board members who'd served as CEOs of the corporations that would replace some of the state-owned enterprises. Each man smiled and nodded. "Another order will allow foreign companies access to every sector of the economy; as we have money, and the Iraqis don't, we'll be well positioned. And another order will allow foreign investors to transfer abroad all funds associated with their investment."

"Ah, Dick," Pappy said, "can you tell us something we don't know?"

I paused, looked him in the eye. "Two words: *seeds* and *security*."

Coker chuckled, looked at Pappy, and back at me. "Would you like to expand on those words, just a little."

"Yes. Seeds. Let's not forget that agriculture in Iraq goes back thousands of years. They've been planting seeds to produce virtually every kind of grain you can think of. With each harvest, farmers traditionally set aside and store seeds, and they vary and blend them with every planting, so that each new crop is naturally disease and pest resistant. Farmers store their own seeds, but should that storage be depleted, because of drought—like the one that's been going on for the last three years—or should it be obliterated—due to aerial bombings and missile strikes, as happened in 1991 and every year after, and as will happen again soon—then farmers turn to the Ministry of Agriculture, which keeps a huge national seed bank in a city called Abu Ghraib. When we invade Iraq, that bank will disappear. The government will have nothing to offer—except the supply of seeds that our corporations will provide."

I paused and watched smiles come to the lips of every man in the audience.

Pappy asked, "Who's our point man on all this?"

"An Under Secretary of Agriculture, who's a former VP of Global Grains. He'll be our agriculture czar."

"And he reports to?"

"To me and to Brunswald."

"So," Earle snickered, "you'll have a czar reporting to you?"

"Yeah. And the czar will report to a proconsul, too."

Minor laughed. "You Americans. Forgive me, but you just reassemble history any way you want. *Pax Americana*, Roman proconsuls, Russian czars …"

Coker smiled at him. "And British prime ministers."

Pappy said, "Let's move on, Dick."

"Brunswald will issue an order on intellectual property rights that will include something we'll call the Plant Variety Protection Provision, or the PVP. This provision will prohibit farmers from re-using seeds of protected varieties."

Pappy asked, "What the hell are 'seeds of protected varieties?'"

"For the most part, GMOs—genetically modified organisms, or plant seeds, developed and patented by our corporations, such as Global Grains. The catch is this: farmers desperate to find seeds after the seed bank at Abu Ghraib has disappeared will find nothing but the patented seeds of our corporations. USAID will provide those seeds free through the Ministry. Iraqi farmers can get the same seeds from our private seed companies that will replace the Iraqi state enterprises, such as the Mesopotamia Seed Company. Our people will also market the benefits of our 'miracle seeds,' which will produce much larger crops."

"So, what's the catch?" one of the CEOs asked.

"The catch is that farmers cannot re-use the seeds and they'll find themselves in the same situation the next year. And the next. Only the seeds will no longer be free. And the farmers will also have to buy our corporations' fertilizers, as well as our pesticides and herbicides, because these plants will be highly vulnerable. Our corporations will play an increasingly important role in agriculture, and Iraq, which was a major exporter of food until 1991, will become *the* major exporter in the Middle East."

Heads nodded.

"I'll be going to St. Louis to visit with the CEO at Global Grains in a couple weeks, and after that, the CEOs of the other Ag corporations that will be working with us, just to make sure we've anticipated everything." I paused for dramatic effect. "Gentlemen, we will soon be sowing the seeds of democracy in Iraq."

Laughter erupted.

"The other word I mentioned is security. I've been in meetings with Don Reynolds. The Department of Defense will be outsourcing security for most U.S. government personnel. Some of you are aware of this. As soon as the invasion is complete and we begin taking over all sectors of the economy, we'll have to deal with security. Secretary Reynolds wants to develop this industry, and Iraq gives us the opportunity to do just that, and on a scale never publicly discussed in this country." I fixed my eyes on Pappy and Coker. I wanted them to understand I was privileged with information that came directly from Reynolds. "We own a good share of the weapons industry. It only makes sense that we would at least partner with an organization that will provide the men who will someday use the weapons we produce."

A few puzzled looks.

"Forgive me. I'm jumping ahead of myself." I paused, and then continued. "In my conversations with Reynolds, he said we'll be going into Iraq with a hundred and seventy thousand of our men. The Brits will contribute another forty-five thousand. That's basically the invasion force. As soon as we pass from the invasion to the occupation, we'll begin moving in people from State, the Pentagon, and various other departments and agencies. Rather than use our military to provide security for them, we'll instead use private contractors."

"And who," Coker interjected, arching his eyebrows, his Texas drawl as warm and smooth as molasses on a hot summer day, "who are these private contractors?"

"There are several. But one is particularly promising: Global Security, or GS. Headed up by a man named Donald King."

One of the CEOs asked, "And who is Donald King?"

Earle chuckled. "I can tell you haven't run for president." He glanced in Pappy's direction, and then scanned the table. "The Kings of Pennsylvania have made significant contributions to our last six presidential campaigns."

"And more to the point for us," I said, "King has already set up a training area for SWAT teams, complete with firing ranges and the like. But he can do a lot more. He's a former Navy Seal, with good connections."

"And he's politically clean," Earle said, looking again down the table toward Pappy. "This guy's a member of the Sovereign Military Order of Malta."

Bartolli scrunched up his face and shook his head. "Sounds like something out of *The Da Vinci Code!*" He snorted a laugh.

"The Sovereign Military Order of Malta ..."

While Earle blathered on in his supercilious tone about the Christian organization founded in the Middle Ages, my mind wandered to the day Elliott and I visited the headquarters of GS, just across the North Carolina border from Virginia. While Elliott drove, I stared out the window at the dense layers of kudzu covering the trees along the edge of a forest. We entered the grounds of GS and passed a swamp. Trees, some of them stripped of foliage and naked as corpses, stood stoically in the dead water, waiting to fall. I lowered my window, saw the water was as black as it appeared through the tinted glass, and breathed the smell of rotting vegetation. A woodpecker hammered away, the toc-toc echoing in the stillness. A heron flew toward us, its wings rising and falling slowly, and landed on a skeletal limb protruding just above the surface. We entered a clearing on a gentle slope, with a manicured lawn as perfect as a golf course. At the top of the slope stood the lodge, a two-story log structure with large windows, and behind and off to either side, several log buildings that must've been the dormitories mentioned on the website.

Elliott chuckled. "Rustic rich!"

The reflection of our black Lexus glided across the tinted windows of the lodge.

When we entered King's office, he stood up from behind his desk and walked toward us, his gait suggesting a powerful, compact body beneath his gray suit. He had a square face, short-cut brown hair, and a solid military look. I commented that his headquarters were closer to DC than I'd thought. He said, "Close enough to the action, far enough away to appear independent."

Enlargements of aerial photographs of the GS site adorned the walls of his office, along with mediocre portraits of Robert E. Lee and Douglas MacArthur. The American flag and another, which I assumed to be that of North Carolina, stood behind the desk, on either side. Between the flags hung a crucifix on the wall. The windows beyond the flags on both sides looked out upon a gravel road that bordered a marsh and led to higher ground with tall pine trees. He boasted about everything the lodge and the adjacent buildings had to offer, such as meeting rooms, a cafeteria, a chapel, a weight room, and a swimming pool. "And then, of course, there's what's out there." He gestured toward one of the windows. "Over thirty thousand acres of marshland, swamp, and what I call jungle terrain. And other areas just as naked as the desert. Perfect for our needs."

Elliott said, "But no one else's. So you got them for a good price."

Donald smiled. "The Lord takes care of those who do his work."

I said, "You have a close relationship to the Lord."

"He and I are like one and the same family. Of course, it's because of the Lord that you're here. He has a higher purpose for me than just training SWAT teams."

"Just think of me as the Lord's messenger," I said. "You've apparently been very successful at recruiting our own Special Operations Forces, after they've left the military."

"I can bring in Seals, Rangers, you name it. I can also assemble my own coalition of the willing—the very willing, from Chile, El Salvador, Guatemala, Nicaragua, and Argentina. Most of them trained by us." He paused and smiled. "I understand you've got quite a background in South America. I've heard you've done pretty well for yourself."

"Everyone did well."

"That's a good sign."

"You can't lose. We can't lose. That's Iraq. Win-win for everyone."

King nodded. "We'll introduce them to a superior religion and a superior culture. They should count themselves lucky."

"Yeah," I said. "Lucky them."

At the end of the meeting, I paused to look out the window at the marsh beneath the late morning sun. I could imagine the buzz of flies and mosquitoes, the whirr of dragonfly wings, frogs resting on lily pads, and a water moccasin gliding across the floating mounds of muck. I turned away, and the American flag and the crucifix again caught my eye.

My mind drifting back to the Advisory Board meeting, I heard a voice saying Donald King would've signed onto the Project for a New American Century's Statement of Principles, if he'd had the opportunity, and I saw the board members still focused on Earle, nodding their heads.

Peter said, "Thank you, Jonathon, for giving us a sense of Mr. King's commitment. Dick, would you please continue."

"As I was saying … once the invasion is complete, we'll start giving out contracts for security. Several of them will go to GS. Iraq will provide an opportunity for GS and the other security companies to recruit people, deploy them, generate revenue, and grow. GS might send only ten thousand men the first year of the occupation. But that number will increase."

Someone asked, "Where are GS and the other companies going to get the men?"

"King has good contacts with a lot of former special forces types," I said.

Bartolli chimed in, his gaze circling the table as he talked. "A lot of Seals, Rangers, and guys who served in the other special-forces units are Top Gun-Rambo wannabes. You've seen them in the movies—wrap-around sunglasses, tight T-shirts, bulging biceps, and the M-16 in the crook of their arm pointed in the air like an appendage." He shook his head and chuckled at the stereotype. "They're in the movies. Only they're not. They're stuck in the real world. They'll sign up in a flash with one of the security companies if they know it'll put them back in their movies. The adrenaline rush is everything. Add good money"—he shook his head—"and they'll fight to get to the front of the line."

Coker looked at me and said, "Jonathon has made it clear we can trust King politically. Are you certain we can trust his competence to get the job done?"

"Based on all the information we have about him, I believe we can. But, as I've pointed out, he's not our only option."

Coker nodded. "I think I know where all this is heading, but I'd like you to spell it out. So tell us what Reynolds is planning and how GS will fit in."

"Reynolds has spoken over the last year about the President developing an elite private military force of fifty to one hundred thousand, over which Congress wouldn't have any oversight. We think GS is one of the most promising companies that might develop that force. As I said, it'll deploy only about ten thousand men the first year of the occupation; but we think they can increase that to twenty thousand the next year, thirty thousand the year after that. We'll continue growing GS, and other security companies, too, all of which are headed up by men with impeccable political credentials."

Earle smiled his satisfaction.

"Iraq will enable us to develop a force that will be outside of Iraqi law, outside the Military Code of Justice, outside the purview of Congress, and outside American law. We will eventually be able to use that force as an arm of our president's foreign policy."

"This president's term is up in two years," Coker shot back. "What happens to plans for those Rambo wannabes if he doesn't win re-election?"

"First, we make sure he wins. I think we have enough power assembled around this table to make that happen. Second, we assess the hardware GS and the other companies will require to be the kind of rapid-deployment force we need and we outfit them."

Bartolli asked, "You're talking about helicopters and weapons systems?"

"Yeah."

Coker interjected, "You know, Congress has oversight authority of our military industries. They'll want to snoop."

"They might want to, but we know if key members have a shared interest in our endeavor, they'll cooperate. Isn't that what we've learned in our business relationship with Saudi Arabia?" I looked directly at the Prince. "If we all share in the profits, we can develop a very lucrative business—that'll be nobody's business but our own."

The Prince nodded in agreement. No one needed more clarification.

"Our goal is to have a force that we can use as an arm of our foreign policy, with our president in the White House. That foreign policy will generate more business for us, and the use of our force, when necessary, will keep our business private." I looked at Coker. "In the event that, someday, we have a president who's not of our choosing, well ..." I shrugged and spread my hands, mimicking that baffled president. "Everything will be in place, people will be making money, and there'll be little he can do."

Coker asked, "Do you actually mean that we, the Lowell Group, might send a private army that we have hired to, say, overthrow a government to advance our economic interests?"

"I'd say that depends on the government and on our interests. But, yes, if everything lined up in a certain way, that's what I'm saying."

Bartolli asked, "And if this rapid-deployment force gets in over its head, do we have another Bay of Pigs?"

"No comparison between that and the kind of force I'm talking about. Our men will have been trained with the most sophisticated weaponry and helicopter gunships in the world. And eventually we'll have about a hundred thousand men."

"You can't recruit a hundred thousand former special forces," Bartolli said. "There aren't that many."

"There are," I said, "if we recruit beyond our borders."

Pappy said, "Congress is not going to look the other way for long. At some point, it will attempt to reassert itself."

"We own much of Congress already," I said. "The only question is whether we own enough."

"That's the real issue," Pappy said. "I'd feel more confident if we owned more."

The Prince spoke for the first time. "I think history bears out what Mr. Rayburn is saying: that if the right people are sharing in the profits—whether those people are from different parties, or different countries—the business endeavor will succeed. Saudi Arabia, for example, will condemn the invasion of Iraq, but the people whose views count support removing Saddam Hussein and opening up Iraq's economy."

"Gentlemen, do you have any questions?" I asked.

The men looked around the table and back at me, shaking their heads.

"Well then, I'd like to conclude my presentation by saying that in the near future, Iraq will be open for business."

The board members applauded, and the admiration I saw in their eyes made me feel I was now one of them.

They broke into small groups to chat. I was thanking Peter for his glowing introduction, when I felt someone touch my arm. I turned and saw the Prince. He looked as if he'd just stepped off his yacht and had somehow managed to assimilate and personify the sunshine and the energy of the Mediterranean *joie de vivre*. He shook my hand and smiled, as if we were the closest of friends. "Dick, it's so good to see you."

I felt flattered at this suggestion of friendship, given that we'd met just a few times, but quickly tempered my excitement by recalling the Prince was known for being expansive in his efforts to make people feel liked. He had earned a reputation for being an adroit salesman, capable of convincing the King of Saudi Arabia, American administrations, and powerful members of Congress to make agreements that no one else could have. Agreements from which he profited.

The Prince gestured toward the living room. "Shall we sit down?" He guided me to a sofa. "How is Alex doing?"

"Fine. His health isn't quite what it used to be, but he's still in good spirits."

"I visited him in the hospital after he had that stroke a year ago. He was very weak. Could hardly talk." The Prince shook his head. "You know, this business of ours is so demanding, sometimes one forgets to do the things that are really important, like staying in touch with Alex. We started working together thirty years ago. He gave me good advice and introduced me to important members of the administration and Congress." The Prince got a wistful smile on his face. "We accomplished a lot together. To show him my appreciation, I offered him my yacht one summer. I think it was in 1978. He took me up on my offer, but only for a couple weeks. He wanted to take his daughter, Valerie—you're married to Valerie, right?"

I nodded.

"Yes, I remember Alex telling me that. Well, he wanted to take Valerie and some friends of hers on a cruise. And during the cruise, Alex and I met …"

I remembered sailing on the yacht with Maria and Valerie, lying on a deck chair, staring up at the seagulls, their white wings in the blue sky, feeling the rocking of the boat and smelling the sea air.

"I was wondering," the Prince continued, "if you and Valerie and your family would like to join my wife and me on my yacht next summer. We'd love to have you."

"Yes, definitely. We'd love to."

"Dick," a voice said.

I looked and saw Pappy, with Coker on one side and Peter on the other. The Prince and I rose, and Pappy shook my hand and said, "Excellent presentation. You'll do a fine job representing our interests in Iraq."

"Mr. President, with your knowledge and experience informing our decisions, I know we'll succeed."

The five of us stood together, beaming and exclaiming our confidence in our success and boasting what it would do for the Middle East. Pappy and Coker left, and the Prince shook my hand, invited me to get together with him for lunch, and followed them out. As I watched him leave, I thought, *I'm working with a prince and a president,* and chuckled to myself.

On the flight home, I was elated by my success at impressing all those powerful men, and feeling I belonged with them, but it didn't take long for thoughts about what I'd done during that meeting, what I was participating in, to seep into my mind, and once again I performed my balancing act, reminding myself that in the end the people of Iraq would benefit from my actions, and so too would my children and Valerie. I sighed and looked out the window at the blue sky and the clouds below and soon felt again that I was flying high. And as the sky darkened, I imagined Valerie's response, the love in her eyes as she drew me close.

CHAPTER 11

VALERIE RETURNED HOME TO take me to my physical-therapy appointment. Sitting next to her as she drove in silence, I waited to speak until we were well on our way, so she'd be trapped in the car. I wanted to hear what she had to say, but I had things to say, too.

"You remember the presentation I gave to the Lowell Group, just a few months before the invasion?"

She kept her eyes on the road and remained silent.

"Well, I remember, and how you responded when I called you after it was over. You laughed and shouted, 'You and the former President! And the Prince wants to take us sailing with him on his yacht, and bring the kids!' Remember that?"

I waited again for her to respond, but she said nothing.

"In the plane and the cab on the way home, I kept thinking about celebrating with you. I couldn't wait to see your face, see the pride and the love in your eyes. It was late when I got home, and the kids had already gone to bed. You poured us a cognac and had me tell you everything about the meeting. And then we went upstairs. You were giggling and pulled me by my tie into our room. You said you were going to give me the best fuck of my life. Valerie, I never kept any secrets from you. So, you're just as complicit in this Lowell-Group thing as I am. And if you're not going to speak to me, then you're a hypocrite."

She looked at me with contempt. "Keep it up, and I'll park the car and call a cab, and you can get yourself to your appointment."

"If anything happens to Jamie, you're just as responsible as I am." I paused. "Do you hear me?"

We arrived at the physical-therapy center. The PT did a double-take when he saw my face and tried to avoid looking at it again. He had me work with several weight machines and repeated, "Motion is lotion," each time I grimaced. After showing me some exercises I could do at home, he told me I'd done good work and he'd see me in a few days. As I was leaving the weight room, I noticed Valerie through the window in the door, walking back and forth, talking on her phone and smiling. When I opened the door, she saw me, and the smile disappeared. She said something into her phone and put it in her purse.

"Who were you talking to?"

"None of your business." After we'd taken a few steps down the hall, she said, "I was talking to my father."

I glanced at the side of her face, but couldn't tell if she was being honest.

By the time we got home, I was exhausted. She went upstairs, and I collapsed on the armchair in the corner of the living room. I thought of lying down on the couch, but I was afraid I'd fall asleep and dream, and Fallujah would come back. I stared at the couch where Jamie and I had sat, watching "Shock and Awe" on television. I'd put my arm around him, and he'd leaned into me and fallen asleep. As I gazed at the couch, the evening of the invasion of Iraq came back. But the invasion wasn't the big event of the day. No, that was Julia's performance in the school play.

Valerie, in a black dress, was standing in the foyer, at the entrance to the dining room, her back turned toward me as I came down the stairs and stopped to listen to her talk on the phone. "He's upstairs getting dressed," she said. "What? Of course you are, Dad." She placed her hand on her hip. "Julia will be devastated if you don't come." Valerie started walking into the dining room. "He's been so busy, he probably didn't get a chance to call." She turned around and saw me. With her hand over the phone, she sighed and said, "Would you please talk to him?"

I looked at my watch. "We're going to see each other in an hour."

She tilted her head, gave me an irritated, imploring look, and handed me the phone.

I took it and crooned, "Alex. How good of you to call."

"Hi, Dick. I called the night before last, after the President's speech about the invasion, but the line was busy. And I don't have your cell number."

Valerie continued watching me, making sure I was kind to the old man. I turned around, walked through the foyer and into the living room, and paced back and forth.

"Well, you know, teenagers. They're always talking on the phone. They've been after us to get them cell phones, but—"

"I thought the President did a great job. Just a really great job reassuring the nation about who we are as a people and why we had to do this."

Alex had obviously rehearsed his comments. But he was right. The President had said all the right things. And in the right way—sitting at his desk, looking at America with his big puppy eyes, telling us what we wanted to hear: "We are a good, noble people. We didn't want this war, we didn't seek it, and we are going to war with great reluctance." Well, he hadn't felt any reluctance. He'd wanted this war from the day after 9/11—maybe earlier—and the neocons had wanted it for years. Weapons of mass destruction, an alliance between Al Qaeda and Saddam—as Peter had said, lies to take the country to war.

"And, Dick, you played a huge role in selling the war to the nation. I mean, your line—'We don't want the smoking gun to be a mushroom cloud.' Brilliant, Dick. Just brilliant."

"The mushroom cloud worked so well in '64, against Goldwater, and it looks like it's working just as well now." I paused. "But I didn't come up with it. Someone else did. In a meeting of the Advisory Board. Then Jonathon Earle repeated it to the President's speech-writer, who brought it to a meeting of the WHIGs, and first thing you know, the National Security Adviser's using it on TV, and now the President uses it." And Hans Blix would allude to it a few days later, when he'd state that none of his inspectors had found any smoking guns in Iraq.

"Well, even if you didn't come up with it, we're lucky to have you on our side."

"Thanks, Alex."

Sometimes I felt Alex thought of me as a member of his family, someone of whom he wanted to feel proud, as if I were his son. And sometimes I felt he was just sucking up. Once he'd become a grandfather and fallen in love with his grandkids, I had him by the balls. I could squeeze them anytime I wanted, simply by controlling access to the kids, and make him sing like a castrato. He treated me with respect, even if he didn't feel any.

"I'm bringing this up now," he said, "because we have to be careful around innocent ears. Sometimes young people are too emotional to see the big picture."

I thanked him again, we said goodbye, and I handed the phone back to Valerie.

"He called because he was afraid you wouldn't be nice to him," she said.

"I'm always nice to him."

"Huh! That's why he's afraid of you? Because you're always nice to him?"

I followed her through the dining room and into the kitchen. "Well, I am, damn it!"

She slammed the phone down on its base. "He tried getting ahold of you all day yesterday at the office, and you didn't return his calls. That's being nice?"

"You know I've been busy."

"I know how hard it is for you to be decent to someone who's helped you so much."

"What?"

"You know what I'm talking about."

"I'm perfectly capable of being decent to someone who's helped me. But Alex—"

She glared at me.

"Yeah. Okay."

I used to go on tirades about her father treating me as if I owed him my life. She'd side with the old man, say maybe I did, and remind me of the job he'd given me in his company. I'd retaliate by saying I'd paid Alex back a thousand times over, and what did I get? And then I'd bring up the way he'd abused Elliott. So heartless. She'd respond by saying her father was not abusive, and I'd say his callous insensitivity to the pain he inflicted on others was abuse in my book. By the time we'd get to the end of one of those arguments, we'd be screaming at one another, and she'd be crying. We'd learned when to stop.

She asked me to call the kids and tell them to set the table.

I stood at the foot of the stairs and shouted, and when they didn't come, I went up, headed for Julia's room, and knocked on the door. No answer. I knocked again. Still no answer. I opened the door. She was sitting in bed, looking at her script, a wire going from the earbuds she was wearing to the iPod next to her. I was still getting used to her new hair style—permed so it cascaded in waves to a froth of curls above her shoulders, like a young woman from the 1940s, like Mom in pictures I'd seen of her. The sight of her adrift in her world of music, reviewing her lines, unwound the tension inside me. My little girl, in her jeans and blouse, looked so adult, and it just wasn't the makeup she'd started to wear. She often had a far-away gaze, as if part of her had already moved on to an exciting future, and the other part, still here, wanted to join that future. The beautiful masks on her walls from Venice and New Orleans, and the posters for *Rent* and *Wicked* and other Broadway productions suggested the star she was following.

I sat down on the bed. She pulled off the earbuds.

"Hi, precious. Got your lines memorized?"

"I've had them memorized for days."

"What time is Ben picking you up?"

"Six-thirty."

"That's in forty-five minutes. Dinner will be ready soon. Your mother wants you downstairs right away."

I crossed the hall to Jamie's room. The door was ajar. I gently pushed it, so he wouldn't notice me. He was lying on his belly, propped up on his elbows, reading a book. I glanced at his posters of soccer players—Pelé, Ronaldo, Zidane, and others whose names I didn't know—and framed photographs of the teams he'd played on—the Bethesda Boys Club and his high school teams. I approached the bed and, when I was standing above him, asked what he was reading. He rolled over on his side, a wing of sandy brown hair falling toward the corner of his eye. I was tempted to brush it back, but that's what Valerie would've done, and one mother was enough.

"*Animal Farm.*"

"Ah! 'All animals are equal, but some are more equal than others.' Well, it's time for us to pig out. Come on, dinner's almost ready."

"You've read this?"

"Yeah. I think I was a senior in high school."

"What did you think of it?"

"That was a long time ago." Jamie looked at me with such reverence, it made me uneasy how much my opinion meant to him. I had to be careful how I worded things. I couldn't tell him that Orwell might've written the novel as an allegorical satire of Stalinist Russia, but, when I was seventeen, I'd read it as a satire of the United States. So I said, "I think it's a great book."

"Why?"

"Because the allegory describes something so complex so simply, and then sums it up perfectly with that one line, all people are equal, but some are more equal than others."

"Animals."

"That's right—animals. Come on. Your mother's waiting for us."

As I headed downstairs, the doorbell rang. I opened the door and looked down at Alex. Not even a half-hour, and here he was.

The once powerful man hazarded a tentative smile. "May I come in?"

I feigned a joyful reception. "Of course, Alex."

He extended his knuckled hand and whispered, "Congratulations again, Dick." His conspiratorial grin irritated me, as if just knowing about what I'd done made him part of it.

I took his coat. "I'd offer you a drink, but Julia has to get to school for the play. She's supposed to be there an hour before the curtain goes up."

We started for the kitchen, when Julia appeared on the stairs.

"There she is! How's my little princess?"

"Hi Grandpa," she exclaimed as she rushed toward him.

He threw his arms open and gave her a hug, pulled back and looked into her eyes and said, "I'm so proud of you. Your mother told me how excited you are. Our little thespian. That's the word, isn't it? Thespian? Now, what's the play called?"

Before she could answer, Jamie appeared, and Julia stepped aside so Alex could give him a hug, too.

"Hey! How's my favorite grandson!"

"I'm your only grandson."

The kids never seemed to tire of Alex's lame jokes. He looked at me with a twinkle in his eye, and I smiled back, seeing the love he felt for them.

Valerie appeared and greeted him with a hug. She suggested he go with me to the living room and I'd fix him a drink, while the kids set the table for dinner.

Alex grinned at me. "I guess I'll get that drink after all."

I accompanied him into the living room and gestured at the armchair at the end of the coffee table, while I went over to the liquor cabinet and poured us each a scotch. I handed him his drink and sat down in the chair at the opposite end. The thing that made sitting with him enjoyable was the pleasure I took in knowing he hated Dad's paintings on the walls. If Alex's eyes drifted to his left, toward the right side of the fireplace, he'd see one of them, *A Woman Alone*—a woman with long blond hair, standing in profile, in a bra and slip, isolated in a rectangle of light coming from a source beyond the frame that she's facing. A yellow curtain furling in a breeze confirms that a window is the source of that light. The woman looks as if she's in her thirties. Her forearm closest to the viewer is extended, and she holds a cigarette between her fingers, smoke rising from it. Between her and the wall in the background, a bed, a red dress tossed across the middle of it, the white sheet and blue cover pulled back from the pillow. Beneath the bed, a pair of high heels that look as if she carelessly kicked them there. The woman is standing just left of center, in the rectangle of light, and her shadow extends behind her, to the end of the rectangle and the edge of the frame. She looks isolated, framed and reframed, and every time I'd look at her, I'd see a woman trapped.

When the chitchat with Alex about the weather ended, he stared at the painting and frowned, and his nose wrinkled, as if he'd gotten a whiff of something that stank. Alex liked pretty paintings, works that were, as he would say, pleasing to the eye. I always had him sit in the same chair, so that his eye would land sooner or later on something with an edge. He looked at me, forced a smile, and tossed down his scotch. Jamie came in to announce dinner was ready.

We sat down at the dining-room table, toasted Julia, our budding actress, passed the platters and bowls of food around, and started eating.

"People my age remember everything that happened sixty years ago," Alex said, "but can't remember what they did yesterday. I can't remember the name of that play."

"*All My Sons*," Julia said.

"Oh! That's it! Maybe I can't remember it because I've never had any sons. And I've never heard of it before. Who wrote it?"

"Arthur Miller."

"Oh. Did he write *Death of a Salesman*?"

"Yes," Julia said.

"You know." Alex looked around the table. "I thought that was the only play he'd ever written. You see, I learn so much from my grandchildren." He looked at Julia. "Now, you said you play a young lady two men are in love with."

"Yes. I play Annie."

"And two young men are jealous over her? Over you? I'm not surprised."

"Actually," Julia said, "she's the fiancée of a young fighter pilot named Larry, who gets killed in the war."

I looked up from my salmon, took a sip of wine, and asked, "Which war?"

"World War II."

"Well, Princess," Alex asked, "what's the play about?"

The doorbell rang.

"That's Ben!" Julia sprang to her feet. "I've got to go."

Valerie said something about her not having eaten anything, and we all shouted good luck as she rushed off to greet her boyfriend, the door slamming behind them.

Tears welled up in Valerie's eyes.

"She'll do well," I said.

"I know she will. She always does. I don't know why I get like this."

"Of course she'll do well," Alex chimed. "She's a brilliant girl. Smith is so lucky to be getting her." He looked at Jamie. "That makes four generations. My mother, my sister, my daughter. And now my granddaughter is going to Smith. Which reminds me, where have you decided to go? Harvard, Princeton, or Yale?"

"I don't know," Jamie said.

"Alex," I said, "he's still got a year to decide."

"I'm pulling for Yale, my alma mater."

"You can pull all you want, Alex. He'll make his own decision. And, I haven't had a chance to tell you yet. Julia has accepted the offer from Fordham. She wants to be in New York."

Alex stared at me with his mouth open, then looked down at his plate.

As I drove us home, I was preoccupied by the play we'd seen, about a man named Joe, whose son commits suicide during the war by crashing his fighter plane on the coast of China.

"That poor mother," Valerie said. "What a horrible thing to have to see."

"She didn't actually see it," I said.

"If I were her, I'd see it every day of my life."

We came in the house, and Valerie and Alex sat down in the living room—Alex in the same armchair he'd sat in before dinner, and Valerie on the couch facing the coffee table. Jamie returned from the kitchen with a Coke and plopped down next to her.

Standing at the liquor cabinet, pouring three glasses of cognac, I asked Alex what he thought of the play.

"My little princess performed magnificently. Just magnificently."

"She did," Valerie said. "She really made you feel what that poor girl went through."

I served Alex. When I handed Valerie her glass, she looked up and smiled through a haze of sadness. I bent over and kissed her on the forehead, wishing I could make her happy. She sighed and took a drink. I sat down in the armchair facing Alex and said, "Julia's performance tonight confirmed what I've thought for a long time. She's so gifted, she can take on any role."

Valerie said, her voice seething with disgust, "Why would the school put on such a horrible play? This is high school!" She took another drink.

"I agree," Alex said. "The play was totally inappropriate for high-school kids."

"The school could've chosen something entertaining," Valerie said, "like *Arsenic and Old Lace*, or *A Midsummer Night's Dream*. Something that would've been fun for the kids to do and for the families to watch."

"Maybe you should talk to the principal," Alex said.

"Can't you just see Julia playing one of those old spinsters," I said, chuckling at the image of Julia wearing a white wig and dressed up as a sweet, homicidal old woman. "She could really get into it."

"Oh, I can see that," Alex said.

"Or, how about Lady Macbeth," I said. "Julia playing one of Shakespeare's greatest roles."

"Is she the one who says, out, out, damned spot, or something like that?" Alex asked.

"Yeah," I said.

"Sounds like a frustrated cleaning lady," he said.

I laughed with Alex and glanced over at Valerie, sitting quietly on the couch, lost in thought, her glass already empty. All our glasses were empty, even though I'd poured generously. We were drinking our cognac faster than usual. I went to the liquor cabinet, got the cognac, filled our glasses again, left the bottle on the table, and sat down.

Valerie said, "I don't understand why people have to make up this kind of stuff. It's disgusting."

Alex said, "Let's not forget, this is just a play. It's just theater."

I thought about the end of the play, felt the father's suicide was just too much, and nodded in agreement. "He's right, Valerie. It's so far-fetched, no one should take it seriously."

She took a drink and stared at the fireplace.

The cognac had calmed the emotions the play had stirred in me, and I was beginning to feel pretty good. I'd hit that zone, like when you're in a plane, you take off, it's kind of rough, the seat-belt lights are on, and then the plane reaches thirty thousand feet, levels off, and the pilot's voice says, "You are now free to walk around the cabin." My mind was walking with total abandon. Quite common for me at night. I generally kept my life well lubricated, so the gears wouldn't grind. Scotch when I got home from work, wine with dinner, and cognac afterwards.

I leaned back into my armchair and admired Dad's paintings. *Woman Alone* was one of my favorites. She seems to have forgotten the cigarette in her hand as she stares in the direction of the window. But she isn't looking at the window. She's looking at something inside her. Something she feels. Like being trapped and knowing there's no way out. Was she an office worker, struggling to survive on a lousy salary? Or a prostitute, with little to hope for? Or just a woman exhausted by life? Or had she suffered some kind of irreparable loss?

Like Mom, after Dad died. She had served as the model, the blonde hue of the woman's hair concealing to some extent Mom's identity. Painters who didn't have money used their wives as models, Dad explained to me, when I was shocked to recognize her in another painting. As his words came back, I felt again the void they would never fill. I took a deep breath, and my eyes wandered to his *Eurydice*, on the other side of the fireplace, and then to the paintings on the opposite wall—*City of Shadows*, in which a boy, who seems to be nothing but a shadow, runs alongside a building's darker shadow, toward the light in an opening and the shadow of a tall, ominous figure, and *Nocturnal Light*, a wood-frame house, seen at night from a street lamp, with daylight above and in the background, and a blue sky and puffy clouds. The eerie nocturnal light haunts the day and makes the sunlight, the lovely serene blue of the sky, appear fake. I'd hired a guy to track down Dad's paintings and find a way to buy them. With each one, I was putting him back together and bringing him home.

"It has nothing to do with reality," Alex said. "In the real world—"

"What has nothing to do with reality?" I asked.

"The play we saw tonight. In the real world, Joe would've told his foreman to stop production, pull back all the flawed parts, fix the problem, and start production again. But this writer—what's his name?"

"Arthur Miller, Grandpa."

"Yeah, Miller. I keep forgetting his name."

"I find everything about Joe repugnant," Valerie said. "Allowing someone else to go to prison, just to save his own skin." She shook her head. "He's repulsive."

Jamie said, "The thing I don't get is all these people act as if they don't know what Joe did. But nearly all of them do. So why don't they just say—"

"I remember Mother saying Marilyn Monroe committed suicide because of Arthur Miller," Valerie said. "She was married to him, and he was so depressing, so negative, she finally killed herself. I remember Mother saying that." Valerie took another drink.

Alex said, "Miller, just to grind his ax, creates this phony story about an incompetent factory owner who causes the death of his own son and twenty other pilots. But what if Miller had actually dealt with reality—like the invasion of Iraq? Someone has to decide, do we risk the lives of a few hundred people to stop Saddam? Do we want to bring freedom, liberty, and democracy to the Iraqi people? Or do we want to spare those few who might die, allow that dictator to continue torturing and murdering his own people, while we run the risk of terrorists using his weapons to destroy us? Now that would be a play based on reality. Something you could take seriously."

"Dad," Valerie said, "didn't Mother say Marilyn Monroe killed herself because of Arthur Miller?"

"I don't know. And so what if she did?"

I was struck by the tension in Alex's voice. His ex was getting huge alimony payments and was now the sole owner of the apartment on Fifth Avenue.

"How long will the Iraq war last?" Jamie asked me.

"Oh, the invasion will probably take a few weeks. And then we'll leave some soldiers behind, while the Iraqis rebuild their country. Not many, because the Iraqi people will be happy to see us. After all, we're liberating them."

The sound of Jamie's voice brought Valerie back. She brushed his hair off his forehead, peered into his eyes, and told him he looked tired. He shook his head, No. Nevertheless, she put her hand on his head and pulled him toward her. Jamie pulled his head away and shrugged her arm off his shoulder. She gave up, poured herself another cognac, and gazed at the fireplace.

I gave my cognac another swirl and tossed it down.

Alex said, "Oh, my God, it's nearly midnight. I should be getting home."

The front door opened, voices whispered, there was a giggle, some more whispering, and the door shut. Julia entered with a smile and bouquets of flowers in her arms. She stopped, struck a pose, and said, "I am the next diva of ..." She paused, as if waiting for a drum roll, and then, with an exaggerated British accent, said, "... the theater."

Everyone laughed, even Valerie, who seemed to come back to life.

Julia held up the bouquets so they framed her face. "Look at them! Aren't they beautiful!"

Valerie sprang up. "They're gorgeous," she said, taking some of them in her arms. Mother and daughter sat down and set the flowers on the coffee table so they could read the cards together, while I gazed at the two women I loved.

I led Jamie off with me to fetch a bottle of champagne, a bottle of apple cider, and glasses. We returned, filled the glasses, and handed them about. I announced, "It's obvious from the applause she received, and from all the bouquets and the tributes on those cards, that our Julia is indeed the diva of high-school actresses. New York, look out!" We laughed and drank until the champagne and cider were gone and the kids had disappeared.

Alex teetered toward the front door, where he paused to say goodnight, and added, in a loud, drunk voice, "Now Val, I want you to be sure to put that play out of your mind. Remember, it's just theater, it has nothing to do with reality. That playwright has an ax to grind, and—"

"Dad, please. I don't want to hear any more about it."

Alex said, "All right, all right, but—"

"Please." And when he looked as if he might try to get in one more word, she repeated, "Please."

Alex nodded, said goodnight, and left.

Valerie stared at the closed door. I ran my fingers across her hair, and she looked at me with weary eyes and said she was going to bed. She started walking up the stairs, paused, put her hand to her head, and swayed. I rushed over and walked her up and into our room. She kicked off her shoes, unzipped her dress, let it fall to the floor, and her bra on top of it, pulled her nightgown out from under her pillow, put it on, and slipped beneath the covers. I sat down next to her and kissed her. She took my hand in hers and closed her eyes.

When I knew she was asleep, I picked up her clothes and laid them across a chair, went downstairs to the living room, and poured myself another cognac. The feeling of celebration had turned into something like mourning, apprehension. I shook my head, as if I were shaking off a bad dream, took a drink, opened the door of the cabinet that housed the television, and turned on CNN so I could watch the first day of the attack on Baghdad. I sat down on the couch, and a little while later Jamie joined me. Father and son, sitting together, watching the bombardment, as if it were a football game.

Missiles whistled like steaming tea kettles and burst in orange and red explosions that filled the screen, before giving way to billowing gray clouds accumulating above the fiery glow. We heard crackling bursts of gunfire and a steady thud-thud between the heavy explosions. A different video stream showed palm trees silhouetted against flaming buildings in the background, and, in the foreground, one- and two-story buildings eerily lit up from inside. And in yet another stream, the city seemed to emanate from a dark green sea, and explosions showed up as intense, shimmering halos of green light. Occasional titles at the top of the screen read, SHOCK & AWE UNDER WAY, and BAGHDAD UNDER HEAVY BOMBARDMENT. At the bottom of the screen, continuous titles scrolled horizontally with the latest reports, the acronym CNN functioning as a period.

A-DAY, THE DAY FOR "SHOCK AND AWE" CAMPAIGN, HAS BEGUN IN BAGHDAD CNN INTELLIGENCE OFFICIALS TOLD CNN THERE IS REAL CONVINCING EVIDENCE SADDAM HUSSEIN & HIS 2 SONS MAY HAVE BEEN INSIDE THE LEADERSHIP COMPOUND AT TIME OF THE ATTACK CNN WASH POST QUOTES AN ADMIN OFFICIAL SAYING THERE'S EVIDENCE

SADDAM HUSSEIN WAS INJURED BECAUSE MEDICAL
ATTENTION WAS URGENTLY SUMMONED ON HIS
BEHALF CNN.

For weeks, journalists, politicos, and generals had been using the
phrase "shock and awe," generating the kind of anticipation that
preceded a well-publicized Hollywood film. As a spectacle, Shock
and Awe outdid the pyrotechnics of the Fourth of July and Bastille
Day combined. Millions of people watched the images and heard
the explosions and gunfire. A major television event. The United
States was the only nation capable of putting on a show like that,
using Baghdad as a stage.

"Are there people in those buildings?" Jamie asked.

"The buildings appear to be empty." I put my arm around his
shoulder, and he leaned into me, as we continued watching the
spectacle, the flashes of light and color. "You have to remember,
Jamie, to keep your eye on the big picture. There will be casualties.
But the goal is a noble one."

CHAPTER 12

I AWOKE IN THE DARK, gasping for air, fleeing Fallujah. It was the same dream—the smoke and fumes of burning propane, the stink of corpses, the lieutenant screaming at me to get away from the bodies, they might be booby-trapped, the old man wailing and crying, the sergeant collapsing to his knees, sobbing, and the boy, his dark eyes staring at me, accusing me. I sat up in bed, panting, holding my head in my hands, trying not to see those eyes. I looked at the clock. After midnight. I fumbled around, found my cane, and hobbled into the hall. No light from beneath Valerie's door. I wanted to go into her room, but the dream had rattled me. And if I woke her, she'd be angry. She'd ridicule me.

I went downstairs to the kitchen and drank some water. When my breathing calmed, I collapsed in a chair and gazed at the skeletal form of the white trellis in the night, the broken stems of all the things that had died in the winter, and the cold statue of Aphrodite shining like a corpse. The war was getting to everyone. Even Peter, the man touched with fairy gold, had lost something. Marie-Thérèse had become increasingly suspicious about the Lowell Group's connections to the administration, and the closer we got to the invasion, the greater the tension between her and Peter. He'd say she was being too French and call her Mother Teresa, and she'd refer to him as *ce petit Napoléon* and serve him cold freedom fries for dinner. By the time of the invasion, when they divorced, she referred to him as *ce petit* Hitler. But she never called him a pathetic excuse for a father.

Peter probably came out of every shitty mess smelling as sweet as his cologne. Its fragrance was the first hint I had of his presence when he visited me in the hospital. A whoosh of air, and I knew he'd sat down in the chair, where Valerie sometimes sat, and another whoosh as the cushion inhaled when he stood up. He came close to the bed and assured me I had nothing to worry about, the Lowell Group was taking care of my family. *Nothing to worry about,* I thought, as he continued talking, *nothing other than dreams, the screams of the ghosts of Fallujah, and me, unable to see or move.* He talked about the Lowell Group moving on. "It's clear we won't be able to transform Iraq into that shining city on the hill, because this administration is incapable of the grandeur of vision that created the free world at the end of World War II. But the big losers are the Iraqi people. When that statue of Saddam was pulled down, it looked like the Middle-Eastern version of the Berlin Wall falling. Freedom was right there, ready for the Iraqis to grab. Instead of thanking us, they tried to kill us." For the first time, I heard bitterness in Peter's voice.

I didn't hear anything for a few minutes and wondered if he'd left. But then he started talking about what we'd accomplished in Iraq. "Between our partners and us, we've made billions in profits over the last eighteen months. Not too difficult, when you think of the way the Coalition Provisional Authority managed the money. People running around with bundles of thousand-dollar bills stuffed in suitcases and duffel bags. The DOD auditors wonder whatever happened to the $8.8 billion that seems to have disappeared." Peter chortled. Silence. And then he added that his son had started a Master's at Johns Hopkins, in the School of Advanced International Studies. "I told him I'd have a job waiting for him. He's an amazing young man." Peter touched my arm. "Dick, are you asleep?" After a long silence, I knew he'd gone.

I was with Valerie the day Jamie came back from Princeton to announce his big surprise. I was expecting something extraordinary, something I'd proudly relate to Elliott and my other colleagues.

Jamie was going to join Valerie and me for dinner, and that's when he'd tell us.

I walked into the kitchen to the smell of meat roasting in the oven. Valerie was slicing something on a cutting board. I put my arms around her waist, rested my cheek on her hair, and slid my hand across her belly. She laid the knife down and leaned back. I snuggled a kiss on her neck, and she giggled. She took a breath, picked up the knife, finished slicing the tomato, asked me to make some vinaigrette, and sipped her wine. I poured myself a scotch and started making the dressing, while she continued cutting up vegetables. It seemed like just another evening—we'd eat, talk, maybe watch a movie. But it wasn't, because we'd have Jamie.

"Where is he?" I asked.

"He used my car to go see his girlfriend. I just hope whatever it is he wants to announce is good news. And not ..."

"A pregnant girlfriend?"

"Oh, my God, I hope not."

The front door opened and shut. I set the cruet on the counter and followed Valerie toward the foyer. Jamie, still wearing his jacket, met us in the dining room.

"Hey! How's my boy?" I asked.

"Hi, Dad."

I gave him a hug, thrilled to hold him, and pulled back to see him grinning at me, his eyes sparkling. He was almost as tall as me and still growing, but just a boy, my boy.

"It's great to have you home," I said.

Valerie and I held him between us as we went into the living room, repeating how happy we were and asking him questions about his life on campus. Jamie and Valerie sat next to one another on the couch, and I sat on the armchair. As I gazed at them, I noticed how he resembled her—the thin face, the delicate features, and the graceful hands with their long fingers. How life was continuing from one generation to the next.

When things calmed down, I said, "Okay, Jamie, what's your announcement?"

He beamed. "I've joined the Army."

I heard the words, but couldn't understand them. I looked at Valerie. She was shocked, her mouth agape. I said, "Joined the Army?"

"Yeah, Dad. Aren't you happy?"

"Oh, my God," Valerie whimpered, bowing her head and sinking into the couch.

"I thought you'd be proud," Jamie said.

"Why?" I asked. "Why did you do this? I thought you love Princeton."

"I do. This has nothing—"

"So, why not stay and finish?" I asked.

"I can't. I've signed up."

"Well, we can get you unsigned. Do you realize how fortunate you are to go to Princeton? And then you throw that away!"

He looked into my eyes. "I had to join."

"No one has to join."

"You said we invaded Iraq because it's exporting terrorism. It has weapons of mass destruction. You told me Saddam used chemical weapons to gas thousands of Kurdish villagers. And now he's developing nuclear weapons."

I'd said those things, without realizing what he'd heard.

"I got so sick of listening to my friends at school saying we'd been lied into this war by a corrupt administration." He looked directly at me. "I knew you wouldn't be part of a lie. You wouldn't do something like that."

My head was floating. I felt cold and clammy and dizzy, like I was about to pass out.

He kept looking at me.

I managed to say, "No, I wouldn't do something like that."

Jamie nodded, pursed his lips, and fixed his eyes on me. "I hope I make you proud."

I nodded. "We are proud. Very proud. We're just … surprised."

He looked at Valerie. "Mom, are you all right?"

"Yes." She forced a smile. "It's like your father said. You took us by surprise. It's not every day you join the Army." She laid her hand on his.

"Thanks, Mom."

She wiped away tears and assumed a stern air. "But I want you to write every week."

"I'll email you."

"And," she continued, "I want you to learn everything you need to, so you can come home safe. That's all I want, Jamie, for you to come home safe. You promise?"

"I promise," he said with a smile. "Well, ah, I wonder if I could use one of the cars. My friends are throwing a party for me tonight."

"But your mom made dinner."

"I'm not hungry." He looked at Valerie. Her whole body seemed to have collapsed upon itself. "Mom, are you sure you're okay?"

"I'm fine." She smiled again. "You can take my car."

"I still have your keys."

She nodded.

"Okay. I'll be home before midnight."

As soon as the front door closed, I said, "I'm calling Reynolds first thing in the morning. He'll take care of this. Our son's never going anywhere he can be a target." My eyes landed on Valerie. She looked pale. "Are you okay?"

She stood up and walked toward the foyer. "I'm sleeping in the guest room tonight."

"What?" I caught up to her and grabbed her arm.

"Don't touch me."

A few days later, I sat across from Don Reynolds, the Secretary of Defense, at a table in the Lafayette Room at the Hay-Adams. His back toward a window, he had a vantage point from which he could survey the room and everyone in it. He leaned into his chair, like he was sitting on a throne, and took a drink of his precious scotch, Laphroaig, neat. He'd commented at a previous lunch that Prince Charles also thought it was the finest scotch in the world, remarkable for its smoky, peaty taste. Whatever Reynolds drank would necessarily be the finest. He brushed a wing of gray hair off his temple, and his eyes squinted at me through his wire-rimmed glasses. He had ashen skin and the look of a man who'd spent most of his life in closed rooms studying reports and maps and writing memos, cleverly crafting the wording. His narrow lips spread repeatedly in a boyish, cocky smirk, which looked weird on a seventy-year-old man. The President had won re-election, and Reynolds saw the victory as validation of his Iraq policy and a rebuke of his critics.

I'd gotten to know him in the 1980s, when I was still working for Alex. They had collaborated on some projects in the Middle East—primarily with Saudi Arabia, Iraq, and Iran—and Alex had introduced us. I met him again after I'd launched my own business. He was between administrations, serving as the CEO of a biotech company. We'd struck up a conversation at a reception in this same hotel, during which he'd praised my work with developing countries and the World Bank. In an off-handed way, while plucking a glass of champagne from a waiter's tray, he asked me if I might have some advice for his son, who'd recently taken over an oil company and was hoping to help countries develop their oil resources. I knew Reynolds would be serving again in someone's cabinet, so I arranged a contract with the government of Ghana that enriched the young Reynolds. And when I found out Reynolds's wife, Eloise, was a Smith alum and served on the alumnae association, I asked Valerie to become a member as well. Soon the four of us were dining and drinking together like friends.

Reynolds had come to trust me, and now I provided him with a sympathetic audience as he vented his contempt for his critics and justified his decisions, speaking just loud enough for me to hear over the sound of muffled voices and silverware clinking on china.

"Some of these critics claim that as no WMDs have been found, there are none. And therefore, the war is unjustified. First of all, we know Saddam Hussein had WMDs. Our intelligence was solid. But even if it weren't, we had to make a decision at the time based on the information we had. And based on that information, we made the right decision. If my critics were in a position where they had to make the decisions I've had to make, they'd understand. But they're not. They might also understand that absence of evidence doesn't mean evidence of absence. We know Saddam Hussein had a program to develop nuclear weapons. We know he had WMDs. But what the hell did he do with them? Destroy them? Hide them? And why did he insist on keeping his actions secret? These were some of the questions we asked him, after we'd captured him. We didn't get any answers. You know, this whole war could've been avoided if he'd just come clean, if he and his government had responded to our efforts to avoid the war. How could they've not known what the next steps would be? We made it clear. But he must've thought we were bluffing, we were a paper tiger and weren't going to do anything. But we did. The first Gulf War left him feeling no one was going to try to take him down. He felt he'd prevailed. He must've assumed he would again. So, we liberate Iraq, and the first thing you know, people are talking about Iraq being chaotic. A mess. Well, when people are liberated, when they can do what they want, stuff happens. Freedom's untidy, democracy's untidy, and free people are free to make mistakes, commit crimes, and do bad things, but they're also free to live their lives and do wonderful things. And that's what's going to happen."

As I listened to him talk, I saw the photographs in the media of two charred, mutilated bodies hanging from the green metal beams of a bridge in Fallujah and felt the hatred that had driven people to do the hanging. But Reynolds—someday he'd write a memoir. It would be very long. And he'd always be right. He would have always made the right decision, based on the best intelligence available. No apologies.

He leaned back and finished his scotch, and the little-boy smirk spread across his lips.

"How's Eloise doing?" I asked.

The smirk vanished, and he sighed. "I'm afraid she's not getting any better. The doctor told me yesterday it, ah, it might be time to start thinking about hospice. She's so doped up, I can't even talk with her." He took his glasses off and wiped his eyes with the back of his hand.

"Valerie and I—our thoughts and prayers are with Eloise and you." I reached across the table and touched his hand. "Don, let me know if there's anything I can do."

He took a deep breath. "Thanks, Dick. I appreciate it."

He noticed our waiter, nodded at his empty glass, and pointed at mine. He surveyed the room, as if his mind were far away, or was looking for something that wasn't there. After a while, his eyes landed on me. He said, "When you told me you wanted to get together for lunch, you mentioned something about your son."

"Yeah. He signed up with the Army."

"Good."

"Well, his mother thinks he's a little young. He's just a freshman in college and, you know how freshmen are, he didn't really think it through."

"Where does he go to school?"

"Princeton."

"Ah! That's where I went. A fantastic place to be at that age, when the only things you think about seriously are women, booze, and having fun."

"Yeah. What else is college for?" I smiled, like nothing was at stake.

The waiter served us our scotch. We both took a drink immediately.

"I'm afraid Jamie doesn't take after me. Not at all like the way I was in college. He's very serious. Kind of shy. Not really suited for the military. His mother, she'd die if anything happened to him."

"That's how parents feel about their boys."

Another waiter served Reynolds his salad, and me, the clam chowder I'd ordered.

Reynolds swallowed his first forkful and asked, "So, what do you want me to do?"

"Get him out."

"Out of the Army?"

"Yeah."

"No. Unless he's under eighteen, he joined, he's in."

"Well, is there someplace safe he can serve?"

Reynolds took a drink. "If you feel so strongly about this, let me check with the Chairman of the Joint Chiefs. He could maybe have a talk with the Army Chief of Staff. I don't think it'll be a big problem."

"Don, I can't thank you enough. Really."

"Happy to help a friend."

I finished my scotch and said, "I think I'll have another. You ready for one?"

He looked startled. He'd only drunk half of his. "Sure, why not. What are you drinking?"

"Bowmore."

"You should give the Laphroaig a try. You might like it."

"Why not?" I caught the waiter's eye and ordered two Laphroaig, neat.

After he walked away, Reynolds said, "I wonder, with the work you're doing in Iraq, if there isn't some way my son's oil company could be of service."

"You know, there might well be. Let me give some thought to that." I gave him a reassuring smile. "I suspect an opportunity might arise."

"Yes, opportunities do arise, don't they."

When our Laphroaig arrived, we toasted opportunity, and then another waiter served us our salmon.

A few days later, I got home from the office and found Valerie waiting for me in the living room. She played back a voice mail from Reynolds, with a phone number to call. I said, "He probably called to let us know where Jamie's going to be stationed."

"I'm going crazy wondering."

I punched the number into the phone. "He's going to be safe, wherever he ends up." The phone rang at the other end. "We should just be happy he's not going to Iraq or Afghanistan."

A female voice answered, and I said I was returning a call to Secretary Reynolds.

A long silence, and then Reynolds's voice. "Afraid I have some bad news. I talked with the Chairman about your boy. He didn't respond in a very positive way. But he did take it to the Chief of Staff. He dug in his heels. Yelled there were no goddamn champagne squadrons in his Army." He paused. "I'd hoped to have good news for you, Dick. I'm afraid your son's going to be treated like anyone else's."

I watched Valerie's face slowly collapse, as she saw my pain.

"You there, Dick?" he asked.

"I'm here."

"Sorry. That's the way it is."

"Yeah."

"Say, we need to talk about this Fallujah thing. I want you to have my secretary schedule an appointment with me before you go to Iraq. I'll transfer you back to her. And, Dick, I'm sorry about your boy, but we'll train him well. He'll come back to you."

"Yeah."

"So long, Dick."

The transfer didn't happen, and the line went dead. My eyes met Valerie's.

"They're not going to do anything for him, are they?" she asked.

I felt as if the blood had drained from my body. I collapsed into a chair.

She stood up, took a few steps, and glared at me. "What a pathetic excuse for a father."

Chapter 13

DISTANT RINGING PIERCED THE fog of my drugged sleep. A hand grabbed my shoulder and shook me, while a voice repeated my name. I knew before I opened my eyes I'd see Valerie glaring down at me, ready to call me pathetic.

I opened them and saw her face, her eyes wide with excitement.

"Jamie's on the phone."

"Jamie? Oh my God, Jamie!" I sat up and took the phone from her.

"I'll listen in downstairs."

"Jamie."

"Hey, Dad, how are you?"

"I'm fine, Jamie. How are you? Are you safe?"

"It's so good to hear your voice, Dad. I was worried. Every time I called, you were in a deep sleep. But Mom and Julia have been keeping me up to date. I can't wait to get home and see you."

"Thanks, Jamie. But, tell me, are you safe?"

"Dad," he said, chuckling, "this is like an eight to five job. Get up in the morning, eat breakfast, and then set out on patrol. Walk, walk, walk. The good thing is I'm getting lots of exercise. I'll be in great shape to play soccer when I get back."

"Do you play soccer over there?" Valerie asked on the phone downstairs.

"Hi, Mom. This isn't Oz. We're safe, but we don't kick the ball around in the streets."

We chuckled.

"My biggest complaint is I can't get any dates, you know. All the women who wear hijabs are off-limits. We're not even supposed to look at them."

"Well, if that's your biggest complaint," I said.

"Yeah, Dad, that and the boredom. The Army didn't plan anything in the way of entertainment. At least, not here in Anbar. No movies, bars, pool tables, nothing. Just patrols."

"Where do you usually go?" I asked.

"On patrol?"

"Yeah."

"Ramadi. A few times in Fallujah. That city's a mess. A lot of the buildings have walls blown away and collapsed roofs." He paused. "Dad, what were you doing there?"

"It's a long story. I'll tell you when you get back. But why were you there?"

"Just doing patrols. I've got to go." He paused. "I miss you. Miss you both."

"I miss you, too, Jamie," Valerie said. "Be careful, honey."

"Say hi to Julia for me. Okay? And don't worry about me. Like the guys in my squad say, I don't plan on becoming 'a sign of progress.'" He snickered.

"What?" Valerie asked. "A sign of progress?"

"It's just a joke, Mom. I'll explain when I get back."

I knew the joke, knew the gallows humor of the soldiers in Iraq and how Jamie had acquired it.

"Really, Mom, Dad, don't worry about me. I'm perfectly safe."

We said I love you and goodbye several times. I went downstairs and found Valerie in the kitchen, facing the counter where she'd hung up the phone, her eyes downcast.

"I'm so afraid," she murmured, without looking at me.

I moved closer to her. "I am, too." I placed my hands on her shoulders. "He'll come back. I know he will."

She slid my hands off her shoulders and left the kitchen.

A cardinal, so red, so beautiful in that faded, lifeless world, perched on a leafless branch outside the window. Such a small creature, how in the hell did it survive winter? How could it be so bright, so alive? The life of every living thing is so fragile, so easily ended.

That afternoon, I was in my room, lying on the floor doing leg lifts, when my phone rang. I knew it wasn't Jamie, so I ignored it. And then, after the fourth ring, I remembered Ron Wolffe and the message I'd left. I grabbed my phone and heard his voice and said, "Hi, Ron."

"How are you?"

"I'm fine, fine. I'm home, now."

"I was going to visit you in the hospital, and suddenly you were gone."

"Yeah, I escaped. After just four months of confinement." I tried to laugh, but my effort sounded phony.

"My secretary said you'd called about something urgent yesterday."

"Jamie, my son. He got it into his head he should join the Army. It was a reaction to what some of the kids at college were saying about the administration lying us into war, you know, all that crap, so he joined to prove he believed the war was the right thing to do and his dad wouldn't be part of a lie. But he's just eighteen, just a kid. He still reads *Harry Potter* and—"

"Well, I—"

"His mother's worried sick. She hardly speaks to me anymore. It's gotten bad."

"What do you want me to do?"

"Anything, anything you can to make sure he's safe."

"Where's he stationed?"

"Iraq."

"Ah."

I gave him information about Jamie's regiment and commanding officer, and he said he'd get back to me in a day or two. I didn't say anything to Valerie.

That night, after a silent dinner, Valerie took a walk, came back a couple hours later, and went up to the guest room. Her room. I went up to our room, my room, but couldn't sleep. I kept wondering whether I had enough pull with Ron. He'd always made sure I had whatever I wanted when I was in Iraq, and we got along well, but was that enough to motivate him to help me? And what if he talked with Reynolds? Ron knew I would've gone to Reynolds first. And he'd guess that Reynolds hadn't come through. But Ron was the kind of guy who might want to do a favor just to prove he had the power. Maybe he thought he'd make a better Secretary of Defense than Reynolds. He'd want something. He'd be calling in a chit down the road.

The next day, late in the afternoon, I was sitting at the desk in my study, reading a newspaper, providing some distance for Valerie, visible through the door to the living room, where she sat on the couch reading a book. My phone rang. It was Ron. He'd talked to a colonel in the Green Zone and to Jamie's commanding officer. Everything was arranged for Jamie to be transferred to the Zone. I couldn't stop thanking him, as I gazed at Valerie. He said he was happy to help me out, and maybe someday I'd be able to return the favor, and I thought, *I'll give you all the goddamn quid pro quo you want.*

I hung up and went into the living room, stopping just a few feet from her. She looked up from her book and studied my face.

"I have good news. Not just good news, great news." I sat down next to her; she stiffened. "Jamie's going to be stationed in the Green Zone in the next few days."

She looked at me with wonder. "What does that mean?"

"He's going to be fine. The Green Zone is so safe, everyone calls it Oz. Even Reynolds and Wolffe and the Secretary of State go there. The worst thing that can happen to Jamie is he might put on weight. He's going to be eating hamburgers, fries, pizzas, and washing it down with beer." Valerie smiled, and her eyes lit up. I took her hands in mine and rested my hands on her leg. She flinched. "But he might come back thinner and in better shape, because he'll be able to work out at the gym, play basketball on the indoor courts, maybe even play some soccer. And he'll get to see all the latest films at the movie theater. He's going to have so much free time, you know what?" She had tears in her eyes. "He might come home with a new sweetheart."

She squeezed my hands, and for the first time in months we laughed together. She leaned back, repeated, "Oh, my God!" and laughed and said, "This is the best thing you've ever done."

We called Julia to tell her the good news, passing the phone back and forth so we could both enjoy listening to her sobs of joy. After we got off the phone, we realized we'd been neglecting her, because of our concern for Jamie and my stay in the hospital. We talked about calling her every day, and then decided maybe we shouldn't, because she was starting rehearsals for Fordham's production of *A Streetcar Named Desire*. We'd see her perform as Blanche in a few weeks, and the thought made me realize we'd stopped living, and now we could start again, because Jamie would be safe in Oz. Valerie burst out laughing and repeated, "Oz, Oz, Oz."

Life with Valerie got better each day. She made breakfast for me every morning and, because I love blueberries, managed to include them in everything—cereal, pancakes, yogurt, or as a dessert after a plate of eggs and sausages. After breakfast we'd sit at the table and talk, looking out from time to time at the yard, the trees with their budding leaves, the gardens with purple, yellow, and white crocuses in bloom, and the songbirds that flocked around the bird feeder and sang their celebration of spring. Then we'd go back up to our room and read in bed and talk some more.

We'd take naps together, and I'd wake up to find her reading, waiting for me to come back to her. She'd go downstairs in the early evening to make dinner and later come up to walk down with me. No scotch before dinner, no wine with dinner, and no cognac after.

"You need to get healthy," she'd say. "We have a lot to live for." She set up a television and a DVD player in our room, so every evening, after dinner, we'd go to bed and watch *film noirs*—*Casablanca*, *The Big Sleep*, *Citizen Kane*, *Touch of Evil*. And I'd do impersonations of Bogie and Orson Welles for her—the voices, if not the facial expressions. I did them well enough to make her laugh, and making her laugh made me want to live.

The first night, after telling her about Jamie being stationed in Oz, she slept in the guest room. But the second night, she slept with me. And the third night, she made love to me—climbing on top of me and moving very gently.

The following afternoon, Valerie and I were sitting on the couch, waiting for the guy I'd hired to search for Dad's paintings to deliver a landscape we'd purchased from an art collector in Santa Fe. I was trying to focus on the newspaper on my lap, when I heard a door slam and looked out the window at a man walking to the back of a van in the driveway. Valerie and I rushed to open the door and greeted the guy and his helper as they approached us with a large shipping crate. The guy, who hadn't seen me in several months, glanced at my new face with a puzzled look, as he and the helper walked past me and followed Valerie through the living room and into my office. They set the case down, pulled out *Canyon Wall*, and leaned the painting against a bookshelf. I told the guy it looked just like the photograph he'd sent, thanked him for his work, and gave him a check. He glanced at it, thanked me, and Valerie saw them to the door.

I gazed at the painting. The perspective suggests someone look-ing at a canyon wall from a distance of about a mile, at ground level, during what Dad used to call the magic hour—the hour before sun-set. He'd caught the soft brilliance of the light on the wall in rich shades of ochre, burnt sienna, and burnt umber. Two black birds, crows or vultures, circle in opposite directions near the summit of the wall, while a third bird, about half-way between the viewer and the wall, glides downward, drawing the eye toward the mutation of the sienna and the umber to the deep black shadows near the base of the summit, where everything seems to disappear in darkness.

The painting is beautiful, but, as so often in Dad's work, there's something that feels terrifying. He used to say, as an artist, you see something three times: the first time, when you literally see it; the second, when you see it with your eyes closed; and the third, when you paint it—when you're in the zone, you feel the texture, the paint, wet on wet, and that feeling takes hold of you and guides the brush, and you create the image that comes from what you feel and exists only in the painting. I see in *Canyon Wall* something I know came from within Dad, something that took possession of him as he painted.

As far as I know, this is his only landscape without human characters. He probably did it while visiting Ghost Ranch, before his marriage. When he'd talk about that place, I'd imagine a ranch haunted by ghosts. Sometimes he'd refer to it with the strange expression, "the faraway," because of the extraordinary colors and the forms of the landscape that were a painter's dream. So, at the dinner table one night, when I was fifteen, and he told Mom, Georgia, and me that an old friend had lent us his cabin in the mountains near Taos and we'd be spending a week there on vacation, I got all excited about seeing the faraway and the ghosts.

He drove our '55 Ford on a narrow blacktop road that wound through the mountains west of Taos, while Mom read the directions guiding us to the cabin. It was early evening when she shouted, "That's it," and we stopped, backed up, and turned onto the gravel road that led down to the cabin in a clearing surrounded by pine trees and boulders. The next day we drove to Ghost Ranch, and I learned that it wasn't a ranch; it was a vast, magical space of twenty-two thousand acres that seemed to extend to infinity. The deep blue sky at once complemented that space and seemed an extension of it. It gave me chills and made me feel as if I were a ghost, a spirit that could step into infinity. Dad felt the same thing. "Intimate infinity," he called it.

During the day, the four of us would go on hikes, in the car and on foot, exploring the mountains and gorges of Ghost Ranch, in awe of the shades of white, yellow, red, and brown of the stone walls, unlike anything I'd ever seen, and I understood why artists would want to paint this land. Dad told us stories about how the canyon walls and gorges created shadows so deep that one could hide almost anything inside, and there had once been two brothers, cattle rustlers, who'd hide entire herds in them from the lawmen crossing the plains. We tried playing hide and seek in the shadows, but it was impossible to find anyone.

At night, we'd sit around the table in the dining area, the lamp suspended above our heads creating an island of light in the dark, and play Monopoly—Mom, gazing at us, seeing our happiness, and smiling back; Georgia, petting her blond hair as she surveyed the board; Dad, his blue eyes sparkling in a sideways glance as he pulled off a *coup*, like buying Park Place, when he already owned Boardwalk, with me just a few spaces away. When I was losing, my buoyant thoughts would drift on the cool mountain air flowing through the open windows. Sometimes we'd hear something scurrying outside and wings flapping, and we'd look at one another, wondering what had just happened, and one of us would get up and close the windows.

We'd also make fires at night in the firepit outside. We'd sit on Adirondack chairs, stare at the flames and the glowing embers, and Dad would tell scary stories, like thump, thump, and a drag, and I'd listen for the footsteps of an escaped mental patient. But often the fire would put us in a kind of trance, and we'd be startled when air pockets in the wood would explode and shoot sparks into the dark. Our last night at the cabin, we sat around the pit and talked about what a great week we'd had. When the sun set and the air cooled, Mom and Georgia went inside, leaving Dad and me. There wasn't much of a moon, but the stars came out and lit the night enough so that with the fire I could see Dad's face in profile. He stared at the flickering flames and the pulsating embers for a while, then reached over and tousled my hair. Looking around he said, "You can't live out here and be afraid of the dark. Even with all the stars." He looked up at them. "Would you like to live out here?"

"That would be so cool."

"Yeah, cool. There's something very seductive about the faraway. Something about being here and feeling part of this space that makes you think in a different way. More like dreaming. And all the great things you dream seem possible. You just need to do them."

"Was it living out here that made you want to become an artist?"

"No, I already was. But the faraway means a lot to me. We all have places that mean a lot to us, and we need to go back and see them from time to time, see them for what they are. Some places get smaller. Like when I go back to Grandpa and Grandma's house, it looks so small."

"It looks smaller to me already."

"You'll probably experience the same thing when you go back to see Mom, years from now."

"Yeah, when I go back to see you and Mom."

He stared at the fire, and then he looked past it, extended his open hands in front of him, as if he were holding something large, like a globe, and said, "This space gets larger all the time. It makes me feel like a speck of dust floating in the air. And that speck doesn't have any understanding of what it is or where it's going. I thought someday I'd find a way, things would work out, and in the end everything would be okay. That's every man's fantasy—I'll make it. I still have all these years ahead of me." He looked back down at the fire.

"Dad, are you okay?"

"I've sometimes felt that the things I did when I wasn't painting were just filler—stuff that filled time, until I could start painting again. When I'm painting, time doesn't exist. Nor anything else that isn't the painting. That's all there is in the world. And I think I see the picture. The big picture. But that's exactly what I didn't see. How you and Georgia and your mom will go on. And what you'll need. That's the big picture."

I heard a tremor in his voice. I panicked and wanted to say something, but couldn't.

He continued gazing at the fire, and then reached over, wrapped his arm around my shoulder, and pulled me toward him. We sat like that for a long time, until we heard a sudden flutter of wings, a pain-filled screech, and a short-lived scuffle in the brush. He let me go and said, "We'd better get to bed. We have a busy day tomorrow."

He emptied a pail of water on the dying fire, making the embers hiss. And then he walked with me, shining the flashlight on our path to the cabin, while I shuffled my feet along the ground, afraid of tripping on one of the protruding roots or rocks.

The next morning, he was fidgety, pacing, smoking one cigarette after another, taking breaks from packing the car to look out over the mountains. One last dream, I guess. Mom knew he wouldn't want to stop for lunch, so she made sandwiches and packed them with some fruit. We arrived home in the evening. By the time I got up the next morning, Dad had already started working in the studio.

I felt Valerie's hand on my back as she stood by my side and gazed at *Canyon Wall* with me. She told me the guy thanked her again for the check. I nodded. It was worth it. I'd found another piece of Dad.

The following morning, while Valerie and I were eating breakfast, we reminisced about our trips with the kids to Denver, to visit Mom and Georgia, and to France the previous summer.

"We showed the kids that bookstore where you lived in Paris. They thought that was so weird, living in a bookstore."

"Julia looked at the little nook where I'd slept and said, 'Here?'"

Valerie and I shook our heads and laughed.

"And then," she said, "we took them to dinner at the *brasserie* on the *Ile Saint-Louis*, and we had *choucroute garnie* and told them about the night you and I celebrated Bastille Day dancing on the island to a live band."

"And the next day we drove down to the *Côte d'Azur* and joined the Prince and his wife on the yacht."

Valerie's happiness vanished, and her eyes narrowed. "And Jamie asked the Prince about having been a fighter pilot. And the Prince said, 'What can be more noble than to defend one's country?' And Jamie asked, 'What are we doing in Iraq? It's not our country.' And the Prince said, 'Removing a dictator and creating a new order.' And then you gave your little speech about bringing to the Iraqi people the same things we want—freedom, liberty, and the pursuit of happiness. I remember every word, because Jamie remembered every word."

She fell silent, closed her eyes, and shook her head. I wondered if she'd ever forgive me.

The doorbell rang. It startled us. It rang again. She said she'd get it and headed for the foyer. I was about to take a sip of coffee, when I heard a strange whimper. I grabbed my cane and rushed to the door.

Valerie was clutching her hair as she circled the foyer, moaning, "No, no, no." She saw me and wailed and staggered upstairs. I wanted to follow her, but I couldn't. I had to know.

I looked out the window of the door and saw two soldiers, square shouldered, in full dress uniform. I opened. They looked at me. One said, "Mr. Richard Rayburn?"

"Yes."

"May we come in?"

They entered, composed themselves, and one said, "The Chief of Staff of the United States Army has entrusted us to express his deep regret that your son, James Rayburn, was killed in action yesterday, by a sniper, in Ramadi, Iraq. The Chief of Staff extends his deepest sympathy to you and your family in your loss."

The soldier continued talking, but nothing seemed to come out of his mouth. All I could hear was Valerie sobbing, the sobs reverberating through me. After his lips stopped, I said, "I want my son."

"I regret your loss, sir, but—"

"I want my son!"

"I regret sir, but—"

"He's supposed to be safe. Bring him to me. Bring him!"

"Sir." He looked scared. "I'm sorry."

I stepped forward, going face to face with the soldier who was talking to me, and screamed, "Don't give me that shit about the Chief of Staff. He doesn't give a fuck about the kids who die. That son of a bitch. And tell that asshole Reynolds he could've saved my boy. Tell him. And the president—that liar. Tell the little puppy and those corrupt, cowardly assholes in Congress, tell them all I want my son back. I want my son!"

The other soldier said, "Let's go." He started to turn, and when the one, at whom I was screaming, didn't follow, he shouted, "Go!" They did an about-face and marched across the lawn, and I hobbled after them crying, "My son died because of greed, corruption, and lies. He died so others could get rich. I know." I stopped. "I know." And what I knew penetrated me like a bullet, and I fell to my knees sobbing, "I know. Oh, I know." I collapsed, my head hit the ground, and I cried, "Oh, God, I know." And I pounded the ground with my fist, as if striking the thing that had killed Jamie, mumbling, "Jamie, Jamie, I failed you. I failed you."

A hand touched my shoulder. A man's voice, a gentle voice, said my name, and repeated it. I looked up and saw my neighbor. He was sorry. So sorry. He lifted my arm, I took a deep breath, and he pulled me to my feet. He picked up my cane, walked me to the house and into the foyer, and called for Valerie. She didn't respond. Between deep breaths and sobs, I told him I'd be okay. He left, and I climbed the stairs and looked in our room. Valerie wasn't there. I staggered to the guest room and found her sitting on the bed, staring at nothing, tears streaming down her face. I sat down next to her. She looked at me, her mouth agape, and I saw the same dead look in her eyes that I'd seen in Mom's, after Dad had died, and I'd sat by her side on the bed and put my hand on her hand with the rosary wrapped around it.

Valerie and Julia stood on the other side of the casket that held
Jamie's body, their eyes downcast at the open grave. I wanted to put
my arms around them and feel we were one in our grief. I heard the
same prayers that had been recited at Dad's burial and remembered
standing next to Mom, feeling her pain as her grasp tightened, her
fingers squeezing my arm. It was a beautiful day. Birds were singing.
But life had stopped for Mom and Georgia and me. Everything inside me had collapsed, had fallen so far, so deep, I felt there was no
coming back. And now, my boy was dead. I'd never see him again.
Never see his eyes, hear his voice, touch his hand. I looked up and
saw Julia's eyes looking at me through a mist of tears. The clap of
the gunfire ripped through me. Julia closed her eyes. She sobbed,
and her body trembled. The honor guard fired their rifles a second
time, and my body flinched. And the third time, the loud crack was
the shot through Jamie's head, the shot that shattered me, and I
wept and felt him die all over again.

Valerie drove us home, each of us entombed in our silence. We
entered the house, and Valerie went upstairs. Julia stopped and
turned toward me. "Dad, what's going on?"

I shook my head. "She won't talk to me."

"Why?"

"She hates me."

"Why?"

"Ask her."

"I asked her last night. She said … she said Jamie died because
of you." Tears welled up in Julia's eyes, as she shook her head. "You
two need to talk. Please." She took a deep breath. "I'm going to call
a cab, and take the train back to New York. I can't stay here. I can't
… can't deal with losing Jamie, and the two of you not speaking to
one another."

I held her in my arms. She trembled, sighed, and moaned, "I
love you, Dad."

"I love you, too."

"I'm going to call the cab and get my things. I'll be down in a
little while."

I watched her walk up the stairs, and then went into the living room and sank into the couch and hung my head. Jamie was dead. He was dead.

A door closed upstairs. Julia's suitcase bumped on one step and another as she came down. And then I remembered she hadn't brought a suitcase.

I got up, went to the foyer, and found her, standing next to Valerie, who had set her purse on her suitcase and was getting her coat out of the closet. She looked at Julia and said, "Go wait in the car, honey. I'll be there in a minute." I wondered what the hell was going on.

Julia looked at me, her eyes misty, lips parted. "Goodbye, Dad."

"Come here." I hugged her. She left.

Valerie said, "I'm driving Julia. I'm going to stay in the apartment in New York. And I'm having the locks changed."

"You're leaving me? You can't do that."

"I *can*. I *am* leaving you."

"Please. We've lost our son—"

"We didn't lose our son, Dick. You killed him. You didn't pull the trigger, but you may as well have."

I shook my head. "I love Jamie. I love him, and I love you."

"I believe you, Dick. I do. But I don't love you. Not anymore. I can't."

"Valerie, you mean everything to me. You and Julia and Jamie—"

"You mean nothing to me. Nothing. Jamie died because of you."

She pushed the door open and walked toward her car in the driveway, and as I followed her, repeating, "I love you, I love you, please, Valerie, please don't leave me," she walked faster. She got in and slammed the door and locked it. I grabbed the handle and pulled, until the hatred in her eyes stopped me. I let go, and she drove away.

I spent the rest of the day remembering Valerie, still young, beautiful, and pregnant. Our sleepless nights during Julia's first year; waking up, taking Julia into our bed, and Valerie nursing her. And the same thing again with Jamie, and Julia joining us, and the four of us asleep in a heap in the morning. And later, weekend mornings, lying in bed, exhausted, the kids, full of energy, playing with their dolls, their trucks and cars, their masks, their magic wands and toy animals. And their birthday parties, and the house ringing with laughter. And the crying, and Valerie and I kissing owies. And Julia performing her little theatrical skits in the living room, and Jamie playing soccer, a midfielder who ran his heart out in every game. Gone. All of it gone.

I walked from room to room, from Jamie's, to Julia's, to the guest room, and to the closet, where Valerie had left some dresses. I pulled one close to me, buried my face in it, and clenched my fists and wept. I leaned against the wall and, after I stopped crying, went to our room, stood in front of her portrait, gazing at the young woman with whom I'd fallen in love, and to her dressing table, where I remembered her sitting on her bench, looking up at me in the mirror, and me, bending over and kissing her neck and her bare shoulders, and getting on my knees, and the two of us making love. I picked up a bottle of perfume, closed my eyes, and inhaled the warm scent. I gazed at the picture of us on one of our trips, our radiant faces pressed together, a white beach and blue water in the background. I went downstairs and walked through the rooms, looking, touching, remembering.

I stopped at the liquor cabinet in the living room, took out a bottle of scotch, filled a tumbler, took a drink, and headed for the foyer, stopping to look out the window at the steps where the soldiers had stood and the driveway where Valerie had gotten into her car. I went up to my room and sat on the edge of the bed. I'd lost Dad. Jamie. Valerie. And probably Julia. That's all there is—losing. You lose and you lose and you lose. That's all life is. Why would anyone want to live, if it's just to suffer one loss after another? I emptied my glass, filled it again, and set the bottle on the night table, next to my pills. Valerie had reminded me of what the doctor had said about morphine—take it with alcohol, and you might not wake up in the morning. I tossed a couple pills in my mouth and washed them down with whiskey.

CHAPTER 14

I OPENED MY EYES AND saw a ceiling. My arms had flopped out, and my hands felt the edge of a mattress on both sides. I was lying on a single bed. I remembered taking pills, drinking, passing out, waking, wandering, staggering through the house, a bottle in my hand. I'd found myself among the charred corpses of Fallujah, recoiling at the sight. And then Jamie was standing in front of me, in his fatigues. His eyes lit up, and he cried, "Dad!" I walked toward him, reaching for him, and as I was about to take him in my arms, his body jolted, his head snapped back, and he looked stunned. He fell, and blood streamed from his head into a dark red pool that spread across the floor. I turned and fled through the other rooms, bumped into chairs and tables, staggered, drank, and again found myself among corpses. I heard Valerie scream, "You killed Jamie. You killed our son," and fled into another room and found him standing in front of me, staring, a bloody hole in his forehead, his eyes begging me to save him.

I sat up. The lights were on. I looked at a window and saw part of Jamie's room reflected on the black surface of the glass. It was night. My eyes wandered. I noticed a bottle on the floor, picked it up, saw some whiskey at the bottom, and took a swig. My eyes landed on the wall where Jamie's photographs hang. I walked over and gazed at the pictures of the teams on which he'd played. My eyes fixed on his image in one of them, and I stared at it, as if by holding it long enough with my eyes, I could bring him back to life. I ran my fingers across the trophies and recalled his dream of playing soccer in college, and maybe as a pro. I stepped back, looked at the shelves below the photographs and medals, eased myself to the floor, and touched the books, wondering what he'd thought, what he'd felt as he'd read them. I left the room and entered Julia's. My eyes landed on the poster for *All My Sons*, with the photograph of the set, the backyard and porch of an old wood-frame house, and I remembered her performance as Annie, the woman who loved the pilot who'd committed suicide. I'd tried calling Julia, but she didn't answer. I took a drink, emptied the bottle, and went downstairs to the living room to get another.

The lights on the main floor were off, but the moon provided enough light for me to find a bottle in the liquor cabinet. I carried it to the kitchen, collapsed onto a chair, and stared out the window. A half-moon shone on the backyard, lighting it like a stage, like a surreal painting—the bent flower stems rising from the ground like broken limbs; the trellis, an arch under which one might pass on the way to nothing; the trees, black, still, and skeletal; and stone-white Aphrodite. Dad could have painted this scene. A rabbit appeared, like a joke, something alive and hopping through the night. I laughed. It stopped and huddled, as if listening for danger, so vulnerable in that open space. I drank to the courageous little bunny, which could be plucked in an instant by an owl. It remained dead still for a minute, then scampered off into the night.

Valerie's voice started reciting her litany again. I killed Jamie. Killed our son. He joined because of me. Because of what I'd said. Because he was defending me. Because he loved me. Because, because, because. Always, because of me.

I reached for the bottle and knocked it over. I turned on the light, blinding myself for a second, and then my eyes landed on the window. It had turned into a mirror, and I saw my monstrous face in the glare from the light, and my eyes stared back at me, accusing me. I grabbed the first thing my hand touched, a glass, and threw it at my face in the middle of the glare. I swayed and nearly fell. I seized the bottle, threw it at my blurred image, and the momentum of the throw hurled me to the floor.

Julia's voice cried, "Dad, Dad." Her hand took hold of my shoulder, her fingers touched the side of my face, and she pleaded with me to answer. I felt my face pressed against the cold floor, opened my eyes and glimpsed her knees. She asked what had happened, and I remembered and started crying, "Jamie, Jamie." "Oh, God," she moaned, as she tried lifting my shoulders, and I continued crying, repeating his name, whimpering it was all because of me. She struggled to lift me, and I tried pushing myself up, but my left arm hurt where it had been fractured in the helicopter crash. I pushed up with my right hand and felt a tingling sensation, as if my hand were full of bees. She got me up, and I fell onto a chair. I saw fear in her face. She touched my cheeks and repeated, "Dad, you're so cold. What happened?" I shook my head and looked around. I was sitting where I'd been before I'd lost it and had started throwing things. The window had a hole near the center of the thick glass, fractures shot out like rays of lightning, and pieces of glass lay scattered across the table. Shivering from the cold air, I looked down, saw my naked chest and legs, and pulled my bathrobe together.

Julia pulled a chair over, sat down, and asked, "What happened?"

I shook my head and mumbled, "I got angry. Angry at the sight of myself."

"Dad—"

"I thought I'd never see you again. Why didn't you return my call?"

"Because I was confused. Mom blames you for Jamie's death. And all I can think about is my brother." She had tears in her eyes. "I didn't want to get in the middle of a fight between you two. I didn't know what to think." She paused. "Mom's so angry. And I was angry, too. That's why I didn't return your call. But I've been thinking about what a good father you are. You love us so much, you've always done everything you could to help us. I can't blame you for what happened to Jamie." She looked into my eyes. "He was lucky to have you as a father. Do you hear me, Dad? He was lucky, and so am I."

"Lucky to have me as a father?" I repeated, in disbelief.

"Yes, lucky." She nodded, her smile radiating love. "Let's get you upstairs and in bed."

She wondered where my cane was. I told her I didn't know, I didn't need it. She helped me out of the chair, had me drape my arm around her as she walked me toward the foyer, where her suitcase stood. By the time we got there, I felt I could make it up the stairs on my own.

"Oh, my God," she said, as she looked at my room—the quilt and the sheet tossed across the foot of the bed and newspapers scattered on the floor, along with an empty bottle. She asked if I wanted to take a shower. I did. When I finished, the bed was made, a pair of pajamas lay on top of it, and the mess had been cleaned. I sat down and put on my pajamas. She called from the foot of the stairs to tell me she was going to fix something to eat and I should get in bed. I was amazed at how mature she seemed. Just twenty, and caring for me as if she were the parent.

She returned with a meal of canned soup, tuna, and crackers. She set the tray on my lap, walked around to the other side of the bed, Valerie's side, and sat next to me, watching me eat. I felt her eyes on me, paused, saw the sadness in her gaze, sensed she was thinking about Jamie, and lost my appetite. I noticed her hand resting on the quilt, placed my hand on hers, and, when our eyes connected, asked about her courses and instructors and the play she was in. She was excited about her role as Blanche. She'd studied Vivien Leigh's performance in the film to better understand this fragile, broken character. She reflected and added that she was dedicating her performance to Jamie. She bit her lip, stared off, and then looked at me and said, "Mom is coming by tomorrow to pick up some things." She paused. "Maybe the two of you can talk."

I imagined Julia, Valerie, and me together, our family reunited, and for a moment felt like the cardinal in the wasteland of our backyard, singing with joy.

Julia left with the tray. Later, as she moved through the house, cleaning, doing the dishes, going through things in her bedroom, she sang to herself, but loud enough for me to hear, and from time to time she reappeared to check on me. The front door closed. She'd gone off to buy groceries. Her tender care was a potent tranquilizer, and I didn't have to wash it down with whiskey. I was sober for the first time since Valerie had left. Valerie. She was coming back. I wasn't anxious, because she'd see Julia, see that I had her support. Julia would lead Valerie to our room and stand next to me as I pleaded my case. She'd tell Valerie how much I love Jamie, how I've always tried to be a good father, how I'd attend his soccer games and talk with him about the books he was reading. How everything I did, I did for the family. And then I'd tell Valerie she meant everything to me. I rehearsed the scene in my head.

I spent the next morning in bed, reading, dozing off, waking up, waiting. I'd just awakened from another nap, when I heard the front door close and Julia say, "Hi, Mom." And the surprise in Valerie's voice, when she exclaimed, "Julia!" And I thought, *Yes, our daughter's here, with me.* Valerie and Julia continued talking, but I couldn't hear what they were saying. Footsteps came up the stairs. I put on my bathrobe and sat back down on the bed. The women had almost reached the door, when Valerie laughed. She had a smile on her lips as she entered our room, but the smile disappeared when she saw me.

"I'll only be a few minutes," she said, her voice suddenly cold.

"It's your house, too. You can stay."

"I know," she snapped.

"I'm happy to see you."

She walked past the foot of the bed to the closet, went inside, and started sliding hangers, looking at clothes she might take.

I moved toward the closet, stopped a few feet away, and glanced back to see Julia behind me. I looked at Valerie and said, "It's so good having Julia home." Valerie continued sorting through her clothes. "And you're here. I'd love for us to come back together. Be a family again."

She froze. "How can you say that? We can never be a family again. Never." She grabbed an armful of clothes and a suitcase in the closet, barged past Julia and me, tossed the case on the bed and started stuffing her clothes in it.

"I love Jamie," I said. "I'll always love him. I've made mistakes, but—"

She pivoted toward me. "You've made mistakes?" She walked toward me, until her eyes were just inches from mine. "Mistakes? Is that what you call what you did to him? A mistake? From the time he was a little boy, he heard his father talk about projects he was heading up all over the world that had *noble goals*. They would liberate people, lift them out of poverty, give them opportunities to create happy lives. Oh,"—she shook her head—"to him, you were God. He couldn't see that you'd never grown up. That you always had to rationalize everything you did, even this war, to satisfy your adolescent idealism. Jamie believed everything you said. That's why he joined the Army. That's why he's dead."

"If my 'adolescent idealism' misled him, then why didn't you step in and set him straight? Why didn't you tell him the truth?"

"Stop!" Julia screamed. "Would you both please stop!" She held her hands toward us, beseeching us. "Please!"

I was about to take Julia in my arms and console her, when Valerie said, "You did it again. You always hurt people."

I pivoted toward her. "What do you mean?"

"Why did you drag Julia into this? Why didn't you think about her, instead of yourself? It's always about you." She returned to the closet and slammed hangers back and forth.

"I didn't try to get Julia involved." I clenched my teeth. "You act as if you're innocent. You never challenged what we were going to do in Iraq. When I talked to you about the invasion, you never said, 'I don't think we should do that. People will get killed.' You never raised any objections. Never!"

"I didn't know so many mothers would lose their sons."

"I told you from the beginning. We had calculated the risks. We knew people were going to die. But we felt, in the balance—"

"Yes, yes, yes." She stood in the closet doorway, facing me. "And you also said the Iraqi people would be lining the streets, cheering our soldiers, throwing flowers. People would be—"

"You knew what I knew, and you had no problem with what we were doing, because you knew it would make us millions. Maybe we could buy a bigger apartment in New York, or a house in the Bahamas. You had your fantasies."

"I never really understood."

"That's bullshit."

"That's the truth."

"The truth doesn't interest you. It never has. It didn't when we were on the Prince's yacht. Remember? Summer of '78? The Mediterranean? Your father's buddy, the Playboy Prince, lent him his yacht so he could take us sailing. And what was Alex doing when he went ashore in Monte Carlo? He was with the Prince, talking about the sale of F15s to the Saudis."

Valerie, rushing past me with another armful of clothes, stopped and glared at me. "Are you trying to suggest my father did something wrong?"

"He was an arms dealer."

She tossed hangers aside and crammed clothes into the suitcase. "Whatever."

"He was part of some of the sleaziest deals of the last forty years in the Middle East. He helped Saddam Hussein get chemical weapons so he could gas the Kurds and the Iranians."

She tried to close the suitcase, but some clothes got stuck in the zipper.

"He helped negotiate the purchase of missiles from us to the Iranians, so they could kill Iraqis in the Iran-Iraq War. Nearly a million people died in that war. But, hey, your daddy made a lot of money. What's wrong with that? Right? After all, he had a family. Had to pay for the beautiful home and apartment and the cars. The education of his little princess. And the presents, like the one you received for graduation—a year in Europe."

She faced me and said, "How dare you. You were nothing when you came to New York, and if it hadn't been for my father, you'd still be nothing."

"Your father is no better than I am, and neither are you."

"I'm not listening to this crap." She headed for the door, strands of clothes protruding from the suitcase that she wheeled behind her.

I followed her, shouting, "Yeah, that's right, run away. Don't look at reality. You wouldn't be able to go on living if you did. Run, run, run!"

She rushed downstairs, and I followed as fast as I could.

"You didn't give a damn about Iraq, until we lost Jamie. And then it was all my fault. Well, you went along with everything. You've always gone along, from the time you were a little girl. You wanted money and everything it could buy. You just never wanted to know where it came from. And you still refuse to see where it came from."

She reached the front door.

I screamed, "You don't have to see what I see every night. You don't have to live with what I live with. Fallujah. The dead staring at me. The eyes of the living accusing me."

She opened the door, turned, and looked at me. "And Jamie. Don't forget Jamie."

I froze, shook my head. "I've never forgotten Jamie. Never."

"You call my father an arms dealer. Well, you're a war dealer. You bring death to people. You brought it to us." She glared. "Your Frankenstein face reveals the horrid person you are."

Her words left me powerless, and I froze. By the time I caught up to her, she'd already put her suitcase in the car and had started the motor. She glared at me, I felt her hatred, and she tore off.

I collapsed on a step and sat there, panting, staring at the empty driveway. And then I thought of Julia and panicked. I looked around, stood up, called her name, went inside and climbed the stairs. I found the door to her room closed. I knocked. No response. I pushed it open and saw her lying on the bed, on her side, facing the other way, her body trembling as she cried. I sat down next to her and placed my hand on her shoulder. Tears flowed from her closed eyes. I told her I was sorry I'd hurt her, sorry her mother had hurt her. Julia opened her eyes and brushed the tears away. I remained close to her, until her eyes closed again and she fell asleep.

In the morning, Julia and I sat at the kitchen table, staring down at our coffee. I felt her pain, but couldn't find anything to say that would help her. I placed my hand on hers. She looked up at me with her bloodshot eyes. I said I was sorry, so sorry. She shook her head, bit her lip, and closed her eyes. She had me drive her to the station, said she'd come back Saturday, and returned to New York.

CHAPTER 15

JULIA HAD GONE. I got up from the chair in the living room and wandered into my office. I stopped to gaze at *Canyon Wall*, at its haunting beauty. I looked to the right of the painting, at the pictures on the wall of the men who were part of my success. I moved over and stared at each photograph—a group-shot of me with the members of the Advisory Board, as well as a few smaller group-shots. We were all wearing our suits and smiles, with an air of entitlement. We were successful, certain of our place in the world and of our accomplishments. Such good men. Family men. Proper, upright members of society. Men who went to church every Sunday, or the synagogue Friday night. Men who prayed to God for guidance. And who wouldn't hesitate a second to have a thousand people killed—or a hundred thousand—if it would make them richer. Men of character. A bunch of psychopaths in suits.

I turned away in disgust and entered the living room and stopped in front of *Eurydice*—the woman painted in flake white, hurrying toward the edge of the city, trapped in the extreme foreshortening of the street and the buildings. And the woman in black, standing in the shadows of a second-story room, staring out the window, spying on Eurydice's vain effort at escape. The memory of Dad painting *Eurydice* came back, and I saw his body shifting and stretching, pulling back, hovering above the canvas, and then plunging, his energy flowing into his work. I looked around at *A Woman Alone*, *City of Shadows*, and *Nocturnal Light*, and headed upstairs to the attic, where I stored Dad's paintings, wanting to be close to him.

I slid them out of the storage unit that I'd had constructed years ago, when I'd started searching for his work, and each painting brought back the world Dad had created—the mountain that dominates a city and casts its shadow across many of the paintings, dividing the space into light and darkness; the sun low in the sky, outside the frame, and the long shadows, some of them cast by objects out of sight, just beyond the corner of a building; the buildings, with empty or closed windows, and the foreshortening of streets; and the different qualities of nocturnal light and daylight. And the solitary figures—a man, a woman, or a child, framed and reframed by light and shadow, isolated and trapped in a closed space, walking or running in the street, their extended shadows accompanying them like doubles. Sometimes the characters themselves look like shadows—shadows projecting shadows. Before I started buying back the paintings, I'd felt the pain of his loss, as if he were a limb that had been amputated. A phantom pain, that never completely disappeared. I'd hoped bringing back the paintings would make the pain less acute. That didn't happen. I still feel the loss. But his work was like a prosthesis that enabled me to walk.

And walk I did, downstairs to the office, where I confronted the psychopaths in their suits. I ripped the pictures off the walls, hurled them into a corner, and swung my arm like a scythe, cutting down those standing on shelves. I tossed the pictures of me with the leaders of developing countries into the same piles of broken frames, bent photos, and shattered glass.

After rummaging through the attic and not finding any of the art materials from the days when I taught the kids to draw and paint, I called an art-supply store and ordered an easel, numerous oil-primed, pre-stretched linen canvases of various sizes, oil paints, linseed oil, turpentine, brushes, a palette, palette knives, rollers, and a staple gun. While waiting for the delivery, I looked around my office, with a bank of windows facing north and a couple windows facing west, and decided it would make a perfect studio. I cleared a space, pushing chairs and tables to the side. I couldn't move the desk, so I cleared the surface, throwing everything on the piles of trash, until I came to a photo of Valerie, Julia, Jamie, and me, standing in front of The Common Good. We were happy then, in the summer of 2003, before everything started to unravel in Iraq.

The doorbell rang. I put the picture in a drawer and answered. The young man standing on the front step was about to say something, but froze and stared at my face. I ignored his response, led him into the studio, and showed him where to put everything—stack the canvases against the walls, put the easel in front of the desk, facing the windows, and the paints, brushes, and everything else on the desk. While he returned to the van, I looked out the window at the sky and around the room filled with light. A perfect day for painting. The man reappeared carrying the first large canvas, which I had him set on the easel. While he carried in the other canvases, I picked up the tubes he'd set on the desk and squeezed them gently to feel the paint inside and stroked my forearms with the brushes.

I spent the evening wandering through the house, looking at the relics of my family, lying on Jamie's bed, staring at the shadows of my thoughts on the ceiling, and returning to my studio to gaze at the canvas on the easel. It glowed white in the dark. I approached the almost incandescent surface, as if it were the entrance to a magical space. Or maybe the entrance to hell, because once I entered, I was going to remember everything. I'd been drinking to forget; now I was doing something to remember. That seemed insane. I considered closing the door to the studio and shunning the canvas. But as I gazed at it, at the white space in front of me, I knew I was going in.

As I stared at the boy's face that I was painting, Julia's face emerged from behind, alongside the canvas, her eyes stunned wide open.

"Dad."

Why is she here? I wondered.

"Dad, didn't you hear me calling? Are you all right?"

"Why are you here?"

"I said I'd be back Saturday." She looked around at the mattress on the floor, the palette and brush in my hands, and the paintings leaning against the wall. "What is all this?"

I followed her eyes and gazed at *Fallujah 1* and remembered staring at the white canvas and wondering if I was entering hell. That was days ago, when the morning sun had peered from behind the trees, and I'd stood here, hesitating, afraid. I hadn't painted in years. But I reminded myself that Dad had spent a thousand hours teaching me to paint, how to work with fat and lean, and how to add depth to colors and make them richer, without producing mud. I squeezed some ivory black from the tube onto the palette, thinned it with turpentine, and, after some hesitation, brushed it onto the flake white. I added more ivory black and worked in some burnt umber, texturing the paint, creating a sense of depth. I moved the brush quickly, feeling the paint on paint, working in some ultramarine blue, adding even greater depth to the darkness—the darkness of my dreams, the depth from which arose the images that haunted me. I applied flake white mixed with raw umber, painting the face that rose from the dark. The face of the boy in Fallujah, the boy standing next to the old man forced to his knees, a gun to his head.

I formed and shaped the face with thick paint, thick like the self-portraits of Van Gogh, almost sculpting it with the brush. I blended in raw sienna, yellow ochre, alizarin crimson, and cerulean blue—enough to turn the flake white into flesh, without toning down the pearlescent glow. The face had to glow as it rose from the dark, as it does in my dreams. And then I started painting the eyes—black, deep, intense. The eyes that had locked onto mine, accusing me, while the Marine threatened to shoot the old man. And by the time I finished painting the tousled hair, the black eyebrows, and the eyes that clutched my heart and made me catch my breath, I'd created the face I was seeking when the helicopter had risen in the tornado of dirt, before the flash in the dark. I stepped back from the canvas, and the eyes riveted me. During the night, I walked through the house, drinking, and returned to the painting and stared.

I rose with the sun, worked some more on the painting, set it next to *Canyon Wall*, put another canvas on the easel, and laid down a ground of ivory black, burnt umber, and ultramarine blue, as I had done in *Fallujah 1*, working wet into wet and creating an illusion of unfathomable darkness. And in that darkness, I painted a wall through which a hole had been blasted, and beyond the hole the rubble of shattered brick and plaster. I laid the figure of a man down across the rubble, feet in the foreground, head in the background, arms lying limp on each side, the body foreshortened like Mantegna's Christ—but seen from a more elevated point of view, as I'd seen it in Fallujah. Charred gray, the hair gone, empty black sockets where the eyes had been, the nose, lips, and cheeks burned off, and the mouth open in a silent scream of white teeth. Parts of his robe had been torched, holes had been burned through the torso, and a forearm ended in two charred bones, where a wrist and hand had been incinerated. I painted and repainted the holes for the empty eye sockets and brushed thick flake white to make the teeth stand out. In a few days I'd go back and lay a glaze of burnt umber over the rubble to create depth and to make the brick appear as if it had melted, cooled, and congealed into a hard glistening surface.

I looked from *Fallujah 2*, leaning against the wall, to the easel and *Fallujah 3*, in which I had again created a dark space, and painted the body of the young teenage boy I'd seen lying on the ground, his legs pulled up toward his torso, suggesting, at the moment he'd died, he was trying to protect himself by curling into the fetal position. I painted the body, which takes up most of the canvas, as if someone were kneeling over it. Painted his dark hair, his open eye, and the clotted blood that had trickled from his mouth and nose onto the ground. And his white tennis shoes—I wanted them very white, like shoes an American kid might wear, like the ones Jamie used to wear. I worked on the details of the face, in particular the fly, standing on the surface of the open eye. And when I finished the fly, I felt again what I'd felt in Fallujah—the desire to brush the fly off the boy's eye. I wanted again to touch his cheek, push his hair back, lift him in my arms, and carry him back to life. But that fly reminds me, as it had in Fallujah, that I can't bring back the dead. I can only paint them.

"Dad. Dad. Look at me."

I looked and saw Julia's anxiety as she implored me.

"What's going on? Why is the mattress here?"

I looked at the mattress on the floor. "I've been sleeping here. When I can sleep."

She moved around to my side of the canvas and gazed at the painting. "Who is this?"

I didn't answer, because once I looked at the boy, I couldn't.

"Dad, who is this?"

"I'm going to call it *Fallujah 3*."

"What do you mean, *Fallujah 3*? What are you doing?"

I nodded toward the other two paintings. "*Fallujah 1* and *2*."

She moved toward them, stopped, and gazed at the burned, charred body. Then she looked at the boy's face. She seemed transfixed by the eyes that stared at her. "You never talk about Fallujah. What happened?"

I shook my head.

She returned and stood close to me. "Please, Dad." Her eyes begged me.

I took a deep breath, the memory of that day seized me, and I gave it voice.

"I'd heard reports about what had gone on during the battle of Fallujah, and I had to find out for myself. So, after the battle, during the mop-up, I used my connection with the Deputy Secretary of Defense to get a helicopter and a crew. When Elliott and I got into that helicopter and lifted off, the sun looked like a ball of fire on the horizon, and its heat beat down on us like a collapsing wall. Within minutes, we were flying over Fallujah, a wasteland of bombed buildings, incinerated remains of cars and trucks and Humvees, and empty streets, and bodies everywhere. In the distance, I saw the green dome of a mosque and the tip of a minaret and thought, *Fallujah, the city of mosques, bombed and burned to hell.*

"Our guide, a lieutenant by the name of Collins, was sitting in front of me. He turned around, saw something that alarmed him, and shouted. When he got my attention, he looked down at the body armor and helmet on the floor and said I had to put on my gear if I didn't want to become another sign of progress. He laughed. You see, the Secretary of Defense had said in a press conference that our forces were taking on the bad guys, and the dead-enders were desperate, because they knew they were finished. That's why they were fighting so hard, and why so many of our guys were getting killed, because we were making progress. That line became the biggest joke in Iraq. Collins had a grin from ear to ear. And then he got serious and said, 'Sir,' and looked even younger, like a kid wearing his dad's uniform. I glanced over at Elliott and saw his eyes bulging with fear and sweat running down his face. He gave me a weird grin and shook his head and shouted, 'We don't want to become signs of progress, do we?' Oh, Elliott, there because of me.

"Well … we flew over an area that resembled a town square, where several small streets converged. A tank stood at one side of the square, and another about a hundred yards away, down one of the streets. Some Marines were walking backward, focused on a building. Flames shot into the sky, hurling fragments of the building and billowing black smoke. Collins turned and shouted, 'They left the mujahedeen a houseguest.' And he explained a houseguest was a couple of propane tanks filled with gas. You ignite it with a C-4, and when it blows, it sucks all the air out of the building—and anyone in it. I pointed at the square and shouted, 'Let's go down.' He shouted it wasn't a good idea. I reminded him who was in charge and told him I wanted to talk to boots on the ground. Huh! Boots on the ground. I'd never used that expression before. It's something a general might say in a press conference. I could never think of Jamie as boots on the ground. But I put him in those boots. That's pretty much what your mom told me in her email that morning.

She pleaded with me to find a way to make sure he'd never get sent to Iraq. I tried. Oh, God, I tried.

"We ... we landed, and then it hit me—the stink of burnt gas and rotting corpses. I looked around the square and saw the black skeletons of trucks, buildings riddled with holes, and corpses in jeans and T-shirts and gray robes. I wandered, with Elliott at my side, staring at the bodies of men and boys. Bodies charred beyond recognition in the rubble of decimated buildings and sprawled out on the street, arms and legs splayed in odd positions, dried pools of blood, flies buzzing around. That's what you see in *Fallujah 2*, the body laid across the rubble like Mantegna's Christ, the eyes gone, the lipless mouth open in a scream of white teeth. The result of white phosphorous. And in *Fallujah 3*, the painting of the boy on the ground, lying in the fetal position, and the fly on his open eye. The fly I want to brush away, every time I see it.

"Collins kept on shouting at me to get away from the bodies, they might be booby-trapped, they could blow up at any time, but I couldn't understand him. I could see, I could hear, I could smell, but I couldn't *understand*. He grabbed me by the arm and pulled me in the direction of the tank parked near a house, where a bunch of Marines were lying in the shade watching us, probably wondering who in the hell we were. Collins said the lieutenant in charge of the platoon might be in the house—a gray building, like the others. Some of them charred, with holes blown through them. Others with one or two walls standing, the roofs and floors gone, and rubble spilling across the streets. A scroungy dog appeared. It had something in its mouth. I wondered, *What the hell?* And then I saw a hand between its jaws. Someone fired several rounds, but the dog leaped away and disappeared around a corner. Collins called that Operation Scooby. They had to shoot dogs on sight, or they'd be feeding on every corpse in the city.

"We passed the tank in front of the house. The crewmembers were smoking and staring at the three of us as we walked by. Collins told them smoking was bad for their health. One of them snickered and said the looey's got a sense of humor. They had to have been in

Iraq for a while to crack jokes like that. Everything I'd seen must've seemed normal to them.

"We approached the house, scarred black by explosions, the door blown away. Inside, in the middle of the room, where the light from the blown-out windows and the open door converged, three men in fatigues and body armor crouched over a map spread out on the floor. They looked up at us, and the guy in the middle asked who the hell we were. Collins introduced us. He said the Deputy Secretary was in Oz and had ordered him to give me everything I wanted. The guy stood up, introduced himself as the lieutenant in charge of the platoon, and presented the other two guys. Sergeant Kelly, a short, stout guy, took a drag off his cigarette, flipped it to the floor, not far from my feet, and nodded his head in our direction, and so did Sergeant Wahl, a wiry guy, with glasses that made him look like Harry Potter.

"The lieutenant wanted to know why the Pentagon had sent us. Kelly said maybe it was to announce mission accomplished. They had a good laugh. Collins explained we wanted to get information about what our military had accomplished in Fallujah, and he was serving as our guide. The lieutenant told me to just look around. They pissed me off. I told them I'd been looking around and wanted to talk to men on the ground. Find out what kind of resistance they'd encountered. Who were these mujahedeen? We'd had reports of Chechen, Filipino, Saudi, Libyan, and Syrian combatants, and of the Iraqi forces having armed them with our weapons. I wanted to know our strategy. The casualties—ours and theirs. The level of destruction. And the message we were sending to the Iraqis.

"The lieutenant slung his rifle over his shoulder and said they had to rendezvous with another platoon. Elliott and I followed him out of the house and into the sun and the heat and the stink of the corpses, with the sergeants in tow behind us, mumbling stuff to one another, just loud enough for me to hear, crap like, 'I hadn't expected to see any more of their kind, now that the elections are over,' and, 'Yeah, politicians, they stay up long nights grieving over every fucking soldier gets killed.'

"I tried to stay abreast of the lieutenant. He explained that before they launched the ground attack, they'd dropped a lot of two-thousand-pound bombs to loosen things up, scare the shit out of the muj, and kill as many as they could. Then, when they moved in, they used rolling mortar and artillery fire in front of their tracks, and called in air strikes anytime they hit resistance. He asked Kelly what kind of message we were sending the Hajjis, as he called them, and Kelly said we were bringing them hell, one block at a time. Wahl said he didn't know how hell was represented in the Koran, but he suspected we might be painting a picture of it right here in Fallujah. And then the lieutenant told Kelly to describe the squeegee for me. Kelly said, 'Go one street at a time, use our tracks to shake and bake, then enter every room with a boom.' And when I asked what he meant by that, Wahl said, 'You saw that building we were in, how it was all charred black on the inside—the guys toss a frag into every room before they go in. And now we're going back through each block, checking each building for weapons and bomb factories. Sometimes we run into a few dead-enders who managed to survive the first sweep and circle around and attack from behind.'

"We continued walking, and had just passed the tank, when the lieutenant stopped and said, 'What the fuck!' I looked and saw an old man, in a gray robe and a red and white kaffiyeh, who'd entered the square from a street off to our right and was walking with his hand on the shoulder of a boy, maybe ten years old, in jeans and a T-shirt. I wondered what they were doing there, how they could still be alive, and where they were going. They continued walking, as if there was nothing unusual about the sight of corpses, a tank, and a bunch of Marines watching them. The lieutenant thought they might know something and ordered Wahl to send a couple of his men over to pick them up. There was an explosion down one of the streets, flames engulfed the other tank, black smoke billowed up, and then smaller explosions. Insurgents, hiding in the buildings, were firing RPGs and automatic weapons at our men who'd been walking alongside and behind the tank. Some of them fell to the ground, others fired back.

"The lieutenant screamed at Wahl to get—and then he stopped, in mid-sentence, and fell forward. Blood flowed out of a hole through the back of his neck. I stared at the wound. Men shouted. A hand grabbed my shirt and yanked me to the side of the tank. I looked into Wahl's face and knew we might die.

"Bullets hammered the tank and spit up dirt around us. Wahl shouted at me to stay down and crept to the rear of the tank, where one of his men was firing bursts from his M-16. When the other man ducked, Wahl rose and fired several bursts from his rifle, then crouched and the other man fired. I looked in the opposite direction and saw Elliott, a few feet away, also cowering against the tank. Collins, huddled near the front, must've thrown him there. There was an explosion, flames, and a marine who'd been at the front, near Collins, flew onto his back. The tank rocked back and forth as it fired its cannon and machine gun in the direction of the RPGs. I rose up just enough to see part of the line of fire. The tank's cannon was destroying a building, chunk by chunk, and the machine gun pocked the walls.

"I slid down and my eyes landed on the Marine lying on his back. Part of his face had been blown away. I looked in the other direction. Wahl was reciting coordinates into a radio. The lieutenant lay face down in the pool of his own blood. Two fighter jets flew in low. Buildings exploded, flames billowed up, and then everything became still. I waited, my heart pumping so hard I could almost hear it. I wondered if they'd gotten all of the enemy.

"The tank's engine rumbled like a monstrous beast, and Kelly appeared from around the rear. Wahl said he'd radioed the other platoon, and it was on its way, and he'd radioed his squad, too, and they were okay. Once they got everyone reassembled, they could move on. He'd also radioed in some birds to take out the dead and the wounded and the visitors from Oz. He looked at Elliott and me and asked if we were okay. I nodded, yes, and laughed, even though my hands wouldn't stop shaking. Wahl looked at the lieutenant, walked over to his body, knelt, and touched his shoulder, as if he might wake him.

"Kelly stared at the obliterated face of the soldier lying on his back and said, 'You poor motherfucker.' He circled the dead man and screamed, 'You poor, fucking bastard!' And then he spun around and faced the rest of us and shouted, 'They told us, second time through, we'd just be cleaning up.' He pointed at the dead man and asked if that looked like cleaning up, and said the fucking city was full of Hajjis.

"Marines converged from all directions on Wahl, Kelly, and the two dead men. A soldier, prodding the old Iraqi and the young boy with his M16, screamed at them to move, or he'd send them to their fucking paradise. He looked around at the other Marines and said he'd found Ali Baba and his little Sinbad and bet they knew where the Hajjis were hiding. He jabbed his M16 into the back of the old man, who staggered and would've fallen if not for the boy's support, and said look at how they work together, Ali Baba and Sinbad, they'd probably coordinated the ambush.

"Kelly called over and asked him to bring those fucking hajjis to him. He took out his pistol and grabbed the old man by his robe, threw him to his knees, and jabbed the gun to his head. The boy tried to shove Kelly away, but Kelly pushed him toward Mackey and screamed at the old man, demanding to know where the Hajjis were hiding. The old man's eyes bulged with fear, while Kelly kept on screaming, calling him Ali Baba and saying he bet he'd set the whole thing up, and if he didn't wanna go to paradise on the bullet express, he'd better talk. The old man whimpered and shook his head. Kelly told Mackey to take the kid to the other side of the track. Mackey grabbed the kid and pulled him around the tank, where they couldn't be seen.

"And then Kelly lit into the old man and said, 'You fucking Ali Baba, you talk or we're gonna kill that boy. Where are the Hajjis?' He got right into the old man's face and shouted, 'Where are the muj? Where are they? You'd better be scared. We'll kill your fucking little Sinbad, if you don't talk.' The old man looked at the ground, tears streaming down his cheeks. Kelly said, 'Okay, Mackey, shoot the Sinbad.' There was a burst of gunfire on the other side of the tank. The old man sunk to the ground in a heap and wailed and beat his head with his fists.

"After a couple minutes, Kelly shouted to Mackey to bring the kid over. Mackey walked the boy out from behind the other side of the tank and pushed him toward the whimpering man. Kelly was still pointing his gun at the man's head, and it looked like he was going to kill him, when Wahl shouted, 'Kelly, that's enough. You don't wanna face a court martial over this.' Kelly continued screaming at the old man, and Wahl warned him again not to kill him. Kelly looked at Wahl, and then at the rest of us. Everyone was staring at him. Someone shouted, 'Let him go,' and someone else, 'He probably doesn't even understand English.' Wahl asked Kelly if he thought the old man would've walked past us with the kid if he'd known we were going to be ambushed. The boy, whom Mackey was still holding, looked around, and his eyes, wide with terror, locked on to mine, like they were accusing me. And that's what you see in that painting, *Fallujah 1*, the boy's eyes, his face glowing as it rises from the dark, the way it does in my dreams.

"Wahl walked up to Kelly and told him to let the old man go, we needed to move on. Kelly lowered his gun. He walked a few feet away. His shoulders started to shake, and he fell to his knees. He was crying. The old man got up, put his hand on the boy's shoulder, and they walked away. I went over to Wahl, stood next to him, and watched them. Three Black Hawks appeared in the sky, flying low. They descended into the square. And then Wahl said, 'You and your friends, you're going to get on one of those birds and fly back to Oz, where you belong.'

"So Elliott and Collins and I boarded one of the Hawks. As it took off, I looked for the boy and the old man, but with all the dirt whirling around, I couldn't see them. I closed my eyes, and saw the boy's face, his hate-filled eyes accusing me. The Hawk was just beginning to move forward, when a ball of fire exploded right in front of me, in front of Elliott. A flash of light, and everything went black. And Elliott, Collins, the pilot, and the co-pilot became signs of progress."

The light was fading, and shadows filled the studio, like a room full of ghosts. The dark soothed my guilt, and I felt relief. I'd told her the truth, at least what I remembered. Told her with the earnestness of a boy, in a confessional, in a church full of shadows.

Julia's voice startled me, even though she spoke almost in a whisper. "I know you love Jamie. And Mom. And me. I know how much Jamie's death hurt you. And Mom leaving you. I don't blame you for his death. You would never intentionally hurt any of us." She fell silent. "I don't know about Fallujah. Or Iraq. Or what you did. I just know I love you."

"I love you, too."

She embraced me, and then walked toward the painting of the boy, gazed at it, and disappeared in the dark, while I stared at the luminous face and the black eyes.

Chapter 16

THE NEXT MORNING, I woke up thinking of Julia. Should I have remained silent about Fallujah? Did I relay something to her that would haunt her? But Fallujah had become part of me. It would've been dishonest not to tell her. And I felt better for having done so. Maybe we'd be able to talk more easily with one another again.

I went downstairs, noticed her suitcase by the front door, and headed for the kitchen. She wasn't there. I crossed the hall, entered the studio, and saw her standing in front of one of the windows, looking out at the backyard. I walked toward her. "Good morning, Sunshine."

She turned toward me, her eyes full of sadness. "We were so happy, before you started working with the Lowell Group. Why did you?"

"Why?" I froze and shook my head. "Because … because I wanted to be able to provide a good life for you and Jamie. That meant, among other things, earning money. The Lowell Group gave me the opportunity to earn a lot. While doing good."

She remained silent, her eyes filled with doubt.

"Look, we had a vision of a modern Iraq, with an open and free economy. And we were going to use Iraq, the leverage we would have gained there, to create similar economies throughout the Middle East, and democratic societies that would bring freedom to everyone. That was our goal."

"Did it justify killing people?"

"We knew lives would be lost. We didn't anticipate the insurgency. It undermined our control. And then Fallujah happened, and by that time so much had gone wrong. The Iraqis hated us, and the longer we stayed, the more they hated us. Nothing went the way we'd planned, but we weren't giving up. We had to send the Iraqis and everyone that message—we weren't giving up. And then reports arrived about Fallujah being punished for the insurgency, and civilians killed, and the use of white phosphorous. I had to see for myself." I closed my eyes, wishing again I'd never gone to Fallujah. I took a deep breath. "We transformed the city of mosques into the city of hatred—ours and theirs."

She glared at me. "When you were working with the Lowell Group to create that free and open market, did you really think you were doing that for your family? Did you think you were doing that for Jamie and Mom and me?"

"Julia—"

"Did you?"

"If things had worked out in Iraq the way we'd hoped, everyone would've benefitted."

"And somehow that justifies killing people?"

I shook my head.

"And now you think doing those paintings is going to make everything okay?"

"Nothing's ever going to be okay again."

She had tears in her eyes. "Mom is right. Jamie died because of you. Because he couldn't believe you'd do it for the money. You didn't do this Iraq thing for us. You did it for yourself."

She tried to walk past me, but I grabbed her by the shoulder and blocked her way. "Julia—"

"Don't use me as your excuse."

"I'm not some kind of psychopath."

She stared at me, and I let go. I turned and followed her, repeating, "Don't go, please don't go." She continued to the foyer, grabbed her suitcase, and rushed out the door to a taxi in the driveway.

Following a night of drinking, of seeing the contempt in Julia's eyes as she glared at me, after I'd said I wasn't some kind of psychopath, I stood in the living room, gazing at *Eurydice* and *A Woman Alone*. The paintings evoke isolation, entrapment, and hopelessness, but they're beautiful. And beauty solicits admiration. I went into the studio and looked at the *Fallujah*s and the luminous figures rising from an oneiric depth and saw beauty in my paintings, too. And that beauty is a problem, because it solicits admiration while muting the terror that the images had seared into me. I didn't experience the shock, the jolt, the burn I'd felt when I'd seen the two bodies and the boy who'd stared at me. The paintings weren't real unless I could see what I'd felt. They shouldn't be beautiful in the ways I'd been taught, based on the traditional values of painting. I had to somehow wrench my work away from what Dad had taught me to get the effect I wanted.

I didn't know what to do. I thought of the paintings he'd talked to me about and those I'd come to admire over the years, trying to find something that could help me—the Rembrandts; the Vermeers and the Hoppers; Van Gogh, Munch, and Dix; Magritte, Dali, and the other surrealists. No ideas. Nothing. What did I want to paint? Pain. Violence. An emotion, a sensation, an impulse. The impulse to kill, to rip something apart. Rage. And self-loathing. How could something beautiful—a Rembrandt, a Vermeer, or a Hopper—make me feel that?

I stood in front of the easel, staring at the blank space, with no idea of what to do or where to start. I felt like applying paint to the canvas, hoping some pattern would emerge, some structure, but I'd end up with something abstract, devoid of tension, and I recalled Dad's tirades about the abstract expressionists. The one he hated most was Pollock. When Dad would talk about how to prepare a canvas, he'd admonish me to never do what Jack the Dripper had done—paint on unprimed canvas. That was crazy. "Unprimed canvas? A few decades down the road, and all those collectors who are buying his paintings will end up owning piles of rot." Dad would shake his head, laugh, and mumble, "Jesus Christ."

My mind latched onto the phrase, *piles of rot*. I was intrigued by the idea of a painting rotting, so I took one of the canvases on which I hadn't painted, put it on the easel, with the back, unprimed side facing me, thinned some ivory black with turpentine and brushed that side with a black wash. I liked the ragged look and the feel of the paint directly on the canvas, and the way the texture of the canvas came through the wash. It felt like something capable of decaying. Of dying. A truly human work. I set that canvas aside, re-stretched another unused canvas, so I could paint on the unprimed side, and covered it with a black wash. I did the same thing with several canvases.

I rummaged through the piles of trash I'd made the day I'd rid my studio of mementoes. I slipped pictures out from behind cracked panes of glass and found crumpled photos in the trash on the floor and studied them. A shot of me with Pappy, smiling together like the best of friends. Another with the former British Prime Minister. And a third with the Playboy Prince. I shuffled through the pictures and stopped at a medium close-up of Peter and me. Peter, with his hair combed in styled waves, gold-rimmed glasses, and self-contented smile. I could almost smell his sweet cologne and, even though I couldn't see them, I knew he was wearing gold cufflinks, with some kind of gem in each one. Real gems. Rubies, or sapphires. He liked to say he didn't buy fakes. He sold them, though. Yeah, Peter the Eloquent, who could make the organization of a campaign of death sound like the realization of Platonic ideals; Peter, who understood that men like him and his son should never risk their lives for the ideals he loved to preach, because the country needed their leadership; Peter, who'd succeeded where I'd failed. I saw again the piercing look in Julia's eyes when I told her I wasn't some kind of psychopath. We were all psychopaths, with our smug smiles and five-thousand-dollar suits. We supported the invasion and the occupation as a business venture costumed in the rhetoric of freedom.

The next morning, I woke with the rising sun, rushed down to my studio, and set to work. I painted a quick, vague sketch of a figure over the black ground. I mixed cobalt blue and ivory black and thinned the paint with turpentine to create a blue that would seem to emerge from the ground and create volume. That volume became a torso in a blue suit, the sleeves resting on the arms of a chair. With a brush and a rag, I applied thick cobalt blue to the suit, making it stand out more from the ground. The undiluted paint dragged in such a way that the lines and smears caught on the fabric of the canvas, creating a rough, uneven finish, which Dad would have found unacceptable. I loved the ragged texture. It felt as if the mortality of the figure—its capacity to decompose and rot—came right to the surface. And then the face and neck, for which I applied a flake-white impasto unevenly with a trowel, rag, and dry brush, so that the black ground in some areas showed through, as if the face hadn't fully emerged from the darkness; in other areas the black ground and the white created a ghostly gray; and in yet other areas, where the paint was thickest, the narrow face seemed a pasty bone white. The dark eyes I set deep in the face, and the mouth I painted open enough to reveal the teeth, dry brushed with a thick white. Using metallic gold paint straight from the tube, I completed the frame of the chair, with a high back like a throne, pulling the paint drily across the canvas. I added two gold eagles, each one perched on the back posts on either side of the chair. I used the same paint to do the gold-rimmed glasses that seem to both mediate the man's vision and restrain his impulses. I finished the gray of the hair, the white of the collar, the blood red tie appearing at the neck and disappearing in the suit, and then the hands, done with a flake-white impasto, like the face and neck.

In the dying sunlight, at the end of that day or the next, I stepped back to look at what I'd done. A male figure of authority in a blue suit, seated on an American throne, emerges out of a darkness from which it never completely separates. The open mouth and the intense eyes glare at me from behind the gold rimmed glasses, as if the man were overwhelmed by an impulse.

I lay on the mattress on the floor, looking at the man in the dark. Unable to sleep, I got up, turned on the light, and stared at the painting. It frustrated and provoked me, but didn't reveal anything visceral. I sensed there was more. I clenched my teeth. There *would* be more.

After a few hours of sleep, I stood in front of the painting again, outraged by all this man concealed. I hadn't even begun to get beyond his facade. He hadn't yet seen what he had to see, feel what he had to feel. I started a new canvas and repainted the figure, working non-stop, painting wet on wet. The ground, the suit, the torso didn't change much, but I made the eyes more intense, and opened the mouth more, revealing the dark red gullet. It looks like the mouth of an animal shrieking in shock and rage. The teeth, whiter, more prominent, more vicious, emerge like the bared teeth of a predator, ready to kill its prey. The chair is more pronounced, with thicker, heavier gold lines, and the bigger, louder scream—the violence and pain concentrated in the face, and in particular in the mouth and eyes—contrasts with the rigidity of the figure, its hands gripping the armrests more desperately, like a body strapped to an electric chair—or a patient to a hospital bed, reliving the horror of what he'd seen.

I worked compulsively, through that day and the next, because to not work was to let my memories, my dreams, my anxiety, tear me to pieces. Painting was becoming a way for me to go on living. It made everything I felt bearable, because everything went from me onto the canvas. I held onto nothing. At the same time, I dreaded painting, because it brought up the feelings I had to channel, or they'd overwhelm me. But if I didn't paint, I'd be washing a handful of pills down with whiskey.

After the last stroke, my hand holding the brush fell to my side, and I stared at the painting. *Study of Psychopath in Blue Suit.* Everything that had gripped me when I was trapped in my head, everything that had been gnawing at me from the inside, everything I hadn't known about myself, all of it had gone on canvas. The orgasmic pleasure of wealth, of power, of superiority, of dominance, and of seeing all of that reflected in the eyes of others. And the masochism of guilt. Oh, that's huge—the incredible pleasure of pain. The constant accusations. The revulsion. And the visions— the dead, the mutilated. Yeah, once this man opens his eyes, once he sees what he's done, the pain he's inflicted, the person he is, he shrieks and cries out. And his pain excites me. It rivets me to him.

I set the palette and the brush on the desk, took another look at the painting, grabbed a rag, and with a single swipe smeared the paint on the face.

A few days later, I made a thin wash of burnt umber and ivory black and brushed it onto the canvas. A wash so thin, so streaky, it suggests a veil, beneath which the psychopath tries to conceal himself, and a wall, as if the veil imprisons him in the darkness from which he comes.

CHAPTER 17

JAMIE DIES AGAIN AND again. Sometimes he smiles. His lips might move, but I can't hear what he's saying. And I don't hear the gunfire. I just see the shock on his face, when the bullet strikes, cutting him off mid-sentence. He's looking at me, but no longer sees me. The bullet severs what united us, and I no longer mean anything to him. I live that last look of non-recognition over and over. He falls to the ground in silence, and blood flows, pooling around his head, the pool getting larger and larger, until it covers the scene, like a red wash over a painting. Other times, instead of falling, he stares at me, his eyes burning through me with the power of white phosphorus, accusing me of the bullet, and I wake up crying.

Every night he died, and every day I tried to bring him back. I found some of his letters in the guest room, where Valerie used to sleep. I read a letter he'd written while in boot camp, which Julia had read to me in the hospital, and the other letters he'd written after joining the Army, and those he'd sent from the various summer and soccer camps he'd attended, from the time he was ten until he'd finished high school.

I went downstairs to the bookshelves in the living room, pulled out old albums, and sat on the couch and looked at photographs. Jamie, the first day of his life, nursing at Valerie's breast. Jamie, at two, wearing a black top hat, his long blond hair hanging out from underneath. At four, carrying Leo, our black cat, who hung limp, draped over his forearms like an armful of laundry. At nine, standing with his foot on a soccer ball, as if he'd conquered it. At fifteen, in three-quarter profile, looking out a window, his long brown hair covering his ear, a sullen look on his face. At sixteen, dribbling the ball in a soccer match, his hair tied in a ponytail. And the last picture—Jamie, at eighteen, his hair cut short, sitting across from me at a table, in an open-air restaurant on the *Côte d'Azur*.

That was the summer Valerie and I took the kids on vacation in France. Jamie and I went off on our own one day and visited the town of Grasse, with its steep cobblestone streets, medieval cathedral, and perfume shops. He'd read the novel *Perfume*, which is set in Grasse, and was curious to see the old city. We returned to the coast for lunch at a restaurant, where we had *bouillabaisse*, and took pictures of each other. In the one I took of him, he looked at me and smiled, his dark eyes warm with happiness. Behind him, people sitting at tables, and beyond, creamy white beaches, cliffs in the distance, the blue sky, and the dark blue sea.

I took some of the photographs to the studio and looked at them again. In nearly each one, Jamie's eyes caught my attention, and I thought of the cliché about the eyes being the window to the soul. I wanted to look through that window and paint his soul. I wanted to hold it close and never let it go.

I selected the picture of Jamie in the restaurant and taped it to the side of the easel, on which I'd set a small canvas, with the primed side facing me. I wanted to bring him back to life. His portrait would live for years. And it would be beautiful. I flooded the canvas with the light of the Mediterranean, giving it both an ethereal and sensual quality. As I painted his face, I felt him return. He was with me, we were together, just as we'd been that day. I finished his eyes—his deep, brown eyes—and stepped back to look at them. As they gazed at me, they seemed to express a premonition of what was going to happen, even though he was smiling. There was something haunting, something sad. I couldn't understand it. If the eyes are the window to the soul, then whose soul were they revealing? Whose knowledge? I wanted to give him eternal life, as if I were God, but all I was doing was reliving a moment I knew was gone.

I couldn't stop painting that knowledge. For the next portrait, I worked from the photograph of him at two, with such an earnest look, putting on the black top hat, his arms raised, his hands holding the brim on each side, his plump cheeks creating dimples in the corners of his mouth. He wore a red flannel shirt and a pair of blue overalls. I felt happy as I brushed the paint, wet on wet, working quickly, confident this time I would succeed. I finished and, as I studied the painting, smiled and whispered, "Topper," the nickname Valerie and I used for him when he'd put on the hat. But, as I continued gazing at the painting, the accusing look of the boy in Fallujah emerged from Jamie's eyes, as if his face had become that boy's.

Every day, I brought him back to life and lost him again. And every night, I'd drink. I started looking at folios, at paintings that dealt with loss, and soon found myself staring at crucifixions, descents from the cross, lamentations, pietas, and entombments—fonts filled with the sorrows of mourners. Sooner or later we all lose our Jesus, and all of the great artists—Michelangelo, Rembrandt, Rubens, El Greco—they all knew that Jesus unites us in our loss.

One night in the studio, I was sitting near the desk, a folio of Rembrandt's work opened on my lap, and found myself gazing at *Flayed Ox*, a painting in which the rear legs of an ox's carcass are tied to a crossbeam in the center foreground of a dark shed and splayed open for air to circulate along the surface of meat, fat, and bone. A woman, peering into the shed from an open door in the background, gazes with reverence, as if in the presence of something sacred, at the carcass hanging from the crossbeam in a way that evokes Christ hanging from the cross. The light from the doorway illuminates the background of the painting, but the carcass, in the center foreground, seems to capture that light and glow, almost as if the light comes from within it. I'd seen the painting several times at the Louvre and had marveled at the texture of meat, fat, and bone that Rembrandt had achieved with the impasto of thick reds and whites. As I gazed at the reproduction, I remembered insisting on the coffin bearing Jamie's body being opened after it had arrived home, so I could look at him, touch his face, feel his cold flesh, and convince myself he was dead. As I gazed at Rembrandt's painting, I felt the truth of my son's death.

I turned a few pages in the folio and came to a reproduction of *Lucretia*. The painting hangs in the art museum in Minneapolis. I'd seen it several times when I lived there. I've always loved this painting. It had affected me so profoundly, I can see it with my eyes closed. Unlike other artists who had turned the rape of Lucretia into an operatic scene, emphasizing the rape and ignoring the emotional impact, Rembrandt had painted Lucretia alone. Her figure is surrounded by darkness—made up probably of several layers of ivory black and burnt umber. She's perhaps sitting on the edge of a bed, it's hard to tell. Beneath a gold dress, spread open, she wears a white undergarment. Her extended hand grasps a gold cord, and the other hand holds the dagger she used to stab herself. Blood flows from the wound and streams down the garment, and her life flows with it. Her face, turned slightly to the side, reveals a complex of emotions difficult to translate—sadness, longing, melancholy, isolation. She's drifting toward death, while casting a dying glance at what she's leaving behind.

Rembrandt's Lucretia was Hendrickje Stoffels, his lover, who'd lived with him for over fifteen years, served as his model for many of his paintings, and had a daughter with him. That's what got them into trouble. When she was pregnant, she was called before a church council for living in sin with Rembrandt and condemned for committing the acts of a whore. The good society of Amsterdam cast Hendrickje and him out, and he lost much of his patronage. They had to move to a poorer area of the city, and the two of them, with their daughter, Cornelia, and his son, Titus, struggled to survive. Hendrickje died less than ten years later, of the plague, and about three years after her death he painted her in a burst of creative energy. Painted her as the victim of men of power, at the moment her life was leaving her body. Painted her as a way of being with her when she died. A work of passion, of love. And of rage. A work that implicitly compares a rapist in Roman history to the church leaders in Amsterdam.

Gazing at the reproduction of *Lucretia*, I thought of Jamie. I wanted to be with him at the moment of his death. Later, as I lay on the mattress on the floor, the reproductions of the *Flayed Ox* and the crucifixions and the pietas came back to me, and in the morning I set to work. I selected a large canvas, with the unprimed side facing me. From now on, I would do all my work on the wrong side.

I set the canvas on the easel and started applying ivory black and ultramarine blue, creating a cold, deep, dark space. In the background, I painted a Humvee. Its headlights illuminate the middle and foreground, but not with a warm light, as in the *Flayed Ox*— that was a spiritual light, the light of auras, of halos. No, this is a cold light. The kind you might use to hunt someone you want to kill. I painted a jeep off to one side, its headlights focused on a cross in the center, and, on the other, men holding flashlights, also focused on the cross. Not a wooden cross—that would have been much too warm. A metal cross. Cold like the bullet that killed Jamie.

I painted him naked on the cross, because he was born naked. Because, for me, he is at once the infant I saw born, the child I held in my arms, the adolescent who rebelled against me, and the young man who went off to war. Jamie's mouth is open in a scream, his face contorted, his arms and legs twisting, his body thrusting forward, as if he were being electrocuted, as if he were trying to leap off the cross to which his hands and feet have been riveted. I painted his body in a thick impasto of whites and reds and blues and blacks, sculpting the limbs, feeling the bone, the tensed muscles, the agony. He screams repeatedly, an animal's shriek of pain. He realizes his life is ending and he's lost everyone and everything, and he's afraid and wails. And then my child cried out, *Why have you abandoned me?* And I answered, my voice trembling with emotion, "I haven't. I never will."

I spent the evening drinking, and returning to the studio to look at the unfinished crucifixion. The vehicles, the lights, the crucifix—all of that seemed a little off. And I remembered the words I'd put in Jamie's mouth, and how they'd elevated me.

Jamie returned that night, and in the morning, I set to work on a new painting. In the bottom foreground and center ground of a large canvas, I painted a flat brown space, foreshortening it to make it appear like a floor that rounds off on either side toward the center middle ground to suggest the curved front of a stage. Following the curve of that stage, in the background, I painted an orange wall, sealing the stage off and turning the space into a closed room.

In the center foreground, I painted Jamie, naked, writhing with pain, as I'd painted him in the crucifixion. But there was no cross. His body is suspended above the floor, at about the same level as if he were riveted to that iron cross. In the left background, just off center, I painted a door—or actually, lines suggesting the edges of a door, the kind that I'd seen in the *hôtels*, the old mansions, in Paris, in which a door might be cut into a wall, and be distinguishable only by the line of that cut and a barely discernible handle. Next to the door stands a small, male figure in a dark blue suit. He looks as if he's trying to sneak away, and then stops, his hand on the door handle, and gazes up at Jamie in front of him.

CHAPTER 18

I WASN'T ABLE TO DO much during the days following my paintings of Jamie. I'd stand in front of a canvas and stare at it, not feel anything, and go stare at something else—the backyard, the flowers, the birds, the trellis. And then one afternoon, I got a call from Julia. She was sorry for the things she'd said. Her voice trembled, and mine did, too, as I told her I was so happy to talk to her, she had nothing to be sorry for. Nothing. I felt her pain. I wept, and she wept, and when we finished weeping, and taking some deep breaths and sighing, she asked if it was okay for her to come home Friday. She had something for me—a ticket for the opening in two weeks of *A Streetcar Named Desire*. I was ecstatic that in just two days she'd be home.

But after we hung up, I panicked. How in the hell could I go to New York? Since returning from the hospital, I hadn't left the house, except for the visit to the physical therapist. I'd skipped my other appointments. I didn't want to go out in public and have people stare at my face. And what about Valerie? Was she going to be there? I should've asked. I'd find out when Julia came home. But then she'd see the new paintings. What would she think? To calm myself, I straightened up the house, searched through Julia's bookshelves, found a collection of plays by Williams that included *Streetcar*, and started reading, my mind wandering as I thought about opening night.

Late Friday afternoon, I was looking at the paper, checking my watch every few minutes, when the front door opened, and Julia shouted, "Dad, I'm home." She rushed into my arms, we hugged, and she sat down on the couch, close to my chair. I told her again I was so happy she'd come home, and paused and asked, "How's your mother?"

"She's okay."

"Is she going to be there opening night?"

"Opening night. Oh, my God! I've been so busy with rehearsals. This is the most difficult role I've ever had. A lot more challenging than Annie."

"Annie?"

"The character I played in *All My Sons*."

"Ah! The play about the factory owner. The war profiteer."

"And the two families."

"There are always families." I thought of Jamie, and guilt like a python tightened its coil around my heart and lungs. "Are you sure you want me to come?"

"The ticket's in my purse. I'll get it in a minute."

"Okay."

"Dad ..."

"If you have your mom's ticket, I can take them both. I could meet her in the lobby. That way you don't have to worry about getting it to her. And I could talk to her, before we take our seats." I paused. "Oh, God, what am I thinking? I'm the last person she'd want to talk to."

Julia looked depressed.

"I'm sorry. I just wanted to make things easy for you. You've got a lot—I mean, you're starting tech rehearsals soon, right?"

"Mom already has her tickets."

"Her tickets? What do you mean, her tickets?"

"She's bringing two guests."

"Who?"

"I don't know."

My mind raced, searching for names, faces.

"Is there anything to eat? I haven't had a thing since breakfast."

I shrugged and mumbled, "Some cans of soup."

"Maybe we can get take-out, and tomorrow I'll go buy groceries."

"You really don't know who she's going with?"

"They're probably old friends from the city."

She didn't have any friends in New York that I knew of, aside from the wives of a few of the men I'd worked with and a couple of women she knew from her college days. But she didn't seem close to them.

"What have you been doing since I saw you last? Dad?"

"What? Oh. Painting."

"That's all?"

"That's it." I was still wondering with whom Valerie might be going, when I heard Julia say, "I'd like to see your paintings. But not tonight." I looked and saw her gazing at *A Woman Alone*, a reflective smile on her face.

We got home from picking up our take-out, sat at the kitchen table, and served ourselves. Julia swallowed her first forkful of food and exclaimed, "Oh, this tastes good!" Her eyes radiated happiness. I nodded in agreement, while thinking about our conversation in the car on the way back, when she'd talked about *Streetcar*, her courses, and her friends—one, in particular, who'd been very supportive in helping her deal with Jamie's death and the separation.

"I'd like to hear more about your friend, Phil. What's he like?"

"Well." She grinned and gave me a coy look. "He's kind of like you." She chuckled. "He likes to talk about changing the world."

"Oh! And how does he plan on doing that?"

"Through theater. He wants to create his own company and stage plays that deal with social justice and politics." She paused. "But, he's also very different from you."

"Well, of course he is."

"Yeah, but … No." She bit her lip.

"No? What do you mean?" I studied her face. "Julia, what are you hiding?"

"He's very critical of the Iraq War … and of the people who got us into it."

I nodded. "Well, he's not wrong to be critical of those people. And, I guess, of me."

"He's really kind of a purist. I mean …" She shook her head and sighed.

"Well, when I was young, I was kind of a purist, too. A big admirer of Che Guevara—"

"You?"

"I moved to Austin, Texas, to do a Ph.D. and work with a historian who specialized in Latin American liberation movements, and I wanted to change the world—through teaching."

"I didn't know that. What happened?"

"How did I go from being a left-wing idealist to a war profiteer?"

"You're not a war profiteer."

"Well, I profited from the war, so I guess I am. But how … why did I go from one to the other?" I looked past her, avoiding her eyes. "As the money increased, I found I liked it, and everything it enabled me to do. I became a man people looked up to. And money was my servant. I ordered whatever I wanted, and, bingo! it appeared, it happened—sailing on yachts, going on wonderful vacations, having a beautiful home and family. And little by little, liberating people became a rationalization, rather than a goal." I looked into her eyes and shook my head. "It happened so gradually, I didn't notice it. Well, from time to time maybe I did, but I could always latch onto the rationalization that my work would help some of the people exploited by a corrupt system."

I paused. This was embarrassing. Humiliating. But I decided to go on. "What I've just said is true, but … things are more complex than that. I always felt a need, from the time I was a kid, to please other people. That was one of the things that defined my relationship with my dad. I performed for him, to see in his eyes his approval, his love. Because what was I, without it?" I paused, thinking how Dad's death changed my life, left me feeling unanchored. I looked at Julia's eyes focused on me. "I've always had this need to see myself in the eyes of the people I love, or whose respect I covet, and making a lot of money enabled me to be the ultimate performer, a performer with status, with power." I paused. "I learned the performer had to succeed if I were to be happy."

Julia's eyes brimmed with tears. She reached across the table and laid her hands on mine.

"The Iraq War ..." I shook my head, feeling tears trickle down my own cheeks. I took a deep breath, and another, until I calmed myself enough to talk. "I ended up a very different person from that graduate student who wanted to write a dissertation on liberation movements in South America." I paused. "But, maybe not. The person I am now was already part of me."

"Did you write a dissertation?"

"No."

"Why not?"

"I moved to Austin for two reasons. One was to do the Ph.D. The other was to be close to a woman, with whom I was in love." I paused, remembering the pain. "She rejected me. Her rejection made me feel worthless. Like a piece of trash." I took a deep breath and sighed. "I dropped out of the program. At the end of the first year." I looked at Julia. "I'm tired. I need to lie down. Maybe we can talk more tomorrow."

She tightened her grip on my hands. "I love you, Dad."

"I love you, too. You mean everything to me. Everything."

The next morning, I came downstairs and found Julia sitting at the kitchen table, in a sweat shirt and jeans, facing the window. I put my hand on her shoulder, kissed her on the top of her head, and asked if she'd slept well. She looked up, and I saw her bloodshot eyes.

"I was going to get some groceries this morning and make breakfast, until I looked at the paintings."

I sat down close to her.

"That crucifixion is Jamie, isn't it?"

I nodded.

"Why did you paint him like that? I thought he died without pain."

"I painted how it felt for me."

She shook her head and bit her lip. "You do this every day? Why?"

"I try to get everything out during the day, but I fill up again at night."

"I don't know how you can live like this."

"Not very well."

"Those men in blue suits, why are they screaming like that? They look insane."

"I call those paintings, *Study of Psychopath in Blue Suit 1* and *2*."

"They have such big mouths. They look like animals, like they're going to attack."

"Yeah. The mouth of the one I painted second is larger. He's screaming because he's about to sink his teeth into something alive, rip it to bloody shreds, and devour it. But he's not an animal— he wears a blue tailored suit. Might be a member of the advisory board of a powerful investment firm, or a CEO. He's very adept at developing ideas that are supposed to help people. Like bringing free and open markets to the Middle East—which would be free and open above all to people like him. And he makes those tough decisions that have to be made—like calculating how many people might die for him to realize his dream. But he knows—he has always known—that his success is worth every life it might cost. So, he screams, because he can hardly control himself.

"But the psychopath I painted is suddenly no longer a psychopath, or maybe was never really a psychopath, and sees and feels what he's doing, what he's done, and having that knowledge and those feelings is almost like being strapped to an electric chair, strapped to who he is. There's no escape. That's how I imagined the psychopath feeling when he sees himself for what he is. That's how I felt."

"Dad, you're not a psychopath."

"If you have to reassure me I'm not, then maybe I am. I think I was. I think I'm recovering. A recovering psychopath. There should be a program for us. People probably get a lot of help becoming psychopaths. We're not born that way. It would be nice if we could get help with the recovery. We could call it Psychopathic Recovery. Would give a new meaning to PR."

The day of opening night of *Streetcar*, nearly two weeks later, I flew to New York. I was so anxious about seeing Valerie, I didn't think about people staring at my face. The cab pulled up in front of the hotel near Lincoln Center, and I hurried into the building to the registration desk and up to my room, wondering all the while how my encounter with Valerie would go. I skipped dinner, took a cab to the theater, and found a place in the lobby, up against a wall, from which I could see nearly everyone. No sight of Valerie. When the lobby was nearly empty, I headed for my seat and scanned the audience again before sitting down.

But when Julia came on stage, I forgot about Valerie. Julia's performance mesmerized me. Her voice—her Southern drawl, sometimes high pitched, even a little shrill, other times fading or drifting off in a fantasy—and the movements of her body—as she extended herself toward another character, or hesitated, or recoiled in fear or shock—made me feel Blanche's emotions as she relived the disappointments and dreams that haunted her. Her eyes dilated at times as if she were amazed by what she heard or saw, in the world she shared with the other characters, or in the one she remembered, or the one that will never be anything but a dream. Julia uttered her last line—"Whoever you are, I have always depended on the kindness of strangers"—the curtain fell, and the audience applauded. The actors returned for two encores, with Julia in the center.

I merged with the crowd as it flowed into the lobby that resonated with explosive exclamations and shrieks of laughter. I weaved past the groups of college kids and family members and friends, peering around people's heads, looking for Julia. Her face appeared.

She still wore her costume—a lacy dress and a shawl draped across her shoulders. A couple stepped aside, and Valerie, in a black dress and white shawl, came into view, with Alex standing next to her. They leaned forward to hear a woman talk amidst all the noise. Julia caught sight of me as I approached and stared at me with her mouth agape. Valerie turned her head to follow Julia's eyes and saw me, and her smile morphed into a glare.

The woman who'd been talking also turned her head, her lips open, as if my approach had stopped her in mid-sentence. She stepped aside so I could embrace Julia. I whispered in her ear, "What a magnificent performance. I'm so proud of you."

I pulled back, our eyes met, she tried to smile and said, "Thanks, Dad." She looked at the woman who'd been talking and said, "Professor Lee, I'd like you to meet my father. Dad, this is Professor Lee. She directed the play."

As I shook the director's hand, she said, "You have such a talented daughter. Her performance of Blanche is one of the best I've ever seen by a student."

"Valerie and I are very proud of her."

Valerie moved closer to Julia, as if taking possession of her, and said to the director, "We thoroughly enjoyed Julia's performance. Every minute of it."

"We certainly did," Alex said. He glanced at me. "Hello, Dick."

Peter Rubin appeared, and Alex stepped aside, so Peter could take what appeared to be his place next to Valerie. She gazed at him with a warm smile as he said, looking around at us, "Wasn't that a fabulous production? Julia is such a gifted young lady."

"Vivien Leigh had better look out." Valerie grinned at him.

"Vivien Leigh's dead," I said.

"Whenever you show up, someone dies," Valerie said.

The director glanced back and forth at Valerie and me and smiled. "It was lovely meeting you. Have a wonderful evening." She leaned toward Julia, murmured, "Good work," and walked away.

Valerie gave Julia a hug, congratulated her, and walked past me as if I didn't exist. Peter and Alex echoed Valerie's congratulation and ignored me as they followed her. I couldn't think or move, frozen by the shock. Julia said, "I'm sorry, Dad." She was shaking her head, tears in her eyes. She offered to meet me in my hotel room as soon as possible. I rushed for the exit, passing Valerie's mother, who also ignored me as she held onto the arm of the man accompanying her.

I took a cab to my hotel and paced back and forth in my room, screaming to myself, *How long has that creep been sleeping with her? That second day home from the hospital, when I woke from a nap and found Valerie had left in the car, had she gone to his apartment? All those times she went out for a walk, did she meet him somewhere? And that night, on the way home in the car, when she talked about how handsome, wealthy, sophisticated Peter had probably charmed the young Marie-Thérèse right out of her panties, had he already charmed Valerie out of hers? Maybe that's what he was doing, when he'd tell stories about sailing in the Caribbean, and Valerie would gaze at him with a bewitched smile. Maybe things had started before I met Peter. Maybe that's why I received the invitation to attend the Lowell Group's banquet at the hotel and found Valerie and I had been assigned to the same table as him and Marie-Thérèse. And then he offered me a position that required I travel out of the country—how convenient! And he probably didn't regret in the least the divorce from Marie-Thérèse. I never saw it coming, but when I told Valerie I hadn't, she said, Really? It was so clear to her.*

I heard a knock at the door, opened, and saw a look on Julia's face that seemed to reflect my depression. I invited her in, gestured toward an armchair, and pulled up a chair and sat down close to her, the questions still screaming in my head.

"I'm so sorry you had to go through that, Dad."

"Do you have any idea how long this has been going on?"

"No," she sighed, shaking her head. She took a breath. "Mom invited me to her apartment, last Friday."

"*Our* apartment. Legally." I heard the anger in my voice and sighed. "Sorry. Go ahead."

"She offered me a glass of wine. I was surprised. She'd never done that before. We toasted our evening together and talked about all kinds of things. She seemed so warm and open. She even served me a second glass. I felt I could open up, so I said, 'I'd love for you and Dad to get back together.'" Julia paused. "Her warmth vanished. She said, 'Never.' She could never live with you again. And she repeated all the horrible things she'd said before, about Jamie dying because of you, because of your adolescent idealism, because of the crazy stuff that led him to join the Army, and on and on. And then the doorbell rang. She stared at me, like she didn't know what to do, and then she wiped her tears and left. And when she returned, she had Peter with her. She introduced us. I didn't know what to do." She shook her head. "He told me he was looking forward to seeing me perform onstage, and then he excused himself, said he had to make some phone calls, and went into her bedroom. I asked if he was living with her. She said they were friends."

I could see Julia didn't want to continue. I took her hands in mine and looked into her eyes. "It might be painful, but I'd rather know. Please tell me everything."

She took a deep breath, closed her eyes, as if she couldn't bear to see what was going to happen, then looked at me. "Mom said, 'Peter has a son. He's in graduate school. And he would never do what Jamie did, because his father is always honest with him about what he does and about the world. He doesn't fill his son's head with crazy ideas that lead him to do crazy things.'"

I looked down at the floor, took a deep breath, and sighed. "Peter's not a pathetic excuse for a father." I paused. "Well, maybe she's right. Maybe if I hadn't talked about how the projects Elliott and I worked on over the years were liberating people and raising them out of poverty, and the invasion of Iraq would lead to the liberation of millions of people ..." I shook my head. "Never being fully honest with him, that's pretty much the same thing as lying." I reflected. "I deceived myself, too. A lot of people have died, and a lot more are going to die."

"Dad, don't do this to yourself."

After I walked her down to her cab and returned to my room, I collapsed onto the bed and continued doing that to myself until I fell asleep.

One night, Valerie came back to me. It had been a long time since we'd made love, but, strangely, I wasn't surprised when she came downstairs to my office, where I was working at my desk. She was wearing nothing but her robe. She moved behind the desk and stood next to me, and as I looked up, she leaned toward me, opened her robe and encircled my head with it, and I leaned into her skin— warm and moist from the shower she'd taken—and started kissing her breast and her belly, and just as I was about to get on my knees, she gave my arm a little pull, and I rose to my feet, and we went upstairs.

The sun was low in the sky, its rays penetrating the lace curtain, and the light was fading from a warm gold to gray. She let her robe fall from her shoulders, helped me undress as we kissed, and I laid her down on the bed, kissing her body from her lips to her thighs. I didn't worry about the kids. They weren't there. It wasn't because they'd gone off to college. It was as if they hadn't been born yet. Valerie and I made love the way we would when we were young. I'd found her again. She'd never left me, never stopped loving me, and never would.

Exhausted, we lay in bed, a slight breeze blowing across our skin, just enough to evaporate the sweat and send a shiver through my body.

She got out of bed and walked toward the bathroom, her long brown hair covering her neck. The curves of her shoulders, her right breast, back, buttocks and thighs caught the warmth of the last light and glowed in the encroaching darkness. She looked like a sculpture. Her right leg bent as she stepped forward and passed, head slightly bowed, through a translucent curtain.

I awoke with that image from the dream, and it stayed with me as I went down to the studio and started working. I created a deep, dark background on the canvas and then began painting Valerie in flake white, stepping into the darkness, her head slightly bowed, her body in a three-quarter view, seen from behind. The white—in particular in those areas of her body closer to the darkness—was so thin, the black beneath created a gray color, as if her body was becoming part of the darkness. I applied fatter layers of white—almost an impasto—to sculpt part of her shoulder and back, her arm closest to me, her buttock, and the curve of her thigh moving forward. I painted a gray wash, like a rain, a translucent curtain with a gap not quite the width of her body, so that she seemed to be both covered by the curtain and walking through it, into an opening in the darkness. Later, to the curtain, I added a few thin streaks of an ochre wash, the color and the warmth of the sun, and pooled some of it in parts of her body. As I stepped back, I could feel the glow of the fading sun touching her skin, playing across the surface. My eyes lingered on the modeling of the underside of her thigh, her beautiful thigh, and on the gray space between her legs. I felt her body move.

She was gone.

CHAPTER 19

I WAS IN THE KITCHEN, making coffee, when the doorbell rang. I opened the front door and saw Maria. My breath caught, and I felt the pain of that night when I left her house for the last time. Now the woman I thought I'd never see again stood in front of me, a little rounder, heavier, with some lines in her face the young Maria didn't have, and dressed casually in jeans, a blouse, and a sweater, as if it were normal for her to be at my door, looking up at me. She was about to say something, but her face froze, her lips open, the words still in her mouth.

"That's what happens when people look at me."

She started to raise her hand, as if she were going to touch my face, but stopped. Her eyes met mine, she smiled, and I remembered how their color used to make me think of warm dark chocolate. "May I come in?"

"Oh, yes. Please."

She stepped into the foyer and looked around at the rooms on either side. "You have a beautiful house," she said, gazing at my face without flinching.

"Yeah. You've lost a lot of your drawl."

"Oh, Mr. Rayburn," she drawled, "I can bring it back whenever I want."

We shared a nervous laugh that left us staring at each other.

"I tried calling, but no one answered."

I nodded. "I stopped answering the landline."

"I finally got Valerie's cell. She said she doesn't live here anymore."

"How did she sound?"

"Cold. But not any colder than the previous time I talked to her. She was angry then about my articles on the war."

"Yeah," I said. "'We know they've got WMDs, because they got them from us.'"

She chuckled at my recitation of one of her lines.

For a second, I caught a glimpse of the young Maria, who might grin like a kid and blow me a kiss, and my breath caught again. I asked her if she'd like a cup of coffee and guided her to the kitchen. She sat down at the table, and I scooped more grounds into the filter and got the coffee started. She asked how I felt.

"Good. Still some pain in my leg, and of course there's the Frankenstein-monster effect every time someone sees me. I almost never go out."

"You move around well."

"And then there's the stuff in my head. The stuff I can't forget."

"Are you getting help?"

"I did for a while, in the hospital." I got two mugs out of the cupboard. "You still take milk and sugar?"

"Got out of that habit when I started my first job as a journalist. With all the coffee I was drinking, I'd weigh two hundred pounds if I'd kept adding milk and sugar."

"Two hundred pounds?" I chuckled. I looked at her and noticed she was staring at the window with its web of cracks.

"What happened?"

"Someone lost his temper. It was a bad night."

"Oh." She nodded as she looked at me.

"Yeah. The mirror has been smashed. Hopefully for good."

The water boiled and gurgled through the grounds. I filled the mugs, carried them to the table, and sat down. She looked at me as if she were trying to read my face, or maybe find it.

"I've read some of your articles," I said.

"I hope they're better than the first one."

"The first one?"

"'Listen up, Austinites.'"

"Oh, yeah." We laughed. It felt good. It seemed forever since I'd laughed.

"I'm publishing a collection of my articles. That one won't be in it."

Our eyes met again. It seemed incomprehensible I could be so close to her. I looked at her hand resting on the table, holding her mug, and imagined touching it.

"Do you ever think about us?" I asked.

"About us?" She nodded. "Yeah. When I have some down time. It's like smoking a joint, or having a couple shots of whiskey. I relax, let myself go, and memories return. And then I put them away."

I grinned. "And then you write an article attacking the assholes who came up with this war."

She arched her eyebrows.

"Don't worry. I think your articles are right on."

"That sounds very seventies."

"It does."

"And reassuring. I didn't know whom I was going to meet when I came here."

"I've changed a lot. Do you remember, when we met up in Paris, at that café on the *Boul'mich*? You'd had your hair cut à la *Cixous* by some stylist on the *Champs Elysées,* and you said something about *le regard de l'Autre.*"

"*Je me suis libérée du regard de l'Autre.*"

"Yeah. I've freed myself from the look of the Other."

"The gaze of the Other. Ah, those were my phallogocentric-deconstruction days. I doubt I understood half of what I was saying. But, who did?"

"I've been performing for the Other most of my life. But not anymore. Now I'm paying. I pay every night. Every day. I'll pay the rest of my life."

She extended her hand toward mine and stopped, her fingers just a couple inches away, her eyes peering into mine.

"I've started painting."

"I've heard that can help with PTSD."

"Is that what this is? PTSD?"

"What do you think?"

"This isn't just some illness from which I want to recover. For the first time in my life, I feel I'm living with the truth." I looked down at the table, knowing if I continued talking about this, I'd fall apart. "You got married."

"To Jake Pringle. The journalist."

"How long after?"

"After you and I separated?"

"Yeah."

"A year. And we got divorced two years later."

"Why? I'm sorry. I'm asking too many questions."

"No, that's okay. I didn't love him. It wasn't his fault. I married him on the rebound. A rebound of my own doing." Her smile fluttered and died. She looked down at her coffee.

"I've seen your articles in a lot of newspapers."

"I've been lucky." She nodded, as she seemed to reflect back on the years. "I earned that luck. Worked my little ass off."

"Twenty-five years ago, I would've said, your pretty little ass."

She chuckled. "That's what you would've said." She took a sip, set her mug down on the table, and wrapped her hands around it.

I looked at her fingers interlaced around the mug, and then at her eyes. "I wonder …" I paused, embarrassed by what I was about to ask. "Did your father approve of Jake?"

"Did he approve? Yeah, at first. Jake came from a rich, conservative family of good ol' boy Texans. But he turned out to be pretty liberal, unlike the rest of his family. And brash. So, by the time we got married, Daddy hated his guts. But, by then, everything was a mess. I was working with a colleague, investigating politicians who'd accepted illegal gifts and campaign contributions, and the people who were buying politicians, and one of the people the investigation led us to was Daddy. About the same time, I learned Jimmy was my half-brother."

"What?"

"Yeah. My half-brother. Peggy told me. I'd suspected, but didn't want to know. After learning that, and after the investigation, I had to reimagine my father. Who was he? And why did he have so much power over me? I'd done everything to avoid those questions. You seemed to push me toward asking them. I chose ignorance over you. Ignorance can make you happy—for a while. But one year, things changed. We all flew to Maine to spend a couple weeks at the summer home of Daddy's family. That meant sailing, tennis, and golf during the day, and martinis, manhattans, and good food and wine at night. My Uncle Elias and Daddy got to drinking one day, and by the time we sat down to dinner they were pickled. Elias said something about a favor he'd done for my father, back when he was a senator—arranging for someone to be called up to serve in the war. The story about my father and Felipe came out. What you'd already guessed. Mom left my father. Then he found out about my role in the investigation. He claimed I'd betrayed him. He didn't go to prison, but by the time it was all over, he and my mom had divorced, she moved to San Antonio, he told me I was an ungrateful little bitch, as trustworthy as a goddamn rattlesnake, and my husband was a goddamn communist. And from then on, Jake and I were pretty much goddamn this and goddamn that."

"And today?"

"My father doesn't talk to me. I went out to the house to visit him a few weeks ago. The lawn had become a field of weeds that had overgrown the gardens. All the blinds and drapes were closed. No one answered the door. I walked around back. The swimming pool was a swamp of brown water and rotting leaves. I walked back to the front and saw a curtain pulled open a few inches in the living room. He was watching me. He closed the curtain as soon as our eyes met. I rang the doorbell again, but he didn't answer. He'd sold his oil company years ago, and I've heard rumors he has women, younger than me, come and stay with him." She paused. "He's still my father. There's all this emotion, all this pain—I don't know what to do with it."

I nodded, feeling the hurt in her voice.

"But, my mother and Anita, my sister, and I, we talk a lot. And the three of us get together for holidays."

"I'm sorry about your father. And sorry, too, I couldn't figure out how to relate to him back then." I shook my head. "I was so immature."

"I don't think what happened between you and my father had anything to do with maturity. He thought you were looking for easy money, he thought that about a lot of men, and no matter what you might've done, he wouldn't have trusted you." She looked down at her coffee, and back up at me, the pain still in her eyes. "Anita and I have talked a lot about him over the years. He loved us very deeply, but he was also very possessive. And controlling. She fled when she was about twenty, so she could live her own life, make her own decisions. Marrying Jake was my way of getting away from him. Dad would love me as if I were a child, but withdraw that love anytime I did something he didn't like. He was amazingly manipulative. It took years of therapy for me to learn how to deal with him."

The front door opened and closed, and Julia cried, "I'm back."

"In the kitchen," I shouted.

Julia burst in with a bag of groceries in each arm and stopped when she saw Maria. She looked at me for an explanation.

"I want you to meet an old friend—Maria."

Maria stood up, Julia set the bags down on the table, and they shook hands.

"Why don't you join us," I said.

"I'm going to put the groceries away first."

She put the bags on the counter, near the refrigerator. When I offered to help, she said, "You have a guest."

"You sort of know Maria already."

Julia gave me a puzzled look.

"Her full name is Maria Cutler."

"The journalist?"

"Yes," Maria said.

Julia finished putting the groceries away, came over, and sat down at the head of the table. "You're the one who always refers to the president as Puppy."

"I am. And Puppy could've never become president without Pappy."

Julia grinned.

"Julia is the actor in the family. The real actor. She just played Blanche in *A Streetcar Named Desire*."

Maria asked her about the production, and soon Julia was talking about how she had prepared herself to play Blanche by studying Vivien Leigh's performance, and about her experience performing in *Hedda Gabler* and some one-acts at Fordham. I felt proud watching her talk about her aspirations and accomplishments, and I thought, as I had frequently, that I'd do anything to help her. The word *anything* stuck in my mind, and I thought about the *anything* I'd done in Iraq, the lives that'd been lost, the families destroyed.

Julia startled me out of my thoughts when she said, "What really helped me understand Blanche was my brother's death." She looked out the window, then back at Maria. "When Blanche talks about the beautiful boy, and losing someone you love, I think of Jamie, and the way his death haunts us. My performance was a gift to him."

"Jamie?" Maria asked.

"My son," I said, wiping a tear from my eye. "He was killed in Iraq."

"I'm so sorry."

After a long silence, Julia took a deep breath and asked, "How did you and Dad meet?"

Maria leaned toward her. "We're old friends. We haven't seen one another in twenty-five years."

"Twenty-five years? Wow! What was he like then?"

Maria told Julia about the college grad, inspired by the film *Easy Rider* to chop a Harley Davidson and ride it from Minnesota to Washington to California and Texas, and who showed up one day in a beer garden, wearing his easy-rider jacket, jeans, and bugs in his teeth—Julia got a good laugh out of that. While Maria described the encounter, I remembered walking toward her in the garden, the way her eyes drew me, and the playful way she looked up and said, "Do I know you?" Maria explained to Julia what an easy-rider jacket was, and Julia said, "Dad, a buckskin jacket with tassels? You?" We laughed. Maria told her about us sewing our bodies together and dancing like mimes, mirroring one another's movements, and about me performing the Who's-on-first skit in the Old Pecan Street Café.

As Julia learned about the things she would've never dreamed I'd done, she'd glance at me, shake her head, and say, "Really?" And sometimes she just cracked up, while Maria beamed. Maria and I had lived something at once ordinary and magical, and now we were living it again and sharing it with Julia. Maria went on about the two of us and Valerie forming a little group, kind of like in *Jules and Jim*, only we were two *nanas* and a *mec*—Julia laughed at the French slang. And about us trying to break the record for racing through the Louvre, our shoes echoing like gunfire through the halls, and being escorted out by the guards. And her and Valerie taking me out for a makeover, and how I'd impressed Julia's grandpa so much he invited me to go on a yacht with them. And the good times she and I'd had in Austin—the movies, the music at the Armadillo, Albion's course we attended together, and the parties, which in the end weren't much fun.

"The parties ended after your father left." Maria's happiness disappeared. She glanced at me, and I could see that remembering for her was not like smoking a joint, and then letting go. She smiled at Julia.

Julia thanked her. "It's been fun learning more about my parents." She looked at me as she stood. "I'm going to change and go for a run."

Maria leaned forward, re-establishing eye contact with her. "I wish you success with your career. I hope I can see you perform sometime."

"If you're in New York this summer, come see me in *Mother Courage*. I have the title role."

After Julia left, Maria said, "She's beautiful."

"She's all that's good in my life."

"And Jamie? Did you give him that name because of Jimmy?"

I nodded. "But he was always Jamie. Never Jimmy."

We remained silent for a while, and then Maria said, "I want to talk to you about something. Would you be willing to work with me on some articles about Iraq? Why we went to war. Who's profiting. Who's telling the truth, and who isn't."

"Is that why you came?"

"You mean, the only reason?"

"Yeah."

"What do you think?"

I looked into her eyes, she looked into mine, and I said, "No."

"Working together will give us an opportunity to talk. I'd like that. It would be good for us."

"Working together, with me as your source."

She nodded. "You know some of the people who got us into this war. They think they can get away with it by saying they made the right decisions based on the evidence that was available, but the occupation has proven Hans Blix was right all along—there were no WMDs. And only an ignorant fool could've believed Saddam Hussein and Osama bin Laden would've worked together. There's nothing bin Laden would've treasured more than Saddam's head on a pike, and vice-versa. Now the Downing Street Memo has come out, proving definitively the cause for war was fabricated, and we have members of Congress claiming to have been misinformed. Poor things. I think it's time the Administration and Congress were held accountable. And you can help."

"It would be like going to confession. I haven't done that since I was a kid. My mother would be shocked. You'd be my confessor. Bless me, Maria, for I have sinned."

"A priest can give you absolution. I can't give you anything."

"You can give me a penance. I have more wealth than my daughter and I need. If you're going to be my confessor, maybe you can think of ways for me to divest myself of money so it'll help others—above all, people hurt by the war. It's kind of like unburdening myself of the person I've become." I chuckled. "But maybe I should

wait until after the divorce. See what's left." I paused. "Come here.
I want to show you something."

I led her into the studio. She saw the face of the boy glowing in
the sunlight and stopped.

"The eyes. They burn right through me."

"When I was in Fallujah, I saw an old man following a boy, his
hand on the boy's shoulder, walking through a square, where there
was a tank, and Marines hanging around, and bodies of dead Iraqis
on the ground. During the months I spent in hospitals, living in the
dark, behind the bandages over my eyes, I'd remember the old man,
and the boy leading him, and I'd see the boy's face and his eyes that
accused me and saw through my lies and unburied the boy in me,
deep in my past, and that boy led me back to where I needed to go,
back to my father's studio, where I first learned to recreate what I
saw and felt." I glanced over, saw her eyes fixed on the painting, and
said, "That's *Fallujah 1*."

When she finally took her eyes off it and started looking
around, I said, "Here are *Fallujah 2* and *3*," and pulled the paintings
out where she could see them.

She gazed at them and shook her head. "How can anyone be
surprised at the PTSD, the suicides? I still don't understand, why
were you even there?"

"Guilt. I'd read reports of what we'd done to the city. To the
people."

"It was a war crime. A crime against humanity."

"From the moment I got into that helicopter, I dreaded seeing
what I was going to see. But I had to."

"You can't blame yourself for this. You didn't do it. You didn't
even have the power to do it. The Advisory Board of the Lowell
Group, with all its well-connected egos, never had as much influence over the administration as it liked to think."

"Ah, the Board. You have to see these."

I moved a large blank canvas and the *Crucifixion* to get to *Study
of Psychopath in Blue Suit 1* and *2*. I carried them toward the opposite side of the room and leaned them against other paintings,

where they could catch the light from the windows. I gestured toward *Psychopath 1* and said, "Do you recognize him?"

She studied the painting and said, "The blue suit, gold-rimmed glasses, and wavy hair ... kind of make me think of Peter Rubin."

"Yeah. Peter, my inspiration. The man who saw the qualities I could bring to the Board and recruited me, made me a member and its representative in Iraq. My patron, who had the nerve to visit me in the hospital and tell me how well his son was doing at Johns Hopkins, while my son was in Iraq. He's fucking my wife. Was probably fucking her when he visited me. Probably had been fucking her for months—who knows, maybe years—without me knowing until a few days ago. How's that for discretion?"

"I'm sorry, Dick."

"I am, too." I sighed, feeling my anger wane.

"You okay?"

"Yeah." I focused on Maria to help me forget Peter and Valerie.

Maria walked back and forth, looking at the two *Psychopaths*. "Can we talk about these?"

"Sure."

"This is the same character, but he changes from one to the other. In the first one, with that tight smile, he looks dangerous, but controlled. But in the second one, there are so many emotions, and they're so intense, it's insane."

"He's a predator. In the first one he's looking at you like he might devour you. He'd have to kill you first, but he'd enjoy that. The pleasure he'd get—oh, he'd go insane with power, crush you, rip you to shreds. An orgy. But all of that is controlled. In the second one, the control has been overwhelmed, and the smile has become a shriek of rage, of insatiable greed. He can already taste the blood. He's so rapacious, he can't loosen his grip. There's something electrifying about that power. And that power is electrocuting him. The throne is an electric chair—but it's still a throne. And all the psychopath can do is cry out in pain. I've played a trick on him. I endowed him with a conscience in the second painting, and he feels what he's doing. And that's part of his rage. And his pleasure. He feels the pain and he can't escape." I stopped in front of *Psychopath 2* and said, "I know this psychopath well. Every portrait is a self-portrait."

"That's why you smeared his face?"

I nodded.

"That's not you. A psychopath doesn't feel guilt. Doesn't feel the way you do."

"The way I do *now*." I continued staring at him.

She walked past me toward *Psychopath 2*, which was leaning against a larger canvas with an orange background, and moved it aside so she could look at the painting. After gazing at it in silence, she said, "This is ..."

"*Jamie dying.*"

"Why did you paint him like this?"

"Like what?"

"It almost looks as if he's been crucified—but there's no cross. He's just suspended in space." She added, in an apologetic tone, "I'm just wondering."

"I could've done portraits that look like photographs. And I did that. Those small paintings leaning against the wall." I pointed in the direction of the wall that separated the studio from the living room. "I did those based on photographs of Jamie. Go ahead and look at them." She walked over and picked them up, one by one, while I sat on the desk and watched. "When I painted them, I relived the moment captured by the photograph. It's a moving experience. The memory comes back, it's so clear, it almost feels as if he's alive, and then it fades, and he's gone. I'd find him ... and lose him with each painting. But I didn't really find him. I just found what the photograph had recorded. I wanted *Jamie dying* to trap that moment of his life in all its violence, in all its intensity, all its complexity and simplicity. I wanted to live that moment with him. I had to be with him. I should've been. I am in my dreams."

She returned to *Jamie dying*. "Who is this man, in the background, with his hand on the door? He looks like he's trying to sneak away, but got caught."

"Caught by his conscience."

She looked at me. "He's you?"

I nodded.

She gazed at the painting. "It's very powerful."

She looked around the room, saw something, walked across the studio, passing before me, stopped in front of *Psychopath 1,* which concealed part of another painting, moved *Psychopath,* and stared at *Gone.* After a long silence, she said, "This is Valerie."

"Yes."

"It feels like a dream."

"That's what it is."

Maria's hand followed her gaze and hovered above the painting, ready to touch it, before falling to her side. "I have a friend, an art critic who writes for the *Times,* who'd love to see your work. I can hear her raving about the *grisaille* in this piece."

"Well, maybe she'd like to see my father's work, too."

I led her into the living room, where she marveled at the four paintings. When we returned to the studio, I showed her *Canyon Wall.* While she gazed at it, I sat down on the desk. She came over, pulled herself up, and sat next to me.

"What a great story. A young man comes out of a mining town in Colorado, starts painting in the, what, late-1940s? Moves to Taos, if I remember correctly, gets married, has two kids—two, right?"

I nodded.

"Trains his son to be an artist, but not his daughter. Why not his daughter?"

"My father could be scary. If something in his work went wrong, or we did something wrong in the studio, he'd lose it. Georgia preferred being with my mother."

She nodded. "Okay. Well, back to the story. So, the father dies young, when his son is just sixteen. A year later, the son goes off to college, continues painting, stops when he finishes college, and nearly thirty years later, begins painting again, as a way of recovering from PTSD."

"Or living with it."

"The son becomes what he perhaps should've become years before, an artist, and the article introduces father and son to the public. And, with that kind of introduction, you might be able to get an exhibit in a gallery."

"Really?"

"One article from this critic could make it happen."

I imagined people standing in front of Dad's work and mine, saying things like, 'Look at the way he uses light and shadow. Look at the *grisaille*. And that deep black—how did he do that?' All the praise and hushed exclamations. And then the whispering subsided, and I was still sitting in my studio, staring at the paintings. They feel personal. I don't want to share them. Not with people who aren't close to me. That would just be another performance.

"Come here." I slid off the desk. "I want you to touch this canvas."

She hesitated.

"Come on."

She jumped off the desk and followed me over to *Psychopath 2*.

"Here, touch it. There's nothing sacred about it. See how it feels? Kind of rough. A little ragged. That's because I violated one of the basic rules of painting. A rule my father taught me when I was a boy. You paint on a surface that's been primed, otherwise the canvas will rot. And when you look at the psychopath's face, you see that texture, you feel it, and you know his image will decay and decompose. The painting will die, the way people do. I like the idea of it dying. It removes the viewer, the spectator, from my head. I don't paint for other people. I paint because painting is a way of living with Jamie, and Dad, and that boy in Fallujah, whose eyes will always make me feel ... feel more than I can say. I don't stop thinking about them. I don't get over the loss of people I love. I don't want to. I don't ever want to get over the loss of Jamie."

After a long silence, she said, "Maybe, instead of a story that my friend would write about the father and the son—a story I was thinking of co-authoring with her—I should write a story about painting as a means of dealing with PTSD and finding meaning."

"Meaning? That sounds a little grandiose. It's personal. I've found the boy in me who worked with Dad, and all three of us are living together in the same head."

"Some of those paintings are very powerful testimonies about the war. They could be meaningful to others." She reflected. "Maybe you and I could work together on an article about them. Those Fallujah paintings," she shook her head, "people need to see them." She chuckled. "It'd be a way for you to do penance."

The front door opened and slammed shut, and footsteps rushed up the stairs.

There were a million things I wanted to talk to Maria about, but all I could think of was how close she was, even as she looked at her watch, thinking of leaving.

"I'd invite you for dinner, but I should—"

"You should spend time with her. She needs you."

"When do you go back to Austin?"

"Tomorrow."

"And when are you coming back?"

"I could come back next weekend, if you have time to do a confession. We can talk about the paintings." She smirked. "And the coconuts. The leaders who lead by misleading. And the irony that the people who tell the truth get fired, and the ones who lie are awarded the Presidential Medal of Freedom. You know, Dick, for a journalist with a bent toward satire, I've never wondered for a moment what I could possibly write about—above all, since this idiot's been president."

"The man who led a legacy life, as you like to say."

"Yes, I have said that, haven't I."

"I've sometimes wondered if Puppy wasn't one of the guys at your parties."

"I wondered that, too, when he was governor, and I covered him for the *Statesman*. I'd try to recall if that face had ever shown up. He would've fit right in. But he is several years older than us."

We gazed at each other.

"I'm not the same little girl you knew in Austin. I'm my own woman."

"I know." But I saw in the warmth of her dark eyes and her smile a friendship that could help me live.

"Okay. I'll see you next weekend. Oh, I should get your cell number."

We traded numbers, I saw her to the door, and we said good-bye again. As I stood in front of the window next to the door and watched her walk to her car, Julia appeared next to me.

"She's the one who threw you away, like a piece of trash."

I nodded.

"She's still in love with you."

"She's a journalist, and I'm a source of information." I looked at Julia. "And I still love your mother, even if she no longer loves me."

As Maria opened her door, she looked up, saw us in the window, and gave us a wave. I waved back.

That evening, Julia and I made dinner together for the first time since the Iraq disaster. When she went shopping, she bought the ingredients to make a dish of my own concoction, ratatouille spaghetti sauce, which I'd often made on weekends for her and Jamie when they were little. I'd stopped making it, because by the time they were teenagers, they'd take one look at my sauce and whine, "Again?" We cut and sautéed onions, garlic, and eggplant, and added Italian sausage, zucchini, tomatoes, and oregano. As we sat at the table, stuffing ourselves with spaghetti, she entertained me with stories about her eccentric profs and college friends, and we heehawed and snorted. And we talked about Phil, who was supposed to drive down to pick her up Sunday, and then they'd drive back to New York. I suggested she see if he'd rather come Saturday afternoon, have dinner with us, spend the night, and then return. She ran up to her room to call him.

I looked out the window, through the web of cracks, at Aphrodite standing on her rock, in the empty fountain full of dead leaves. She appears so modest, so virginal, but there's that dolphin full of desire leaping next to her calf. Julia's full of desire, too. She wants to accomplish a lot, but if I wash a handful of pills down with whiskey ...

I have to go on living, and the only way I can do that is to keep painting. And maybe it's time I clean out those dead leaves and turn on Aphrodite's fountain.

CHAPTER 20

I DIDN'T KNOW WHAT I was going to create, but after applying a wash of ivory black and ultramarine blue on the canvas, I started painting a face, building it up with flecks of white, raw sienna, yellow ochre, alizarin crimson, and cerulean blue, accumulating the strokes, creating with the impasto a boy's face—a young man's face, Jamie's face—that almost rose from the surface of the canvas. No lines, nothing drawn, just the strokes accumulating, the paint getting thicker and thicker, until I could feel the texture of the skin. And as I painted, I felt the brush caress his skin, its firmness, and that feeling guided the brush.

I built up the impasto to define the cheek, the chin, and the nose, and I set the brown eyes beneath the brows of dark, flecked paint. The lips I painted slightly open, while his eyes gaze off, fixed on a point far beyond my shoulder as I worked. He had perhaps just looked up from a book, and maybe he was thinking about what he was reading, or about the life he'd led, or might've led. I'd seen him like this so often, his mind drifting, and I loved him for that. Loved him for being young, for thinking and daydreaming and wanting things and ... everything.

As the image of Jamie became clearer, and the form took shape, I became more excited and worked faster. I was living with him. We were in the same time, the same space. A space that included sight, touch, sound, smell, and feelings. I could hear him breathing, feel the blood, the energy pulsing through him.

I responded to the smooth surface of the skin and the impasto of the features with darker colors—burnt umber blended with ivory black—to create waves of long hair. Waves of energy, like cascading water. That energy took hold of me, and I wanted to sustain it, extend it, prolong it. I blended ivory black with ultramarine blue and applied the blend with a loaded brush, extending the black from the waves of hair into the blue-black waves of the background, painted so thick you could see the brushwork. The waves whirled around, like a halo, an aura of energy radiating from Jamie's head.

I finished, and my hand fell to my side. The way Dad's would fall to his, after he'd put all his energy and emotion onto the canvas. I was still with him, even in the motion of my body. With him, with Jamie, all three of us together. I gazed at Jamie—at his eyes, at the expression on his face, which I couldn't define, even though I'd painted it. His eyes reflected what he was thinking and feeling, but I couldn't find the right words to translate what was so clearly reflected. Whatever it was, it made me feel alive, and that feeling flowed from his face into his hair and into the energy that surrounded his head.

I turned around and looked out the window. Many hours had passed, but I hadn't noticed. What's time to a painter? Or that cardinal, singing a song that rippled through me?

Julia fluttered around the house in the afternoon like a bird preparing its nest. She went shopping for flowers, pastries, and more groceries, because what we had in the refrigerator wouldn't do with Phil coming for dinner. I sat in the living room and read. The second the doorbell rang, she flew to answer it, and I heard the excited voices of the lovers chirping in the foyer.

I rose to greet him. He wore a blue sports jacket, a dark red shirt, and blue jeans. Handsome, cool, and dramatic. He asked me about the paintings in the living room, and I told him about Dad's work and the painters whom he'd admired. Phil knew how to get someone to talk and feel comfortable.

Julia appeared, announced dinner was ready, led us into the dining room, pointed at the head of the table, and said, "Dad sits here, so Phil, how about if you sit there, across from me." She grinned at him. "So I can keep my eye on you." We chuckled and sat down.

She said, "Help yourselves to the Caesar salad, and then we can move on to our main course—*linguine frutti di mare.*" After Phil and I had complimented Julia on the meal, served ourselves some salad, and begun eating, I grinned at him and said, "I'm sure you've heard this question before: What do you want to do in life?"

He responded without hesitation, as if he'd been waiting for this opportunity. "I want to create my own theatrical troupe. That's been my dream for years, and that's what Julia and I are doing now." He paused, glanced at her, and the look in their eyes suggested they shared the dream. "We have four friends who want to build the company with us—all theater students in New York. We're going to stage plays that deal with the important issues of the day—or the issues that should be important. Like war. So, our first production will be Bertolt Brecht's *Mother Courage and Her Children.* It's a brilliant play, one of the greatest ever written on the subject of war. And we'll do other plays by Brecht."

Julia said, "And other classics—like *All My Sons, A Doll's House, An Enemy of the People.*"

"*All My Sons,*" I repeated. "So would you play Annie again?"

Her hand holding the fork she was raising toward her mouth froze, and her joy disappeared. I wondered how what I'd said could've hurt her. She set the fork down on her plate, shook her head, and wiped the corners of her eyes with her napkin.

"There are times …" Her voice caught. "There are times when I think of that play, and my thoughts go back to Jamie. And … when he was alive, and we were all together."

I reached over, placed my hand on her shoulder, wishing I could take her in my arms and hold her. "I'm sorry. I shouldn't have mentioned that play."

"That's all right, Dad. We're going to have to learn how to live with him gone."

"We're going to have to learn how to live all over again."

"Yeah." She paused. "I was talking about …" She took a breath. "… talking about the theater company Phil and I want to develop. We're going to produce contemporary work, too."

Phil, who'd been watching her, looked at me and said, "And we're going to write plays and produce them."

"And one of those plays will deal with this fucking war," she said, "and all of the lies."

I smiled. She'd never used that word in my presence. "I can be a resource for that."

"Great!" she said. "There's another way in which you can support us." She looked me in the eye. "We need financial help launching our first production." She glanced at Phil, giving him his cue.

"There's an abandoned warehouse in lower Manhattan that we've looked at. It would be a perfect space for staging *Mother Courage.*"

"If you could help us with renting that space and some of the other costs …"

I laughed and shook my head, as I realized I'd been listening to a sales pitch. "Of course I'll help you." She beamed victory as she looked from me to Phil. "But," I focused on Julia, "I have one concern. You're finishing your second year of college. Are you planning on dropping out?"

"No. I'll finish my degree and work with Phil."

"How is that possible?"

"You know, Dad, there are a lot of students who have to work part-time jobs to get through school, the way you did when you were an undergraduate. I've met kids who work thirty hours a week. I don't know how they do it. I can carve out the time I need to do the kind of theater that might help change the world." She looked at Phil. "That's what we've been talking about." They smiled at one another.

Phil looked at me and explained. "I have two more years to go, as well. Our plan is to do one major production every summer, and then two one-act plays each academic year, until we graduate. And then we'll work full-time."

I nodded, relieved. "That makes sense. Well, I'm happy to work with you—with both of you—on this." I became aware of our salads, which we'd hardly touched. "Shall we eat?"

Phil's phone rang. He took it out of his pocket, checked to see who was calling, and said, "I have to take this. Do you mind if I go in the living room?"

"Not at all," I said.

As soon as he disappeared, Julia said, "Dad, do you remember talking to me about when you were an undergraduate, and you described yourself as a serial monogamist?"

"Oh, God!" I chuckled and shook my head.

"Well, Phil's not one of those. We've been together for eight months." She paused. "I stay at his apartment sometimes, and sometimes he stays at mine. Tonight, he's sleeping in the guest room, which has a double bed ..."

I nodded and smiled. "Of course."

She placed her hand on mine, her eyes radiating love. "Thanks, Dad."

Later, as I lay in bed, thinking about serving as a source for Maria and providing assistance to Julia and Phil—my post-psychopath projects, as I called them in my mind—I heard their hushed voices and laughter, and Julia shushing Phil and giggling. And then quiet. I remembered my days as a serial monogamist and the women whom I'd hurt, and hoped Phil wouldn't hurt Julia. But there's nothing I can do to protect her. She's no longer a little girl. She's a woman, making decisions, and some of them might open the door to the life she'll live for years, perhaps decades. Will she and Phil remain together? Will they realize what they want to accomplish with Brecht's *Mother Courage*? Will she succeed as an actress? It's one thing to stand out in a school production, quite another to make it on Broadway, or in Hollywood. And I'm making decisions, too. I won't try to go back to the life I lived with Valerie. I've decided to be an artist. I don't know that I can succeed, any more than Dad did. I've made the decision, chosen my way, and there's no turning back. I'm afraid, anxious, and excited. And I'm sure Julia is, too.

My thoughts had generated too much energy for me to sleep, so, after not hearing any sounds from the other room for a while, I got up, found my robe, and went downstairs to the studio. Moonlight illuminated the stacked canvases, the easel, and the desk. I walked around to the other side of the easel to look at the portrait of Jamie, facing me and the windows. The painting almost glowed in the night. I leaned forward and discerned the brushwork in the face, the hair, and the background. I'd found life in this painting—not in the object, but in the process of creating it.

I went over to the desk and sat down. I thought again of Rembrandt's *Lucretia*. He'd painted his dead lover from memory. She'd continued living in him, and he'd continued loving her, just as Jamie will continue living in me, and I will continue loving him. With all the billions of people in the world, why should the loss of one mean so much? Because he's my son, and through him, and through Dad, and Elliott, I'm connected to everyone. All those who carry their dead inside. All those who live with the loss of anyone they've loved, and even if that person still lives, there's the longing that never ends. People talk of getting over it, recovering from it, as if we need to be separated from those whom we've lost. But they're part of us. Like phantom pain, they live on. Painting is a way of living with them. And with what I've done.

We lose and we lose and we lose. And then we die. Maybe that's what you were thinking, Dad, when you said life is overrated. But I don't think it is. I know, when you said that, you'd already done all your smoking and drinking, and you were going to die. You were probably trying to bring a little light into the dark. A little humor. A little irony. Well, I'm being straight with you. Life really isn't overrated. And I will love you and work with you and continue living with you—and with all those I love—until the end.

ACKNOWLEDGEMENTS

WE ALL KNOW THE SAYING, It takes a village to raise a child. The same thing is true for the production of a book. The village that helped me produce *Ivory Black* includes some gifted writers— Peter Geye, Mary Logue, and Brian Malloy—who critiqued early drafts of the book. My village also includes literary friends, some of whom—Jeff Kellgren, Amy McCumber, and Victoria Tirrel—read several drafts.

Writing for me is a way of exploring the world. *Ivory Black* drew me into the world of a painter. My novel would have included some embarrassing gaffes if my partner, Jane Bassuk, a visual artist, hadn't helped me assemble a group of six very talented painters who reviewed the first draft. I want to thank Jane, Barbara Kreft, Joyce Lyon, Michelle Ranta, Nancy Robinson, and Andrée Tracey. And I want to pay tribute to the painter, Lance Kiland, who was part of our group, but died not long after we met to discuss my book.

From my perspective, a book isn't finished until it's been published. I want to thank Michael Mirolla, Publisher and Editor-in-Chief at Guernica Editions, for offering publication and ensuring high-quality production, as well as my editor, Scott Walker, cover designer Allen Jomoc Jr., and book designer Jill Ronsley.

And, above all, thanks to my loving family—Jane, Cathy, Neil, Michael, and Daniel.

About the Author

Brian Duren was born and raised in Minnesota. A former French professor and university administrator, he holds doctorates from the University of Paris and the University of Minnesota. His first novel, *Whiteout*, described by the *St. Paul Pioneer Press* as a "stunning debut novel, worthy of national recognition," won the Independent Publisher Gold Medal for Midwestern Fiction. Duren is also the author of *The Gravity of Love*. He is working on his next novel, *Day Brings Back the Night*.

www.brianduren.com